P9-COP-191

**"TOM CLANCY HAS PASSED THE TORCH
TO A NEW GENERATION."**
—*St. Louis Post-Dispatch*

A man named Mohammed sits in a café in Vienna, about to propose a deal to a Colombian. What if they combined his network of Middle East agents and sympathizers with the Colombian's drug network in America? The potential for profits would be enormous—and the potential for destruction unimaginable.

A young man in suburban Maryland, who has grown up around intrigue, is about to put his skills to the test. Taught the ways of the world firsthand by agents, statesmen, analysts, Secret Servicemen, and black-ops specialists, he crosses the radar of "The Campus"—a secret organization set up to identify local terrorist threats and deal with them by any means necessary.

His name:
JACK RYAN, JR.

"INCREDIBLY ADDICTIVE . . . 400-odd tightly-woven, adrenaline-fueled pages of intelligence interception, 6 A.M. fitness training, shootings, and hard men. Such fun!"
—*Daily Mail* (London)

"THE AUTHOR KNOWS THIS STUFF LIKE NO ONE ELSE and delivers it all in his inimitable clipped manner."
—*Publishers Weekly*

"CLANCY TAKES A NEW PATH WITH *TIGER* . . . [He] is still the top draw in a field filled with contemporaries."
—*San Antonio Express-News*

"SATISFYING . . . CHILLINGLY PLAUSIBLE."
—*Orlando Sentinel*

"ENTERTAINING . . . SUSPENSEFUL."
—*The Seattle Times*

Created by Tom Clancy and Steve Pieczenik
TOM CLANCY'S OP-CENTER
TOM CLANCY'S OP-CENTER: MIRROR IMAGE
TOM CLANCY'S OP-CENTER: GAMES OF STATE
TOM CLANCY'S OP-CENTER: ACTS OF WAR
TOM CLANCY'S OP-CENTER: BALANCE OF POWER
TOM CLANCY'S OP-CENTER: STATE OF SIEGE
TOM CLANCY'S OP-CENTER: DIVIDE AND CONQUER
TOM CLANCY'S OP-CENTER: LINE OF CONTROL
TOM CLANCY'S OP-CENTER: MISSION OF HONOR
TOM CLANCY'S OP-CENTER: SEA OF FIRE
TOM CLANCY'S OP-CENTER: CALL TO TREASON

TOM CLANCY'S NET FORCE
TOM CLANCY'S NET FORCE: HIDDEN AGENDAS
TOM CLANCY'S NET FORCE: NIGHT MOVES
TOM CLANCY'S NET FORCE: BREAKING POINT
TOM CLANCY'S NET FORCE: POINT OF IMPACT
TOM CLANCY'S NET FORCE: CYBERNATION
TOM CLANCY'S NET FORCE: STATE OF WAR
TOM CLANCY'S NET FORCE: CHANGING OF THE GUARD

Created by Tom Clancy and Martin Greenberg
TOM CLANCY'S POWER PLAYS: POLITIKA
TOM CLANCY'S POWER PLAYS: RUTHLESS.COM
TOM CLANCY'S POWER PLAYS: SHADOW WATCH
TOM CLANCY'S POWER PLAYS: BIO-STRIKE
TOM CLANCY'S POWER PLAYS: COLD WAR
TOM CLANCY'S POWER PLAYS: CUTTING EDGE
TOM CLANCY'S POWER PLAYS: ZERO HOUR

THE TEETH OF THE TIGER

TOM CLANCY

BERKLEY BOOKS, NEW YORK

If you purchased this book without a cover, you should be aware that this book is stolen property. It was reported as "unsold and destroyed" to the publisher, and neither the author nor the publisher has received any payment for this "stripped book."

This is a work of fiction. Names, characters, places, and incidents either are the product of the author's imagination or are used fictitiously, and any resemblance to actual persons, living or dead, business establishments, events, or locales is entirely coincidental.

THE TEETH OF THE TIGER

A Berkley Book / published by arrangement with
Rubicon, Inc.

PRINTING HISTORY
G. P. Putnam's Sons hardcover edition / August 2003
Berkley mass-market edition / August 2004

Copyright © 2003 by Rubicon, Inc.
Front cover photograph by Paul Edmondson/Gettyimages.
Cover design by Anthony Romondo.

All rights reserved.
This book, or parts thereof, may not be reproduced in any form without permission. The scanning, uploading, and distribution of this book via the Internet or via any other means without the permission of the publisher is illegal and punishable by law. Please purchase only authorized electronic editions, and do not participate in or encourage electronic piracy of copyrighted materials.
Your support of the author's rights is appreciated.
For information address: The Berkley Publishing Group,
a division of Penguin Group (USA) Inc.,
375 Hudson Street, New York, New York 10014.

ISBN: 0-425-19740-9

BERKLEY®
Berkley Books are published by The Berkley Publishing Group,
a division of Penguin Group (USA) Inc.,
375 Hudson Street, New York, New York 10014.
BERKLEY and the "B" design
are trademarks belonging to Penguin Group (USA) Inc.

PRINTED IN THE UNITED STATES OF AMERICA

10 9 8 7 6 5 4 3 2 1

To Chris and Charlie.
Welcome aboard

...and, of course, Lady Alex, whose light burns
as brightly as ever

ACKNOWLEDGMENTS

Marco, in Italy, for navigation instructions
Ric and Mort for the medical education
Mary and Ed for the maps
Madam Jacque for the records
UVA for the look at TJ's place
Roland, again, for Colorado
Mike for the inspiration
And a raft of others for small but important tidbits of
knowledge

"People sleep peaceably in their beds at night only because rough men stand ready to do violence on their behalf."

—GEORGE ORWELL

"This is a war of the unknown warriors; but let all strive without failing in faith or in duty..."

—WINSTON CHURCHILL

Whether the State can loose and bind
    In Heaven as well as on Earth:
If it be wiser to kill mankind
    Before or after the birth—
These are matters of high concern
    Where State-kept schoolmen are;
But Holy State (we have lived to learn)
    Endeth in Holy War.

Whether The People be led by The Lord,
    Or lured by the loudest throat:
If it be quicker to die by the sword
    Or cheaper to die by vote—
These are things we have dealt with once,
    (And they will not rise from their grave)
For Holy People, however it runs,
    Endeth in wholly Slave.

Whatsoever for any cause,
    Seeketh to take or give
Power above or beyond the Laws,
    Suffer it not to live!
Holy State or Holy King—
    Or Holy People's Will—
Have no truck with the senseless thing.
    Order the guns and kill!
Saying—after—me:—

Once there was The People—Terror gave it birth;
Once there was The People and it made a Hell of Earth
Earth arose and crushed it. Listen, O ye slain!
Once there was The People—it shall never be again!

        —RUDYARD KIPLING, "Macdonough's Song"

THE TEETH OF THE TIGER

||||||||||||||||||||||||||||||||||||||||||||||||||||

THE OTHER SIDE
OF THE RIVER

DAVID GREENGOLD had been born in that most American of communities, Brooklyn, but at his Bar Mitzvah, something important had changed in his life. After proclaiming "Today I am a man," he'd gone to the celebration party and met some family members who'd flown in from Israel. His uncle Moses was a very prosperous dealer in diamonds there. David's own father had seven retail jewelry stores, the flagship of which was on Fortieth Street in Manhattan.

While his father and his uncle talked business over California wine, David had ended up with his first cousin, Daniel. His elder by ten years, Daniel had just begun work for the Mossad, Israel's main foreign-intelligence agency, and, a quintessential newbie, he had regaled his cousin with stories. Daniel's obligatory military service had been with the Israeli paratroopers, and he'd made eleven jumps, and had seen some action in the 1967 Six Day War. For him, it had been a happy war, with no serious casualties in his company, and just enough kills to make it seem to have been a sporting adventure—a hunting trip against game that was dangerous, but not overly so, with a conclusion that had fitted very well indeed with his prewar outlook and expectations.

The stories had provided a vivid contrast to the gloomy TV coverage of Vietnam that led off every evening news broadcast then, and with the enthusiasm of his newly reaffirmed religious identity, David had decided on the spot to emigrate to his Jewish homeland as soon as he graduated from high school. His father, who'd served in the U.S. Second Armored Division in the Second World War, and on the whole found the adventure less than pleasing, had been even less happy by the possibility of his son's going to an Asian jungle to fight a war for which neither he nor any of his acquaintances had much enthusiasm—and so, when graduation came, young David flew El Al to Israel and really never looked back. He brushed up on his Hebrew, served his uniformed time, and then, like his cousin, he was recruited by the Mossad.

In this line of work, he'd done well—so well that today he was the Station Chief in Rome, an assignment of no small importance. His cousin Daniel, meanwhile, had left and gone back to the family business, which paid far better than a civil servant's wage. Running the Mossad Station in Rome kept him busy. He had three full-time intelligence officers under his command, and they took in a goodly quantity of information. Some of this information came from an agent they called Hassan. He was Palestinian by ancestry, and had good connections in the PFLP, the Popular Front for the Liberation of Palestine, and the things he learned there he shared with his enemies, for money—enough money, in fact, enough to finance a comfortable flat a kilometer from the Italian parliament building. David was making a pickup today.

The location was one he'd used before, the men's room of the Ristorante Giovanni near the foot of the Spanish Steps. First taking the time to enjoy a lunch of Veal Francese—it was superb here—he finished his white wine and then rose to collect his package. The dead drop was on the underside of the leftmost urinal, a theatrical choice but it had the advantage of never being inspected or cleaned. A steel plate had been glued there, and even had it been noticed, it would have looked innocent enough, since the plate bore the embossed name of the manufacturer, and a number that meant nothing at all. Approaching it, he decided to take advantage of the opportunity by doing what men usually do with a urinal, and, while engaged, he heard the door creak open. Whoever it was took no interest in him, however, but, just to make sure, he dropped his cigarette pack, and as he bent down to retrieve it with his right hand, his left snatched the magnetic package off its hiding place. It was good fieldcraft, just like a professional magician's, attracting attention with the one hand and getting the work done with the other.

Except in this case it didn't work. Scarcely had he made the pickup when someone bumped into him from behind.

"Excuse me, old man—*signore,* that is," the voice corrected itself in what sounded like Oxford English. Just the sort of thing to make a civilized man feel at ease with a situation.

Greengold didn't even respond, just turned to his right to wash his hands and take his leave. He made it to the sink, and turned on the water, when he looked in the mirror.

Most of the time, the brain works faster than the hands. This time he saw the blue eyes of the man who had bumped into him. They were ordinary enough, but their expression was not. By the time his mind had commanded his body to react, the man's left hand had reached forward to grab his forehead, and something cold and sharp bit into the back of his neck, just below the skull. His head was pulled sharply backward, easing the passage of the knife into his spinal cord, severing it completely.

Death did not come instantly. His body collapsed when all of the electrochemical commands to his muscles ceased. Along with that went all feeling. Some distant fiery sensations at his neck were all that remained, and the shock of the moment didn't allow them to grow into serious pain. He tried to breathe, but couldn't comprehend that he would never do that again. The man turned him around like a department store mannequin and carried him to the toilet stall. All he could do now was look and think. He saw the face, but it meant nothing to him. The face looked back, regarding him as a thing, an object, without even the dignity of hatred. Helplessly, David scanned with his eyes as he was set down on the toilet. The man appeared to reach into his coat to steal his wallet. Was that what this was, just a robbery? A robbery of a senior Mossad officer? Not possible. Then the man grabbed David by the hair to lift up his drooping head.

"Salaam aleikum," his killer said: Peace be unto you. So, this was an Arab? He didn't look the least bit Arabic. The puzzlement must have been evident on his face.

"Did you really trust Hassan, Jew?" the man asked. But he displayed no satisfaction in his voice. The emotionless delivery proclaimed contempt. In his last moments of life, before his brain died from lack of oxygen, David Greengold realized that he'd fallen for the oldest of espionage traps, the False Flag. Hassan had given him information so as to be able to identify him, to draw him out. Such a stupid way to die. There was time left for only one more thought:

Adonai echad.

The killer made sure his hands were clean, and checked his clothing. But knife thrusts like this one didn't cause much in the way of bleeding. He pocketed the wallet, and the dead-drop package, and after adjusting his clothing made his way out. He stopped at his table to leave twenty-three Euros for his own meal, including only a few cents for the tip. But he would not be coming back soon. Finished with Giovanni's, he walked across the square. He'd noticed a Brioni's on his way in, and he felt the need for a new suit.

* * *

HEADQUARTERS, United States Marine Corps, is not located in the Pentagon. The largest office building in the world has room for the Army, Navy, and Air Force, but somehow or other the Marines got left out, and have to satisfy themselves with their own building complex called the Navy Annex, a quarter of a mile away on Lee Highway in Arlington, Virginia. It isn't that much of a sacrifice. The Marines have always been something of a stepchild of the American military, technically a subordinate part of the Navy, where their original utility was to be the Navy's private army, thus precluding the need to embark soldiers on warships, since the Army and the Navy were never supposed to be friendly.

Over time, the Marine Corps became a rationale unto itself, for more than a century the only American land fighting force that foreigners ever saw. Absolved of the need to worry about heavy logistics, or even medical personnel—they had the squids to handle that for them—every Marine was a rifleman, and a forbidding, sobering sight to anyone who did not have a warm spot in his heart for the United States of America. For this reason, the Marines are respected, but not always beloved, among their colleagues in America's service. Too much show, too much swagger, and too highly developed a sense of public relations for the more staid services.

The Marine Corps acts like its own little army, of course—it even has its own air force, small, but possessed of sharp fangs—and that now included a chief of intelligence, though some uniformed personnel regarded that as a contradiction in terms. The Marine intelligence headquarters was a new establishment, part of the Green Machine's effort to catch up with the rest of the services. Called the M-2—"2" being the numerical identifier of someone in the information business—the chief's name was Major General Terry Broughton, a short, compact professional infantryman who'd been stuck with this job in order to bring a little reality to the spook trade: The Corps had decided to remember that at the end of the paper trail was a man with a rifle who needed good information in order to stay alive. It was just one more secret of the Corps that the native intelligence of its personnel was second to none—even to the computer wizards of the Air Force whose attitude was that anyone able to fly an airplane just *had to be* smarter than anybody else. Eleven months from now, Broughton was in line to take command of the Second Marine Division, based at Camp Lejeune, North Carolina. This welcome news had just arrived a week before, and he was still in the best of good moods from it.

That was good news for Captain Brian Caruso as well, for whom an audience with a general officer was, if not exactly frightening, certainly reason for a little circumspection. He was wearing his Class-A olive-colored uniform, complete to the Sam Browne belt, and all the ribbons to which he was entitled, which wasn't all that many, though some of them were kind of pretty, as well as his gold parachute-jumper's wings, and a collection of marksmanship awards large enough to impress even a lifelong rifleman like General Broughton.

The M-2 rated a lieutenant-colonel office boy, plus a black female gunnery sergeant as a personal secretary. It all struck the young captain as odd, but nobody had ever accused the Corps of logic, Caruso reminded himself. As they liked to say: two hundred thirty years of tradition untrammeled by progress.

"The General will see you now, Captain," she said, looking up from the phone on her desk.

"Thank you, Gunny," Caruso said, coming to his feet and heading for the door, which the sergeant held open for him.

Broughton was exactly what Caruso had expected. A whisker under six feet, he had the sort of chest that might turn away a high-speed bullet. His hair was a tiny bit more than stubble. As with most Marines, a bad hair day was what happened when it got to half an inch, and required a trip to the barber. The general looked up from his paperwork and looked his visitor up and down with cold hazel eyes.

Caruso did not salute. Like naval officers, Marines do not salute unless under arms or "covered" with a uniform cap. The visual inspection lasted about three seconds, which only felt like a week or so.

"Good morning, sir."

"Have a seat, Captain." The general pointed to a leather-covered chair.

Caruso did sit down, but remained at the position of attention, bent legs and all.

"Know why you're here?" Broughton asked.

"No, sir, they didn't tell me that."

"How do you like Force Recon?"

"I like it just fine, sir," Caruso replied. "I think I have the best NCOs in the whole Corps, and the work keeps me interested."

"You did a nice job in Afghanistan, says here." Broughton held up a folder with red-and-white-striped tape on the edges. That denoted top-secret material. But special-operations work often fell into that category, and, sure as hell, Caruso's Afghanistan job had not been something for the *NBC Nightly News.*

"It was fairly exciting, sir."

"Good work, says here, getting all your men out alive."

"General, that's mostly because of that SEAL corpsman with us. Corporal Ward got shot up pretty bad, but Petty Officer Randall saved his life, and that's for sure. I put him in for a decoration. Hope he gets it."

"He will," Broughton assured him. "And so will you."

"Sir, I just did my job," Caruso protested. "My men did all—"

"And that's the sign of a good young officer," the M-2 cut him off. "I read your account of the action, and I read Gunny Sullivan's, too. He says you did just fine for a young officer in his first combat action." Gunnery Sergeant Joe Sullivan had smelled the smoke before, in Lebanon and

Kuwait, and a few other places that had never made the TV news. "Sullivan worked for me once," Broughton informed his guest. "He's due for promotion."

Caruso bobbed his head. "Yes, sir. He's sure enough ready for a step up in the world."

"I've seen your fit-rep on him." The M-2 tapped another folder, this one not with TS formatting. "Your treatment of your men is generous in its praise, Captain. Why?"

That made Caruso blink. "Sir, they did very well. I could not have expected more under any circumstances. I'll take that bunch of Marines up against anybody in the world. Even the new kids can all make sergeant someday, and two of them have 'gunny' written all over them. They work hard, and they're smart enough that they start doing the right thing before I have to tell them. At least one of them is officer material. Sir, those are my people, and I am damned lucky to have them."

"And you trained them up pretty well," Broughton added.

"That's my job, sir."

"Not anymore, Captain."

"Excuse me, sir? I have another fourteen months with the battalion, and my next job hasn't been determined yet." Though he'd happily stay in Second Force Recon forever. Caruso figured he'd screen for major soon, and maybe jump to battalion S-3, operations officer for the division's reconnaissance battalion.

"That Agency guy who went into the mountains with you, how was he to work with?"

"James Hardesty, says he used to be in the Army Special Forces. Age forty or so, but he's pretty fit for an older guy, speaks two of the local languages. Doesn't wet his pants when bad things happen. He—well, he backed me up pretty well."

The TS folder went up again in the M-2's hands. "He says here you saved his bacon in that ambush."

"Sir, nobody looks smart getting into an ambush in the

first place. Mr. Hardesty was reconnoitering forward with Corporal Ward while I was getting the satellite radio set up. The bad guys were in a pretty clever little spot, but they tipped their hand. They opened up too soon on Mr. Hardesty, missed him with their first burst, and we maneuvered uphill around them. They didn't have good enough security out. Gunny Sullivan took his squad right, and when he got in position, I took my bunch up the middle. It took a total of ten to fifteen minutes, and then Gunny Sullivan got our target, took him right in the head from ten meters. We wanted to take him alive, but that wasn't possible the way things played out." Caruso shrugged. Superiors could generate officers, but not the exigencies of the moment, and the man had had no intention of spending time in American captivity, and it was hard to put the bag on someone like that. The final score had been one badly shot-up Marine, and sixteen dead Arabs, plus two live captives for the Intel pukes to chat with. It had ended up being more productive than anyone had expected. The Afghans were brave enough, but they weren't madmen—or, more precisely, they chose martyrdom only on their own terms.

"Lessons learned?" Broughton asked.

"There is no such thing as too much training, sir, or being in too good a shape. The real thing is a lot messier than exercises. Like I said, the Afghans are brave enough, but they are not trained. And you can never know which ones are going to slug it out, and which ones are going to cave. They taught us at Quantico that you have to trust your instincts, but they don't issue instincts to you, and you can't always be sure if you're listening to the right voice or not." Caruso shrugged, but he just went ahead and spoke his mind. "I guess it worked out okay for me and my Marines, but I can't really say I know why."

"Don't think too much, Captain. When the shit hits the fan, you don't have time to think it all the way through. You think beforehand. It's in how you train your people, and assign responsibilities to them. You prepare your mind for action, but you never think you know what form the action is going to take. In any case, you did everything pretty well. You impressed this Hardesty guy—and he *is* a fairly serious customer. That's how this happened," Broughton concluded.

"Excuse me, sir?"

"The Agency wants to talk to you," the M-2 announced. "They're doing a talent hunt, and your name came up."

"To do what, sir?"

"Didn't tell me that. They're looking for people who can work in the field. I don't think it's espionage. Probably the paramilitary side of the house. I'd guess that's the new counterterror shop. I can't say I'm pleased to lose a promising young Marine. However, I have no say in the matter. You are free to decline the offer, but you do have to go up and talk to them beforehand."

"I see." He didn't, really.

"Maybe somebody reminded them of another ex-Marine who worked out fairly well up there..." Broughton half observed.

"Uncle Jack, you mean? Jesus—excuse me, sir, but I've been dodging that ever since I showed up at the Basic School. I'm just one more Marine O-3, sir. I'm not asking for anything else."

"Good," was all Broughton felt like saying. He saw before him a very promising young officer who'd read the *Marine Corps Officer's Guide* front to back, and hadn't forgotten any of the important parts. If anything he was a touch too earnest, but he'd been the same way once himself. "Well, you're due up there in two hours. Some guy named Pete Alexander, another ex–Special Forces guy. Helped run the Afghanistan operation for the Agency back in the 1980s. Not a bad guy, so I've heard, but he doesn't want to grow his own talent. Watch your wallet, Captain," he said in dismissal.

"Yes, sir," Caruso promised. He came to his feet, into the position of attention.

The M-2 graced his guest with a smile. "Semper Fi, son."

"Aye, aye, sir." Caruso made his way out of the office, nodded to the gunny, never said a word to the half-colonel, who hadn't bothered looking up, and headed downstairs, wondering what the hell he was getting into.

HUNDREDS OF miles away, another man named Caruso was thinking the same thing. The FBI had made its reputation as one of America's premier law-enforcement agencies by investigating interstate kidnappings, beginning soon after passage of the Lindbergh Law in the 1930s. Its success in closing such cases had largely put an end to kidnapping-for-money—at least for smart criminals. The Bureau closed *every single one* of those cases, and professional criminals had finally caught on that this form of crime was a sucker's game. And so it had remained for years, until kidnappers with objectives other than money had decided to delve into it.

And those people were much harder to catch.

Penelope Davidson had vanished on her way to kindergarten that very morning. Her parents had called the local police within an hour after her disappearance, and soon thereafter the local sheriff's office had called the FBI. Procedure allowed the FBI to get involved as soon as it was possible for the victim to have been taken across a state line. Georgetown, Alabama, was just half an hour from the Mississippi state line, and so the Birmingham office of the FBI had immediately jumped on the case like a cat on a mouse. In FBI nomenclature, a kidnapping case is called a "7," and nearly every agent in the office got into his car and headed southwest for the small farming-market town. In the mind of each agent, however, was the dread of a fool's errand. There was a clock on kidnapping cases. Most victims were thought to be sexually exploited and killed within four or six hours. Only a miracle could get the child back alive that quickly, and miracles didn't happen often.

But most of them were men with wives and children themselves, and so they worked as though there were a chance. The office ASAC—Assistant Special Agent in Charge—was the first to talk to the local sheriff, whose name was Paul Turner. The Bureau regarded him as an amateur in the business of investigations, out of his depth, and Turner thought so as well. The thought of a raped and murdered little girl in his jurisdiction turned his stomach, and he welcomed federal assistance. Photos were passed out to every man with a badge and a gun. Maps were consulted. The local cops and FBI Special Agents headed to the area between the Davidson house and the public school to which she'd walked five blocks every morning for two months. Everyone who lived on that pathway was interviewed. Back in Birmingham, computer checks were made of possible sex offenders living within a hundred-mile radius, and agents and Alabama state troopers were sent to interview them, too. Every house was searched, usually with permission of the owner, but often enough without, because the local judges took a stern view of kidnapping.

For Special Agent Dominic Caruso, it wasn't his first major case, but it was his first "7," and while he was unmarried and childless, the thought of a missing child caused his blood first to chill, and then to boil. Her "official" kindergarten photo showed blue eyes and blond hair turning brown, and a cute little smile. This "7" wasn't about money. The family was working class and ordinary. The father was a lineman for the local electric co-op, the mother worked part-time as a nurse's aide in the county hospital. Both were churchgoing Methodists, and neither, on first inspection, seemed a likely suspect for child abuse, though that would be looked into, too. A senior agent from the Birmingham Field Office was skilled in profiling, and his initial read was frightening: This unknown subject could be a serial kidnapper and killer, someone who found children sexually attractive, and who knew that the safest way to commit this crime was to kill the victim afterward.

He was out there somewhere, Caruso knew. Dominic Caruso was a young agent, hardly a year out of Quantico, but already in his second field assignment—unmarried FBI agents had no more choice in picking their assignments than a sparrow in a hurricane. His initial assignment had been in Newark, New Jersey, all of seven months, but Alabama was more to his taste. The weather was often miserable, but it wasn't a beehive like that dirty city. His assignment now was to patrol the area west of Georgetown, to scan and wait for some hard bit of information. He wasn't experienced enough to be an effective interviewer. The skill took years to develop, though Caruso thought he was pretty smart, and his college degree was in psychology.

Look for a car with a little girl in it, he told himself, *one* not *in a car seat?* he wondered. It might give her a better way to look out of the car, and maybe wave for help... So, no, the subject would probably have her tied up, cuffed, or wrapped with duct tape, and probably gagged. *Some little girl, helpless and terrified.* The thought made his hands tighten on the wheel. The radio crackled.

"Birmingham Base to all '7' units. We have a report that the '7' suspect might be driving a white utility van, probably a Ford, white in color, a little dirty. Alabama tags. If you see a vehicle matching that description, call it in, and we'll get the local PD to check it out."

Which meant, don't flash your gum-ball light and pull him over yourself unless you have to, Caruso thought. It was time to do some thinking.

If I were one of those creatures, where would I be...? Caruso slowed down. He thought... a place with decent road access. Not a main road per se... a decent secondary road, with a turnoff to something more private. Easy in, easy out. A place where the neighbors couldn't see or hear what he's up to...

He picked up his microphone.

"Caruso to Birmingham Base."

"Yeah, Dominic," responded the agent on the radio

desk. The FBI radios were encrypted, and couldn't be listened into by anyone without a good descrambler.

"The white van. How solid is that?"

"An elderly woman says that when she was out getting her paper, she saw a little girl, right description, talking to some guy next to a white van. The possible subject is male Caucasian, undetermined age, no other description. Ain't much, Dom, but it's all we got," Special Agent Sandy Ellis reported.

"How many child abusers in the area?" Caruso asked next.

"A total of nineteen on the computer. We got people talking to all of them. Nothing developed yet. All we got, man."

"Roger, Sandy. Out."

More driving, more scanning. He wondered if this was anything like his brother Brian had experienced in Afghanistan: alone, hunting the enemy... He started looking for dirt paths off the road, maybe for one with recent tire tracks.

He looked down at the wallet-sized photo again. A sweet-faced little girl, just learning the ABC's. A child for whom the world has always been a safe place, ruled by Mommy and Daddy, who went to Sunday school and made caterpillars out of egg cartons and pipe cleaners, and learned to sing "Jesus loves me, this I know / 'Cause the Bible tells me so..." His head swiveled left and right. There, about a hundred yards away, a dirt road leading into the woods. As he slowed, he saw that the path took a gentle S-curve, but the trees were thin, and he could see...

... cheap frame house... and next to it... the corner of a van...? But this one was more beige than white...

Well, the little old lady who'd seen the little girl and the truck... how far away had it been... sunlight or shadows...? So many things, so many inconstants, so many variables. As good as the FBI Academy was, it couldn't prepare you for everything—hell, not even close to every-thing. That's what they told you, too—told you that you had to trust your instinct and experience...

But Caruso had hardly a year's experience.

Still...

He stopped the car.

"Caruso to Birmingham Base."

"Yeah, Dominic," Sandy Ellis responded.

Caruso radioed in his location. "I'm going 10-7 to walk in and take a look."

"Roger that, Dom. Do you request backup?"

"Negative, Sandy. It's probably nothing, just going to knock on the door and talk to the occupant."

"Okay, I'll stand by."

Caruso didn't have a portable radio—that was for local cops, not the Bureau—and so was now out of touch, except for his cell phone. His personal side arm was a Smith & Wesson 1076, snug in its holster on his right hip. He stepped out of the car, and closed the door without latching it, to avoid making noise. People always turned to see what made the noise of a slammed car door.

He was wearing a darker than olive green suit, a fortu-nate circumstance, Caruso thought, heading right. First he'd look at the van. He walked normally, but his eyes were locked on the windows of the shabby house, halfway hop-ing to see a face, but, on reflection, glad that none appeared.

The Ford van was about six years old, he judged. Minor dings and dents on the bodywork. The driver had backed it in. That put the sliding door close to the house, the sort of thing a carpenter or plumber might do. Or a man moving a small, resisting body. He kept his right hand free, and his coat unbuttoned. Quick-draw was something every cop in the world practiced, often in front of a mirror, though only a fool fired as part of the motion, because you just couldn't hit anything that way.

Caruso took his time. The window was down on the

driver-side door. The interior was almost entirely empty, bare, unpainted metal floor, the spare tire and jack...and a large roll of duct tape...

There was a lot of that stuff around. The free end of the roll was turned down, as though to make sure he'd be able to pull some off the roll without having to pick at it with his fingernails. A lot of people did that, too. There was, finally, a throw rug, tucked—no, *taped,* he saw, to the floor, just behind the right-side passenger seat...and was that some tape dangling from the metal seat framing? What might that mean?

Why there? Caruso wondered, but suddenly the skin on his forearms started tingling. It was a first for that sensation. He'd never made an arrest himself, had not yet been involved in a major felony case, at least not to any sort of conclusion. He'd worked fugitives in Newark, briefly, and made a total of three collars, always with another, more experienced agent to take the lead. He was more experienced now, a tiny bit seasoned...But not all that much, he reminded himself.

Caruso's head turned to the house. His mind was moving quickly now. What did he really have? Not much. He'd looked into an ordinary light truck with no direct evidence at all in it, just an empty truck with a roll of duct tape and a small rug on the steel floor.

Even so...

The young agent took the cell phone out of his pocket and speed-dialed the office.

"FBI. Can I help you?" a female voice asked.

"Caruso for Ellis." That moved things quickly.

"What you got, Dom?"

"White Ford Econoline van, Alabama tag Echo Romeo Six Five Zero One, parked at my location. Sandy—"

"Yeah, Dominic?"

"I'm going to knock on this guy's door."

"You want backup?"

Caruso took a second to think. "Affirmative—roger that."

"There's a county mountie about ten minutes away. Stand by," Ellis advised.

"Roger, standing by."

But a little girl's life was on the line...

He headed toward the house, careful to keep out of the sight lines from the nearest windows. That's when time stopped.

He nearly jumped out of his skin when he heard the scream. It was an awful, shrill sound, like someone looking at Death himself. His brain processed the information, and he suddenly found that his automatic pistol was in his hands, just in front of his sternum, pointed up into the sky, but in his hands even so. It had been a woman's scream, he realized, and something just went *click* inside his head.

As quickly as he could move without making much noise, he was on the porch, under the uneven, cheaply made roof. The front door was mostly wire screening to keep the bugs out. It needed painting, but so did the whole house. Probably a rental, and a cheap one at that. Looking through the screen he could see what seemed to be a corridor, leading left to the kitchen and right to a bathroom. He could see into it. A white porcelain toilet and a sink were all that was visible from this perspective.

He wondered if he had probable cause to enter the house, and instantly decided that he had enough. He pulled the door open and slipped in as stealthily as he could manage. A cheap and dirty rug leading down the corridor. He headed that way, gun up, senses sandpapered to ultimate alertness. As he moved, the angles of vision changed. The kitchen became invisible, but he could see into the bathroom better...

Penny Davidson was in the bathtub, naked, china blue eyes wide open, and her throat cut from ear to ear, with a whole body's supply of blood covering her flat chest and the sides of the tub. So violently had her neck been slashed that it lay open like a second mouth.

Strangely, Caruso didn't react physically. His eyes recorded the snapshot image, but for the moment all he thought about was that the man who'd done it was alive, and just a few feet away.

He realized that the noise he heard came from the left and ahead. The living room. A television. The subject would be in there. Might there be a second one? He didn't have time for that, nor did he particularly care at the moment.

Slowly, carefully, his heart going like a trip-hammer, he edged forward and peeked around the corner. There he was, late thirties, white male, hair thinning, watching the TV with rapt attention—it was a horror movie, the scream must have come from that—and sipping Miller Lite beer from an aluminum can. His face was content and in no way aroused. He'd probably been through that, Dominic thought. And right in front of him—Jesus—was a butcher knife, a bloody one, on the coffee table. There was blood on his T-shirt, as if sprayed. From a little girl's throat.

"The trouble with these mutts is that they never resist," an instructor had told his class at the FBI Academy. "Oh, yeah, they're John Wayne with an attitude when they have little kids in their hands, but they don't resist armed cops— ever. And, you know, that's a damned shame," the instructor had concluded.

You are not going in to jail today. The thought entered Caruso's mind seemingly of its own accord. His right thumb pulled back the spurless hammer until it clicked in place, putting his side arm fully in battery. His hands, he noted briefly, felt like ice.

Just at the corner, where you turned left to enter the room, was a battered old end table. Octagonal in shape, atop it was a transparent blue glass vase, a cheap one, maybe from the local Kmart, probably intended for flowers, but none were there today. Slowly, carefully, Caruso cocked his leg, then kicked the table over. The glass vase shattered loudly on the wooden floor.

The subject started violently, and turned to see an unexpected visitor in his house. His defensive response was instinctive rather than reasoned—he grabbed for the butcher knife on the coffee table. Caruso didn't even have time to smile, though he knew the subject had made the final mistake of his life. It's regarded as holy gospel in American police agencies that a man with a knife in his hand less than twenty-one feet away is an immediate and lethal threat. He even started to rise to his feet.

But he never made it.

Caruso's finger depressed the trigger of his Smith, sending the first round straight through the subject's heart. Two more followed in less than a second. His white T-shirt blossomed in red. He looked down at his chest, then up at Caruso, total surprise on his face, and then he sat back down, without speaking a word or crying out in pain.

Caruso's next action was to reverse direction and check out the house's only bedroom. Empty. So was the kitchen, the rear door still locked from the inside. There came a moment's relief. Nobody else in the house. He took another look at the kidnapper. The eyes were still open. But Dominic had shot true. First he disarmed and handcuffed the dead body, because that was how he'd been trained. A check of the carotid pulse came next, but it was wasted energy. The guy saw nothing except the front door of hell. Caruso pulled his cell phone out and speed-dialed the office again.

"Dom?" Ellis asked when he got the phone.

"Yeah, Sandy, it's me. I just took him down."

"What? What do you mean?" Sandy Ellis asked urgently.

"The little girl, she's here, dead, throat cut. I came in, and the guy came up at me with a knife. Took him down, man. He's dead, too, dead as fuckin' hell."

"Jesus, Dominic! The county sheriff is just a couple of minutes out. Stand by."

"Roger, standing by, Sandy."

Not another minute passed before he heard the sound of a siren. Caruso went out on the porch. He decocked and holstered his automatic; then he took his FBI credentials out of his coat pocket, and held them up in his left hand as the sheriff approached, his service revolver out.

"It's under control," Caruso announced in as calm a voice as he could muster. He was pumped up now. He waved Sheriff Turner into the house, but stayed outside by himself while the local cop went inside. A minute or two later, the cop came back out, his own Smith & Wesson holstered.

Turner was the Hollywood image of a southern sheriff, tall, heavyset, with beefy arms, and a gun belt that dug deeply into his waistline. Except he was black. Wrong movie.

"What happened?" he asked.

"Want to give me a minute?" Caruso took a deep breath and thought for a moment how to tell the story. Turner's understanding of it was important, because homicide was a local crime, and he had jurisdiction over it.

"Yeah." Turner reached into his shirt pocket and pulled out a pack of Kools. He offered one to Caruso, who shook his head.

The young agent sat down on the unpainted wooden deck and tried to put it all together in his head. What, exactly, had happened? What, exactly, had he just done? And how, exactly, was he supposed to explain it? The whispering part of his mind told him that he felt no regret at all. At least not for the subject. For Penelope Davidson—too damned late. An hour sooner? Maybe even a half hour? That little girl would not be going home tonight, would never more be tucked into bed by her mother, or hug her father. And so Special Agent Dominic Caruso felt no remorse at all. Just regret for being too slow.

"Can you talk?" Sheriff Turner asked.

"I was looking for a place like this one, and when I drove past, I saw the van parked..." Caruso began.

Presently, he stood and led the sheriff into the house to relate the other details.

"Anyway, I tripped over the table. He saw me, and went for his knife, turned toward me—and so, I drew my pistol and shot the bastard. Three rounds, I think."

"Uh-huh." Turner went over to the body. The subject hadn't bled much. All three rounds had gone straight through the heart, ending its ability to pump almost instantly.

Paul Turner wasn't anywhere nearly as dumb as he looked to a government-trained agent. He looked at the body, and turned to look back at the doorway from which Caruso had taken his shots. His eyes measured distance and angle.

"So," the sheriff said, "you tripped on that end table. The suspect sees you, grabs his knife, and you, being in fear of your life, take out your service pistol and take three quick shots, right?"

"That's how it went down, yeah."

"Uh-huh," observed a man who got himself a deer almost every hunting season.

Sheriff Turner reached into his right-side pants pocket and pulled out his key chain. It was a gift from his father, a Pullman porter on the old Illinois Central. It was an old-fashioned one, with a 1948 silver dollar soldered onto it, the old kind, about an inch and a half across. He held it over the kidnapper's chest, and the diameter of the old coin completely covered all three of the entrance wounds. His eyes took a very skeptical look, but then they drifted over toward the bathroom, and his eyes softened before he spoke his verdict on the incident.

"Then that's how we'll write it up. Nice shootin', boy."

FULLY A dozen police and FBI vehicles appeared within as many minutes. Soon thereafter came the lab truck from the Alabama Department of Public Safety to perform the crime-scene investigative work. A forensic photographer shot twenty-three rolls of 400-speed color film. The knife was taken from the subject's hand and bagged for fingerprints and blood-type matching with the victim—it was all less than a formality, but criminal procedure was especially strict in a murder case. Finally, the body of the little girl was bagged and removed. Her parents would have to identify her, but blessedly her face was reasonably intact.

One of the last to arrive was Ben Harding, the Special Agent in Charge of the Birmingham Field Office of the Federal Bureau of Investigation. An agent-involved shooting meant a formal report from his desk to that of Director Dan Murray, a distant friend. First, Harding came to make sure that Caruso was in decent physical and psychological shape. Then he went to pay respects to Paul Turner, and get his opinion of the shooting. Caruso watched from a distance, and saw Turner gesture through the incident, accompanied by nods from Harding. It was good that Sheriff Turner was giving his official stamp of approval. A captain of state troopers listened in as well, and he nodded, too.

The truth of the matter was that Dominic Caruso didn't really give a damn. He knew he'd done the right thing, just an hour later than it ought to have been. Finally, Harding came over to his young agent.

"How you feeling, Dominic?"

"Slow," Caruso said. "Too damned slow—yeah, I know, unreasonable to expect otherwise."

Harding grabbed his shoulder and shook it. "You could not have done much better, kid." He paused. "How'd the shooting go down?"

Caruso repeated his story. It had almost acquired the firmness of truth in his mind now. He could probably have spoken the exact truth and not been hammered for it, Dom knew, but why take the chance? It was, officially, a clean shoot, and that was enough, so far as his Bureau file was concerned.

Harding listened, and nodded thoughtfully. There'd be paperwork to complete and FedEx up the line to D.C. But it would not look bad in the newspapers for an FBI agent to have shot and killed a kidnapper the very day of the crime. They'd probably find evidence that this was not the only such crime this mutt had committed. The house had yet to be thoroughly searched. They'd already found a digital camera in the house, and it would surprise no one to see that the mutt had a record of previous crimes on his Dell personal computer. If so, Caruso had closed more than one case. If so, Caruso would get a big gold star in his Bureau copybook.

Just how big, neither Harding nor Caruso could yet know. The talent hunt was about to find Dominic Caruso, too.

And one other.

CHAPTER 1

||||||||||||||||||||||||||||||||||||||||||||||||||||||||||||||||

THE
CAMPUS

THE TOWN of West Odenton, Maryland, isn't much of a town at all, just a post office for people who live in the general area, a few gas stations and a 7-Eleven, plus the usual fast-food places for people who need a fat-filled breakfast on the drive from Columbia, Maryland, to their jobs in Washington, D.C. And half a mile from the modest post office building was a mid-rise office building of government-undistinguished architecture. It was nine stories high, and on the capacious front lawn a low decorative monolith made of gray brick with silvery lettering said HENDLEY ASSOCIATES, without explaining what, exactly, Hendley Associates was. There were few hints. The roof of the building was flat, tar-and-gravel over reinforced concrete, with a small penthouse to house the elevator machinery and another rectangular structure that gave no clue about its identity. In fact, it was made of fiberglass, white in color, and radio-transparent. The building itself was unusual only in one thing: Except for a few old tobacco barns that barely exceeded twenty-five feet in height, it was the only building higher than two stories that sat on a direct line of sight from the National Security Agency located at Fort Meade, Maryland, and the headquarters of the Central Intelligence Agency at Langley, Virginia. Some other entrepreneurs had wished to build on that sight line, but zoning approval had never been granted, for many reasons, all of them false.

Behind the building was a small antenna farm not unlike that found next to a local television station—a half-dozen six-meter parabolic dishes sat inside a twelve-foot-high, razor-wire-crowned Cyclone fence enclosure and pointed at various commercial communications satellites. The entire complex, which wasn't terribly complex at all, comprised fifteen and a third acres in Maryland's Howard County, and was referred to as "The Campus" by the people who worked there. Nearby was the Johns Hopkins University Applied Physics Laboratory, a government-consulting establishment of long standing and well-established sensitivity of function.

To the public, Hendley Associates was a trader in stocks, bonds, and international currencies, though, oddly, it did little in the way of public business. It was not known to have any clients, and while it was whispered to be quietly active in local charities (the Johns Hopkins University School of Medicine was rumored to be the main recipient of Hendley's corporate largesse), nothing had ever leaked to the local media. In fact, it had no public-relations department at all. Neither was it rumored to be doing anything untoward, though its chief executive officer was known to have had a somewhat troubled past, as a result of which he was shy of publicity, which, on a few rare occasions, he'd dodged quite adroitly and amiably, until, finally, the local media had stopped asking. Hendley's employees were scattered about locally, mostly in Columbia, lived upper-middle-class lifestyles, and were generally as remarkable as Beaver's father, Ward Cleaver.

Gerald Paul Hendley, Jr., had had a stellar career in the commodities business, during which he'd amassed a sizable personal fortune and then turned to elected public service in his late thirties, soon becoming a United States senator from South Carolina. Very quickly, he'd acquired a reputation as a legislative maverick who eschewed special interests and their campaign money offers, and followed a rather ferociously independent political track, leaning toward liberal on civil-rights issues, but decidedly conservative on defense and foreign relations. He'd never shied away from speaking his mind, which had made him good and entertaining copy for the press, and eventually there were whispered-about presidential aspirations.

Toward the end of his second six-year term, however, he'd suffered a great personal tragedy. He'd lost his wife and three children in an accident on Interstate 185 just outside of Columbia, South Carolina, their station wagon crushed beneath the wheels of a Kenworth tractor-trailer. It had been a predictably crushing blow, and soon thereafter, at the very beginning of the campaign for his third term, more misfortune had struck him. It became known through a column in the *New York Times* that his personal investment portfolio—he'd always kept it private, saying that since he took no money for his campaigning, he had no need to disclose his net worth except in the most general of terms—showed evidence of insider trading. This suspicion was confirmed with deeper delving by the newspapers and TV, and despite Hendley's protest that the Securities and Exchange Commission had never actually published guidelines about what the law meant, it appeared to some that he'd used his inside knowledge on future government expenditures to benefit a real-estate investment enterprise which would profit him and his co-investors over fifty million dollars. Worse still, when challenged on the question in a public debate by the Republican candidate—a self-described "Mr. Clean"—he'd responded with two mistakes. First, he'd lost his temper in front of rolling cameras. Second, he'd told the people of South Carolina that if they doubted his honesty, then they could vote for the fool with whom he shared the stage. For a man who'd never put a political foot wrong in his life, that surprise alone had cost him five percent of the state's voters. The remainder of his lackluster campaign had only slid downhill, and despite the lingering sympathy vote from those who remembered the annihilation of his family, his seat had ended up an upset-loss for the Democrats, which had further been exacerbated by a venomous concession statement. Then he'd left public life for good, not even returning to his antebellum plantation northwest of Charleston but rather moving to Maryland and leaving his life entirely behind. One further flamethrower statement at the entire congressional process had burned whatever bridges might have remained open to him.

His current home was a farm dating back to the eighteenth century, where he raised Appaloosa horses—riding and mediocre golf were his only remaining hobbies—and lived the quiet life of a gentleman farmer. He also worked at The Campus seven or eight hours per day, commuting back and forth in a chauffeured stretch Cadillac.

Fifty-two now, tall, slender and silver haired, he was well known without being known at all, perhaps the one lingering aspect of his political past.

"YOU DID well in the mountains," Jim Hardesty said, waving the young Marine to a chair.

"Thank you, sir. You did okay, too, sir."

"Captain, anytime you walk back through your front door after it's all over, you've done well. I learned that from my training officer. About sixteen years ago," he added.

Captain Caruso did the mental arithmetic and decided that Hardesty was a little older than he looked. Captain in the U.S. Army Special Forces, then CIA, plus sixteen years made him closer to fifty than forty. He must have worked very hard indeed to keep in shape.

"So," the officer asked, "what can I do for you?"

"What did Terry tell you?" the spook asked.

"He told me I'd be talking with somebody named Pete Alexander."

"Pete got called out of town suddenly," Hardesty explained.

The officer accepted the explanation at face value. "Okay, anyway, the general said you Agency guys are on some kind of talent hunt, but you're not willing to grow your own," Caruso answered honestly.

"Terry is a good man, and a damned fine Marine, but he can be a little parochial."

"Maybe so, Mr. Hardesty, but he's going to be my boss soon, when he takes over Second Marine Division, and I'm trying to stay on his good side. And you still haven't told me why I'm here."

"Like the Corps?" the spook asked. The young Marine nodded.

"Yes, sir. The pay ain't all that much, but it's all I need, and the people I work with are the best."

"Well, the ones we went up the mountain with are pretty good. How long did you have them?"

"Total? About fourteen months, sir."

"You trained them pretty well."

"It's what they pay me for, sir, and I had good material to start with."

"You also handled that little combat action well," Hardesty observed, taking note of the distant replies he was getting.

Captain Caruso was not quite modest enough to regard it as a "little" combat action. The bullets flying around had been real enough, which made the action big enough. But his training, he'd found, had worked just about as well as his officers had told him it would in all the classes and field exercises. It had been an important and rather gratifying discovery. The Marine Corps actually did make sense. Damn.

"Yes, sir," was all he said in reply, however, adding, "And thank you for your help, sir."

"I'm a little old for that sort of thing, but it's nice to see that I still know how." And it had been quite enough, Hardesty didn't add. Combat was still a kid's game, and he was no longer a kid. "Any thoughts about it, Captain?" he asked next.

"Not really, sir. I did my after-action report."

Hardesty had read it. "Nightmares, anything like that?"

The question surprised Caruso. Nightmares? Why would he have those? "No, sir," he responded with visible puzzlement.

"Any qualms of conscience?" Hardesty went on.

"Sir, those people were making war on my country. We made war back. You ought not to play the game if you can't handle the action. If they had wives and kids, I'm sorry about that, but when you screw with people, you need to understand that they're going to come see you about it."

"It's a tough world?"

"Sir, you'd better not kick a tiger in the ass unless you have a plan for dealing with his teeth."

No nightmares and no regrets, Hardesty thought. That was the way things were supposed to be, but the kinder, gentler United States of America didn't always turn out its people that way. Caruso was a warrior. Hardesty rocked back in his seat and gave his guest a careful look before speaking.

"Cap'n, the reason you're here ... you've seen it in the papers, all the problems we've had dealing with this new spate of international terrorism. There have been a lot of turf wars between the Agency and the Bureau. At the operational level, there's usually no problem, and there isn't all that much trouble at the command level—the FBI director, Murray, is solid troop, and when he worked Legal Attaché in London he got along well with our people."

"But it's the midlevel staff pukes, right?" Caruso asked.

He'd seen it in the Corps, too. Staff officers who spent a lot of their time snarling at other staff officers, saying that their daddy could beat up the other staff's daddy. The phenomenon probably dated back to the Romans or the Greeks. It had been stupid and counterproductive back then, too.

"Bingo," Hardesty confirmed. "And you know, God Himself might be able to fix it, but even He would have to have a really good day to bring it off. The bureaucracies are too entrenched. It's not so bad in the military. People there shuffle in and out of jobs, and they have this idea of 'mission,' and everybody generally works to accomplish it, especially if it helps them all hustle up the ladder individually. Generally speaking, the farther you are from the sharp end, the more likely you are to immerse yourself in the minutiae. So, we're looking for people who know about the sharp end."

"And the mission is—what?"

"To identify, locate, and deal with terrorist threats," the spook answered.

"'Deal with'?" Caruso asked.

"Neutralize—shit, okay, when necessary and convenient, kill the son of a bitches. Gather information on the nature and severity of the threat, and take whatever action is necessary, depending on the specific threat. The job is fundamentally intelligence-gathering. The Agency has too many restrictions on how it does business. This special sub-group doesn't."

"Really?" *That* was a considerable surprise.

Hardesty nodded soberly. "Really. You won't be working for CIA. You may use Agency assets as resources, but that's as far as it goes."

"So, who am I working for?"

"We have a little way to go before we can discuss that." Hardesty lifted what had to be the Marine's personnel folder. "You score in the top three percent among the Marine officers in terms of intelligence. Four-point-oh in nearly everything. Your language skills are particularly impressive."

"My dad is an American citizen—native-born, I mean—but his dad came off the boat from Italy, ran—still runs—a restaurant in Seattle. So, Pop actually grew up speaking mostly Italian, and a lot of that came down on me and my brother, too. Took Spanish in high school and college. I can't pass for a native, but I understand it pretty well."

"Engineering major?"

"That's from my dad, too. It's in there. He works for Boeing—aerodynamicist, mainly designs wings and control surfaces. You know about my mom—it's all in there. She's mainly a mom, does things with the local Catholic schools, too, now that Dominic and I are grown."

"And he's FBI?"

Brian nodded. "That's right, got his law degree and signed up to be a G-man."

"Just made the papers," Hardesty said, handing over a faxed page from the Birmingham papers. Brian scanned it.

"Way to go, Dom," Captain Caruso breathed when he got to the fourth paragraph, which further pleased his host.

IT WAS scarcely a two-hour flight from Birmingham to Reagan National in Washington. Dominic Caruso walked to the Metro station and hopped a subway train for the Hoover Building at Tenth and Pennsylvania. His badge absolved him of the need to pass through the metal detector. FBI agents were supposed to carry heat, and his automatic had earned a notch in the grip—not literally, of course, but FBI agents occasionally joked about it.

The office of Assistant Director Augustus Ernst Werner was on the top floor, overlooking Pennsylvania Avenue. The secretary waved him right in.

Caruso had never met Gus Werner. He was a tall, slender, and very experienced street agent, an ex-Marine, and positively monkish in appearance and demeanor. He'd headed the FBI Hostage Rescue Team and two field divisions, and been at the point of retirement before being talked into his new job by his close friend, Director Daniel E. Murray. The Counter-Terrorism Division was a stepchild of the much larger Criminal and Foreign Counter-Intelligence divisions, but it was gaining in importance on a daily basis.

"Grab yourself a seat," Werner said, pointing, as he finished up a call. That just took another minute. Then Gus replaced the phone and hit the DO NOT DISTURB button.

"Ben Harding faxed this up to me," Werner said, holding the shooting report from the previous day. "How did it go?"

"It's all in there, sir." He'd spent three hours picking his own brain and putting it all down on paper in precise FBI bureaucratese. Strange that an act requiring less than sixty seconds to perform should require so much time to explain.

"And what did you leave out, Dominic?" The question was accompanied by the most penetrating look the young agent had ever encountered.

"Nothing, sir," Caruso replied.

"Dominic, we have some very good pistol shots in the Bureau. I'm one of them," Gus Werner told his guest. "Three shots, all in the heart from a range of fifteen feet, is pretty good range shooting. For somebody who just tripped over an end table, it's downright miraculous. Ben Harding didn't find it remarkable, but Director Murray and I do—Dan's a pretty good marksman, too. He read this fax last night and asked me to render an opinion. Dan's never whacked a subject before. I have, three times, twice with HRT—those were cooperative ventures, as it were—and once in Des Moines, Iowa. That one was a kidnapping, too. I'd seen what he'd done to two of his victims—little boys—and, you know, I really didn't want some psychiatrist telling the jury that he was the victim of an adverse childhood, and that it really wasn't his fault, and all that bullshit that you hear in a nice clean court of law, where the only thing the jury sees are the pictures, and maybe not even them if the defense counsel can persuade the judge that they're overly inflammatory. So, you know what happened? I got to be the law. Not to enforce the law, or write the law, or explain the law. That one day, twenty-two years ago, I got to *be* the law. God's Own Avenging Sword. And you know, it felt good."

"How did you know ... ?"

"How did I know for sure that he was our boy? He kept souvenirs. Heads. There were eight of them there in his house trailer. So, no, there wasn't any doubt at all in my mind. There was a knife nearby, and I told him to pick it up, and he did, and I put four rounds in his chest from a range of ten feet, and I've never had a moment's regret." Werner paused. "Not many people know that story. Not even my wife. So, don't tell me you tripped over a table, drew your Smith, and printed three rounds inside the subject's ventricle standing on one foot, okay?"

"Yes, sir." Caruso responded ambiguously. "Mr. Werner—"

"Name's Gus," the Assistant Director corrected.

"Sir," Caruso persisted. Senior people who used first names tended to make him nervous. "Sir, were I to say something like that, I'd be confessing to the next thing to murder, in an official government document. He *did* pick up that knife, he *was* getting up to face me, he *was* just ten or twelve feet away, and at Quantico they taught us to regard that as an immediate and lethal threat. So, yes, I took the shot, and it was righteous, in accordance with FBI policy on the use of lethal force."

Werner nodded. "You have your law degree, don't you?"

"Yes, sir. I'm admitted to the bar in Virginia and D.C. both. I haven't taken the Alabama bar exam yet."

"Well, stop being a lawyer for a minute," Werner advised. "This was a righteous shooting. I still have the revolver I whacked that bastard with. Smith Model 66 four-inch. I even wear it to work sometimes. Dominic, you got to do what every agent would like to do just once in his career. You got to deliver justice all by yourself. Don't feel bad about it."

"I don't, sir," Caruso assured him. "That little girl, Penelope—I couldn't save her, but at least that bastard won't ever do it again." He looked Werner right in the eye. "You know what it feels like."

"Yeah." He looked closely at Caruso. "And you're sure you have no regrets?"

"I caught an hour's nap on the flight up, sir." He delivered the statement without a visible smile.

But it generated one on Werner's face. He nodded. "Well, you'll be getting an official attaboy from the office of the Director. No OPR."

OPR was the FBI's own "Internal Affairs" office, and while respected by rank-and-file FBI agents, was not beloved of them. There was a saying, "If he tortures small animals and wets his bed, he's either a serial killer or he works for the Office of Professional Responsibility."

Werner lifted Caruso's folder. "Says here you're pretty smart...good language skills, too...Interested in coming to Washington? I'm looking for people who know how to think on their feet, to work in my shop."

Another move, was what Special Agent Dominic Caruso heard.

GERRY HENDLEY was not an overly formal man. He wore a jacket and tie to work, but the jacket ended up on a clothes tree in his office within fifteen seconds of arrival. He had a fine executive secretary—like himself, a native of South Carolina—named Helen Connolly, and after running through his day's schedule with her, he picked up his *Wall Street Journal* and checked the front page. He'd already devoured the day's *New York Times* and *Washington Post* to get his political fix for the day, grumbling as always how they never quite got it right. The digital clock on his desk told him that he had twenty minutes before his first meeting, and he lit up his computer to get the morning's *Early Bird* as well, the clipping service that went to senior government officials. This he scanned to see if he'd missed anything in his morning read of the big-time papers. Not much, except for an interesting piece in the *Virginia Pilot* about the annual Fletcher Conference, a circle-think held by the Navy and Marine Corps every year at the Norfolk Navy Base. They talked about terrorism, and fairly intelligently, Hendley thought. People in uniform often did. As opposed to elected officials.

We kill off the Soviet Union, Hendley thought, *and we expected everything in the world to settle down. But what we* didn't *see coming was all these lunatics with leftover AK-47s and education in kitchen chemistry, or simply a willingness to trade their own lives for those of their perceived enemies.*

And the other thing they hadn't done was prepare the intelligence community to deal with it. Even a president experienced in the black world and the best DCI in American history hadn't managed to get all that much done. They'd added a lot more people—an extra five hundred personnel in an agency of twenty thousand didn't sound like a lot, but it had doubled the operations directorate. That had given the CIA a force only half as horribly inadequate as it had been before, but that wasn't the same as adequate. And in return for it, the Congress had further tightened oversight and restrictions, thus further crippling the new people hired to flesh out the governmental skeleton crew. They never learned. He himself had talked at infinite length to his colleagues in the World's Most Exclusive Men's Club, but while some listened, others did not, and almost all of the remainder vacillated. They paid too much attention to the editorial pages, often of newspapers not even native to their home states, because *that,* they foolishly figured, was what the American People thought. Maybe it was this simple: Any newly elected official was seduced into the game the same way Cleopatra had snookered Gaius Julius Caesar. It was the staffs, he knew, the "professional" political helpers who "guided" their employers into the right way to be reelected, which had become the Holy Grail of public service. America did not have a hereditary ruling class, but it did have plenty of people happy to lead their employers onto the righteous path of government divinity.

And working inside the system just didn't work.

So, to accomplish anything, you just had to be outside the system.

Way the hell outside the system.

And if anybody noticed, well, he was already disgraced anyway, wasn't he?

He spent his first hour discussing financial matters with some of his staff, because that was how Hendley Associates made its money. As a commodities trader, and as a currency arbitrageur, he'd been ahead of the curve almost from the beginning, sensing the momentary valuation differences—he always called them "Deltas"—which were generated by psychological factors, by perceptions that might or might not turn out to be real.

He did all his business anonymously through foreign banks, all of which liked having large cash accounts, and none of which were overly fastidious about where the money came from, so long as it was not overtly dirty, which his certainly was not. It was just another way of keeping outside the system.

Not that every one of his dealings was strictly legal. Having Fort Meade's intercepts on his side made the game a lot easier. In fact, it was illegal as hell, and not the least bit ethical. But in truth Hendley Associates did little in the way of damage on the world stage. It could have been otherwise, but Hendley Associates operated on the principle that pigs got fed and hogs got slaughtered, and so they ate only a little out of the international trough. And, besides, there was no real governing authority for crimes of this type and this magnitude. And tucked away in a safe within the company vault was an official Charter signed by the former President of the United States.

Tom Davis came in. The titulary head of bond trading, Davis's background was similar in some ways to Hendley's, and he spent his days glued to his computer. He didn't worry about security. In this building all of the walls had metal sheathing to contain electronic emanations, and all of the computers were tempest-protected.

"What's new?" asked Hendley.

"Well," Davis answered, "we have a couple of potential new recruits."

"Who might they be?"

Davis slid the files across Hendley's desk. The CEO took them and opened both.

"Brothers?"

"Twins. Fraternals. Their mom must have punched out two eggs instead of one that month. Both of them impressed the right people. Brains, mental agility, fitness, and between them a good mix of talents, plus language skills. Spanish, especially."

"This one speaks Pashtu?" Hendley looked up in surprise.

"Just enough to find the bathroom. He was in country eight weeks or so, took the time to learn the local patois. Acquitted himself pretty well, the report says."

"Think they're our kind of people?" Hendley asked. Such people did not walk in the front door, which was why Hendley had a small number of very discreet recruiters sprinkled throughout the government.

"We need to check them out a little more," Davis conceded, "but they do have the talents we like. On the surface, both appear to be reliable, stable, and smart enough to understand why we're here. So, yeah, I think they're worth a serious look."

"What's next for them?"

"Dominic is going to transfer to Washington. Gus Werner wants him to join the counterterror office. He'll probably be a desk man to start with. He's a little young for HRT, and he hasn't proven his analytical abilities yet. I think Werner wants to see how smart he is first. Brian will fly to Camp Lejeune, back to working with his company. I'm surprised the Corps hasn't seconded him to intelligence. He's an obvious candidate, but they do like their shooters, and he did pretty well over in camel-land. He'll be fast-tracked to major's rank, if my sources are correct. So, first, I think I'll fly down and have lunch with him, feel him out some, then come back to D.C. And do the same with Dominic. Werner was impressed with him."

"And Gus is a good judge of men," the former senator noted.

"That he is, Gerry," Davis agreed. "So—anything new shaking?"

"Fort Meade is buried under a mountain, as usual." The NSA's biggest problem was that they intercepted so much raw material it would take an army to sort through it all. Computer programs helped by homing in on key words and such, but nearly all of it was innocent chatter. Programmers were always trying to improve the catcher program, but it had proven to be virtually impossible to give a computer human instincts, though they were still trying. Unfortunately, the really talented programmers worked for game companies. That was where the money was, and talent usually followed the money path. Hendley couldn't complain about that. After all, he'd spent his twenties and half of his thirties doing the same. So, he often went looking for rich and very successful programmers for whom the money chase had become not so much boring as redundant. It was usually a waste of time. Nerds were often greedy bastards. Just like lawyers, but not quite as cynical. "I've seen half a dozen interesting intercepts today, though..."

"Such as?" Davis asked. The company's chief recruiter, he was also a skilled analyst.

"This." Hendley handed the folder across. Davis opened it and scanned down the page.

"Hmm," was all he said.

"Could be scary, if it turns into anything," Hendley thought aloud.

"True. But we need more." That was not earthshaking. They *always* needed more.

"Who do we have down there right now?" He ought to have known, but Hendley suffered from the usual bureaucratic disease: He had trouble keeping all the information current in his head.

"Right now? Ed Castilanno is in Bogotá, looking into the Cartel, but he's in deep cover. Real deep," Davis reminded his boss.

"You know, Tom, this intelligence business sometimes sucks the big one."

"Cheer up, Gerry. The pay's a hell of a lot better—at least for us underlings," he added with a tiny grin. His bronze skin contrasted starkly with the ivory teeth.

"Yeah, must be terrible to be a peasant."

"At least da massa let me get educated, learn my letters and such. Could have been worse, don' have to chop cotton no more, Mas Gerry." Hendley rolled his eyes. Davis had, in fact, gotten his degree from Dartmouth, where he took a lot less grief for his dark skin than for his home state. His father grew corn in Nebraska, and voted Republican.

"What's one of those harvesters cost now?" the boss asked.

"You kidding? Far side of two hundred thousand. Dad got a new one last year and he's *still* bitching about it. 'Course, this one'll last until his grandchildren die rich. Cuts through an acre of corn like a battalion of Rangers going through some bad guys." Davis had made a good career in CIA as a field spook, becoming a specialist in tracking money across international borders. At Hendley Associates he'd discovered that his talents were also quite useful in a business sense, but, of course, he'd never lost his nose for the real action. "You know, this FBI guy, Dominic, he did some interesting work in financial crimes in his first field assignment in Newark. One of his cases is developing into a major investigation into an international banking house. He knows how to sniff things out pretty well for a rookie."

"All that, and he can kill people on his own hook," Hendley agreed.

"That's why I like his looks, Gerry. He can make decisions in the saddle, like a guy ten years older."

"Brother act. Interesting," Hendley observed, eyes on the folders again.

"Maybe breeding tells. Grandfather was a homicide cop, after all."

"And before that in the 101st Airborne. I see your point, Tom. Okay. Sound them both out soon. We're going to be busy soon."

"Think so?"

"It's not getting any better out there." Hendley waved at the window.

THEY WERE at a sidewalk café in Vienna. The nights were turning less cold, and the patrons of the establishment were enduring the chill to enjoy a meal on the wide sidewalk.

"So, what is your interest with us?" Pablo asked.

"There is a confluence of interests between us," Mohammed answered, then clarified: "We share enemies."

He gazed off. The women passing by were dressed in the formal, almost severe local fashion, and the traffic noise, especially the electric trams, made it impossible for anyone to listen in on their conversation. To the casual, or even the professional, observer, these were simply two men from other countries—and there were a lot of them in this imperial city—talking business in a quiet and amiable fashion. They were speaking in English, which was also not unusual.

"Yes, that is the truth," Pablo had to agree. "The enemies part, that is. What of the interests?"

"You have assets for which we have use. We have assets for which you have use," the Muslim explained patiently.

"I see." Pablo added cream to his coffee and stirred. To his surprise, the coffee here was as good as in his own country.

He'd be slow to reach an agreement, Mohammed expected. His guest was not as senior as he would have preferred. But the enemy they shared had enjoyed greater success against Pablo's organization than his own. It continued to surprise him. They had ample reason to employ effective security measures, but as with all monetarily motivated people they lacked the purity of purpose that his own colleagues exercised. And from that fact came their higher vulnerability. But Mohammed was not so foolish as to assume that made them his inferiors. Killing one Israeli spy didn't make him Superman, after all. Clearly they had ample expertise. It just had limits. As his own people had limits. As everyone but Allah Himself had limits. In that knowledge came more realistic expectations, and gentler disappointments when things went badly. One could not allow emotions to get in the way of "business," as his guest would have misidentified his Holy Cause. But he was dealing with an unbeliever, and allowances had to be made.

"What can you offer us?" Pablo asked, displaying his greed, much as Mohammed had expected.

"You need to establish a reliable network in Europe, correct?"

"Yes, we do." They'd had a little trouble of late. European police agencies were not as restrained as the American sort.

"We have such a network." And since Muslims were not thought to be active in the drug trade—drug dealers often lost their heads in Saudi Arabia, for example—so much the better.

"In return for what?"

"You have a highly successful network in America, and you have reason to dislike America, do you not?"

"That is so," Pablo agreed. Colombia was starting to make progress with the Cartel's uneasy ideological allies in the mountains of Pablo's home country. Sooner or later, the FARC would cave in to the pressure and then, doubtless, turn on their "friends"—really "associates" was a loose enough word—as their price of admission to the democratic process. At that time, the security of the Cartel might be seriously threatened. Political instability was their best friend in South America, but that might not last forever. The same was true of his host, Pablo considered, and that *did* make them allies of convenience. "Precisely what services would you require of us?"

Mohammed told him. He didn't add that no money would be exchanged for the Cartel's service. The first shipment that Mohammed's people shepherded into—Greece? Yes, that would probably be the easiest—would be sufficient to seal the venture, wouldn't it?

"That is all?"

"My friend, more than anything else we trade in ideas, not physical objects. The few material items we need are quite compact, and can be obtained locally if necessary. And I have no doubt that you can help with travel documents."

Pablo nearly choked on his coffee. "Yes, that is easily done."

"So, is there any reason why this alliance cannot be struck?"

"I must discuss it with my superiors," Pablo cautioned, "but on the surface I see no reason why our interests should be in conflict."

"Excellent. How may we communicate further?"

"My boss prefers to meet those with whom he does business."

Mohammed thought that over. Travel made him and his associates nervous, but there was no avoiding it. And he did have enough passports to see him through the airports of the world. And he also had the necessary language skills. His education at Cambridge had not been wasted. He could thank his parents for that. And he blessed his English mother for her gift of complexion and blue eyes. Truly he could pass for a native of any country outside of China and Africa. The remains of a Cambridge accent didn't hurt, either.

"You need merely tell me the time and the place," Mohammed replied. He handed over his business card. It had his e-mail address, the most useful tool for covert communications ever invented. And with the miracle of modern air travel, he could be anywhere on the globe in forty-eight hours.

||||||||||||||||||||||||||||||||||||||||||||||||||||

CHAPTER 2

JOINING UP

HE CAME in at a quarter to five. Anyone who passed him on the street would not have given him a second look, though he might have caught the eye of the odd unattached female. At six-one, a hundred eighty or so pounds—he worked out regularly—black hair and blue eyes, he wasn't exactly movie star material, but neither was he the sort of man that a pretty young female professional would have summarily kicked out of bed.

He also dressed well, Gerry Hendley saw. Blue suit with a red pinstripe—it looked English-made—vest, red-and-yellow-striped tie, nice gold tie bar. Fashionable shirt. Decent haircut. The confident look that came from having both money and a good education to go with a youth that would not be misspent. His car was parked in the visitors' lot in front of the building. A yellow Hummer 2 SUV, the sort of vehicle favored by people who herded cattle in Wyoming, or money in New York. And, probably, that was why . . .

"So, what brings you here?" Gerry asked, waving his guest to a comfortable seat on the other side of his mahogany desk.

"I haven't decided what I want to do yet, just sort of bumping around, looking for a niche I might fit into."

Hendley smiled. "Yeah, I'm not so old that I can't remember how confusing it is when you get out of school. Which one did you go to?"

"Georgetown. Family tradition." The boy smiled gently. That was one good thing about him that Hendley saw and appreciated—he wasn't trying to impress anyone with his name and family background. He might even be a little uneasy with it, wanting to make his own way and his own name, as a lot of young men did. The smart ones, anyway. It was a pity that there was no place for him on The Campus.

"Your dad really likes Jesuit schools."

"Even Mom converted. Sally didn't go to Bennington. She got through her premed up at Fordham in New York. Hopkins Med now, of course. Wants to be a doc, like Mom. What the hell, it's an honorable profession."

"Unlike law?" Gerry asked.

"You know how Dad is about that," the boy pointed out with a grin. "What was your undergraduate degree in?" he asked Hendley, knowing the answer already, of course.

"Economics and mathematics. I took a double major." It had been very useful indeed for modeling trading patterns in commodities markets. "So, how's your family doing?"

"Oh, fine. Dad's back writing again—his memoirs. Mostly he bitches that he isn't old enough to do that sort of book, but he's working pretty hard to get it done right. He's not real keen on the new President."

"Yeah, Kealty has a real talent for bouncing back. When they finally bury the guy, they'd better park a truck on top of his headstone." That joke had even made the *Washington Post*.

"I've heard that one. Dad says it can only take one idiot to unmake the work of ten geniuses." That adage had *not* made the *Washington Post*. But it was the reason the young man's father had set up The Campus, though the young man himself didn't know it.

"That's overstating things. This new guy only happened by accident."

"Yeah, well, when it comes time to execute that klukker retard down in Mississippi, how much you want to bet he commutes the sentence?"

"Opposition to capital punishment is a matter of principle to him," Hendley pointed out. "Or so he says. Some people do feel that way, and it is an honorable opinion."

"Principle? To him that's the nice old lady who runs a grammar school."

"If you want to have a political discussion, there's a nice bar and grill a mile down Route 29," Gerry suggested.

"No, that's not it. Sorry for the digression, sir."

This boy is holding his cards pretty close, Hendley thought. "Well, it's not a bad subject for one. So, what can I do for you?"

"I'm curious."

"About what?" the former senator asked.

"What you do here," his visitor said.

"Mainly currency arbitrage." Hendley stretched to show his weary relaxation at the end of a working day.

"Uh-huh," the kid said, just a slight bit dubiously.

"There's really money to be made there, if you have good information, and if you have the nerves to act on it."

"You know, Dad likes you a lot. He says it's a shame you and he don't see each other anymore."

Hendley nodded. "Yeah, and that's my fault, not his."

"He also said you were too smart to fuck up the way you did."

Ordinarily, it would have been a positively seismic faux pas, but it was obvious from looking in the boy's eyes that he hadn't meant it as any sort of insult but rather as a question . . . or was it? Hendley suddenly asked himself.

"It was a bad time for me," Gerry reminded his guest. "And anybody can make a mistake. Your dad even made a few himself."

"That's true. But Dad was lucky to have Arnie around to

cover his ass." That left his host an opening, which he jumped at.

"How's Arnie doing?" Hendley asked, making the dodge to maneuver for time, still wondering why the kid was here, and actually starting to get a little uneasy about it, though he was not sure why he should feel that way.

"Fine. He's going to be the new chancellor for the University of Ohio. He ought to be good at it, and he needs a calm sort of job, Dad thinks. I think he's right. How that guy managed not to have a heart attack is beyond me and Mom both. Maybe some people really do thrive on the action." His eyes never left Hendley's through the entire discourse. "I learned a lot talking to Arnie."

"What about from your father?"

"Oh, a thing or two. Mainly, I learned things from the rest of the bunch."

"Who do you mean?"

"Mike Brennan for one. He was my Principal Agent," Jack Jr. explained. "Holy Cross graduate, career Secret Service. Hell of a pistol shot. He's the guy who taught me to shoot."

"Oh?"

"The Service has a range on the Old Post Office Building, couple of blocks from the White House. I still get to go there occasionally. Mike's an instructor in the Secret Service Academy now, up at Beltsville. Really good guy, smart and laid-back. Anyway, you know, he was my babysitter, like, and I used to ping on him about stuff, ask him what Secret Service people do, how they train, how they think, the things they look for while they're protecting Mom and Dad. I learned a lot from him. And all the other people."

"Like?"

"FBI guys, Dan Murray, Pat O'Day—Pat's the Major Case Inspector for Murray. He's getting ready to retire. Can you believe it, he's going to raise beef cattle up in Maine. Funny damned place to punch cattle. He's a shooter, too, like Wild Bill Hickock with an attitude, but it's too easy to forget he's a Princeton grad. Pretty smart guy, Pat is. He taught me a lot about how the Bureau runs investigations. And his wife, Andrea, she's a mind reader. Ought to be, she ran Dad's detail during a very scary time, master's degree in psychology from University of Virginia. I learned a shitload from her. And the Agency people, of course, Ed and Mary Pat Foley—God Almighty, what a pair they are. But you know who the most interesting one of all was?"

He did. "John Clark?"

"Oh yeah. The trick was getting him to talk. I swear, compared to him, the Foleys are Desi and Lucy. But once he trusts you, he will open up some. I cornered him when he got his Medal of Honor—it was on TV briefly, retired Navy chief petty officer gets his decoration from Vietnam. About sixty seconds of videotape on a slow news day. You know, not one reporter asked what he did after he left the Navy. Not one. Jesus, they are *thick*. Bob Holtzman knew part of it, I think. He was there, standing in the corner, across the room from me. He's pretty smart for a newsie. Dad likes him, just doesn't trust him as far as he can sling an anchor. Anyway, Big John—Clark, I mean—he's one serious honcho. He's been there, and done that, and he has the T-shirt. How come he isn't here?"

"Jack, my boy, when you come to the point, you do come to the point," Hendley said, with a touch of admiration in his voice.

"When you knew his name, I knew I had you, sir." A briefly triumphant look in the eyes. "I've been checking you out for a couple of weeks."

"Oh?" And with that, Hendley felt his stomach contract.

"It wasn't hard. It's all on the public record, just a question of mix and match. Like the connect-the-dots things they give to little kids in their activity books. You know, it amazes me that this place never made the news—"

"Young man, if that's a threat—"

"What?" Jack Jr. was surprised by the interruption. "You mean, blackmail you? No, Senator, what I meant to say is that there's so much raw information lying around out there, that you have to wonder how reporters miss it. I mean, even a blind squirrel will find an acorn once in a while, y'know?" He paused for a moment before his eyes lit up. "Oh, I get it. You handed them what they expected to find, and they ran with it."

"It's not that hard, but it's dangerous to underestimate them," Hendley warned.

"Just don't talk to them. Dad told me a long time ago: 'A closed mouth gathers no foot.' He always let Arnie do the leaks. Nobody else said anything to the press without Arnie's guidance. I swear, I think the media was scared of that guy. He's the one who lifted a *Times* reporter's White House pass and made it stick."

"I remember that," Hendley responded. There had been quite a stink about it, but soon enough even the *New York Times* realized that having no reporter in the White House Press Room hurt in a very tender spot. It had been an object lesson in manners which had lasted for almost six months. Arnie van Damm had a longer and nastier memory than the media, which was quite something in and of itself. Arnold van Damm was a serious player of five-card-draw poker.

"What's your point, Jack? Why are you here?"

"Senator, I want to play in the bigs. This here, I think, is the bigs."

"Explain," Hendley commanded. Just how much had the boy put together?

John Patrick Ryan, Jr., opened his briefcase. "For starters, this is the only building taller than a private residence on the sight line from NSA Fort Meade to CIA Langley. You can download satellite photos off the Internet. I printed them all up. Here." He handed a small binder across. "I checked with the zoning offices, and I found out that three other office buildings were planned for this area, and all were denied construction permits. The records didn't say why, but nobody made a fuss about it. The medical center down the road, however, got really nice finance terms from Citibank on their revised plans. Most of your personnel are former spooks. Your security people are all former military police, rank E-7 or higher. The electronic security system here is better than they have at Fort Meade. How the hell did you manage that, by the way?"

"Private citizens have a lot more freedom negotiating with contractors. Go on," the former senator said.

"You never did anything illegal. That conflict-of-interest charge that killed your Senate career was a crock of shit. Any decent lawyer could have had it tossed right out of court on a summary judgment, but you rolled over and played dead on it. I remember how Dad always liked you for your brains, and he always said you were a straight shooter. He didn't say that about all that many people on The Hill. The senior people at CIA liked working with you, and you helped with funding for a project some other folks on The Hill had a conniption fit over. I don't know why it is, but a lot of people there hate the intelligence services. Used to drive Dad nuts, how every time he had to sit down with senators and congressmen over that stuff, had to bribe them with pet projects for their districts and stuff. Jeez, Dad *hated* that. Whenever he did it, he'd grumble for a week before and after. But you helped him a lot. You used to be pretty good working inside the Capitol Building. But when you had your political problem, you just caved in. I thought it was pretty hard to believe. But what I really had trouble swallowing was how Dad never talked about it at all. He never said a single word. When I asked, he changed the subject. Even Arnie never talked about it—and Arnie answered every question I ever hit him with. So, the dogs didn't bark, y'know?" Jack leaned back, keeping his eyes on his host at all times. "Anyway, I never said anything either, but I sniffed around during my senior year at Georgetown, and I kept talking to people, and those folks taught me how to look into things quietly. Again, it's not all that hard."

"And so, what conclusion did you reach?"

"You would have been a good president, Senator, but losing your wife and kids was a big hit. We were all busted up about that. Mom really liked your wife. Please excuse me for bringing it up, sir. That's why you left politics, but I think you're too much of a patriot to forget about your country, and I think Hendley Associates is your way of serving your country—but off the books, like. I remember Dad and Mr. Clark talking over drinks upstairs one night—my senior year of high school, it was. I didn't catch much of it. They didn't want me there, and so I went back to watching the History Channel. Coincidence, they had a show about SOE that night, the British Special Operations Executive from World War Two. They were mostly bankers. 'Wild Bill' Donovan recruited lawyers to start up the OSS, but the Brits used bankers to screw over people. I wondered why, and Dad said bankers are smarter. They know how to make money in the real world, whereas lawyers aren't quite as smart—that's what Dad said, anyway. I guess he figured that's what he did. With his trading background, I mean. But you're a different sort of pirate, Senator. I think you're a spook, and I think Hendley Associates is a privately funded spook shop that works off the books—completely outside the federal budget process. So, you don't have to worry about senators and congress-critters snooping around and leaking stuff because they think you do *bad* things. Hell, I did a Google search and there's only six mentions of your company on the Internet. You know, there's more pieces than that about my mom's hairstyle. *Women's Wear Daily* used to like clobbering her. Really pissed Dad off."

"I remember." Jack Ryan, Sr., had once cut loose in front of reporters on that issue, and paid the price of being laughed at by the chattering classes. "He talked to me about how Henry VIII would have given the reporters some special haircuts for that."

"Yeah, with an ax at the Tower of London. Sally used to laugh about it some. She needled Mom about her hair, too. I guess that's one nice thing about being a man, eh?"

"That and shoes. My wife didn't like Manolo Blahniks. She liked sensible shoes, the sort that didn't make her feet hurt," Hendley said, remembering, and then running into a concrete wall. It still hurt to talk about her. It probably always would, but at least the pain did affirm his love for her, and that was something. Much as he loved her memory, he could not smile in public about her. Had he remained in politics, he'd have had to do that, pretend that he'd gotten over it, that his love was undying but also unhurtful. Yeah, sure. One more price of political life was giving up your humanity along with your manhood. And it was not worth that price. Even to be President of the United States. One of the reasons why he and Jack Ryan, Sr., had always gotten along was that they were so alike.

"You really think this is an intelligence agency?" he asked his guest as lightly as the situation allowed.

"Yes, sir, I do. If NSA, say, pays attention to what the big central banks are doing, you are ideally located to take advantage of the signals-intelligence they gather and cross-deck to Langley. Must give your currency-trading troops the best sort of insider information, and if you play your cards carefully—that is, if you don't get greedy—you can make a ton of long-term money without anybody really noticing. You do that by not attracting investors. They'd talk way too much. So, that activity funds the things you do here. Exactly what it is you do, that I have not speculated on very much."

"Is that a fact?"

"Yes, sir, that is a fact."

"You haven't talked to your father about this?"

"No, sir." Jack Jr. shook his head. "He'd just blow it off. Dad told me a lot when I asked, but not stuff like this."

"What did he tell you?"

"People stuff. You know, dealing with politicians, which

foreign president likes little girls or little boys. Jeez, a lot of that going around, especially overseas. What sort of people they were, how they think, what their individual priorities and eccentricities are. Which country took good care of its military. Which country's spook services were good, and which ones were not. A lot of things about the people on The Hill. The sort of stuff you read in books or the papers, except what Dad told me was the real shit. I knew not to repeat it anywhere," the young Ryan assured his host.

"Even in school?"

"Nothing I didn't see in the *Post* first. The papers are pretty good about finding stuff out, but they're too quick to repeat damaging things about people they don't like, and they frequently don't publish stuff about people they do like. I guess the news business is pretty much the same as women trading gossip over the phone or the card table. Less a matter of hard facts than sniping at people you don't care for."

"They're as human as everybody else."

"Yes, sir, they are. But when my mom operates on somebody's eyes, she doesn't care if she likes the person or not. She swore an oath to play her game by the rules. Dad's the same way. That's how they raised me to be," John Patrick Ryan, Jr., concluded. "Same thing every dad tells every son: If you're going to do it, do it right or don't do it at all."

"Not everybody thinks that way anymore," Hendley pointed out, though he'd told his two sons, George and Foster, exactly the same thing.

"Maybe so, Senator, but that's not my fault."

"What do you know about the trading business?" Hendley asked.

"I know the basics. I can talk the talk, but I haven't learned the nitty-gritty enough to walk the walk."

"And your degree from Georgetown?"

"History, strong minor in economics, kinda like Dad.

Sometimes I'd ask him about his hobby—he still likes to play the market, and he has friends in the business, like George Winston, his Secretary of the Treasury. They talk a lot. George has tried and tried to get Dad to come inside his company, but he won't do anything more than go in and schmooze. They're still friends, though. They even hack away at golf together. Dad's a lousy golfer."

Hendley smiled. "I know. Ever try it yourself?"

Little Jack shook his head. "I already know how to swear. Uncle Robby was pretty good. Jeez, Dad really misses him. Aunt Sissy still comes to the house a lot. She and Mom play piano together."

"That was pretty bad."

"That redneck racist fuck," Junior observed. "Excuse me. Robby was the first guy I ever knew who got murdered." The amazing thing was that his murderer had been taken alive. The Secret Service detail had been half a second behind the Mississippi State Police in getting to him, but some civilian had tackled the bastard before anyone could get a round off, and so he'd gone to jail alive. That fact had at least eliminated any conspiracy nonsense. It had been a Ku Klux Klan member, sixty-seven years old, who just couldn't abide the thought that Ryan's retirement had brought his black Vice President to the position of President of the United States. His trial, conviction, and sentencing had gone off with startling speed—the assassination had all been on videotape, not to mention there'd been six witnesses all within two yards of the killer. Even the Stars and Bars atop the State House in Jackson had flown at half-staff for Robby Jackson, to the dismay and disgust of some. *"Sic volvere Parcas,"* Jack observed.

"What's that?"

"The Fates, Senator. One spins the thread. One measures the thread. And one cuts the thread. 'So spin the Fates,' the Roman adage is. I never saw Dad so broken up about anything. Mom handled it better, really. I guess docs are used to people dying. Dad—well, he just wanted to whack the guy himself. It was pretty tough." The news cameras had caught the President weeping at the funeral service at the Naval Academy Chapel. *Sic volvere Parcas.* "So, Senator, how does my fate spin out here?"

It didn't catch Hendley short. He'd seen this question coming a quarter mile away, but it was not an especially easy question even so. "What about your father?"

"Who says he has to know? You have six subsidiary corporations that you probably use to hide your trading activities." Finding that out hadn't been all that easy, but Jack knew how to dig.

"Not 'hide,'" Hendley corrected. "'Disguise,' maybe, but not 'hide.'"

"Excuse me. As I told you, I used to hang out with spooks."

"You learned a lot."

"I had some pretty good teachers."

Ed and Mary Pat Foley, John Clark, Dan Murray, and his own father. Damned Skippy, he's had some pretty good teachers, Hendley thought.

"What exactly do you think you'd do here?"

"Sir, I'm pretty smart, but not that smart. I'll have to learn a lot. I know that. So do you. What do I want to do? I want to serve my country," Jack said evenly. "I want to help get things done that need doing. I don't need money. I have trust funds set up from Dad and Granddad—Joe Muller, Mom's dad, I mean. Hell, if I wanted, I could get a law degree and end up like Ed Kealty, working my way toward the White House on my own, but my dad isn't a king and I'm not a prince. I want to make my own way and see how things play out."

"Your dad can't know about this, at least not for a while."

"So? He kept a lot of secrets from *me*." Jack thought that was pretty funny. "Turnabout is fair play, isn't it?"

"I'll think about it. You have an e-mail address?"

"Yes, sir." Jack handed across a card.

"Give me a couple of days."

"Yes, sir. Thanks for letting me in to see you." He stood, shook hands, and made his way out.

The boy had grown up in a hurry, Hendley thought. Maybe having a Secret Service detail helped with that—or hurt, depending on what sort of person you happened to be. But this boy had come from good stock, as much from his mother as his father. And clearly he was smart. He had a lot of curiosity, usually a sign of intelligence.

And intelligence was the only thing there was never enough of, anywhere in the world.

"SO?" Ernesto asked.

"It was interesting," Pablo replied, lighting a Dominican cigar.

"What do they want of us?" his boss asked.

"Mohammed began by talking about our common interests, and our common enemies."

"If we tried to do business over there, we would lose our heads," Ernesto observed. With him, it was always business.

"I pointed that out. He replied that theirs is a small market, hardly worth our time. They merely export raw materials. And that is true. But he can help us, he said, with the new European market. Mohammed tells me that his organization has a good base of operations in Greece, and with the demise of international borders in Europe that would be the most logical point of entry for our consignments. They will not charge us for their technical assistance. They say they wish to establish goodwill only."

"They must want our help very badly," Ernesto observed.

"They have their own considerable resources, as they have demonstrated, *jefe*. But they seem to need some expertise for smuggling weapons in addition to people. In any case, they ask little, and they offer much."

"And what they offer will make our business more convenient?" Ernesto wondered.

"It will certainly make the *Yanquis* devote their resources to different tasks."

"It could create havoc in their country, but the political effects could be serious..."

"*Jefe,* the pressure they put upon us now can scarcely get worse, can it?"

"This new *norteamericano* president is a fool, but dangerous even so."

"And so, we can have our new friends distract him, *jefe,*" Pablo pointed out. "We will not even use any of our assets to do so. We have little risk, and the potential reward is large, isn't it?"

"I see that, but, Pablo, if it is traced to us, the cost could be serious."

"That's true, but again, how much additional pressure can they put on us?" Pablo asked. "They're attacking our political allies through the Bogotá government, and if they succeed in producing the effect they desire then the harm to us will be very serious indeed. You and the other members of the Council might become fugitives in our own land," the Cartel's intelligence chief warned. He didn't have to add that such an eventuality would take much of the fun out of the immense riches the Council members enjoyed. Money has little utility without a comfortable place to spend it. "There is an adage in that part of the world: The enemy of my enemy is my friend. *Jefe,* if there is a major downside to this proposal venture, I do not see it."

"You think I should meet with this man, then?"

"*Sí,* Ernesto. There should be no harm. He is more wanted by the *gringos* than we are. If we fear betrayal, then he should fear it even more so, shouldn't he? And in any case, we will take proper precautions."

"Very well, Pablo. I will discuss this with the Council with a recommendation that we hear him out," Ernesto conceded. "How difficult would it be to set up?"

"I would expect him to fly through Buenos Aires. Surely he knows how to travel safely. He probably has more false passports than we do, and he truly does not look conspicuously Arabian."

"His language skills?"

"Adequate," Pablo answered. "Speaks English like an Englishman, and that is a passport all its own."

"Through Greece, eh? Our product?"

"His organization has used Greece as a sally port for many years. *Jefe,* it's easier to smuggle our product than a group of men, and so on first inspection their methods and assets seem to be adaptable to our purposes. Our own people will have to examine them, of course."

"Any idea what his plans for North America might be?"

"I did not ask, *jefe.* It does not really concern us."

"Except insofar as it tightens border security. That could be an inconvenience"—Ernesto held up his hand—"I know, Pablo, not a serious one.

"As long as they help us out, I don't care what they want to do to America."

||||||||||||||||||||||||||||||||||||||||||||||||||||||||||||||||||

CHAPTER 3

GRAY FILES

ONE OF Hendley's advantages was that most of his assets worked elsewhere. They didn't have to be paid, housed, or fed. The taxpayers paid all of the overhead without knowing it, and, indeed, the "overhead" itself didn't know exactly what it was. Recent evolution in the world of international terrorism had caused America's two principal intelligence agencies, CIA and NSA, to work even more closely than they had in the past, and since they were an inconvenient hour's drive apart—negotiating the northern part of the D.C. Beltway can be like driving through a shopping mall parking lot during Christmas week—they did most of their communication via secure microwave links, from the top of NSA's headquarters building to the top of CIA's. That this sight line transited the roof of Hendley Associates had gone unnoticed. And it ought not to have mattered anyway, since the microwave link was encrypted. It had to be, since microwaves leaked off their line of transmission due to all manner of technical reasons. The laws of physics could be exploited, but not changed to suit the needs of the moment.

The bandwidth on the microwave channel was immense, due to compression algorithms that were little different from those used on personal computer networks. The King James Version of the Holy Bible could have flown from one building to another in seconds. These links were always up and running, most of the time swapping nonsense and random characters in order to befuddle anyone who might try to crack the encryption—but since this system was TAPDANCE encrypted, it was totally secure. Or so the wizards at NSA claimed. The system depended on CD-ROMs stamped with totally random transpositions, and unless you could find a key to atmospheric RF noise, that was the end of that. But every week, one of the guard detail from Hendley, accompanied by two of his colleagues—all of them randomly chosen from the guard force—drove to Fort Meade and picked up the week's encryption disks. These were inserted in the jukebox attached to the cipher machine, and when each was ejected after use, it was hand-carried to a microwave oven to be destroyed, under the eyes of three guards, all of them trained by years of service not to ask questions.

This somewhat laborious procedure gave Hendley access to all of the activity of the two agencies, since they were government agencies and they wrote everything down, from the "take" from deep-cover agents to the cost of the mystery meat served in the cafeteria.

Much—even most—of the information was of no interest to Hendley's crew, but nearly all of it was stored on high-density media and cross-referenced on a Sun Microsystems mainframe computer that had enough power to administer the entire country, if need be. This enabled Hendley's staff to look in on the stuff the intelligence services were generating, along with the top-level analysis being done by experts in a multitude of areas and then cross-decked to others for comment and further analysis. NSA was getting better at this sort of work than CIA, or so Hendley's own top analyst thought, but many heads on a single problem often worked well—until the analysis became so convoluted as to paralyze action, a problem not unknown to the intelligence community. With the new Department of Homeland Security—for whose authorization Hendley thought he would have voted "Nay"—in the loop, CIA and NSA were both recipients of FBI analysis. That often just added a new layer of bureaucratic complexity, but the truth of the matter was the FBI agents took a slightly different take on raw intelligence. They thought in terms of building a criminal case to be put before a jury, and that was not at all a bad thing when you got down to it.

Each agency had its own way of thinking. The Federal Bureau of Investigation was composed of cops who had one slant. The Central Intelligence Agency had quite another, and it did have the power—occasionally exercised—to take some action, though that was quite rare. The National Security Agency, on the third hand, just got information, analyzed it, and passed it on to others—whether those individuals did anything with it was a question beyond Agency purview.

Hendley's chief of Analysis/Intelligence was Jerome Rounds. Jerry to his friends, he had a doctorate in psychology from the University of Pennsylvania. He'd worked in the State Department's Office of Intelligence and Research—I&R—before moving on to Kidder, Peabody as a different sort of analyst for a different sort of paycheck, before then-Senator Hendley had personally spotted him during lunch in New York. Rounds had made a name for himself in the trading house as the in-house mind reader, but though he'd made himself a goodly pile of money, he'd found that money faded in importance once your kids' education was fully guaranteed and your sailboat was paid off. He'd chafed on Wall Street, and he'd been ready for the offer Hendley had made four years earlier. His duties included reading the minds of other international traders, which was something he'd learned to do in New York. He worked very closely with Sam Granger, who was both the head of currency trading at The Campus and also chief of the Operations Department.

It was near closing time when Jerry Rounds came into Sam's office. It was the job of Jerry and his staff of thirty to go over all the downloads from NSA and CIA. They all had to be speed-readers with sensitive noses. Rounds was the local equivalent of a bloodhound.

"Check this out," he said, dropping a sheet of paper on Granger's desk and taking a seat.

"Mossad lost a—Station Chief? Hmmph. How did that happen?"

"The local cops are thinking robbery. Killed with a knife, wallet missing, no sign of a protracted struggle. Evidently, he wasn't carrying heat with him at the time."

"Civilized place like Rome, why bother?" Granger observed. But they would now, for a while at least. "How did we find out?"

"Made the local papers that an official at the Israeli Embassy got whacked while taking a leak. The Agency Chief of Station fingered him for a spook. Some people at Langley are running around in circles trying to figure what it all means, but they'll probably fall back on Occam's razor and buy what the local cops think. Dead man. No wallet. Robbery where the crook got a little carried away."

"You think the Israelis will buy that?" Granger wondered.

"About as soon as they serve roast pork at an embassy dinner. He was knifed between the first and second vertebrae. A street hood is more likely to slash the throat, but a pro knows that's messy and noisy. The Carabinieri are working the case—but it sounds as though they don't have dick to work with, unless somebody at the restaurant has a hell of a good memory. I wouldn't want to wager much on that one."

"So, what's it all mean?"

Rounds settled back in the chair. "When's the last time a Station Chief of any service got killed?"

"It's been a while. The Agency lost one in Greece—that local terrorist group. The COS was fingered by some prick... one of their own, defector, skipped over the wall, drinking vodka now and feeling lonely, I imagine. The Brits lost a guy a few years ago in Yemen..." He paused. "You're right. You don't gain much by killing a Station Chief. Once you know who he is, you watch him, find out who his contacts and sub-officers are. If you whack one, you lose assets instead of gaining any. So, you're thinking a terrorist, maybe sending a message to Israel?"

"Or maybe eliminating a threat they especially disliked. What the hell, the poor bastard was Israeli, wasn't he? Embassy official. Maybe just that was enough, but when a spook—especially a senior spook—goes down, you don't assume it's an accident, do you?"

"Any chance Mossad will ask for our help?" But Granger knew better. The Mossad was like the kid in the sandbox who never, ever, shared toys. They'd ask for help only if they were, A, desperate, and, B, convinced someone else could give them something they'd never get on their own. Then they'd act like the returning prodigal son.

"They won't confirm that this guy—named Greengold—was Mossad. That might be a little helpful to the Italian cops, might even get their counter-spook agency involved, but if it's been said, there is no evidence of it that Langley knows about."

But Langley would not think in such terms, Granger realized. So did Jerry. He could see it in his eyes. CIA didn't think in those terms because the intelligence business had become very civilized. You didn't kill off the other guy's assets, because that was bad for business. Then he might do something to your assets, and if you were fighting a guerrilla war on the streets of some foreign city, you were not getting the actual job done. The actual job was to get information back to your government, not to carve notches on your pistol grips. So, the Carabinieri would think in terms of a street crime because any diplomat's person was inviolable to the forces of any other country, protected by international treaty and by a tradition that went all the way back to the Persian Empire under Xerxes.

"Okay, Jerry, you're the man with the trained nose," Sam observed. "What are you thinking?"

"I'm thinking there's a nasty ghost out on the street, maybe. This Mossad guy is at a gilt-edged restaurant in Rome, having lunch and a glass of nice wine. Maybe he's making a pickup at a dead drop—I checked the map, the restaurant is a brisk walk from the embassy building, a little too far for a regular lunch place, unless this Greengold guy was a jogging type, and it was the wrong time of day for that. So, unless he was really hot for the chef at Giovanni's, even money it's a dead drop or a meet of some sort. If so, he was set up. Not set up to be ID'd by his opposition, whoever that may be, but ID'd to be whacked. To the local cops, it may look like a robbery. To me, it looks like a deliberate assassination, and expertly done. The victim was instantly incapacitated. No chance to resist in any way. That's how you'd want to take a spook down—you never know how good he might be at self-defense, but if I were an Arab, I'd figure a Mossad guy for the bogeyman. I would not take many chances. No pistol, so he left nothing behind in the form of physical evidence, no bullet, no cartridge case. He takes the wallet to make it look like a robbery, but he killed a Mossad *rezident,* and he delivered a message, probably. Not that he dislikes Mossad, but that he can kill their people as easy as zipping his pants."

"You planning a book on the subject, Jerry?" Sam asked lightly. The chief analyst was taking a single factoid of hard information and spinning it into a complete soap opera.

Rounds just tapped his nose and smiled. "Since when do you believe in coincidences? Something smells about this one."

"What's Langley think?"

"Nothing yet. They've assigned it to the Southern Europe Desk for evaluation. I expect we'll see something in a week or so, and it won't say much. I know the guy who runs that shop."

"Dumb?"

Rounds shook his head. "No, that's not fair. He's smart enough, but he doesn't stick his neck out. Nor is he especially creative. I bet this doesn't even go as far as the Seventh Floor."

A new CIA Director had replaced Ed Foley, who was now retired and reportedly doing his own "I Was There" book, along with his wife, Mary Pat. In their day, they'd been pretty good, but the new DCI was a politically attractive judge beloved of President Kealty. He didn't do anything without Presidential approval, which meant it had to be run through the mini-bureaucracy of the National Security Council team in the White House, which was about as leaky as RMS *Titanic,* and hence beloved of the press. The Directorate of Operations was still growing, still training new field officers at The Farm in Tidewater, Virginia, and the new DDO wasn't a bad man at all—Congress had insisted on someone who knew how to work the field, somewhat to Kealty's dismay, but he knew how to play the game with Congress. The Directorate of Operations might be growing back into proper shape, but it would never do anything overtly bad under the current administration. Nothing to make Congress unhappy. Nothing to make the freelance haters of the intelligence community get loud about anything other than their routine complaints about historical wives' tales and grand conspiracy theories, and how CIA had caused Pearl Harbor and the San Francisco Earthquake.

"So, nothing will come of this, you figure?" Granger asked, knowing the answer.

"Mossad will look around, tell its troops to stay awake, and that'll work for a month or two, and then most of them will settle down to their normal routines. Same with other services. Mainly, the Israelis will try to figure how their guy got fingered. Hard to speculate on that with the information at hand. Probably something simple. Usually is. Maybe he recruited the wrong guy and it bit him, maybe their ciphers got cracked—a bribed cipher clerk at the embassy, for example—maybe somebody talked to the wrong guy at the wrong cocktail party. The possibilities are pretty wide, Sam. It only takes one little slip to get a guy killed out there, and the best of us can make that sort of error."

"Something to put in the manual about what to do on the street, and what not to do." He'd done his own street time, of course, but mainly in libraries and banks, rooting around for information so dry as to make dust look moist, and finding the occasional diamond in a pile of it. He'd always maintained a cover and stuck to it until it had become as real to him as his birthday.

"Unless some other spook craps out on the street somewhere," Rounds observed. "Then we'll know if there really is a ghost out there."

THE AVIANCA flight from Mexico touched down at Cartagena five minutes early. He'd flown Austrian Air to London Heathrow, and then a British Airways flight to Mexico City before taking Colombia's flag carrier to the South American country. It was an old American Boeing, but he was not one to worry about the safety of air travel. The world had far greater dangers. At the hotel, he opened his bag to retrieve his day planner, took a walk outside, and spotted a public phone to make his call.

"Please tell Pablo that Miguel is here . . . *Gracias.*" And with that he walked to a cantina for a drink. The local beer wasn't all that bad, Mohammed found. Though it was contrary to his religious beliefs, he had to fit in to this environment, and here everybody drank alcohol. After sitting for fifteen minutes, he walked back to his hotel, scanning twice for a tail, which he did not see. So, if he was being shadowed, it was by experts, and there was little defense against that, not in a foreign city where everyone spoke

Spanish and no one knew the direction to Mecca. He was traveling on a British passport that said his name was Nigel Hawkins of London. There was indeed a flat at the indicated address. That would protect him even from a routine police stop, but no cover legend went forever, and if it came to that... then it came to that. You could not live your life in fear of the unknown. You made your plans, took the necessary precautions, and then you played the game.

It was interesting. The Spanish were ancient enemies of Islam, and this country was composed mostly of the children of Spain. But there were people in this country who loathed America almost as much as he did—only *almost*, because America was to them a source of vast income for their cocaine... as America was a source of vast income for the oil of his homeland. His own personal net worth was in the hundreds of millions of American dollars, stored in various banks around the world, Switzerland, Liechtenstein, and most recently, the Bahamas. He could afford his own private plane, of course, but that would be too easy to identify, and, he was sure, too easy to shoot down over water. Mohammed was contemptuous of America, but he was not blind to her power. Too many good men had gone unexpectedly to Paradise for forgetting that. It was hardly a bad destiny, but his work was among the living, not the dead.

"HEY, CAPTAIN."

Brian Caruso turned to see James Hardesty. It wasn't even seven in the morning. He'd just finished leading his short company of Marines through their morning routine of exercise and the three-mile run, and like all his men he'd worked up a good sweat in the process. He'd dismissed his people to their showers, and was on his way back to his quarters when he'd encountered Hardesty. But before he could say anything, a more familiar voice called.

"Skipper?" the captain turned to see Gunnery Sergeant Sullivan, his senior NCO.

"Yeah, Gunny. The people looked pretty sharp this morning."

"Yes, sir. You didn't work us too hard. Good of you, sir," the E-7 observed.

"How did Corporal Ward do?" Which was why Brian hadn't worked them too hard. Ward had said he was ready to get back into the swing, but he was still coming off some nasty wounds.

"He's puffing some, but he didn't cave on us. Corpsman Randall is keeping an eye on the lad for us. You know, for a squid, he isn't too bad," the gunny allowed. Marines are typically fairly solicitous to their Navy corpsmen, especially the ones tough enough to play in the weeds with Force Recon.

"Sooner or later the SEALs are going to invite him out to Coronado."

"True enough, Skipper, and then we're gonna have to break in a new squid."

"What you need, Gunny?" Caruso asked.

"Sir—oh, he's here. Hey, Mr. Hardesty. Just heard you were down to see the boss. Beg pardon, Captain."

"No problem. See you in an hour, Gunny."

"Aye, aye, sir." Sullivan saluted smartly and headed back to the barracks.

"He's a pretty good NCO," Hardesty thought aloud.

"Big time," Caruso agreed. "Guys like him run the Corps. They just tolerate people like me."

"How's about some breakfast, Cap'n?"

"Need a shower first, but sure."

"What's on the agenda?"

"Today's class work is on comms, to make sure we can all call in air and artillery support."

"Don't they know that?" Hardesty asked in surprise.

"You know how a baseball team does batting practice before every game, with the batting coach around? They all know how to swing a bat, right?"

"Gotcha." The reason they were called fundamentals was

because they really were fundamental. And these Marines, like ballplayers, wouldn't object to the day's lesson. One trip into the tall weeds had taught them all how important the fundamentals were.

It was a short walk to Caruso's quarters. Hardesty helped himself to some coffee and a newspaper, while the young officer showered. The coffee was pretty good for a single man's making. The paper, as usual, didn't tell him much he didn't already know, except for late sports scores, but the comics were always good for a laugh.

"Ready for breakfast?" the youngster asked, all cleaned up.

"How's the food here?" Hardesty stood.

"Well, kinda hard to screw up breakfast, isn't it?"

"True enough. Lead on, Captain." Together they drove the mile or so to the Consolidated Mess in Caruso's C-class Mercedes. The car marked him as a single man, to Hardesty's relief.

"I didn't expect to see you again for a while," Caruso said, from behind the wheel.

"Or at all?" the former Special Forces officer asked lightly.

"That, too, yes, sir."

"You passed the exam."

It was enough to turn his head. "What exam was that, sir?"

"I didn't think you'd notice," Hardesty observed with a chuckle.

"Well, sir, you have succeeded in confusing me this morning." Which, Captain Caruso was sure, was part of to-day's plan.

"There's an old saying: 'If you're not confused, you're misinformed.'"

"That sounds a little ominous," Captain Caruso said, turning right into the parking lot.

"It can be." He got out and followed the officer toward the building.

It was a large single-story building full of hungry Marines. The cafeteria line had racks and trays of the usual American breakfast foods, Frosted Flakes to bacon and eggs. And even some—

"You can try the bagels, but they aren't all that good, sir," Caruso warned as he got two English muffins and real butter. He was clearly too young to worry about cholesterol and the other difficulties that came with increasing years. Hardesty got himself a box of Cheerios, because he *had* gotten that old, rather to his annoyance, along with low-fat milk and non-sugar sweetener. The coffee mugs were large, and the seating permitted a surprising amount of anonymity, though there had to be four hundred people in here, of various ranks from corporal to full-bull colonel. His host steered him to a table in a crowd of young sergeants.

"Okay, Mr. Hardesty, what can I do for you?"

"Number one, I know you have security clearances, up to TS, right?"

"Yes, sir. Some compartmented stuff, but that doesn't concern you at all."

"Probably," Hardesty conceded. "Okay, what we're about to discuss goes a little higher than that. You cannot repeat this to anyone at all. Are we clear on that?"

"Yes, sir. This is code-word stuff. I understand." In fact, he didn't, thought Hardesty. This was actually beyond code word, but that explanation would have to wait for another venue. "Please go on, sir."

"You've been noticed by some fairly important people as a prime recruit prospect for a rather . . . a rather special organization that does not exist. You've heard this sort of thing before in movies or read it in books. But this is quite real, son. I am here to offer you a place in that organization."

"Sir, I am a Marine officer, and I like that."

"It will not prejudice your career in the Marines. As a matter of fact, you've been deep-dipped for promotion to major. You'll be getting that letter next week. So, you'll have to leave your current billet anyway. If you stay in the

Marine Corps, you'll be sent to Headquarters Marine Corps next month, to work in the intelligence/special-operations shop. You're also going to get a Silver Star for your action in Afghanistan."

"What about my people? I put them in for decorations, too." It was the mark of this kid that he'd worry about that, Hardesty thought.

"Everyone's been approved. Now, you'll be able to return to the Corps whenever you wish. Your commission and routine advancement will not suffer from this at all."

"How did you manage that?"

"We have friends in high places," his guest explained. "So do you, as a matter of fact. You will continue to be paid through the Corps. You may have to set up new banking arrangements, but that's routine stuff."

"What will this new posting entail?" Caruso asked.

"It will mean serving your country. Doing things that are necessary to our national security, but doing them in a somewhat irregular manner."

"Doing what, exactly?"

"Not here, not now."

"Can you be any more mysterious, Mr. Hardesty? I might start understanding what you're talking about and spoil the surprise."

"I don't make the rules," he replied.

"Agency, eh?"

"Not exactly, but you'll find out in due course. What I need now is a yes or a no. You can leave this organization at any time if you find it not to your liking," he promised. "But this isn't the proper venue for a fuller explanation."

"When would I have to decide?"

"Before you finish your bacon and eggs."

The reply caused Captain Caruso to set his muffin down. "This isn't some sort of joke, right?" He'd taken his share of razzing due to his family connections.

"No, Captain, it isn't a joke."

The pitch was deliberately designed to be nonthreatening. People like Caruso, however courageous they might be, often regarded the unknown—more properly, the not-understood unknown—with some degree of trepidation. His profession was dangerous enough already, and the intelligent among us do not blissfully go seeking after danger. Theirs is usually a reasoned approach to hazard, after first making sure their training and experience are adequate to the task. And so Hardesty had made sure to tell Caruso that the womb of the United States Marine Corps would always be available to take him back. It was almost true, and that was close enough for his purposes, if not, perhaps, to the young officer's.

"What's your love life like, Captain?"

The question surprised him, but he answered it truthfully. "No attachments. There's a few girls I date, but nothing very serious yet. Is that a concern?" Just how dangerous might this be? he wondered.

"Only from a security point of view. Most men cannot keep secrets from their wives." But girlfriends were a different question altogether.

"Okay, how dangerous will this job be?"

"Not very," Hardesty lied, not skillfully enough to be entirely successful.

"You know, I've been planning to stay in the Corps at least long enough to be a light colonel."

"Your evaluator at Headquarters Marine Corps thinks you're good enough to make full-bull someday, unless you step on your crank along the way. Nobody thinks that's likely, but it has happened to a lot of good men." Hardesty finished his Cheerios and returned his attention to the coffee.

"Nice to know I have a guardian angel up there somewhere," Caruso observed dryly.

"As I say, you've been noticed. The Marine Corps is pretty good at spotting talent and helping it along."

"And so have some other people—spotted me, I mean."

"That's correct, Captain. But all I am offering you is a

chance. You'll have to prove yourself along the way." The challenge was well considered. Capable young men had trouble turning away from one. Hardesty knew he had him.

IT HAD been a long drive from Birmingham to Washington. Dominic Caruso did it in one long day because he didn't much like cheap motels, but even starting at five in the morning didn't make it any shorter. He drove a white Mercedes C-class four-door much like his brother's, with lots of luggage piled in the back. He had been stopped twice, but on both occasions the state police cars had responded favorably to his FBI credentials—called "creedos" by the Bureau—and pulled away with nothing more than a friendly wave. There was a brotherhood among law-enforcement officers that extended at least as far as ignoring speeding violations. He arrived at Arlington, Virginia, just at ten that night, where he let a bellman unpack his car for him and took the elevator to his room on the third floor. The in-room bar had a split of a decent white wine, which he downed after the needed shower. The wine and boring TV helped him sleep. He left notice for a seven o'clock wake-up call, and faded out with the help of HBO.

"GOOD MORNING," Gerry Hendley said at 8:45 the next morning. "Coffee?"

"Thank you, sir." Jack availed himself of a cup and took his seat. "Thanks for calling back."

"Well, we looked at your academic records. You did okay at Georgetown."

"For what it costs, you might as well pay attention—and, besides, it wasn't all that hard." John Patrick Ryan, Jr., sipped at his coffee and wondered what would be coming next.

"We're prepared to discuss an entry-level job," the former senator told him right away. He'd never been one for beating about the bush, which was one of the reasons he and his visitor's father had gotten along so well.

"Doing what, exactly?" Jack asked, with his eyes perked up.

"What do you know about Hendley Associates?"

"Only what I've already told you."

"Okay, nothing of what I'm about to tell you can be repeated anywhere. Not anywhere. Are you clear on that?"

"Yes, sir." And just that fast, everything was clear as hell. He'd guessed right, Jack told himself. Damn.

"Your father was one of my closest friends. I say 'was' because we can't see each other anymore, and we talk very rarely. Usually because he calls here. People like your dad never retire—never all the way, anyway. Your father was one of the best spooks who ever lived. He did some things that were never written down—at least not on government paper—and probably never will be written down. In this case, 'never' means fifty years or so. Your father is doing his memoirs. He's doing two versions, one for publication in a few years, and another that won't see the light of day for a couple of generations. It will not be published until after his death. That's his order."

It stuck hard at Jack that his father was making plans for after his own death. His dad—dead? It was a lot to grasp except in a distant, intellectual sense. "Okay," he managed to say. "Does Mom know this stuff?"

"Probably—no, almost certainly not. Some of it may not exist even at Langley. The government occasionally does things that are not committed to paper. Your father had a gift for stumbling into the middle of stuff like that."

"And what about you?" Junior asked.

Hendley leaned back and took a philosophical tone. "The problem is that no matter what you do, there's somebody who won't like it much. Like a joke. No matter how funny it is, somebody will be offended by it. But at a high level, when somebody is offended, instead of calling you on it to your face, he goes off and cries his eyes out to a member of the press, and it goes public, usually with a great big disapproving tone attached to it. Most often that's careerism raising its ugly head—getting ahead by backstabbing somebody senior to you. But it's also because people in senior positions like to make policy in accordance with their own version of right and wrong. That's called ego. Problem is, everyone has a different version of right and wrong. Some of them can be downright crazy.

"Now, take our current President. In the Senate Cloakroom, once Ed told me he was so opposed to capital punishment that he couldn't even have abided executing Adolf Hitler. That was after a few drinks—he tends to be verbose when he's been drinking, and the sad fact is that he drinks a little too much on occasion. When he said that to me, I joked about it. I told him not to say it in a speech—the Jewish vote is big and powerful and they might see it less as a deeply held principle than as a high-order insult. In the abstract a lot of people oppose capital punishment. Okay, I can respect that, though I do not agree with it. But the drawback to that position is that you cannot then deal decisively with people who do harm to others   sometimes serious harm—without violating your principles, and to some people, their consciences or political sensibilities will not let them do it. Even though the sad fact of the matter is that due process of law is not always effective, frequently outside our borders, and, on rare occasions, inside them.

"Okay, how does this affect America? CIA doesn't kill people—ever. At least not since the 1950s. Eisenhower was very skillful at using CIA. He was, in fact, so brilliant at exercising power that people never knew anything was happening and thought him a dullard because he didn't do the old war dance in front of cameras. More to the point, it was a different world back then. World War Two was recent history, and the idea of killing a lot of people—even innocent civilians—was a familiar one, mainly from the bombing campaigns," Hendley clarified. "It was just a cost of doing business."

"And Castro?"

"That was President John Kennedy and his brother Robert. They had a hard-on for doing Castro. Most people think it was embarrassment over the Bay of Pigs fiasco. I personally think it might have come more from reading too many James Bond novels. There was a glamour in murdering people back then. Today we call it sociopathy," Hendley noted sourly. "Problem was, first, that it's a lot more fun to read about than actually to do it, and, second, it's not an easy thing to accomplish without highly trained and highly motivated personnel. Well, I guess they found out. Then, when it became public, somehow the involvement of the Kennedy family was glossed over, and CIA paid the price for doing—badly—what the sitting President had told them to do. President Ford's Executive Order put an end to it all. And so, CIA doesn't deliberately kill people anymore."

"What about John Clark?" Jack asked, remembering the look in that guy's eyes.

"He's an aberration of sorts. Yes, he has killed people more than once, but he was always careful enough to do it only when it was tactically necessary at the moment. Langley *does* allow people to defend themselves in the field, and he had a gift for making it tactically necessary. I've met Clark a couple of times. Mainly, I know him by reputation. But he's an aberration. Now that he's retired, maybe he'll write a book. But even if he does, it'll never have the full story in it. Clark plays by the rules, like your dad. Sometimes he bends those rules, but to my knowledge he's never once broken them—well, not as a federal employee," Hendley corrected himself. He and the elder Jack Ryan had once had a long talk about John Clark, and they were the only two people in all the world who knew the whole story.

"Once I told Dad that I wouldn't want to be on Clark's bad side."

Hendley smiled. "That's true enough, but you could also trust John Clark with the lives of your children. When we met last, you asked me a question about Clark. I can answer now: If he were younger, he'd be here," Hendley said revealingly.

"You just told me something," Jack said at once.

"I know. Can you live with it?"

"Killing people?"

"I didn't say that, exactly, did I?"

Jack Jr. put his coffee cup down. "Now I know why Dad says you're smart."

"Can you live with the fact that your father has taken a few lives in his time?"

"I know about that. Happened the night I was born. It's practically a family legend. The newsies made a lot of it while Dad was President. They kept bringing it up like it was leprosy or something. Except there's a cure for leprosy."

"I know. In a movie it's downright cool, but in real life people get the heebie-jeebies about it. The problem with the real world is that sometimes—not often, but sometimes—it's necessary to do that sort of thing, as your father discovered . . . on more than one occasion, Jack. He never flinched. I think he even had bad dreams about it. But when he had to do it, he did it. That's why you're alive. That's why a lot of other people are alive."

"I know about the submarine thing. That's pretty much in the open, but—"

"More than just that. Your father never went out looking for trouble, but when it found him—as I said, he did what was necessary."

"I sorta remember when the people who attacked Mom and Dad—the night I was born, that is—were executed. I asked Mom about it. She's not real big on executing people, you see. In that case, she didn't mind very much. She was uncomfortable with it, but I suppose you'd say she saw the logic of the situation. Dad—you know, he didn't really like it either, but he didn't cry any tears over it."

"Your father had a gun to that guy's—the leader, I

mean—his head, but he didn't squeeze off the round. It wasn't necessary, and so he held back. Had I been in his position, well, I don't know. It was a hard call, but your father made the right choice when he had ample reason not to."

"That's what Mr. Clark said. I asked him about it once. He said the cops were right there, so why bother? But I never really believed him. That's one hardcase mother. I asked Mike Brennan, too. He said it was impressive for a civilian to hold off. But he would not have killed the guy. Training, I guess."

"I'm not sure about Clark. He's not really a murderer. He doesn't kill people for fun or for money. Maybe he would have spared the guy's life. But no, a trained cop is not supposed to do anything like that. What do you think you would have done?"

"You can't know until you're there," Jack answered. "I thought it through once or twice. I decided Dad handled it okay."

Hendley nodded. "You're right. He handled the other part right, too. The guy in the boat he drilled in the head, he had to do it to survive, and when you have that choice, there's only one way to go."

"So, Hendley Associates does what, exactly?"

"We gather and act upon intelligence information."

"But you're not part of the government," Jack objected.

"Technically, no, we're not. We do things that have to be done, when the agencies of the government are unable to handle them."

"How often does that happen?"

"Not very," Hendley replied offhandedly. "But that may change—or it might not. Hard to tell right now."

"How many times—"

"You do not need to know," Hendley replied, with raised eyebrows.

"Okay. What does Dad know about this place?"

"He's the guy who persuaded me to set it up."

"Oh . . ." And just that fast it was all clear. Hendley had

kissed off his political career in order to serve his country in a way that would never be recognized, never be rewarded. Damn. Did his own father have the stones to try this one? "And if you get into trouble somehow... ?"

"In a safety-deposit box belonging to my personal attorney are a hundred presidential pardons, covering any and all illegal acts that might have been committed between the dates that my secretary will fill in when she types up the blanks, and signed by your father, a week before he left office."

"Is that legal?"

"It's legal enough," Hendley replied. "Your dad's Attorney General, Pat Martin, said it would pass muster, though it would be pure dynamite if it ever became public."

"Dynamite, hell, it would be a nuke on Capitol Hill," Jack thought aloud. It was, in fact, something of an understatement.

"That's why we're careful here. I cannot encourage my people to do things that might end them up in prison."

"Just lose their credit rating forever."

"You have your father's sense of humor, I see."

"Well, sir, he *is* my dad, you know? Comes along with the blue eyes and black hair."

The academic records said that he had the brains. Hendley could see that he had the same inquisitive nature, and the ability to sort the wheat from the chaff. Did he have his father's guts... ? Better never to have to find out. But even his best people couldn't predict the future, except in currency fluctuations—and on that they cheated. That was the one illegal thing he could get prosecuted for, but, no, that would never happen, would it?

"Okay, time for you to meet Rick Bell. He and Jerry Rounds do the analysis here."

"Have I met them before?"

"Nope. Neither has your father. That's one of the problems with the intelligence community. It's gotten too damned big. Too many people—the organizations are always tripping over themselves. If you have the best hundred people in pro football on the same team, the team will self-destruct from internal dissension. Every man was born with an ego, and they're like the proverbial long-tailed cat in a room full of rocking chairs. Nobody objects too much because the government isn't supposed to function too efficiently. It would scare people if it did. That's why we're here. Come on. Jerry's office is right down the hall."

"CHARLOTTESVILLE?" Dominic asked. "I thought—"

"Since the time of Director Hoover, the Bureau has had a safe house facility down there. Technically, it doesn't belong to the FBI. It's where we keep the Gray Files."

"Oh." He'd heard about that from a senior instructor at the Academy. The Gray Files—outsiders never even knew the term—were supposed to be Hoover's files on political figures, all manner of personal irregularities, which politicians collected as other men collected stamps and coins. Supposedly destroyed at Hoover's death in 1972, in fact they'd been sequestered in Charlottesville, Virginia, in a large safe house on a hilltop across the gentle valley from Tom Jefferson's Monticello and overlooking the University of Virginia. The old plantation house had been built with a capacious wine cellar, which for more than fifty years had held rather more precious contents. It was the blackest of Bureau secrets, known only to a handful of people, which did not necessarily include the sitting FBI Director, but rather controlled by only the most trusted of career agents. The files were never opened, at least not the political ones. That junior senator during the Truman administration, for example, did not need to have his penchant for underage females revealed to the public. He was long dead in any case, as was the abortionist. But the fear of these records, whose continuation was widely believed to be carried on, explained why Congress rarely attacked the FBI on matters of appropriations. A really good archivist with a computerized memory might have inferred their existence from subtle holes in the Bureau's voluminous records, but that would have been a task worthy of Heracles. Besides, there were much juicier secrets than that to be found in the White Files squirreled off in a former West Virginia coal mine—or so an historian might think.

"We're going to detach you from the Bureau," Werner said next.

"What?" Dominic Caruso asked. "Why?" The shock of that pronouncement nearly ejected him from his chair.

"Dominic, there's a special unit that wants to talk to you. Your employment will continue there. They will fill you in. I said 'detach,' not 'terminate,' remember. Your pay will continue. You'll be kept on the books as a Special Agent on special assignment to counterterrorism investigations directly under my office. You'll continue to get normal promotions and pay raises. This information is secret, Agent Caruso," Werner went on. "You cannot discuss it with anyone but me. Is that clear?"

"Yes, sir, but I cannot say I understand."

"You will in due course. You will continue to investigate criminal activity, and probably to act upon it. If your new assignment turns out to be not to your liking, you can tell me, and we'll reassign you to a new field division for more conventional duties. But, I repeat, you cannot discuss your new assignment with anyone but me. If anyone asks, you're still a Special Agent of the FBI, but you are unable to discuss your work with anyone. You will not be vulnerable to any adverse action of any kind as long as you do your job properly. You will find that the oversight is looser than you're used to. But you will be accountable to someone at all times."

"Sir, this is still not very clear," Special Agent Caruso observed.

"You will be doing work of the highest national importance, mainly counterterrorism. There will be danger attached to it. The terrorist community is not a civilized one."

"This is an undercover assignment, then?"

Werner nodded. "Correct."

"And it's run out of this office?"

"More or less," Werner dodged with a nod.

"And I can bail out whenever I want?"

"Correct."

"Okay, sir, I'll give it a look. What do I do now?"

Werner wrote on a small pad of paper and handed it across. "Go to that address. Tell them you want to see Gerry."

"Right now, sir?"

"Unless you have something else to do."

"Yes, sir." Caruso stood, shook hands, and took his leave. At least it would be a pleasant drive into the Virginia horse country.

CHAPTER 4

BOOT CAMP

THE DRIVE back across the river to the Marriott allowed Dominic to collect his bags—with a twenty-dollar bill to the bellman—and then punch in his destination on the Mercedes's navigation computer. Soon he was southbound on Interstate 95, leaving Washington behind. The skyline of the national capital actually looked pretty good in his rearview mirror. The car drove well, about what you'd expect of a Mercedes; the local talk radio was pleasingly conservative—cops tended to be that way—and traffic wasn't too bad, though he found himself pitying the poor bastards who had to drive into D.C. every day to push paper in the Hoover Building and all the other government-grotesque buildings surrounding The Mall. At least FBI Headquarters had its own pistol range for stress management. Probably well used, Dominic thought.

Just before hitting Richmond, the female voice on his computer told him to take a right onto the Richmond Beltway, which presently delivered him to I-64 west toward the rolling, wooded hills. The countryside was pleasant, and green enough. Probably a lot of golf courses and horse farms. He'd heard that the CIA had its safe houses here from back when they had to debrief Soviet defectors. He wondered what the places were used for now. Chinese, maybe? Frenchmen, perhaps. Certainly they hadn't been sold. The government didn't like letting go of things, except maybe to close down military bases. The clowns from the Northeast and Far West loved to do that. They didn't much like the Bureau either, though they were probably afraid of it. He didn't know what it was about cops and soldiers that bothered some politicians, but he didn't much worry about it. He had his rice bowl, and they had theirs.

After another hour and fifteen minutes or so, he started looking for his exit sign, but the computer didn't need him.

"PREPARE TO TURN RIGHT AT THE NEXT EXIT," the voice said, about two minutes ahead of time.

"Fine, honey," Special Agent Caruso replied, without getting an acknowledgment. A minute later, he took the suggested exit—without so much as a VERY GOOD from the computer—and then took some ordinary city streets through the pleasant little town and up some gentle hills to the north wall of this valley, until finally:

"TAKE THE NEXT LEFT AND YOU HAVE ARRIVED AT YOUR DESTINATION . . ."

"That's nice, honey, thank you," he observed.

"YOUR DESTINATION" was the end of an entirely ordinary-looking country road, maybe a driveway, since it had no lines painted on it. A few hundred yards farther and he saw two redbrick abutments and a white-rail gate that was conveniently swung open. There was a house another three hundred yards off, with six white pillars holding up the front part of the roof. The roof appeared to be slate— rather old slate, at that—and the walls were weathered brick that hadn't been red in over a hundred years. This place had to be over a century old, maybe two. The driveway was recently raked pea-sized gravel. The grass—there was a *lot* of grass here—was a luscious golf-course green. Someone came out of a side door and waved him around to the left. He twisted the wheel to head behind the house, and got a surprise. The mansion—what *did* you call a house this big?—was larger than it first appeared, and had a fair-sized parking lot, which at the moment held a Chevy Suburban, a Buick SUV, and—another Mercedes C-class just like his, with North Carolina tags. The likelihood of this coincidence was too remote even to enter his imagina—

"Enzo!"

Dominic snapped his head around. "Aldo!"

People often remarked on their resemblance, though it was even more apparent when they were apart. Both had dark hair and fair skin. Brian was the taller by twenty-four millimeters. Dominic was perhaps ten pounds heavier. Whatever differences in mannerisms they'd had as boys had stayed with them as they'd grown up together. Since both were partly Italian in ancestry, they hugged warmly—but they didn't kiss. They weren't *that* Italian.

"What the hell are you doing here?" Dominic was the first to ask.

"Me? What about you?" Brian shot back, heading to help with his brother's bags. "I read about your shoot in Alabama. What's the story?"

"Pedophile," Dominic replied, pulling out his two-suiter. "Raped and killed a cute little girl. I got there about half an hour too late."

"Hey, ain't nobody perfect, Enzo. Papers said you put an end to his career."

Dominic looked right into Brian's eyes. "Yeah, I managed to accomplish that."

"How, exactly?"

"Three in the chest."

"Works every time," Captain Brian Caruso observed. "And no lawyers to cry over his body."

"No, not this time." His words were not the least bit jolly, but his brother heard the cold satisfaction.

"With this, eh?" The Marine lifted his brother's automatic from its holster. "Looks nice," he said.

"It shoots pretty good. Loaded, bro, do be careful."

Brian ejected the magazine and cleared the chamber. "Ten millimeter?"

"That's right. FBI-issue. Makes nice holes. The Bureau went back to it after Inspector O'Day had that shoot-out with the bad guys—you know, Uncle Jack's little girl."

Brian remembered the story well: the attack on Katie Ryan at her school shortly after her dad had become President, the shoot-out, the kills.

"That dude had his shit wired pretty tight," he said. "And you know, he's not even an ex-Marine. He was a Navy puke before he turned cop. That's what they said at Quantico, anyway."

"They did a training tape of the job. I met him once, just shook his hand with twenty other guys. Son of a bitch can shoot. He talked about waiting for your chance and making the first shot count. He double-tapped both their heads."

"How did he keep his cool?" The rescue of Katie Ryan had struck home for both Caruso boys. She was, after all, their first cousin, and a nice little girl, the image of her mother.

"Hey, you smelled the smoke over there. How did you keep yours?"

"Training. I had Marines to look after, bro."

Together, they manhandled Dominic's things inside. Brian showed the way upstairs. They had separate bedrooms, next to each other. Then they came back to the kitchen. Both got coffee and sat at the kitchen table.

"So, how's life in the Marine Corps, Aldo?"

"Gonna make major soon, Enzo. Got myself a Silver Star for what I did over there—wasn't that big a deal, really, I just did what they trained me to do. One of my men got shot up, but he's okay now. We didn't bag the guy we were after—he wasn't in a mood to surrender, so Gunny Sullivan sent him off to see Allah—but we got two live ones and they talked some, gave us some good information, the Intel guys told me."

"What did you get the pretty ribbon for?" Dominic asked pointedly.

"Mainly for staying alive. I shot three of the bad guys myself. Weren't even hard shots, really. I just took 'em. Later they asked me if I had any nightmares about it. The Marine Corps just has too many doctors around—and they're all squids."

"Bureau's the same way, but I blew it off. No bad dreams about that bastard. The poor little girl. I should've shot his dick off."

"Why didn't you?"

"'Cause that doesn't kill your ass, Aldo. But three in the heart does."

"You didn't shoot him on the spur of the moment, did you?"

"Not exactly, but—"

"And that's why you're here, Special Agent Caruso," a man said, entering the room. He was over six feet, a very fit fifty, both of the others thought.

"Who are you, sir?" Brian asked.

"Pete Alexander," the man answered.

"I was supposed to meet you last—"

"No, actually you weren't, but that's what we told the general." Alexander sat down with his own cup of coffee.

"So, who are you, then?" Dominic asked.

"I'm your training officer."

"Just you?" Brian asked.

"Training for what?" Dominic asked at the same time.

"No, not just me, but I'm the one who'll be here all the time. And the nature of the training will show you what you're training for," he answered. "Okay, you want to know about me. I graduated Yale thirty years ago, in political science. I was even a member of Skull and Bones. You know, the boys' club that conspiracy theorists like to prattle about. Jesus, like people in their late teens can really accomplish anything beyond getting laid, on a *good* Friday night." His brown eyes and the look in them hadn't come from a college, however, even an Ivy League one. "Back in the old days, the Agency liked to recruit people from Yale and Harvard and Dartmouth. The kids there have gotten over it. They all want to be merchant bankers now and make money. I worked twenty-five years in the Clandestine Service, and then I got recruited by The Campus. Been with them ever since."

"The Campus? What's that?" the Marine asked. Alexander noticed that Dominic Caruso did not. He was listening and watching very closely. Brian would never stop being a Marine, and Dominic would never stop being FBI. They never did. It was both good and bad, in both cases.

"*That* is a privately funded intelligence service."

"Privately funded?" Brian asked. "How the hell—"

"You'll see how it works later, and when you do, you will be surprised how easily it's done. What concerns you right here and right now is *what* they do."

"They kill people," Dominic said immediately. The words came out seemingly of their own accord.

"Why do you think that?" Alexander asked innocently.

"The outfit is small. We're the only people here, judging by the parking pad outside. I'm not experienced enough to be an expert agent. All I did was whack somebody who needed it, and next day I'm up in Headquarters talking to an assistant director, and a couple of days after that I drive to D.C. and get sent down here. This place is very, very special, very, very small, and it has top-level approval for whatever it does. You're not selling U.S. Savings Bonds here, are you?"

"The book on you is that you have good analytical ability," Alexander said. "Can you learn to keep your mouth shut?"

"It's not needed in this particular place, I should think. But, yeah, I know how, when the situation calls for it," Dominic said.

"Okay, here's the first speech. You guys know what 'black' means, right? It means a program or project that is not acknowledged by the government. People pretend it doesn't exist. The Campus takes that one step further: We really do not exist. There is not a single written document in the possession of any government employee that has a single word about us. From this moment on, you two young gentlemen do not exist. Oh, sure, you, Captain—or is it Major already?—Caruso, you get a paycheck that's going to be direct-deposited into whatever bank account you set up this week, but you are no longer a Marine. You are on detached duty, whose nature is unknown. And you, Special Agent Dominic Caruso—"

"I know. Gus Werner told me. They dug a hole and pulled it in after them."

Alexander nodded. "You will both leave your official identification documents, dog tags, everything, here before you leave. You can keep your names, maybe, but a name is just a couple of words, and nobody believes a name in this business anyway. That's the funny part about my time in the field with the Agency. Once on a job, I changed names without thinking about it. Damned embarrassing when I realized it. Like an actor: All of a sudden I'm Macbeth when I'm supposed to be Hamlet. No harm came of it, though, and I didn't croak at the end of the play."

"What, exactly, will we be doing?" This was Brian.

"Mostly, you'll be doing investigative work. Tracking money. The Campus is particularly good at that. You'll find out how and why later. You will probably deploy together. You, Dominic, will do most of the heavy lifting on the investigative side. You, Brian, will back him up on the muscle side, and along the way you'll learn to do what—what was it you called him a little while ago?"

"Oh, you mean Enzo? I call him that because he had a heavy foot when he got his driver's license. You know, like Enzo Ferrari."

Dominic pointed to his brother and laughed. "He's Aldo because he dresses like a dweeb. Like in that wine commercial, Aldo Cella: 'He's not a slave to fashion'? It's a family joke."

"Okay, go to Brooks Brothers and dress better," Pete Alexander told Brian. "Your cover mainly will be as a businessman or a tourist. So, you'll have to dress neatly, but not like the Prince of Wales. You'll both let your hair grow out, especially you, Aldo."

Brian rubbed a hand over his head stubble. It marked him anywhere in the civilized world as a United States Marine. It could have been worse. Army Rangers were even more radical in the hair department. Brian would look like a fairly normal human being in a month or so. "Damn, I'll have to buy a comb."

"What's the plan?"

"For today, just relax and settle in. Tomorrow we wake up early and make sure you two are in decent physical shape. Then there's weapons proficiency—and the sit-down classwork. You're both computer-literate, I presume."

"Why do you ask?" This was Brian.

"The Campus mainly works like a virtual office. You'll be issued computers with built-in modems, and that's how you'll communicate with the home office."

"What about security?" Dominic asked.

"The machines have pretty good security built in. If there's a way to crack them, nobody's found it yet."

"That's good to know," Enzo observed, dubiously. "They use computers in the Corps, Aldo?"

"Yeah, we have all the modern conveniences, even toilet paper."

"AND YOUR name is Mohammed?" Ernesto asked.

"That is correct, but for now, call me Miguel." Unlike with Nigel, it was a name he'd be able to remember. He had not begun by invoking Allah's blessing on this meeting. These unbelievers would not have understood.

"Your English is—well, you *sound* English."

"I was educated there," Mohammed explained. "My mother was English. My father was Saudi."

"Was?"

"Both are dead."

"My sympathies," Ernesto offered with questionable sincerity. "So, what can we do for each other?"

"I told Pablo here about the idea. Has he filled you in?"

"*Sí*, he has, but I wish to hear it directly from you. You understand that I represent six others who share my business interests."

"I see. Do you have the power to negotiate for all of them?"

"Not entirely, but I will present what you say to them— you need not meet with them all—and they have never rejected my suggestions. If we come to an agreement here, it can be fully ratified by the end of the week."

"Very well. You know the interests I myself represent. I am empowered to make an agreement, as well. Like you, we have a major enemy nation to the north. They are putting ever-greater pressure on my friends. We wish to retaliate, and to deflect their pressure in other directions."

"It is much the same with us," Ernesto observed.

"Therefore, it is in our mutual interests to cause unrest and chaos within America. The new American president is a weak man. But for that reason he can be a dangerous one. The weak are quicker to use force than the strong. Even though they use it inefficiently, it can be an annoyance."

"Their methods of intelligence-gathering concern us. You also?"

"We have learned caution," Mohammed replied. "What we do not have is a good infrastructure in America. For this we need assistance."

"You don't? That's surprising. Their news media is full of reports about the FBI and other agencies busily tracking your people within their borders."

"At the moment, they are chasing shadows—and sowing discord in their own land by doing so. It complicates the task of building a proper network so that we can conduct offensive operations."

"The nature of those operations does not concern us?" Pablo asked.

"That is correct. It is nothing you have not done yourselves, of course." *But not in America,* he did not add. Here in Colombia the gloves were all the way off, but they'd been careful to limit themselves in the U.S., their "customer" nation. So much the better. It would be entirely out of character with anything they'd done. Operational security was a concept both sides fully understood.

"I see," the senior Cartel man noted. He was no fool. Mohammed could see that in his eyes. The Arab was not going to underestimate these men or their capabilities . . .

Nor would he mistake them for friends. They could be as ruthless as his own men, he knew that. Those who denied God could be every bit as dangerous as those who worked in His Name.

"So what can you offer us?"

"We have conducted operations in Europe for a long time," said Mohammed. "You wish to expand your marketing efforts there. We've had a highly secure network in place for over twenty years. The changes in European commerce—the diminution of the importance of borders, and so forth—works in your favor, as it has worked in ours. We have a cell in the port city of Piraeus that can easily accommodate your needs, and contacts within the transnational trucking companies. If they can transport weapons and people for us, they can surely transport your products easily enough."

"We will need a list of names, the people with whom we can discuss the technical aspects of this business," Ernesto told his guest.

"I have it with me." Mohammed held up his personal laptop computer. "They are accustomed to doing business in return for monetary considerations." He saw his hosts nod without asking about how much money. Clearly, this was not a matter of great concern for them.

Ernesto and Pablo were thinking: There were over three hundred million people in Europe, and many of them would doubtless enjoy the Colombians' cocaine. Some European countries even allowed the use of drugs in discreet, controlled—and taxed—settings. The money involved was insufficient to make a decent profit, but it did have the advantage of setting the proper atmosphere. And nothing, not even medicinal-quality heroin, was as good as Andean coca. For that they would pay their Euros, and this time it would be enough to make this venture profitable. The danger, of course, was in the distribution side. Some careless street dealers would undoubtedly be arrested, and some of them would talk. So, there had to be ample insulation between the wholesale distribution and retail sides, but that was something they knew how to do—no matter how professional the European policemen were, they could not be all that different from the Americans. Some of them would even happily take the Cartel's Euros, and grease the skids. Business was business. And if this Arab could help with that—for free, which was truly remarkable—so much the better. Ernesto and Pablo did not react physically to the business offer on the table. An outsider might have taken their demeanor for boredom. It was anything but that, of course. This offer was heaven-sent. A whole new market was going to open up, and with the new revenue stream it brought, maybe they could buy their country entirely. They'd have to learn a new way of doing business, but they'd have the money to experiment, and they were adaptable creatures: fish, as it were, swimming in a sea of peasants and capitalists.

"How do we contact these people?" Pablo inquired.

"My people will make the necessary introductions."

Better and better, Ernesto thought.

"And what services will you require of us?" he finally asked.

"We will need your help to transport people into America. How would we go about this?"

"If you mean physically moving people from your part of the world into America, the best thing is to fly them into Colombia—right here to Cartagena, in fact. Then we will arrange for them to be flown into other Spanish-speaking countries to the north. Costa Rica, for example. From there, if they have reliable travel documents, they can fly there directly, via an American airline, or through Mexico. If they appear Latin and speak Spanish, they can be smuggled across the Mexican-American border—it is a physical challenge, and some of them might be apprehended, but if so, they'd simply be returned to Mexico, for another attempt. Or, again with proper documents, they could just walk across the border into San Diego, California. Once in America, it's a question of maintaining your cover. If money is not an issue—"

"It isn't," Mohammed assured him.

"Then you retain a local attorney—few of them have much in the way of scruples—and arrange the purchase of a suitable safe house to serve as a base of operations. Forgive me—I know we agreed that such operations need not concern us—but if you gave me some idea of what you have in mind, I could advise you."

Mohammed thought for a few moments, and then explained.

"I see. Your people must be properly motivated to do such things," Ernesto observed.

"They are." Could this man have any doubt of that? Mohammed wondered.

"And with good planning and nerve, they can even survive. But you must never underestimate the American police agencies. In our business we can make financial arrangements with some of them, but that is very unlikely in your case."

"We understand that. Ideally, we would want our people to survive, but sadly we know that some will be lost. They understand the risk." He didn't talk about Paradise. These people would not understand. The God they worshipped folded into their wallets.

What sort of fanatic throws his people away like that? Pablo asked himself. His men freely took their risks, measuring the money to be gained against the consequences of failure, and made decisions out of their own free will. Not these people. Well, one couldn't always choose one's business associates.

"Very well. We have a number of blank American passports. It is your job to be certain that the people you send us can speak proper English or Spanish, and can present themselves properly. I trust none of them will partake in flying lessons?" Ernesto meant it as a joke.

Mohammed did not take it as one.

"The time for that is past. Success rarely succeeds twice in my field of endeavor."

"Fortunately, we have a different field," Ernesto responded. And it was true. He could send shipments in cargo container boxes via commercial vessels and trucks all over America. If one of them was lost, and the programmed destination discovered, America had many legal protections for his downstream employees. Only the foolish ones went to prison. Over the years, they'd learned to defeat sniffer dogs and all the other means of discovery. The most important thing was that they used people who were willing to take risks, and most of them survived to retire back to Colombia and join the upper middle class, their prosperity the result of something in the distant, fading past, never to be repeated or spoken of.

"So," Mohammed said. "When can we commence operations?"

This man is anxious, Ernesto noted. But he would accommodate him. Whatever he managed to accomplish would draw manpower away from America's counter-smuggling operations, and that was good. The relatively minor cross-border losses he had learned to endure would shrink to even more trivial levels. The street price of cocaine would drop, but demand would increase somewhat, and so there would be no net loss in sales revenue. That would be the tactical profit. More to the point, America would become less interested in Colombia, and shift her focus of intelligence operations elsewhere. That would be his strategic advantage from this endeavor...

...and he always had the option of sending information to the CIA. Terrorists had appeared unexpectedly in his backyard, he could say, and their operations would be understood to be beyond the pale even for the Cartel. While that would not gain him the affection of America, it would not hurt him, either. And any of his own people who'd provided assistance to the terrorists could be dealt with internally, as it were. The Americans would actually respect that.

So, there was a real upside, and a controllable downside. On the whole, he decided, this had the makings of a valuable and profitable operation.

"Señor Miguel, I will propose this alliance to my colleagues, with my recommendation that we undertake it. You can expect a final decision by the end of this week. Will you remain in Cartagena, or will you be traveling?"

"I prefer not to remain in one place too long. I fly out tomorrow. Pablo can reach me via the Internet with your decision. For the moment, I thank you for a cordial business meeting."

Ernesto stood and took his guest's hand. He decided then and there to consider Miguel as a businessman in a similar but not competitive field of endeavor. Not a friend, certainly, but an ally of convenience.

"**HOW THE** hell did you manage this?" Jack asked.

"Ever hear of a company called INFOSEC?" Rick Bell asked in return.

"Encryption stuff, right?"

"Correct. Information Systems Security Company. The

company's domiciled outside of Seattle. They have the best information-security program there is. Headed by a former deputy head of the Z-Division over at Fort Meade. He and three colleagues set the company up about nine years ago. I'm not sure NSA can crack it, short of brute-forcing it with their new Sun Workstations. Just about every bank in the world uses it, especially the ones in Liechtenstein and the rest of Europe. But there's a trapdoor in the program."

"And nobody's found it?" Buyers of computer programs had learned over the years to have outside experts go over such programs line by line, as a defense against playful software engineers, of which there were far too many.

"Those NSA guys do good code," Bell responded. "I have no idea what's in there, but these guys still have their old NSA school ties hanging in the closet, y'know?"

"And Fort Meade listens in, and we get what they dig up when they fax it to Langley," Jack said. "Anybody at CIA good at tracking money?"

"Not as good as our people."

"Takes a thief to catch a thief, eh?"

"Helps to know the mind-set of the adversary," Bell confirmed. "It's not a large community we're dealing with here. Hell, we know most of them—we're in the same business, right?"

"And that makes me an additional asset?" Jack asked. He was not a prince under American law, but Europeans still thought in such terms. They'd bow and scrape just to shake his hand, regard him as a promising young man however thick his head might turn out to be, and seek his favor, first because of the possibility he might speak a kind word into the right ear. It was called corruption, of course, or at least the atmosphere for it.

"What did you learn in the White House?" Bell asked.

"A little, I suppose," Jack responded. Mostly, he'd learned things from Mike Brennan, who'd cordially detested all the diplomatic folderol, to say nothing of the political stuff that happened there every day. Brennan had talked it over with his foreign colleagues often enough, who saw the same things in their own capitals, and who thought much the same of it, from behind the same blank faces when they stood post. It was probably a better way to learn all this stuff than his father had, Jack thought. He hadn't been forced to learn to swim while struggling not to drown. It was something his father had never spoken about, except when angry at the whole corrupting process.

"Be careful talking to Gerry about it," said Bell. "He likes to say how clean and upright the trading business is by comparison."

"Dad really likes the guy. I guess maybe they're a little alike."

"No," Bell corrected, "they're a *lot* alike."

"Hendley got out of politics because of the accident, right?"

Bell nodded. "That's it. Wait until you have a wife and kids. It's about the biggest hit a man can take. Even worse than you might think. He had to go and identify the bodies. It wasn't pretty. Some people would eat a gun after that. But he didn't. He'd been thinking about a run for the White House himself, thought maybe Wendy would make a good First Lady. Maybe so, but his lust for that job died along with his wife and kids." He didn't go further. The senior people at The Campus protected the boss, in reputation at least. They thought him a man who deserved loyalty. There was no considered line of succession at The Campus. Nobody had thought that far forward, and the subject never came up in board meetings. Those were mainly concerned with non–business matters anyway. He wondered if John Patrick Ryan, Jr., would take note of that one blank spot in the makeup of The Campus. "So," Bell went on, "what do you think so far?"

"I read the transcripts they gave me of what the central bank heads say back and forth to each other. It's surprising how venal some of that stuff is." Jack paused. "Oh, yeah, shouldn't be surprised, should I?"

"Any time you give people control of that much money or power, some corruption is bound to happen. What surprises me is the way their friendships cross national lines. A lot of these guys profit personally when their own currencies are hurt, even if it means a little inconvenience for their fellow citizens. Back in the old-old days, the nobility frequently felt more at ease with foreign nobility than with the people on their own estates who bowed down to the same king. That characteristic hasn't died yet—at least not over there. Here the big industrialists might work together to lobby Congress, but they don't often hand freebies to them, and they don't trade secrets. Conspiracy at that level isn't impossible, but concealing it for a long time is pretty tough. Too many people, and every one has a mouth. Europe's getting the same way. There's nothing the media likes better than a scandal, here or there, and they'd rather clobber a rich crook than a cabinet minister. The latter is often a good source, after all. The former is just a crook."

"So, how do you keep your people honest?"

It was a good question, Bell thought, and one they worried about all the time, though it wasn't spoken about much.

"We pay our people pretty well, and everyone here is part of a group investment plan that makes them feel comfortable. The annualized return is about nineteen percent over the last few years."

"That's not bad," Junior understated. "All within the law?"

"That depends on the lawyer you talk to, but no U.S. Attorney is going to make a big deal about it, and we're very careful how we manage it. We don't like greed here. We could turn this place into the biggest thing since Ponzi, but then people would notice. So, we don't flaunt anything. We make enough to cover our operations and to make sure the troops are well provided for." They also kept track of the employees' money, and the trades they made, if any. Most didn't, though some worked accounts through the office, which, again, was profitable but not greedy. "You'll give us account numbers and codes to all of your personal finances, and the computers will keep track of them."

"I have a trust account through Dad, but it's managed through an accounting firm in New York. I get a nice allowance, but no access to the principal. What I make on my own is mine alone, however, unless I send it into the CPAs. Then they build it up and send me a statement every quarter. When I turn thirty, I'm allowed to play with it on my own." Turning thirty was a little distant for young Jack to concern himself about at the moment, however.

"We know," Bell assured him, "it's not a question of lack of trust. It's just that we want to make sure nobody's developed a gambling habit."

Probably the best mathematicians of all time were the ones who'd made up the rules for gambling games, Bell thought. They'd provided just enough illusion that you had a chance to sucker you in. Born inside the human mind was the most dangerous of drugs. That was called "ego," too.

"So, I start out on the 'white' side of the house? Watching currency fluctuations and stuff?" said Jack.

Bell nodded. "Correct. You need to learn the language first."

"Fair enough." His father had started off a lot more humbly than this, as a junior accounting manager at Merrill Lynch who'd had to cold-call people. Paying one's dues was probably bad for the ego but good for the soul. His father had often lectured him on the Virtue of Patience. He'd said that it was a pain in the ass to acquire, even after acquiring it. But the game had rules, even in this place. *Especially in this place,* Jack realized on reflection. He wondered what happened to people on The Campus who crossed over the line. Probably nothing good.

"BUON VINO," Dominic observed. "For a government installation, the wine cellar isn't half bad." The year on the bottle read 1962, long before he and his brother had been born...for that matter, so long ago their mom had just been thinking about Mercy High School, a few blocks from their grandparents' place on Loch Raven Boulevard in Baltimore...toward the end of the last Ice Age, probably. But Baltimore was a hell of a long way from the Seattle they'd grown up in. "How old is this place?" he asked Alexander.

"The property? It goes back to before the Civil War. The house was started in seventeen-something. Burned down and rebuilt in 1882. Government got hold of it just before Nixon was elected. The owner was an old OSS guy, J. Donald Hamilton, worked with Donovan and his crowd. He got a fair price when he sold it, moved out to New Mexico and died there in 1986, I think, aged ninety-four. They say he was a mover and shaker in his day, stuck it out pretty far in World War One, and helped Wild Bill work against the Nazis. There's a painting of him in the library. Looks like a guy to step aside for. And, yeah, he did know his wines. This one's from Tuscany."

"Goes nicely with veal," Brian said. He'd done the cooking.

"This veal goes well with anything. You didn't learn that in the Marine Corps," Alexander observed.

"From Pop. He is a better cook than Mom," Dominic explained. "You know, it's an old-country thing. And Grandpop, that son of a bitch, can still do it, too. He's what, Aldo, eighty-two?"

"Last month," Brian confirmed. "Funny old guy, travels the whole world to get to Seattle, and then he never leaves the city for sixty years."

"Same house for the last forty," Dominic added, "a block from the restaurant."

"This his recipe for the veal?"

"Bet your bippy, Pete. The family goes back to Florence. Went up there two years when the Med FMF was making a port call in Naples. His cousin has a restaurant just upriver from the Ponte Vecchio. When they found out who I was, they went nuts feeding me. You know, Italians love the Marines."

"Must be the green suit, Aldo," Dominic said.

"Maybe I just cut a manly figure, Enzo. Ever think of that?" Captain Caruso demanded.

"Oh, sure," Special Agent Caruso replied, taking another bite of the Veal Francese. "The next Rocky sits before us."

"You boys always like this?" Alexander asked.

"Just when we drink," Dominic replied, and his brother laughed.

"Enzo can't hold his liquor worth a damn. Now, we Marines, we can do anything."

"I have to take this from somebody who thinks Miller Lite is really beer?" the FBI Caruso asked the air.

"You know," Alexander said, "twins are supposed to be alike."

"Only identical twins. Mom punched out two eggs that month. It had Mom and Dad fooled until we were a year old or so. We're not at all alike, Pete." Dominic delivered this pronouncement with a smile shared by his brother.

But Alexander knew better. They only dressed differently—and that would soon be changing.

CHAPTER 5

|||||||||||||||||||||||||||||||||||||||||||||||||||||||||||||||||||||||||

ALLIANCES

MOHAMMED TOOK the first Avianca flight to Mexico City and there he waited for British Airways Flight 242 to London. He felt safe in airports, where everything was anonymous. He had to be careful of the food, since Mexico was a nation of unbelievers, but the first-class lounge protected him from their cultural barbarism, and the many armed police officers ensured that people rather like himself did not crash the party, such as it was. So, he picked a corner seat away from windows and read a book he'd picked up in one of the shops and managed not to be bored to death. He never read the Koran in such a place, of course, nor anything about the Middle East, lest someone ask him a question. No, he had to live his cover "legend" as well as any professional intelligence officer, so that he did not come to an end as abrupt as the Jew Greengold in Rome. Mohammed even used the bathroom facilities carefully, in case someone tried the same trick on him.

He didn't even make use of his laptop computer, though there was ample opportunity to do so. Better, he judged, to sit still like a lump. In twenty-four hours he'd be back on the European mainland. It hit him that he lived in the air more than anywhere else. He had no home, just a series of safe houses, which were places of dubious reliability. Saudi Arabia was closed to him, and had been for nearly five years. Afghanistan was similarly out-of-bounds. How strange that the only lands where he could feel something close to safe were the Christian countries of Europe, which Muslims had struggled and failed to conquer on more than one occasion. Those nations had a nearly suicidal openness to strangers, and one could disappear in their vastness with only modest skills—hardly any, in fact, if you had money. These people were so self-destructively open, so afraid to offend those who would just as soon see them and their children dead and their entire cultures destroyed. It was a pleasing vision, Mohammed thought, but he didn't live within dreams. Instead, he worked *for* them. This struggle would last longer than his lifetime. Sad, perhaps, but true. But it was better to serve a cause than one's own interests. There were enough of those in the world.

He wondered what his supposed allies from yesterday's meeting were saying and thinking. They were certainly not true allies. Oh, yes, they shared enemies, but that was not the summation of an alliance. They would—might—facilitate matters, but no more than that. Their men would not assist his men in any real endeavor. Throughout history, mercenaries had never been really effective soldiers. To fight effectively, you had to *believe*. Only a believer would risk his life, because only a believer had nothing to fear. Not with Allah Himself on his side. What was there to fear, then? Only one thing, he admitted to himself. Failure. Failure was not an option. The obstacles between him and success were things to be dealt with in any way that was convenient. Just things. Not people. Not souls. Mohammed fished a cigarette out of his pocket and lit it. In this sense, at least, Mexico was a civilized country, though he refused to speculate on what the Prophet would have said about tobacco.

* * *

"EASIER IN a car, isn't it, Enzo?" Brian teased his brother as they crossed the finish line. The three-mile run wasn't a big deal for the Marine, but for Dominic, who had just maxed out his PT test for the FBI, it had been a bit of a stretch.

"Look, turkey," Dominic gasped out, "I just have to run faster than my subjects."

"Afghanistan would've killed your ass." Brian was running backward now, the better to observe his struggling brother.

"Probably," Dominic admitted. "But Afghans don't rob banks in Alabama and New Jersey." Dominic had never in his life traded toughness to his brother, but clearly the Marines had made him maintain greater fitness than the FBI did. But how good was he with a pistol? At last it was over, and he walked back toward the plantation house.

"Do we pass?" Brian asked Alexander on the way in.

"Easy, both of you. This isn't Ranger School, guys. We don't expect you to try out for the Olympics team, but, out in the field, running away is a nice ability to have."

"At Quantico, Gunny Honey liked to say that," Brian agreed.

"Who?" Dominic asked.

"Nicholas Honey, Master Gunnery Sergeant, United States Marine Corps, and, yeah, he probably took a lot of razzing because of his name—but probably not from the same guy twice. He was one of the instructors at the Basic School. They also called him 'Nick the Prick,'" Brian said, grabbing a towel and tossing it to his brother. "He's one bad-ass Marine. But he said that running away is the one skill an infantryman needs."

"Did you?" Dominic asked.

"I've only seen combat once, and that was just for a couple of months. Mostly, we were looking down at mountain goats who had heart attacks from climbing those fucking hills."

"That bad, eh?"

"Worse." Alexander joined in. "But fighting wars is for kids, not sensible adults. You see, Agent Caruso, out in the weeds you also wear sixty-five pounds on your back."

"That must be fun," Dominic said to his brother, not without respect.

"Big time. Okay, Pete, what other pleasant things are on the plan of the day?"

"Get cleaned up first," Alexander advised. Now that he was certain that both were in reasonable physical shape—though he'd had little doubt of that, and it wasn't all *that* important anyway, despite what he'd said—they could look into the hard stuff. The important stuff.

"THE BUCK is going to take a hit," Jack told his new boss.

"How bad?"

"Just a scratch. The Germans are going to short the dollar against the Euro, about five hundred million worth."

"Is that a big deal?" Sam Granger asked.

"You're asking me?" Jack responded.

"That's right. You have to have an opinion. It doesn't have to be correct, but it has to make some kind of sense."

Jack Ryan, Jr., handed over the intercepts. "This guy Dieter's talking with his French counterpart. He makes it sound like a routine transaction, but the translator says the tone of his voice has some nastiness to it. I speak a little German, but not well enough for that sort of nuance," the young Ryan told his boss. "I cannot say that I understand why the Germans and French would be in any sort of conspiracy against us."

"It suits current German interests to cozy up to the French. I do not see a long-term bilateral alliance of any sort, however. Fundamentally, the French are afraid of the Germans, and the Germans look down on the French. But the French have imperial ambitions—well, they always have. Look at their relations with America. Kind of like brother and sister, age twelve or so. They love each other, but they can't get along very well. Germany and France, that's similar but more complex. The French used to kick their ass, but then the Germans got organized and kicked the French ass. And both countries have long memories. That's the curse of Europe. There's a lot of contentious history over there, and they have trouble forgetting it."

"What does that have to do with this?" the young Ryan asked.

"Directly, nothing at all, but as background maybe the German banker wants to get close to this guy to make a future play. Maybe the Frenchman is letting him think he's getting close so that the French central bank can score points on Berlin. This is a funny game. You can't clobber your adversary too hard because then he won't play with you anymore, and, besides that, you don't go out of your way to make enemies. All in all, it's like a neighborhood poker game. If you do too well, then you make enemies, and it's a lot less fun to live there because nobody will come over to your house to play. If you're the dumbest at the table, the others will gang up on you in the nicest possible way and steal from you—not enough to hurt you but enough to tell themselves how smart they are. So what happens is that everyone plays a touch under his game, and it stays fairly friendly. Nobody over there is any farther than a general strike away from a major national liquidity crisis, and when that happens you need friends. I forgot to tell you, the central bankers regard everyone else on the continent as peasants. That can include the heads of the various governments."

"And us?"

"Americans? Oh, yeah. Meanly born, poorly educated—but exceedingly lucky—peasants."

"With big guns?" Little Jack asked.

"Yeah, peasants with guns always make the aristocracy nervous," Granger agreed, stifling a laugh. "They still have that class crap over there. They have trouble understanding how badly it holds them back in the marketplace, because the big shots rarely come up with a really new idea. But that's not our problem."

Oderint dum metuant, Jack thought. One of the few things he remembered from Latin. Supposedly the personal motto of the Emperor Gaius Caligula: *Let them hate so long as they fear.* Hadn't civilization advanced any further than that in the past two millennia?

"What is our problem?" he asked.

Granger shook his head. "I didn't mean it that way. They don't like us much—they never have liked us, really—but at the same time they can't live without us. Some of them are starting to think they can, after the death of the Soviet Union, but if they ever try reality will bite them on the ass hard enough to draw blood. Don't confuse the thoughts of the aristocracy with those of the people. That's the problem with them. They really do think that people follow their lead, but they don't. They follow their own wallets, and the average guy in the street will figure things out all by himself if he has enough time to think it through."

"So, The Campus just makes money off their fantasy world?"

"You got it. You know, I hate soap operas. Do you know why I hate them?" He got a blank look. "Jack, it's because they reflect reality so precisely. Real life, even at this level, is full of petty bullshit and egos. It isn't love that makes the world go 'round. It isn't even money. It's bullshit."

"Hey, I've heard cynicism in my time, but—"

"Granger cut him off with a raised hand. "Not cynicism. Human nature. The one thing that hasn't changed in ten thousand years of recorded history. I wonder if it ever will. Oh, sure, there's the good part of human nature, too: nobility, charity, self-sacrifice, even courage in some cases— and love. Love counts. It counts a lot. But along with it comes envy, covetousness, greed, all the seven deadly sins. Maybe Jesus knew what He was talking about, eh?"

"Is this philosophy or theology?" *I thought this was supposed to be the intelligence business,* the young Ryan thought.

"I turn fifty next week. Too soon old and too late smart. Some cowboy said that a hundred or so years ago." Granger smiled. "Problem is, you're too damned old when you realize it to be able to do anything about it."

"What would you do, start a new religion?"

Granger had himself a good laugh as he turned to refill his coffee cup from his personal Gevalia machine. "No, none of the bushes around my house burn. The trouble with thinking deep thoughts is that you still have to cut the grass, and put food on the table. And, in our case, protect our country."

"So, what do we do about this German thing?"

Granger gave the intercept another look and thought for a second. "Nothing, not right now, but we remember that Dieter has earned a point or two with Claude, which he may cash in on in six months or so. The Euro is still too new to see how it's going to play out. The French think that the financial leadership of Europe will slide to Paris. The Germans think it'll go to Berlin. In fact, it'll go to the country with the strongest economy, the most efficient workforce. That won't be France. They have pretty good engineers, but their population isn't as well organized as the Germans are. If I had to bet, I'd bet on Berlin."

"The French won't like that."

"That's a fact, Jack. That's a fact," Granger repeated. "What the hell. The French have nukes, and the Germans don't—for now, anyway."

"You serious?" the young Ryan demanded.

A smile. "No."

"THEY TAUGHT us some of that at Quantico," Dominic said. They were in a medium-sized shopping mall that catered to the college crowd due to the proximity of UVA.

"What did they say?" Brian asked.

"Don't stay in the same place relative to your subject. Try to alter your appearance—sunglasses, like that. Wigs if they're available. Reversible jackets. Don't stare at him, but don't turn away if he looks at you. It's a lot better if it's more than one agent on a target. One man can't track a trained adversary for very long without being made. A trained subject is hard to tail under the best of circumstances. That's why the big offices have the SSGs, Special Surveillance Groups. They're FBI employees, but they're not sworn, and they don't carry guns. Some guys call them the Baker Street Irregulars, as in Sherlock Holmes. They look like anything except a cop, street people—bums—workers in coveralls. They can be dirty. They can be panhandlers. I met some at the New York Field Office once, they work OC and FCI—organized crime and foreign counterintelligence. They're pros, but they're the most unlikely-looking damn pros you ever want to meet."

"Hardworking people like that?" Brian asked his brother. "Surveillance, I mean."

"Never tried it myself, but from what I've heard, it takes a lot of manpower, like fifteen or twenty, to work one subject, plus cars, plus aircraft—and a really good bad guy can outfox us even then. The Russians especially. Those bastards are trained pretty well."

"So, what the hell are we supposed to do?" Captain Caruso asked.

"Just learn the basics," Alexander told them. "See the woman over there with the red sweater?"

"Long dark hair?" Brian asked.

"That's the one," Pete confirmed. "Determine what she buys, what sort of car she drives, and where she lives."

"Just the two of us?" Dominic demanded. "You're not asking much, are you?"

"Did I tell you this was easy work?" Alexander asked innocently. He handed over two radios. "The earpieces go in your ears, and the microphones clip to your collars.

Range is about three kilometers. You both have your car keys." And with that he walked away, toward an Eddie Bauer store to buy himself a pair of shorts.

"Welcome to the shit, Enzo," Brian said.

"At least he gave us a mission brief."

"It was brief, all right."

Their subject had walked into an Ann Taylor store. They both headed down that way, each getting a large cup of coffee at the Starbucks as a jackleg disguise.

"Don't throw the cup away," Dominic told his brother.

"Why?" Brian asked.

"In case you gotta take a piss. The perversity of the world has a way of impinging on your carefully made plans in situations like this. That's a practical lesson from a class at the Academy."

Brian didn't comment, but it seemed sensible enough. One at a time they donned their radios and made sure they worked properly.

"Aldo to Enzo, over," Brian called on Channel 6.

"Enzo copies, bro. Let's switch off on visual surveillance, but we'll stay within sight of each other, okay?"

"Makes sense. Okay, I'll head toward the store."

"Ten-four. That's roger to you, bro." Dominic turned to see his brother draw off. Then he settled down to sipping his coffee and looking off the subject—never directly at her, but about 20 degrees to the side.

"What's she up to?" Aldo asked.

"Picking a blouse, looks like." The subject was thirty or so, with shoulder-length brown hair, fairly attractive, wearing a wedding band but no diamond, and a cheap gold-colored necklace probably purchased at Wal-Mart on the other side of the road. Peach-colored blouse/shirt. Pants rather than a skirt, black in color, black flat "sensible" shoes. Fairly large purse. Did not appear overly alert to her surroundings, which was good. She appeared to be alone. She finally settled on a blouse, white silk by the look of it, paid for it with a credit card, and walked out of Ann Taylor.

"Subject is moving, Aldo."

Seventy yards away, Brian's head perked up and turned directly toward his brother. "Talk to me, Enzo."

Dominic raised his coffee cup as though to take a drink. "Turning left, coming your way. You can take over in a minute or so."

"Ten-four, Enzo."

They'd parked their cars on opposite sides of the shopping mall. That turned out to be a good thing, as their subject turned right and headed for the door out to the parking lot.

"Aldo, get close enough to make her tag," Dominic ordered.

"What?"

"Read her tag number to me, and describe the car. I'm heading for my car."

"Okay, roger that, bro."

Dominic didn't run to his car, but he walked as fast as circumstances allowed. He got in, started the engine, and lowered all his windows.

"Enzo to Aldo, over."

"Okay, she's driving a dark green Volvo station wagon, Virginia tag Whiskey Kilo Romeo Six One Niner. Alone in the car, starting up, turning north. I'm on the way to my wheels."

"Roger that. Enzo is in pursuit." He got around the Sears department store that anchored the east end of the mall as quickly as traffic allowed, and reached in his coat pocket for his cell phone. And called information to get the number of the Charlottesville FBI office, which the phone company dialed for him for an additional charge of fifty cents. "Heads up, this is Special Agent Dominic Caruso. My creed-o number is one six five eight two one. I need a tag number run, right now, Whiskey Kilo Romeo Six One Niner."

Whoever was on the other end of the phone typed his credentials number into a computer and verified Dominic's identity.

"What are you doing this far from Birmingham, Mr. Caruso?"

"No time for that. Please run the tag."

"Roger, okay, it's a Volvo, green in color, a year old, registered to Edward and Michelle Peters, at Six Riding Hood Court, Charlottesville. That's just inside the city line on the west side of town. Anything else? Do you need backup?"

"Negative. Thank you, I can handle it from here. Caruso out." He killed his cell phone and relayed the address to his brother over the radio. Both then did the same thing, and entered the address into their navigation computers.

"This is cheating," Brian observed, smiling as he did so.

"Good guys don't cheat, Aldo. They just get the job done. Okay, I have eyeballs on the subject. She's heading west on Shady Branch Road. Where are you?"

"About five hundred yards back of you—shit! I have a red light."

"Okay, sit it out. Looks like she's heading home, and we know where that is." Dominic closed his target to within a hundred yards, keeping a pickup truck between himself and the subject car. He'd rarely done this sort of thing before, and he was surprised at how tense it was.

"PREPARE TO TURN RIGHT IN FIVE HUNDRED FEET," the computer told him.

"Thanks, honey," Dominic grumbled.

But then the Volvo turned at the corner suggested by the computer. So, it wasn't so bad after all, was it? Dominic took a breath and settled down some.

"Okay, Brian, looks like she's going right home. Just follow me in," he said over the radio.

"Roger, following you in. Any idea who this broad is?"

"Michelle Peters, so says the DMV." The Volvo turned left, then right, into a cul-de-sac, where it pulled into a driveway that ended at a two-car garage attached to a medium-sized house of two stories and white aluminum siding. He parked his car a hundred yards up the street and took a sip of his coffee. Brian showed up thirty seconds later, doing the same half a block up.

"See the car?" Dominic called.

"That's affirmative, Enzo." The Marine paused. "Now what do we do?"

"You come on down for a cup of my coffee," a female voice suggested. "I'm the broad in the Volvo," the voice clarified.

"Oh, shit," Dominic whispered away from the microphone. He got out of his Mercedes and waved to his brother to do the same.

Upon joining up, the Caruso brothers walked to 6 Riding Hood Court. The door opened as they came up the driveway.

"Set up all the way," Dominic said quietly. "Should have figured that one out from the beginning."

"Yep. Color us dumb," Brian thought.

"Not really," Mrs. Peters said from the door. "But getting my address from the DMV really was cheating, you know."

"Nobody told us anything about rules, ma'am," Dominic told her.

"There aren't any—not very often, anyway, not in this business."

"So, you listened in on the radio circuit the whole time?" Brian asked.

She nodded as she led them to the kitchen. "That's right. The radios are encrypted. Nobody else knew what you were talking about. How do you boys like your coffee?"

"So, you spotted us all the way?" This was Dominic.

"Actually, no. I didn't use the radios to cheat—well, not all that much." She had an engaging smile, which helped to soften the blows to her visitors' egos. "You're Enzo, right?"

"Yes, ma'am."

"You were a little close, but only a really sharp-eyed target would have noticed, given the limited time frame.

The make of the car helped. A lot of those little Benzes in this area. But the best choice of car would be a pickup—a dirty one. A lot of the yokels *never* wash them, and some of the academics at the school have adopted the same sort of behavior to fit in, like. Out on Interstate 64, well, you'd better have an aircraft, of course, and a Porta-Potti. Discreet surveillance can be the toughest job in the business. But now you boys know that."

Then the door opened and Pete Alexander came in. "How'd they do?" he asked Michelle.

"I'll give them a B."

And suddenly Dominic thought that was generous.

"And forget what I said before—calling the FBI to get a DMV on me was pretty smart."

"Not cheating?" Brian asked.

Alexander took that one. "The only rule is to accomplish the mission without being compromised. We don't tally up style points at The Campus."

"Just body count," Mrs. Peters confirmed, to Alexander's evident annoyance.

That was enough to make Brian's stomach contract a little. "Uh, guys, I know I've asked it before, but what exactly *are* we training for?" Dominic leaned in visibly as well.

"Patience, fellas," Pete cautioned.

"Okay." Dominic nodded submission. "I'll give you that this time." But not too much longer, he didn't have to add.

"SO, YOU'RE not going to exploit this?" Jack asked at closing time.

"We could, but it's not really worth the time. We'd only turn a couple of hundred thousand at best, probably not that much. But you did okay spotting it," Granger allowed.

"How much message traffic like this comes through here on a weekly basis?"

"One or two, four in a really busy week."

"And how many plays do you make?" Junior asked.

"One in five. We do so carefully, but even so, we always

run the risk of being noticed. If the Europeans saw that we were outguessing them too much, then they'd look into how we were doing it—they'd probably shake down their own people, looking for a human leaker. That's how they think over there. It's a big place for conspiracy theory, you see, because of the way they operate themselves. But the game they play regularly sort of militates against it."

"What else do you look into?"

"Starting next week, you'll have access to the secure accounts—people call them numbered accounts because they're supposedly identified by code numbers. Now it's mainly code words, because of computer technology. They probably picked that up from the intelligence community. They often hire spooks to look after their security—but not good ones. The good ones stay away from money-management businesses, mainly out of snobbery. It's not important enough for a senior spook," Granger explained.

"The 'secured' accounts, do they identify the owners?" Jack asked.

"Not always. Sometimes it's all done via code word, though sometimes the banks have internal memoranda that we can tap into. Not always, though, and the bankers never speculate internally about their clients—at least not in written form. I'm sure they chat back and forth over lunch, but you know, a lot of them, they really don't care very much about where the money comes from. Dead Jews in Auschwitz, some Mafia capo in Brooklyn—it's all money fresh off the presses."

"But if you turned this over to the FBI—"

"We can't, because it's illegal, and we don't, because then we'd lose a way to track the bastards and their money. On the legal side, there's more than one jurisdiction, and for some of the European countries—well, banking is a big moneymaker, and no government ever turns its back on tax revenue. The dog doesn't bite anybody in their backyard. What it does down the block, they don't care about."

"I wonder what Dad thinks of that?"

"Not much, I'll bet," Granger opined.

"Not hardly," Jack agreed. "So, you track the secured accounts to follow the bad guys and their money?"

"That's the idea. It's a lot harder than you might imagine, but when you score, you score big."

"So, I'm going to be a bird dog?"

"That's right. If you're good enough," Granger added.

MOHAMMED WAS almost directly overhead at that moment. The Great Circle Route from Mexico City to London passed close enough to Washington, D.C., for him to look down from thirty-seven thousand feet and see the American capital laid out like a paper map. Now, were he a member of the Department of Martyrdom, he might have climbed the spiral stairs to the upper level and used a gun to kill the flight crew and dive the aircraft...but that had been done before, and now the cockpit doors were protected, and there might well be an armed policeman up there in business class to spoil the show. Worse yet, an armed soldier in civilian clothes. Mohammed had little respect for police officers, but he'd learned the hard way not to disregard Western soldiers. However, he was not a member of the Department of Martyrdom, much as he admired those Holy Warriors. His ability to seek out information made him too valuable to be thrown away in such a noble gesture. That was good, and that was bad, but good or bad, it was a fact, and he lived in the world of facts. He would meet Allah and enter Paradise at the time written by God's Own Hand in God's Own Book. For the moment, he had another six and a half more hours of confinement in this seat.

"More wine, sir?" the pink-faced stewardess asked. What a prize she might be in Paradise...

"Ah, yes, thank you," he replied in his best Cambridge English. It was contrary to Islam, but not to drink would look suspicious, he thought again, and his mission was much too important to risk. Or, at least, so he often told himself, Mohammed admitted to himself, with a minor chink in his conscience. He soon tossed off the drink and then adjusted the seat controls. Wine might be contrary to the laws of Islam, but it did help one sleep.

"MICHELLE SAYS the twins are competent for beginners," Rick Bell told his boss.

"The tracking exercise?" Hendley asked.

"Yeah." He didn't have to say that a proper training exercise would have entailed eight to ten cars, two aircraft, and a total of twenty agents, but The Campus didn't have anything approaching those assets. Instead, it had a wider latitude in dealing with its subjects, a fact which had advantages and disadvantages. "Alexander seems to like them. He says they're bright enough, and they have mental agility."

"Good to know. Anything else happening?"

"Rick Pasternak has something new, he says."

"What might that be?" Gerry asked.

"It's a variant on succinylcholine, a synthetic version of curare, shuts down the skeletal muscles almost immediately. You collapse and can't breathe. He says it would be a miserable death, like taking a bayonet through the chest."

"Traceable?" Hendley asked.

"That is the good news. Esterases in the body break the drug down rapidly into acetylcholine, so it is also likely to be undetectable, unless the target happens to croak right outside a primo medical center with a very sharp pathologist who is looking for something out of the ordinary. The Russians looked at it—would you believe it, back in the 1970s. They were thinking about battlefield applications, but it proved to be impractical. It's surprising KGB didn't make use of it. It'll look like a big-time myocardial infarction, even on a marble slab an hour later."

"How'd he get it?"

"A Russian colleague was visiting with him at Columbia. Turned out he was Jewish and Rick got him talking. He talked enough that Rick developed a delivery system right there in his lab. It's being perfected right now."

"You know, it's amazing that the Mafia never figured it out. If you want somebody killed, you hire a doc."

"Goes against the old school tie for most of them." But most of them didn't have a brother at Cantor Fitzgerald who'd ridden the ninety-seventh floor down to sea level one Tuesday morning.

"Is this variant better than what we have already?"

"Better than what anyone has, Gerry. He says it's almost a hundred percent reliable if used properly."

"Expensive?"

Bell shook his head. "Not hardly."

"It's tested, it really works?"

"Rick says it killed six dogs—all big ones—pretty as you please."

"Okay, approved."

"Roger that, boss. Ought to have them in two weeks."

"What's happening out there?"

"We don't know," Bell admitted with downcast eyes. "One of the guys at Langley is saying in his memos that maybe we hurt them badly enough to slow them down, if not shut them down, but I get nervous when I read stuff like that. Like the 'there's no top to this market' shit that you get before the bottom falls out. *Hubris ante nemesis*. Fort Meade can't track them on the 'Net, but maybe that means they're just getting a little smarter. There's a lot of good encryption programs out on the market, and two of them NSA hasn't cracked yet—at least, not reliably. They're working on that one a couple of hours every day with their big mainframes. As you always say, Gerry, the smartest programmers don't work for Uncle anymore—"

"—they develop video games." Hendley finished the sentence. The government had never paid people well enough to attract the best—and that would never be fixed. "So, just an itchy nose?"

Rick nodded. "Until they're dead, in the ground, with a

wood stake through the heart, I'm going to worry about them."

"Kinda hard to get them all, Rick."

"Sure as hell." Even their personal Dr. Death at Columbia couldn't help with that.

||||||||||||||||||||||||||||||||||||||||||||||||||||||||

CHAPTER 6

ADVERSARIES

THE 747-400 touched down gently at Heathrow five minutes early at 12:55 P.M. Like most of the passengers, Mohammed was all too eager to get out of the Boeing wide-body. He cycled through passport control, smiling politely, availed himself of a washroom, and, feeling somewhat human again, walked to the Air France departure lounge for his connecting flight to Nice. It was ninety minutes to departure time, and then ninety minutes to his destination. In the cab, he demonstrated the sort of French that one might learn in a British university. The cab driver corrected him only twice, and on checking in to the hotel he surrendered his British passport—reluctantly, but the passport was a secure document which he'd used many times. The bar-code strip found on the inside of the cover page of the new passports troubled him. His didn't have that feature, but when it expired in another two years he'd have to worry about some computer tracking him wherever he went. Well, he had three solid and secure British identities, and it was just a matter of getting passports for all three of them, and keeping a very low profile so that no British police constable would check into those identities. No cover could ever stand up to even a casual investigation, much less an in-depth one, and that bar code could someday mean that the immigration officer would get a flashing light on his panel, which would be followed by the appearance of a policeman or two. The infidels were making things hard on the faithful, but that was what infidels did.

The hotel did not have air-conditioning, but the windows could be opened, and the ocean breeze was pleasant. Mohammed hooked up his computer to the phone on the desk. Then the bed beckoned him, and he succumbed to its call. As much as he traveled, he had not found a cure for jet lag. For the next couple of days, he'd live on cigarettes and coffee until his body clock decided that it knew where he was at the moment. He checked his watch. The man meeting him would not be there for another four hours, which, Mohammed thought, was decent of him. He'd be eating dinner when his body would be expecting breakfast. Cigarettes and coffee.

IT WAS breakfast time in Colombia. Pablo and Ernesto both preferred the Anglo-American version, with bacon or ham and eggs, and the excellent local coffee.

"So, do we cooperate with that towel-headed thug?" Ernesto asked.

"I don't see why not," Pablo replied, stirring cream into his cup. "We will make a great deal of money, and the opportunity to create chaos within the house of the *norteamericanos* will serve our interests well. It will set their border guards to looking at people rather than at container boxes, and it will not do any harm to us, either directly or indirectly."

"What if one of these Muslims is taken alive and made to talk?"

"Talk about what? Who will they meet, except some Mexican *coyotes*?" Pablo asked in reply.

"*Sí,* there is that," Ernesto agreed. "You must think me a frightened old woman."

"*Jefe,* the last man who thought that of you is long dead." That earned Pablo a grunt and a crooked smile.

"Yes, that is true, but only a fool is not cautious when the police forces of *two* nations pursue him."

"So, *jefe,* we give them others to pursue, do we not?"

This was potentially a dangerous game he was entering into, Ernesto thought. Yes, he'd be making a deal with allies of convenience, but he was not so much cooperating with them as making use of them, creating straw men for the Americans to seek after and kill. But these fanatics didn't *mind* being killed, did they? They *sought after* death. And so, by making use of them, he was really doing *them* a service, wasn't he? He could even—very carefully—betray them to the *norteamericanos* and not incur their wrath. And besides, how could these men possibly harm him? On his turf? Here in Colombia? Not likely. Not that he planned to betray them, but if he did how would they find out? If their intelligence services were all that good, they would not be needing his assistance in the first place. And if the *Yanqui*—and his *own*—governments had not been able to get to him here in Colombia, how could these people?

"Pablo, how exactly will you communicate with this fellow?"

"Via computer. He has several e-mail addresses, all with European service providers."

"Very well. Tell him, yes, it is approved by the council." Not too many people knew that Ernesto *was* the council.

"*Muy bien, jefe.*" And Pablo went to his laptop. His message went out in less than a minute. Pablo knew his computers. Most international criminals and terrorists did.

IT WAS in the third line of the e-mail: "And, Juan, Maria is pregnant. She's having twins." Both Mohammed and Pablo had the best encryption programs commercially available—programs which, the vendors said, could not be cracked by anyone. But Mohammed believed in that as much as he believed in Santa Claus. All those companies lived in the West, and owed allegiance to their own homelands and to no other. Moreover, using programs like this only highlighted his e-mails for whichever watcher programs were being used by the National Security Agency, British Government Communications Headquarters (GCHQ), and French Director General Security Exterior (DGSE). Not to mention whatever additional unknown agencies might be tapping into international communications, legally or not, none of whom had any love for him and his colleagues. The Israeli Mossad would certainly pay a lot to have his head atop a pike, even though they didn't—couldn't—know of his role in the elimination of David Greengold.

He and Pablo had arranged a code, innocent phrases that could mean anything, which could be couriered around the world to cutouts who would then deliver them. Their electronic accounts were paid by anonymous credit cards, and the accounts themselves were in large and completely reputable Europe-based Internet Service Providers. In its way, the Internet was as effective as Swiss banking laws in terms of anonymity. And too many e-mail messages transited the ether every day for anyone to screen them all, even with computer assistance. As long as he didn't use any easily predicted buzzwords, his messages should be secure, Mohammed judged.

So, the Colombians would cooperate—Maria was pregnant. And she was having twins—the operation could begin at once. He would tell his guest this evening over dinner, and the process would begin immediately. The news was even worth a glass of wine or two, in anticipation of the merciful forgiveness of Allah.

THE PROBLEM with the morning run was that it was more boring than the society page of an Arkansas newspaper—but it had to be done, and each of the brothers used the time to think...mainly about how boring it was. It only took half an hour. Dominic was thinking about getting a small portable radio, but he'd never do it. He never managed to think about such things when he was in a shopping mall. And his brother probably enjoyed this crap. Being in the Marines had to be bad for you.

Then came breakfast.

"So, boys, are we all awake?" said Pete Alexander.

"How come you don't break a sweat in the morning?" Brian asked. The Marines had many inside stories about the Special Forces, none of them complimentary and few of them accurate.

"There are some advantages to getting old," the training officer replied. "One of them is taking it easy on the knees."

"Fine. What's today's lesson plan?" *You lazy bastard,* the captain didn't add. "When are we getting those computers?"

"Pretty soon."

"You said the encryption security is pretty good," Dominic said. "How good is 'pretty good'?"

"NSA can crack it, if they direct their mainframes to it for a week or so and brute-force it. They can crack anything, given the time to apply. Most commercial systems they can already break. They have an arrangement with most of the programmers," he explained. "And they play ball...in return for some NSA algorithms. Other countries could do it, too, but it requires a lot of expertise to understand cryptology fully, and few people have the resources or time to acquire it. So, a commercial program can make it hard, but not too hard if you have the source code. That's why our adversaries try to relay messages in face-to-face meetings, or use codes instead of ciphers, but since that is so time-inefficient they're gradually getting away from it. When they have time-urgent material to transfer, we can often crack it."

"How many messages going across the 'Net?" Dominic asked.

Alexander let out a breath. *"That's* the hard part. There're billions of them, and the programs we have to sweep them aren't good enough yet. Probably never will be. The trick is to ID the address of the target and key in on that. It takes time, but most bad guys are lazy about how they log on to the system—and it's hard to keep track of a bunch of different identities. These guys are not supermen, and they don't have microchips wired into their heads. So, when we get a computer belonging to a bad guy, the first thing we do is print up his address book. That's like striking gold. Even though they can sometimes transmit gibberish, which can cause Fort Meade to spend hours—even days—trying to crack something that isn't supposed to make any sense. The pros used to do that by sending names from the Riga phone book. It's gibberish in every language *but* Latvian. No, the biggest problem is linguists. We don't have enough Arab speakers. It's something they're working on out at Monterey, and at some universities. There are a lot of Arab college students on the payroll right now. Not at The Campus, though. The good news for *us* is that we get the translations from NSA. We don't need much in the way of linguistics."

"So, we're not here to gather intelligence, are we?" Brian asked. Dominic had already figured that one out.

"No. What you can scare up, fine, we'll find a way to make use of it, but our job is to act upon intelligence, not to accumulate it."

"Okay, so we're back to the original question," Dominic observed. "What the hell is the mission?"

"What do you think it is?" Alexander asked.

"I think it's something Mr. Hoover would not have been happy about."

"Correct. He was a nasty son of a bitch, but he was a stickler for civil rights. We at The Campus are not."

"Keep talking," Brian suggested.

"Our job is to act upon intelligence information. To take decisive action."

"Isn't the term for that 'executive action'?"

"Only in the movies," Alexander replied.

"Why us?" Dominic asked.

"Look, the fact of the matter is that CIA is a government organization. A whole lot of chiefs and not enough Indians. How many government agencies encourage people to put their necks on the line?" he asked. "Even if you do it successfully, the lawyers and accountants nibble you to death like ducks. So, if somebody needs to depart this mortal coil, the authorization has to come from up the line, up the chain of command. Gradually—well, not all that gradually—the decisions went to the Big Boss in the West Wing. And not many presidents want that sheet of paper to turn up in their personal archives, where some historian might find it and do an exposé. So, we got away from that sort of thing."

"And there are not many problems that can't be solved by a single .45 bullet at the right time and place," Brian said like a good Marine.

Pete nodded again. "Correct."

"So, we are talking political assassination? That could be dangerous," Dominic observed.

"No, that has too many political ramifications. That sort of thing hasn't happened in centuries, and not very often even then. However, there are people out there who rather urgently need to meet God. And sometimes, it's up to us to arrange the rendezvous."

"Damn." This was Dominic.

"Wait a minute. Who authorizes this?" Major Caruso asked.

"We do."

"Not the President?"

A shake of the head. "No. As I said before, there aren't too many Presidents with the stones to say yes to something like that. They worry too much about the newspapers."

"But what about the law?" Special Agent Caruso asked, predictably.

"The law is, as I've heard one of you once say, so memorably, if you want to kick a tiger in his ass, you'd better have a plan for dealing with his teeth. You guys will be the teeth."

"Just us?" Brian wondered.

"No, not just you, but what others there might or might not be, you do not need to know."

"Shit . . ." Brian sat back in his chair.

"Who set this place—The Campus—up?"

"Somebody important. It's got deniable authorization. The Campus has no ties to the government at all. None," Alexander emphasized.

"So, we'll be shooting people technically on our own?"

"Not much shooting. We have other methods. You will probably not be using firearms much. They're too hard to move around, with airports and all."

"In the field naked?" Dominic asked. "No cover at all?"

"You will have a good cover legend, but no diplomatic protection of any kind. You will live by your wits. No foreign intelligence service will have any way of finding you. The Campus does not exist. It's not on the federal budget, even the black part. So, nobody can trace any money to us. That's how it's done, of course. That's one of the ways we have of tracking people. Your cover will be as international businessmen, bankers and investment stuff. You'll be educated in all the terminology so that you can carry on a conversation on an airplane, for example. Such people don't talk much about what they're up to, to keep their business secrets close. So, if you're not overly talkative, it will not be seen as unusual."

"Secret Agent Man . . ." Brian said quietly.

"We pick people who can think on their feet, who are self-starters, and who don't faint at the sight of blood. Both of you have killed people out in the real world. In both of your cases, you were faced with the unexpected, and both of you handled the situation efficiently. Neither of you had any regrets. That will be your job."

"What about protection for us?" The FBI agent again.

"There's a get-out-of-jail-free card for both of you."

"My ass," Dominic said again. "There isn't any such thing."

"A signed presidential pardon," Alexander clarified.

Fuck... Brian thought for a second. "It was Uncle Jack, wasn't it?"

"I can't answer that, but if you wish you can see your pardons before you go into the field." Alexander set down his coffee cup. "Okay, gentlemen. You'll have a few days to think this one over, but you'll have to make your decisions. This is not a small thing I'm asking of you. It's not going to be a fun job, nor will it be easy or pleasant, but it will be a job which will serve the interests of your country. It's a dangerous world out there. Some people need to be dealt with directly."

"And if we whack the wrong guy?"

"Dominic, there is that possibility, but, no matter who it is, I can promise you that you will not be asked to kill Mother Teresa's little brother. We're pretty careful about who we target. You'll know who it is, plus how and why we need to deal with him or her before we send you out."

"Kill women?" Brian asked. That was not part of the Marine ethos.

"It's never happened, as far as I know, but it's a theoretical possibility. So, if that's enough for breakfast, you guys need to think it over."

"Jesus," Brian said after Alexander left the room. "What's lunch going to be like?"

"Surprised?"

"Not completely, Enzo, but the way he just said it like that..."

"Hey, bro, how many times have you wondered why we couldn't simply take care of business ourselves?"

"You're the cop, Enzo. *You're* the guy who's supposed to say *Oh, shit,* remember?"

"Yeah, but that shoot of mine in Alabama—well, I kinda

stepped a little over the line some, y'know? All the way driving to D.C., I thought over how I'd explain it to Gus Werner. But he didn't blink even a little."

"So, what do you think?"

"Aldo, I'm willing to listen some more. There's a saying in Texas that there's more men need killin' than horses need stealin'."

The reversal of roles struck Brian as more than a little surprising. After all, he was the gung ho Marine. Enzo was the guy who was trained to give people their constitutional rights before he slapped the cuffs on.

That they were both able to take a life without having bad dreams later was obvious to the brothers, but this went a little farther than that. This was premeditated murder. Brian usually went into the field with an exquisitely trained sniper under his command, and he knew what they did wasn't far removed from murder, either. But being in uniform made it different. It put some sort of blessing on it. The target was an enemy, and on the battlefield it was everyone's job to look after his own life, and if he failed to do it, well, that was his failing, not that of the man who killed him. But this would be more than that. They'd be hunting individual people down with the deliberate intent of killing them, and that wasn't what he'd been brought up and trained to do. He'd be dressed in civilian clothes—and killing people under those circumstances made him a *spy,* not an officer of the United States Marine Corps. There was honor in the latter, but damned little in the former, or so he'd been trained to think. The world no longer had a Field of Honor, and real life wasn't a duel in which men had identical weapons and an open field on which to make use of them. No, he'd been trained to plan his operations in a way that gave his enemy no chance at all, because he had men under his command whose lives he was sworn to preserve. Combat had rules. Harsh rules, to be sure, but rules even so. Now he was being asked to set those rules aside and become—what? A paid assassin? The teeth of some notional wild beast? The masked avenger from some old movie on Nick at Nite? This didn't fit into his tidy picture of the real world.

When he'd been sent to Afghanistan, he hadn't—hadn't what? He hadn't disguised himself as a fishmonger on a city street. There'd been no city street in those goddamned mountains. It had been more like a big-game hunt, one in which the game had weapons of its own. And there was honor in such a hunt, and for his efforts he'd gotten the approval of his country: a combat decoration for bravery that he might or might not display.

All in all, it was a lot to consider over his second cup of morning coffee.

"Jesus, Enzo," he breathed.

"Brian, you know what the dream of every cop is?" Dominic asked.

"To break the law and get away with it?"

Dominic shook his head. "I had this talk with Gus Werner. No, not to break the law, but just once to *be* the law. To be God's Own Avenging Sword, was the way he put it—to strike down the guilty without lawyers and other bullshit to get in the way, to see justice done all by yourself. It doesn't happen very often, they say, but, you know, I got to do it down in Alabama, and it felt pretty good. You just have to be sure you're bagging the right mutt."

"How can you be sure?" Aldo asked.

"If you're not, you back off the mission. They can't hang you for *not* committing murder, bro."

"So, it is murder?"

"Not if the mutt has it coming, it isn't." It was an aesthetic point, but an important one to someone who had already committed murder under the shelter of the law, and had had no bad dreams about it.

"IMMEDIATELY?"

"Yes. How many men do we have already?" Mohammed asked.

"Sixteen."

"Ah." Mohammed took a sip of a fine French white from the Loire Valley. His guest was drinking Perrier and lemon. "Their language skills?"

"Sufficient, we think."

"Excellent. Tell them to make preparations to travel. We'll fly them in to Mexico. There they will meet with our new friends, and travel to America. And once there, they can do their work."

"*Insh'Allah,*" he observed. God willing.

"Yes, God willing," Mohammed said in English, reminding his guest of what language he should be using.

They were in a sidewalk restaurant overlooking the river, off to one side, with no one nearby. Both men spoke normally, two well-dressed men over a friendly dinner, not huddled or conspiratorial in their demeanor. This took some amount of concentration, since some degree of conspiratorial posture came naturally to what they were doing. But neither of them was a stranger to such meetings.

"So, how was it to kill the Jew in Rome?"

"It was very satisfactory, Ibrahim, to feel his body go slack as I cut his spine, and then the surprised look on his face."

Ibrahim smiled broadly. It wasn't every day they got to kill a Mossad officer, much less a Station Chief. The Israelis would always be their most hated enemies, if not the most dangerous. "God was good to us that day."

The Greengold mission had been a recreational exercise for Mohammed. It hadn't even been strictly necessary. Setting up the meet and feeding the Israeli juicy information had been...fun. Not terribly difficult, even. Though it would not soon be repeated. No, Mossad would not let any of its officers do anything without overwatch for some time. They were not fools, and they *did* learn from their mistakes. But killing a tiger had satisfactions all its own. A pity he had no pelt. But where would he hang it? He had no fixed home anymore, only a collection of safe houses that might or might not be totally safe. But you couldn't worry about everything. You'd never get anything done. Mohammed and his colleagues didn't fear death, only failure. And they had no plans to fail.

"I need the meeting arrangements and so forth. I can take care of travel. Arms will be provided by our new friends?"

A nod. "Correct."

"And how will our warriors enter America?"

"That is for our friends to handle. But you will send in a group of three at first, to make sure the arrangements are satisfactorily secure."

"Of course." They knew all about operational security. There had been many lessons, none of them gentle. Members of his organization peopled many prisons around the world, those who were unlucky enough to have avoided death. That was a problem, one which his organization had never been able to fix. To die in action, that was noble and courageous. To be caught by a policeman like a common criminal was ignoble and humiliating, but somehow his men found it preferable to die without accomplishing a mission. And Western prisons were not all that terrible for many of his colleagues. Confining, perhaps, but at least the food was regular, and Western nations did not violate their dietary rules.

These nations were so weak and foolish regarding their enemies, they showed mercy to those who gave them none in return. But that was not Mohammed's fault.

"DAMN," Jack said. It was his first day on the "black" side of the house. His training in high finance had gone very rapidly, due to his upbringing. His grandfather Muller had taught him well during his infrequent visits to the family home. He and Jack's father were civil to each other, but Grandpa Joe thought real men worked in the trading business rather than in the dirty world of politics—though he had to admit, of course, that his son-in-law had worked out fairly well in Washington. But the money he could have made on Wall Street... why would any man turn away from that? Muller had never said that to Little Jack, of course, but his opinion was clear enough. In any case, Jack could have gotten an entry-level job in any of the large houses, and probably worked up the line pretty fast from there. But what mattered to him now was that he had skipped through the financial side of The Campus and was now in the Operations Department—it wasn't actually named that, but that's what it was called by its members. "They're that good?"

"What's that, Jack?"

"NSA intercept." He handed the sheet across. Tony Wills read it.

The intercept had identified a known associate of terrorists—exactly what function he performed was not known yet, but he'd been positively identified from voiceprint analysis.

"It's the digital phones. They generate a very clean signal, easy for the voiceprint computer to ID the voices. I see they haven't ID'd the other guy." Wills handed the sheet back.

The nature of the conversation was innocuous, so much so that one might wonder why the call had been placed. But some people just liked to chat on the phone. And, maybe, they were talking in code, discussing biological warfare, or a campaign to set bombs in Jerusalem. Perhaps. More likely, they were just passing the time. There was a lot of that in Saudi Arabia. What impressed Jack was that the call had been picked up and read in real time.

"Well, you know how digital phones work, right? They're always broadcasting the HERE I AM signal to the local cell, and every phone has its unique addressing code. Once we identify that code, it's just a matter of listening in when the phone rings, or the phone holder makes a call. Similarly, we can ID the number and phone of the inbound caller. The hard part is to get the identity in the first place. Now they have another phone ident for the computer to monitor."

"How many phones do they keep track of?" Jack asked.

"Just over a hundred thousand, and that's just in Southwest Asia. Nearly all of them are dry holes, except for the one in ten thousand that counts—and sometimes they can show real results," Wills told him.

"So, to bag a cold call, a computer listens in and keys on 'hot' words?"

"Hot words and hot names. Unfortunately, so many people are named Mohammed over there—it's the most popular given name in the world. A lot of them go by patronymics or nicknames. Another problem is that there's a big market in cloned phones—they clone them in Europe, mainly London, where most of the phones have the international software. Or a guy can get six or seven phones and use them once each before tossing them. They're not dumb. They *can* get overconfident, though. Some of them end up telling us a lot of things, and occasionally it's useful. It all goes in the big NSA/CIA book, to which we have access on our terminals."

"Okay, who's this guy?"

"His name is Uda bin Sali. Rich family, close friends of the king. The big daddy's a very senior Saudi banker. He has eleven sons and nine daughters. Four wives, a man of commendable vigor. Not a bad guy, supposedly, but he's a little too doting with his kids. Gives them money instead of attention, like a Hollywood big shot. Uda here discovered Allah in a big way back in his late teens, and he's on the extreme right of the Wahabi branch of Sunni Islam. Doesn't like us very much. This boy we keep track of. He might be a gateway into their banking arrangements. His CIA file has a picture. He's about twenty-seven, five-eight, slender build, neatly trimmed beard. Flies to London a lot. Likes the ladies he can purchase by the hour. Not married yet. That's unusual, but if he's gay he conceals it well. The Brits have gotten girls into his bed. They report that he's vigorous, about what you'd expect for his age, and fairly inventive."

"Hell of a thing for a trained intelligence officer to do," Jack observed.

"Lots of services enlist the help of hookers," Wills explained. "They don't mind talking, and for the right wad of cash they'll do just about anything. Uda here likes chicken-in-a-basket. Never tried that myself. Asian specialty. Know how to call up his dossier?"

"Nobody taught me," Jack replied.

"Okay." Wills frog-walked his swivel chair over and demonstrated. "This is the general index. Your access password is SOUTHWEST 91."

Junior duly typed in the password, and the dossier came up as an Acrobat graphics file.

The first photo was probably from his passport, followed by six more, in a more informal format. Jack Jr. managed not to blush. He'd seen his share of *Playboys* while growing up, even in Catholic schools. Will continued the day's lesson.

"You can learn a lot from how a guy does it with women. Langley has a shrink who analyzes that in great detail. It's probably one of the annexes on this file. At Langley, it's called 'Nuts and Sluts' information. The doc is named Stefan Pizniak. Harvard Medical School professor. As I recall, he says this kid is normal in his drives, given his age, liquidity, and his social background. As you'll see, he hangs out a lot with merchant bankers in London, like a new kid learning the business. The word is that he's smart, affable, and handsome. Careful and conservative in his money work. He does not drink. So, he is somewhat religious. Doesn't flaunt it or lecture others about it, but lives in accordance with the major rules of his religion."

"What makes him a bad guy?" Jack asked.

"He talks a lot to people we know about. There's no

word on who he hangs with in Saudi. We've never put any coverage on him in his own backyard. Even the Brits haven't, and they have a lot more assets in place. CIA doesn't have much, and his profile isn't high enough to merit a closer look, or so they think. It's a shame. His daddy's supposed to be a good guy. It'll break his heart to find out his son's hanging with the wrong crowd at home." With that wisdom imparted, Wills went back to his own workstation.

Junior examined the face on his computer screen. His mom was pretty good at reading people from a single look, but it was a skill she hadn't passed along to him. Jack had trouble enough figuring women out—along with most of the men in the world, he comforted himself. He continued to stare at the face, trying to read the mind of someone six thousand miles away, who spoke a different language and adhered to a different religion. What thoughts circulated behind those eyes? His father, he knew, liked the Saudis. He was especially close to Prince Ali bin Sultan, a prince and senior official in the Saudi government. Young Jack had met him, but only in passing. A beard and a sense of humor were the only two things he remembered. It was one of Jack Sr.'s core beliefs that all men were fundamentally the same, and he'd passed that opinion along to his son. But that also meant that, just as there were bad people in America, so there were also bad people elsewhere in the world, and his country had recently had some hard lessons from that sad fact. Unfortunately, the sitting President hadn't quite figured out what to do about it yet.

Junior read on through the dossier. So, this was how it began here at The Campus. He was working a case—well, kinda working some sort of case, he corrected himself. Uda bin Sali was working at being an international banker. Sure enough, he moved money around. His father's money? Jack wondered. If so, his daddy was one very wealthy son of a bitch. He played with all the big London banks—London was still the world's banking capital. Jack would never have guessed that the National Security Agency had the sort of ability to crack this kind of thing.

A hundred million here, a hundred million there, pretty soon you were talking about real money. Sali was in the capital-preservation business, which meant not so much growing the money entrusted to him as making sure the lockbox had a really good lock. There were seventy-one subsidiary accounts, sixty-three of which were identified by bank, number, and password, so it seemed. Girls? Politics? Sports? Money management? Cars? The oil business? What did rich Saudi princelings talk about? That was a big blank spot in the files. Why didn't the Brits listen in? The interviews with his hookers hadn't revealed very much, except that he was a good tipper for those girls who'd shown him an especially good time in his house in Berkeley Square . . . an upscale part of town, Jack noted. He mainly got around by taxi. Owned a car—a black Aston Martin convertible, no less—but didn't drive it much, the British information revealed. Did *not* have a chauffeur. Went to the embassy a lot. All in all, it was a lot of information that revealed not very much. He remarked on this to Tony Wills.

"Yeah, I know, but if he turns up hinky, you can be sure there're two or three things in there that ought to have jumped off the page at you. That's the problem with this damned business. And, remember, we're seeing the processed 'take.' Some poor schlub had to take really raw data and distill it down to this. Exactly what significant facts got lost along the way? No way to tell, my boy. No way to tell."

This is what my dad used to do, Junior reminded himself. *Trying to find diamonds in a bucket full of shit.* He'd expected it to be easier, somehow. All right, so what he had to do was find money moves that were not easily explained. It was the worst sort of scut work, and he couldn't even go to his father for advice. His dad would probably have flipped out to learn that he was working here. Mom would not be overly pleased, either.

Why did that matter? Wasn't he a man now, able to do what he wanted to do with his life? Not exactly. Parents had power over you that never went away. He'd always be trying to please them, to show them that they'd raised him the right way, and that he was doing the right thing. Or something like that. His father had been lucky. They'd never learned about all the things he'd had to do. Would they have liked it?

No. They would have been upset—furious—with all the chances he'd taken with his life. And that was just the stuff his son knew about. There were a lot of blank spots in his memory, times his father hadn't been home, and Mom hadn't explained why... and so, now, here he was, if not doing the same thing, then sure as hell heading in that direction... Well, his father had always said that the world was a crazy place, and so here he was, figuring out just how crazy it might really be.

||||||||||||||||||||||||||||||||||||||||||||||||||||||||||||||||||||||

CHAPTER 7

TRANSIT

IT STARTED in Lebanon, with a flight to Cyprus. From there, a KLM flight to Schipol Airport in the Netherlands, and from there to Paris. In France the sixteen men overnighted in eight separate hotels, taking the time to walk the streets and exercise their English—there had been little point in having them learn French, after all—and struggle with a local population that could have been more helpful. The good news, as they saw it, was that certain female French citizens went out of their way to speak decent English, and were very helpful indeed. For a fee.

They were ordinary in most details, all in their late twenties, clean-shaven, average in size and looks, but better dressed than was the average. They all concealed their unease well, albeit with lingering but furtive glances at the cops they saw—they all knew not to attract the attention of anyone in a police officer's uniform. The French police had a reputation for thoroughness which did not appeal to the new visitors. They were traveling on Qatari passports at the moment, which were fairly secure, but a passport issued from the French Foreign Minister himself would not stand up to a directed inquiry. And so they kept a low profile. They had all been briefed not to look around much, to be polite, and to make the effort to smile at everyone they encountered. Fortunately for them, it was tourist season in France, and Paris was jammed with people like them, many of whom also spoke little French, much to the bemused contempt of the Parisians, who in every case took their money anyway.

THE NEXT day's breakfast hadn't concluded with any new explosive revelations, and neither had lunch. Both Caruso brothers listened to their lessons from Pete Alexander, doing their best not to doze off, because these lessons seemed pretty straightforward.

"Boring, you think?" Pete asked over lunch.

"Well, none of it's earthshaking," Brian responded after a few seconds.

"You'll find it's a little different in a foreign city, out on the street in a market, say, looking for your subject in a crowd of a few thousand. The important part is to be invisible. We'll work on that this afternoon. You had any experience in that, Dominic?"

"Not really. Just the basic stuff. Don't look too directly at the subject. Reversible clothes. Different ties, if you're in an environment that calls for a necktie. And you depend on others to switch off on coverage. But we won't have the same backup we have in the Bureau for a discreet surveillance, will we?"

"Not even close. So, you keep your distance until it's time to move in. At that point, you move in as quickly as circumstances allow—"

"And whack the guy?" Brian asked.

"Still uneasy about it?"

"I haven't walked out yet, Pete. Let's say I have my concerns, and leave it at that."

Alexander nodded. "Fair enough. We prefer people who know how to think, and we know that thinking carries its own penalties."

"I guess that's how you have to look at it. What if the guy we're supposed to do away with turns out to be okay?" the Marine asked.

"Then you back off and report in. It's theoretically possible that an assignment can be erroneous, but to the best of my knowledge it's never happened."

"Never?"

"Not ever, not once," Alexander assured him.

"Perfect records make me nervous."

"We try to be careful."

"What are the rules? Okay, maybe I don't need to know—right now—who sends us out to kill somebody, but it would be nice to know what the criteria are to write up some fucker's death warrant, y'know?"

"It will be someone who has, directly or indirectly, caused the death of American citizens, or is directly involved in plans to do so in the future. We're not after people who sing too loud in church or who have books overdue at the library."

"You're talking about terrorists, right?"

"Yup," Pete replied simply.

"Why not just arrest them?" Brian asked next.

"Like you did in Afghanistan?"

"That was different," the Marine protested.

"How?" Pete asked.

"Well, for one thing we were uniformed combatants operating in the field under orders from legally constituted command authority."

"You took some initiative, right?"

"Officers are supposed to use their heads. My overall mission orders came from up the chain of command, however."

"And you don't question them?"

"No. Unless they're crazy, you're not supposed to do that."

"What about when *not* doing something is crazy?" Pete asked. "What if you have a chance to take action against people who are planning to do something very destructive?"

"That's what CIA and FBI are for."

"But when they can't get the job done, for one reason or another, then what? Do you just let the bad guys move ahead with their plans and handle them afterward? That can be expensive," Alexander told him. "Our job is to do the things that are necessary when the conventional methods are unable to accomplish the mission."

"How often?" This was Dominic, seeking to protect his brother.

"It's picking up."

"How many hits have you made?" Brian again.

"You don't need to know."

"Oh, I do love hearing that one," Dominic observed with a smile.

"Patience, boys. You're not in the club yet," Pete told them, hoping they were smart enough not to object at this point.

"Okay, Pete," Brian said, after a moment's thought. "We both gave our word that what we learn here stays here. Fine. It's just that murdering people in cold blood isn't exactly what I've been trained to do, y'know?"

"You're not supposed to feel good about it. Over in Afghanistan, did you ever shoot anybody looking the other way?"

"Two of them," Brian admitted. "Hey, the battlefield isn't the Olympic Games," he semiprotested.

"Neither is the rest of the world, Aldo." The look on the Marine's face said, *Well, you got me there.* "It's an imperfect world, guys. If you want to try to make it perfect, go ahead, but it's been tried before. Me, I'd settle for something safer and more predictable. Imagine if somebody had taken care of Hitler back in 1934 or so, or Lenin in 1915 in Switzerland. The world would have been better, right? Or maybe bad in a different way. But we're not in that business. We will not be involved in political assassinations. We're after the little sharks who kill innocent people in such a way that conventional procedures cannot handle them. It's not the best system. I know that. We all know that. But it's something, and we're going to try to see if it works. It can't be much worse than what we have already, can it?"

Dominic's eyes never left Pete's face during that discourse. He'd just told them something that maybe he hadn't meant to tell them. The Campus didn't have any killers yet. They were going to be the first. There had to be a lot of hopes riding on them. That was a lot of responsibility. But it all made sense. It was plain that Alexander was not teaching them from his own real-world experience. A training officer was supposed to be somebody who'd actually gone out and done it. That was why most of the instructors at the FBI Academy were experienced field agents. They could tell you how it felt. Pete could only tell them what had to be done. But why, then, had they picked him and Aldo?

"I see your point, Pete," Dominic said. "I'm not leaving yet."

"Neither am I," Brian told his training officer. "I just want to know what the rules are."

Pete didn't tell them they'd be making the rules up as they went along. They'd figure that one out soon enough.

AIRPORTS ARE the same all over the world. Instructed to be polite, they all checked their bags, waited in the correct lounges, smoked their cigarettes in the designated smoking areas, and read the books they'd purchased in the airport kiosks. Or pretended to. Not all of them had the language skills they would have wished. Once at cruising altitude, they ate their airline meals, and most of them took their airline naps. Nearly all of them were seated in the aft rows of their seating sections, and when they stirred, they wondered which of their seatmates they might meet again in a few days or weeks, however long it took to work out the details. Each of them hoped to meet Allah soon, and to garner the rewards that would come for fighting in their Holy Cause. It occurred to the more intellectual of them that even Mohammed, blessings and peace be upon him, was limited in his ability to communicate the nature of Paradise. He'd had to explain it to people with no knowledge of passenger jet aircraft, automobiles, and computers. What, then, was its true nature? It had to be so thoroughly wonderful as to defy description, but even so, a mystery yet to be discovered. And they would discover it. There was a degree of excitement in that thought, a sort of anticipation too sublime to discuss with one's colleagues. A mystery, but an infinitely desirable one. And if others had to meet Allah, too, as a result, well, that also was written in the Great Book of Destiny. For the moment, they all took their naps, sleeping the sleep of the just, the sleep of the Holy Martyrs yet to be. Milk, honey, and virgins.

SALI, JACK found, had some mystery about him. The CIA file on the guy even had the length of his penis appended in the "Nuts and Sluts" section. The British whores said he was grossly average in size but uncommonly vigorous in application—and a fine tipper, which appealed to their commercial sensibilities. But unlike most men, he didn't talk about himself much. Talked mainly about the rain and chill of London, and complimentary things about his companion of the moment, which appealed to her vanity. His occasional gift of a nice handbag—Louis Vuitton in most cases—sat well with his "regulars," two of whom reported to Thames House, the new home of both the British Secret Service and the Security Service. Jack wondered if they were getting paid by both Sali and H.M. Government for services rendered. Probably a good deal for the girls involved, he was sure, though Thames House probably wouldn't spring for shoes and a bag.

"Tony?"

"Yeah, Jack?" Wills looked up from his workstation.

"How do we know if this Sali is a bad guy?"

"We don't for sure. Not until he actually does something, or we intercept a conversation between him and somebody we don't like."

"So, I'm just checking this bird out."

"Correct. You'll be doing a lot of that. Any feel for the guy yet?"

"He's a horny son of a bitch."

"It's hard to be rich and single, in case you haven't noticed, Junior."

Jack blinked. Maybe he had that coming. "Okay, but I'll be damned if I pay for it, and he's paying a lot."

"What else?" Wills asked.

"He doesn't talk a hell of a lot."

"What's that tell you?"

Ryan sat back in his swivel chair to think it over. *He* didn't talk to his girlfriends much, either, at least not about his new job. As soon as you said "financial management," most women tended to doze off in self-defense. Did *that* mean anything? Maybe Sali just wasn't a talker. Maybe he was sufficiently secure that he didn't feel the need to impress his lady friends with anything but his cash—he always used cash, not credit cards. And why that? To keep his family from knowing? Well, Jack didn't talk to Mom and Dad about his love life, either. In fact, he rarely took a girlfriend to the family home. His mom tended to scare girls away. Not his dad, strangely enough. The M.D. Dr. Ryan struck other women as powerful, and while most young women found it admirable, many also found it intimidating as hell. His father dialed all the power stuff way back and came off as a slender and distinguished gray-haired teddy bear to family guests. More than anything else, his dad liked to play catch with his son on the grass overlooking the Chesapeake Bay, maybe harkening back to a simpler time. He had Kyle for that. The littlest Ryan was still in grammar school, at the stage where he asked furtive questions about Santa Claus, but only when Mom and Dad weren't around. There was probably a kid in class who wanted to let everybody know what he knew—there was always one of those—and Katie had wised up by now. She still liked to play Barbies, but she knew that her mom and dad bought them at the Toys R Us in Glen Burnie, and assembled the accoutrements on Christmas Eve, a process his father truly loved, much as he might bitch about it. When you stopped believing in Santa Claus, the whole damn world just started a downhill slide . . .

"It tells us he's not a talker. Not much else," Jack said after a moment's reflection. "We're not supposed to convert inference into facts, are we?"

"Correct. A lot of people think otherwise, but not here. Assumption is the mother of all fuckups. That shrink at Langley specializes in spinning. He's good, but you need to learn to distinguish between speculation and facts. So, tell me about Mr. Sali," Wills commanded.

"He's horny, and he doesn't talk much. He plays very conservatively with the family's money."

"Anything that makes him look like a bad guy?"

"No, but he's worth watching because of his religious— well, extremism's the wrong word. There are some things missing here. He's not boisterous, not showy the way rich people his age usually are. Who started the file on him?" Jack asked.

"The Brits did. Something about this guy tweaked the interest of one of their senior analysts. Then Langley took a brief look and started a file of their own. Then he was intercepted talking to a guy who's also got a file at Langley—the conversation wasn't about anything important, but there it was," Wills explained. "And you know, it's a lot easier to open a file than it is to close one. His cell phone is coded in to the NSA computers, and so they report on him whenever he turns it on. I've been through the file, too. He's worth keeping an eye on, I think—but I'm not sure why. You learn to trust your instincts in this business, Jack. So, I'm nominating you to be the in-house expert on this kid."

"And I'm looking for how he handles his money . . . ?"

"That's right. You know, it doesn't take much to finance a bunch of terrorists—at least not much by his reckoning. A million bucks a year is a lot of money to those people. They live hand-to-mouth, and their maintenance expenses aren't that high. So, you're supposed to look at the margins. Chances are he'll try to hide whatever he does in the shadows of his big transactions."

"I'm not an accountant," Jack pointed out. His father had gotten his CPA a long time ago, but never used it, even to do his own taxes. He had a law firm for that.

"Can you do arithmetic?"

"Well, yeah."

"So, attach a nose to it."

Oh, great, John Patrick Ryan, Jr., thought. Then he reminded himself that actual intelligence operations weren't about shoot-the-bad-guy-and-bang-Ursula-Undress while the credits rolled. That was only in the movies. This was the real world.

"OUR FRIEND is in that much of a hurry?" Ernesto asked in considerable surprise.

"So it would seem. The *norteamericanos* have been hard on them of late. I imagine they want to remind their enemies that they still have fangs. A thing of honor for them, perhaps," Pablo speculated. His friend would understand that readily enough.

"So, what do we do now?"

"When they are settled in Mexico City, we arrange for transport into America, and, I presume, we arrange for weapons."

"Complications?"

"If the *norteamericanos* have our organizations penetrated, they might have some prewarning, plus whispers of our involvement. But we have considered this already."

They'd considered it briefly, yes, Ernesto reflected, but that had been at a convenient distance. Now the knocker on the door was rattling, and it was time for further reflection. But he couldn't renege on this deal. That, too, was a matter both of honor and of business. They were preparing an initial shipment of cocaine to the E.U. That promised to be a really sizable market.

"How many people are coming?"

"Fourteen, he says. They have no weapons at all."

"What will they need, do you suppose?"

"Light automatics should do it, plus pistols, of course," Pablo said. "We have a supplier in Mexico who can handle it for less than ten thousand dollars. For an additional ten, we can have the weapons delivered to the end users in America, to avoid complications during the crossing."

"*Bueno*, make it so. Will you fly to Mexico yourself?"

Pablo nodded. "Tomorrow morning. I will coordinate with them and the *coyotes* this first time."

"You will be careful," Ernesto pointed out. His suggestions had the force of an explosive device. Pablo took some chances, but his services were very important to the Cartel. He would be hard to replace.

"Of course, *jefe*. I need to evaluate how reliable these people are if they are to assist us in Europe."

"Yes, that is so," Ernesto agreed warily. As with most deals, when it came time to take action, there were second thoughts. But he was not an old woman. He had never been afraid to act decisively.

THE AIRBUS pulled up to its gate, the first-class passengers were allowed to deplane first, and they followed the colored arrows on the floor to immigration and customs, where they assured the uniformed bureaucrats that they had nothing to declare, and their passports were duly stamped, and they walked off to collect their luggage.

The leader of the group was named Mustafa. A Saudi by birth, he was clean-shaven, which he didn't like, though it exposed skin that the women seemed to like. He and a colleague named Abdullah walked together to get their bags, and then out to where their rides were supposed to be waiting. This would be the first test of their newfound friends in the Western Hemisphere. Sure enough, someone was holding a cardboard square with "MIGUEL" printed on it. That was Mustafa's code name for this mission, and he walked over to shake the man's hand. The greeter said nothing, but motioned them to follow him. Outside, a brown Plymouth minivan waited. The bags went in back, and the passengers slid into the middle seat. It was warm in Mexico City, and the air was fouler than anything they'd ever experienced. What ought to have been a sunny day was ruined by a gray blanket over the city—air pollution, Mustafa thought.

The driver continued to say nothing as he drove them to their hotel. This actually impressed them. If there was nothing to say, then one should keep quiet.

The hotel was a good one, as expected. Mustafa checked in using the false Visa card that had been faxed ahead, and in five minutes he and his friend were in their spacious room on the fifth floor. They looked around for obvious bugs before speaking.

"I didn't think that damned flight would ever end," Abdullah groused, looking in the minibar for bottled water. They'd been briefed to be careful drinking the stuff that came out of the tap.

"Yes, I agree. How did you sleep?"

"Not well. I thought the one good thing about alcohol was that it made you unconscious."

"For some. Not for all," Mustafa told his friend. "There are other drugs for that."

"Those are hateful to God," Abdullah observed. "Unless a physician administers them."

"We have friends now who do not think that way."

"Infidels," Abdullah almost spat.

"The enemy of your enemy is your friend."

Abdullah twisted the top off an Evian bottle. "No. You can trust a true friend. Can we trust these men?"

"Only as far as we must," Mustafa allowed. Mohammed had been careful in his mission brief. These new allies would help them only as a matter of convenience, because they also wished harm to the Great Satan. That was good enough for now. Someday these allies would become enemies, and they'd have to deal with them. But that day had not yet come. He stifled a yawn. Time to get some rest. Tomorrow would be a busy day.

JACK LIVED in a condo in Baltimore, a few blocks from Orioles Park at Camden Yards, where he had season tickets, but which was dark tonight because the Orioles were in Toronto. Not a good cook, he ate out as he usually did, alone this time because he didn't have a date, which was not as unusual as he might have wished. Finished, he walked back to his condo, switched on his TV, and then thought better of it, went to his computer instead, and logged on to check his e-mail and surf the 'Net. That's when he made a note to himself. Sali lived alone as well, and while he often had whores for company, it wasn't every night. What did he do on the other nights? Log on to his computer? A lot of people did. Did the Brits have a tap on his phone lines? They must. But the file on Sali didn't include any e-mails . . . why? Something worth checking out.

"WHAT YOU thinking, Aldo?" Dominic asked his brother. ESPN had a baseball game on; the Mariners were playing the Yankees, to the current detriment of the former.

"I'm not sure I like the idea of shooting some poor bastard down on the street, bro."

"What if you know he's a bad guy?"

"And what if I whack the wrong guy just because he drives the same kind of car and has the same mustache? What if he leaves a wife and kids behind? Then I'm a fucking murderer—a contract killer, at that. That's not the sort of thing they taught us at the Basic School, y'know?"

"But if you *know* he's a bad guy, then what?" the FBI agent asked.

"Hey, Enzo, that's not what they trained you to do, either."

"I know that, but this here's a different situation. If I know the mutt's a terrorist, and I know we can't arrest him, and I know he's got more plans, then I think I can handle it."

"Out in the hills, in Afghanistan, you know, our intel wasn't always gold-plated, man. Sure, I learned to put my own ass on the line, but not some poor other schlub's."

"The people you were after over there, who'd they kill?"

"Hey, they were part of an organization that made war on the United States of America. They probably weren't Boy Scouts. But I never saw any direct evidence of it."

"What if you had?" Dominic asked.

"But I didn't."

"You're lucky," Enzo responded, remembering a little girl whose throat had been slashed ear to ear. There was a legal adage that hard cases made for bad law, but the books could not anticipate all the things that people did. Black ink on white paper was a little too dry for the real world sometimes. But he'd always been the passionate one of the two. Brian had always been a touch cooler, like Fonzie on *Happy Days*. Twins, yes, but fraternal ones. Dominic was more like his father, Italian and passionate. Brian had turned out more like Mom, chillier from a more northerly climate. To an outsider, the differences might have appeared less than trivial, but to the twins themselves it was frequently the subject of jabs and jokes. "When you see it,

Brian, when it's right there in front of you, it sets you off, man. It lights a fire in the gut."

"Hey, been there, done that, got the T-shirt, okay? I whacked five men all by myself. But it was business, not personal. They tried to ambush us, but they didn't read the manual right, and I used fire and maneuver to fake 'em out and roll 'em up, just like they taught me to do. It's not my fault they were inept. They could have surrendered, but they preferred to shoot it out. That was a bad call on their part, but 'a man should do what he thinks is best.'" His all-time favorite movie was John Wayne's *Hondo*.

"Hey, Aldo, I'm not saying you're a wuss."

"I know what you're saying, but, look, I don't want to turn into one of them, okay?"

"That's not the mission here, bro. I got my doubts, too, but I'm going to stay around and see how it plays out. We can always kiss it off whenever we want."

"I suppose."

Then Derek Jeter doubled up the middle. Pitchers probably thought of *him* as a terrorist, didn't they?

ON THE other side of the building, Pete Alexander was on a secure phone to Columbia, Maryland.

"So, how are they doing?" he heard Sam Granger ask.

Pete sipped at his glass of sherry. "They're good kids. They both have doubts. The Marine talks openly about it, and the FBI guy keeps his mouth shut about it, but the wheels are turning over slowly."

"How serious is it?"

"Hard to say. Hey, Sam, we always knew that training would be the hard part. Few Americans want to grow up to be professional killers—at least not the ones we need for this."

"There was a guy at the Agency who would have fit right in—"

"But he's too damned old, and you know it," Alexander

countered at once. "Besides, he has his sunset job over across the pond in Wales, and he seems to be comfortable in it."

"If only..."

"If only your aunt had balls, she'd be your uncle," Pete pointed out. "Selecting candidates is your job. Getting them trained up is mine. These two have the brains and they have the skills. The hard part is temperament. I'm working on that. Be patient."

"In the movies, it's a lot easier."

"In the movies, everybody is borderline psychopath. Is that who we want on the payroll?"

"I guess not." There were plenty of psychopaths to be found. Every large police department knew of several. And they'd kill people for modest monetary considerations, or a small quantity of drugs. The problem with such people was that they didn't take orders well, and they were not very smart. Except in the movies. Where was that little Nikita girl when you really needed her?

"So, we have to deal with good, reliable people who have brains. Such people think, and they do not always think predictably, do they? A guy with a conscience is nice to have, but every so often he's going to wonder if he's doing the right thing. Why did you have to send two Catholics? Jews are bad enough. They're born with guilt— but Catholics learn it all in school."

"Thank you, Your Holiness," Granger responded, dead-pan.

"Sam, we knew going in that this was not going to be easy. Jesus, you send me a Marine and an FBI agent. Why not a couple of Eagle Scouts, y'know?"

"Okay, Pete. It's your job. Any idea on timing? There's some work piling up on us," Granger observed.

"Maybe a month and I'll know if they'll play or not. They *will* need to know the why in addition to the who, but I always told you that," Alexander reminded his boss.

"True," Granger admitted. It really *was* a lot easier in

the movies, wasn't it? Just let your fingers do the walking to "Assassins R Us" in the Yellow Pages. They had thought about hiring former KGB officers at first. They all had expert training, and all wanted money—the going rate was less than twenty-five thousand dollars per kill, a pittance—but such people would probably report back to Moscow Centre in the hope of being rehired, and The Campus would then become known within the global "black" community. They couldn't have that.

"What about the new toys?" Pete asked. Sooner or later, he'd have to train the twins with the new tools of the trade.

"Two weeks, they tell me."

"That long? Hell, Sam, I proposed them nine months ago."

"It's not something you get at the local Western Auto. They have to be manufactured from scratch. You know, highly skilled machinists in out-of-the-way places, people who don't ask questions."

"I told you, get the guys who do this sort of thing for the Air Force. They're always making up clever little gadgets." Like tape recorders that fit in cigarette lighters. Now, *that* was probably inspired by the movies. And for the really good things, the government almost never had the right people in-house, which was why they employed civilian contractors, who took the money, did the job, and kept their mouths shut because they wanted more such contracts.

"They're all being worked on, Pete. Two weeks," he emphasized.

"Roger that. Until then, I have all the suppressed pistols I need. They're both doing nicely with the tracking and tailing drills. Helps that they're so ordinary-looking."

"So, bottom line, things are going well?" Granger asked.

"Except for the conscience thing, yeah."

"Okay, keep me posted."

"Will do."

"See ya."

Alexander set the receiver back down. Goddamned consciences, he thought. It would be nice to have robots, but somebody might notice Robby striding down the street. And they couldn't have that. Or maybe the Invisible Man, but in the H. G. Wells story, the drug that made him transparent also made him mad, and this gig was already crazy enough, wasn't it? He tossed off the last of his sherry, and then on reflection, went off to refill his glass.

||||||||||||||||||||||||||||||||||||||||||||||||||||||||||||||||||||||

CHAPTER 8

CONVICTION

MUSTAFA AND Abdullah arose at dawn, said their morning prayers, and ate, and then hooked up their computers and checked their e-mail. Sure enough, Mustafa had an e-mail from Mohammed, forwarding a message from someone else, supposedly named Diego, with instructions for a meeting at...10:30 A.M. local time. He sorted through the rest of his electronic mail, most of it something the Americans called "spam." He'd learned that this was a canned pig product, which seemed entirely appropriate. Both of them walked outside—but separately—just after 9:00, mainly to get the blood moving and examine the neighborhood. They checked carefully but furtively for tails and found none. They got to the planned rendezvous point at 10:25.

Diego was already there, reading a paper, wearing a white shirt with blue stripes.

"Diego?" Mustafa asked pleasantly.

"You must be Miguel," the contact replied with a smile, rising to shake hands. "Please be seated." Pablo scanned around. Yes, there was "Miguel's" backup, sitting alone and ordering coffee, doing overwatch like a professional. "So, how do you like Mexico City?"

"I did not know it was so large and bustling." Mustafa waved around. The sidewalks were crowded with people heading in all directions. "And the air is so foul."

"That is a problem here. The mountains hold in the pollution. It takes strong winds to clear the air. So, coffee?"

Mustafa nodded. Pablo waved to the waiter and held up the coffeepot. The sidewalk café was European in character, but not overly crowded. The tables were about half occupied, in knots of people meeting for business or socially, doing their talking and minding their own business. The new coffeepot arrived. Mustafa poured and waited for the other to speak.

"So, what can I do for you?"

"All of us are here as requested. How soon can we go?"

"How soon do you wish?" Pablo asked.

"This afternoon would be fine, but that might be a little soon for your arrangements."

"Yes. But what about tomorrow, say about thirteen hundred hours?"

"That would be excellent," Mustafa responded in pleasant surprise. "How will the crossing be arranged?"

"I will not be directly involved, you understand, but you will be driven to the border and handed over to someone who specializes in getting people and certain goods into America. You will be required to walk about six kilometers. It will be warm, but not greatly so. Once in America, you will be driven to a safe house outside Santa Fe, New Mexico. There you can either fly to your final destinations or rent cars."

"Weapons?"

"What exactly will you require?"

"Ideally, we would like AK-47s."

Pablo shook his head at once. "Those we cannot supply, but we can get you Uzi and Ingram submachine guns.

Nine-millimeter Parabellum caliber, with, say, six thirty-round magazines each, fully loaded for your purposes."

"More ammunition," Mustafa said at once. "Twelve magazines, plus three additional boxes of ammunition for each weapon."

Pablo nodded. "That is easily done." The increased expense would be only a couple of thousand dollars. The weapons would have been bought on the open market, along with the ammunition. They were technically traceable to their origin and/or purchaser, but that was only a theoretical problem, not a practical one. The guns would be mainly Ingrams, not the better-made and more accurate Israeli Uzis, but these people wouldn't care. Who knows, they might even have religious or moral objections to touching a Jewish-made weapon. "Tell me, how are you set for traveling expenses?"

"We have five thousand American dollars each in cash."

"You can use that for minor expenses, like food and gasoline, but for other things you need credit cards. Americans will not accept cash to rent cars, and *never* to buy airplane tickets."

"We have them," Mustafa replied. He and each member of the team had Visa cards issued to them in Bahrain. They even had consecutive numbers. All were drawn on an account in a Swiss bank, whose account held just over five hundred thousand dollars. Sufficient to their purposes.

The name on the card, Pablo saw, was JOHN PETER SMITH. Good. Whoever had set this up hadn't made the mistake of using explicitly Middle Eastern names. Just as long as the card didn't fall into the hands of a police officer who might ask Mr. Smith where exactly he came from. He hoped they had been briefed on the American police and their habits.

"Other documents?" Pablo asked.

"Our passports are Qatari. We have international driver's licenses. We all speak acceptable English and can read maps. We know about American laws. We will keep within the speed limits and drive carefully. The nail that sticks up is hammered down. So we will not stick up."

"Good," Pablo observed. So, they had been briefed. Some might even remember it. "Remember that one mistake can ruin the entire mission for all of you. And it is easy to make mistakes. America is an easy country in which to live and move about, but their police are very efficient. If you are not noticed, you are safe from them. Therefore, you must avoid being noticed. Fail in that, and you could all be doomed to failure."

"Diego, we will not fail," Mustafa promised.

Fail at what? Pablo wondered, but did not ask. *How many women and children will you kill?* But it didn't really matter to him. It was a cowardly way to kill, but the rules of honor in his "friend's" culture were very different from his own. This was business, and that was all he needed to know.

THREE MILES, push-ups, and a coffee chaser, and that was life in southern Virginia.

"Brian, you used to carrying a firearm?"

"Usually an M16 and five or six extra mags. Some fragmentation grenades, too, go in the basic load, yeah, Pete."

"I was talking about side arms, actually."

"M9 Beretta, that's what I'm used to."

"Any good with it?"

"It's in my package, Pete. I qualified expert at Quantico, but so did most of my class. No big deal."

"You used to carrying it around?"

"You mean in civilian clothes? No."

"Okay, get used to it."

"Is it legal?" Brian asked.

"Virginia is a shall-issue state. If you've got a clean record, the commonwealth will grant you a concealed-carry permit. What about you, Dominic?"

"I'm still FBI, Pete. I'd feel kinda naked out on the street without a friend."

"What do you carry?"

"Smith & Wesson 1076. Shoots the ten-millimeter cartridge, double action. The Bureau's gone to the Glock lately, but I like the Smith better." *And, no, I didn't carve a notch in the grips,* he didn't add. Though he had thought about it.

"Okay, well, when you're off-campus here, I want you both to carry, just to get used to the idea, Brian."

A shrug. "Fair enough." It beat the hell out of a sixty-five-pound rucksack.

THERE WAS a lot more to it than just Sali, of course. Jack was working on a total of eleven different people, all but one of them Middle Eastern, all in the money business. The one European lived in Riyadh. He was German, but had converted to Islam, which had struck someone as odd enough to deserve electronic surveillance. Jack's university German was good enough to read the guy's e-mails, but they didn't reveal very much. He'd evidently gone native in his habits, didn't even drink beer. He was evidently popular with his Saudi friends—one thing about Islam was that if you obeyed the rules and prayed the correct way, they didn't much care what you looked like. It would have been admirable except for the fact that most of the world's terrorists prayed to Mecca. But that, Jack reminded himself, wasn't the fault of Islam. The night he himself had been born, people had tried to kill him while he was still in his mother's womb—and they'd identified themselves as Catholics. Fanatics were fanatics, the world around. The idea that people had tried to murder his mother was enough to make him want to pick his Beretta .40. His father, well, his dad was able to look after himself, but messing with women constituted a big step over the line, and that was a line you could cross only once and in one direction. There was no coming back.

He didn't remember any of it, of course. The ULA terrorists had all gone off to meet their God—courtesy of the State of Maryland—before he'd entered first grade, and his parents had never talked about it. His sister Sally had, though. She still had dreams about it. He wondered if Mom and Dad had them, too. Did events like that go away eventually? He'd seen things on the History Channel to suggest that World War II veterans still had images of combat return to them at night, and that had been over sixty years ago. Such memories had to be a curse.

"Tony?"

"Yeah, Junior?"

"This guy Otto Weber, what's the big deal? He's about as exciting as vanilla ice cream."

"If you're a bad guy, do you suppose you wear a neon sign on your back, or do you think you try to hide down in the grass?"

"With the snakes," Junior completed the thought. "I know—we're looking for little things."

"Like I told you. You can do fourth-grade arithmetic. Attach a nose to it. And, yes, you're looking for things that are *supposed* to be damned near invisible, okay? That's why this job is so much fun. And innocent little things are mostly innocent little things. If he downloads kiddie porn off the 'Net, it's not because he's a terrorist. It's because he's a pervert. That's not a capital offense in most countries."

"I bet it is in Saudi."

"Probably, but they don't chase after it, I bet."

"I thought they were all puritans."

"Over there, a man keeps his libido to himself. But if you do something with a real live kid, you're in big trouble. Saudi Arabia is a good place to abide by the law. You can park your Mercedes and leave the keys in the ignition and the car'll be there when you get back. You can't even do that in Salt Lake City."

"Been there?" Jack asked.

"Four times. The people are friendly as long as you treat

them properly, and if you make a real friend over there, he's a friend for life. But their rules *are* different, and the price for breaking them can be pretty steep."

"So, Otto Weber plays by the rules?"

Wills nodded. "Correct. He's bought all the way into the system, religion and all. They like him for that. Religion is the center of their culture. When a guy converts and lives by Islamic rules, it validates their world, and they like that, just like anybody would. I don't think Otto's a player, though. The people we're looking for are sociopaths. They can happen anywhere. Some cultures catch them early and change them—or kill them. Some cultures don't. We're not as good at that as we ought to be, and I suspect the Saudis probably are. But the really good ones can skate in any culture, and some of them use the disguise of religion. Islam is not a belief system for psychopaths, but it can be perverted to the use of such people, just like Christianity can. Ever take psych courses?"

"No, wish I had," Ryan admitted.

"So, buy some books. Read them. Find people who know about that stuff and ask questions. Listen to the answers." Wills turned back to his computer screen.

Shit, Junior thought. This job just kept getting worse. How long, he wondered, before they expected him to turn up something useful? A month? A year? What the hell was a passing grade at The Campus...

...and what, exactly, would happen when he did turn up something useful?

Back to Otto Weber...

THEY COULDN'T stay in their room all day without having people wonder why. Mustafa and Abdullah left just after eating a light lunch in the coffee shop, and took a walk. Three blocks away they found an art museum. Admission was free, but inside they found out why. It was a museum of modern art and its painting and sculpture were well beyond their comprehension. They wandered through it over a period of two hours, and both of them concluded that paint must be cheap in Mexico. Nevertheless, it gave them the chance to burnish their covers, as they pretended to appreciate the garbage hanging on the walls and sitting on the floors.

Then they strolled back to their hotel. The one good thing was the weather. It was warm to those of European extraction, but quite pleasant to the visiting Arabs, gray haze and all. Tomorrow they would see desert again. One last time, perhaps.

IT WAS impossible, even for a well-supported government agency, to search all the messages that flew through cyberspace every night, and so the NSA used computer programs to screen for key phrases. The electronic addresses of some known or suspected terrorists or suspected stringers had been identified over the years, and these were watched, as were the server computers of Internet Service Providers, or ISPs. All in all, it used up vast amounts of storage space, and as a result delivery trucks were constantly bringing new disk storage devices to Fort Meade, Maryland, where they were hooked up to the mainframe computers so that if a target person was identified, then his e-mails dating back for months or even years could be screened. If there were ever a game of falcon and mouse, this was it. The bad guys, of course, knew that the screening program looked for specific words or phrases, and so they had taken to using their own code words—which was another trap in itself, since codes gave a false sense of security, one that was easily exploited by an agency with seventy years of experience reading the minds of America's enemies.

The process had its limits. Too free a use of signal-intelligence information revealed its existence, causing the targets to change their methods of encryption, and so compromising the source. Using it too little, on the other hand, was as bad as not having it at all. Unfortunately, the intelligence services leaned more to the latter than the former. The creation of a new Department of Homeland Security had, theoretically, set up a central clearinghouse for all threat-related information, but the size of the new super-agency had crippled it from the get-go. The information was all there, but in too great a quantity to be processed, and with too many processors to turn out a viable product.

But old habits died hard. The intelligence community remained intact, a superagency overtop its own bureau-cracy or not, and its segments talked to each other. As al-ways, they savored what the insiders knew as opposed to those who knew it not . . . and wished to keep it that way.

The National Security Agency's principal means of com-munication with the Central Intelligence Agency was essen-tially to say *This is interesting, what do you think?* That was because each of the two agencies held a different corporate ethos. They talked differently. They thought differently. And insofar as they acted at all, they acted differently.

But at least they thought in parallel directions, not diver-gent ones. On the whole, CIA had the better analysts, and NSA was better at gathering information. There were ex-ceptions to both general rules; and in both cases, the really talented individuals knew one another, and, among them-selves, they mostly spoke the same language.

THAT BECAME clear the next morning with the inter-agency cable traffic. A senior analyst at Fort Meade headed it as FLASH-traffic to his counterpart at Langley. That en-sured that it would be noticed at The Campus. Jerry Rounds saw it at the top of his morning e-mail pile, and he brought it to the next morning's conference.

"'We will sting them badly this time,' the guy says. What could that mean?" Jerry Rounds wondered aloud. Tom Davis had overnighted in New York. He had a break-fast meeting with the bond people at Morgan Stanley. It was annoying when business got in the way of business.

"How good's the translation?" Gerry Hendley asked.

"The footnote says there's no problem on that end. The intercept is clear and static-free. It's a simple declarative sentence in literate Arabic, no particular nuances to worry about," Rounds declared.

"Origin and recipient?" Hendley went on.

"The originator is a guy named Fa'ad, last name unknown. We know this guy. We think he's one of their mid-level operations people—a plans rather than field guy. He's based somewhere in Bahrain. He only talks on his cell phone when he's in a moving car or a public place, like a market or something. Nobody's gotten a line on him yet. The recipient," Bell went on, "is supposedly a new guy—more likely an old guy on a newly cloned phone. It's an old analog phone, and so they couldn't generate a voiceprint."

"So, they probably have an operation running..." Hendley observed.

"Looks that way," Rounds agreed. "Nature and location unknown."

"So, we don't know dick." Hendley reached for his coffee cup and managed a frown best measured on the Richter scale. "What are they going to do about it?"

Granger took that one: "Nothing useful, Gerry. They're in a logic trap. If they do anything at all, like upgrading the color on the threat rainbow, they're sounding the alarm, and they've done that so much that it's become counterproductive. Unless they disclose the text and the source, nobody'll take it seriously. If they do disclose anything, we burn the source for fair."

"And if they don't sound the alarm, Congress will shove whatever ends up happening right up their ass." Elected officials were much more comfortable being the problem rather than the solution. There was political hay to be made from nonproductive screaming. So, CIA and other services would continue to work at identifying the people with the distant cell phones. That was unglamorous, slow police work, and it ran at a speed that grossly impatient politicians could not dictate—and throwing money at the problem didn't make it any better, which was doubly frustrating to people who didn't know how to do anything else.

"So, they straddle the issue, and do something they know won't work—"

"—and hope for a miracle," Granger agreed with his boss.

Police departments all across America would be alerted, of course—but for what purpose, and against what threat, nobody knew. And cops were always looking for Middle Eastern faces to pull over and question anyway, to the point that cops were bored with what was almost always a nonproductive exercise in doing something the ACLU was already raising hell about. There were six Driving While Arab cases pending in various federal district courts, four involving physicians, and two with demonstrably innocent students whom the local police had hassled a little too vigorously. Whatever case law resulted from those incidents would do far more harm than good. It was just what Sam Granger called it, a logic trap.

Hendley's frown got a little deeper. It was echoed, he was sure, at a half-dozen government agencies which, for all their funding and personnel, were about as useful as tits on a boar hog. "Anything we can do?" he asked.

"Stay alert and call the cops if we see anything unusual," Granger answered. "Unless you have a gun handy."

"To shoot some innocent clown who's probably taking citizenship classes," Bell added. "Not worth the trouble."

I should have stayed in the Senate, Hendley thought. At least being part of the problem had its satisfactions. It was good for the spleen to vent it once in a while. Screaming here was totally counterproductive, and bad for the morale of his people.

"Okay, then, we pretend we're ordinary citizens," the boss said at last. The senior staff nodded agreement, and went on to the remaining routine business of the day. Toward the end, Hendley asked Rounds how the new boy was doing.

"He's smart enough to ask a lot of questions. I have him reviewing known or suspected stringers for unaccountable money transfers."

"If he can stand doing that, God bless him," Bell observed. "That can drive a man crazy."

"Patience is a virtue," Gerry noted. "It's just a son of a bitch to acquire."

"We alert all of our people to this intercept?"

"Might as well," Bell responded.

"Done," Granger told them all.

"SHIT," Jack observed fifteen minutes later. "What's it mean?"

"We might know tomorrow, next week—or never," Will answered.

"Fa'ad . . . I know that name . . ." Jack turned back to his computer and keyed up some files. "Yeah! He's the guy in Bahrain. How come the local cops haven't sweated him some?"

"They don't know about him yet. Tracking him's an NSA gig so far, but maybe Langley will see if they can learn some more about him."

"Are they as good as the FBI for police work?"

"Actually, no, they're not. Different training, but it's not that removed from what a normal person can do—"

Ryan the Younger cut him off. "Bullshit. Reading people is something cops are good at. It's an acquired skill, and you also have to learn how to ask questions."

"Says who?" Wills demanded.

"Mike Brennan. He was my bodyguard. He taught me a lot."

"Well, a good spook has to read people, too. Their asses depend on it."

"Maybe, but if you want your eyes fixed, you talk to my mom. For ears, you talk to somebody else."

"Okay, maybe so. For now, check out our friend Fa'ad."

Jack turned back to his computer. He scrolled back to

the first interesting conversation they'd intercepted. Then he thought better of it and went back to the very beginning, the first time he'd attracted notice. "Why doesn't he change phones?"

"Maybe he's lazy. These guys are smart, but they have blind spots, too. They fall into habits. They're clever, but they do not have formal training, like a trained spook, KGB or like that."

NSA had a large but covert listening post in Bahrain, covered in the American Embassy, and supplemented by U.S. Navy warships that called there on a regular basis, but were not seen as an electronic threat in that environment. The NSA teams that regularly sailed on them even intercepted people walking the waterfront with their cell phones.

"This guy is dirty," he observed a minute later. "This guy's a bad guy, sure as hell."

"He's been a good barometer, too. He says a lot of things we find interesting."

"So, somebody ought to pick him up."

"They're thinking about that at Langley."

"How big's the station in Bahrain?"

"Six people. Station Chief, two field spooks, and three sundry employees, signals and stuff."

"*That's all?* There? Just a handful?"

"That's right," Wills confirmed.

"Damn. I used to ask Dad about this. He usually shrugged and grumbled."

"He tried pretty hard to get CIA more funding and more employees. Congress wasn't always accommodating."

"Have we ever taken a guy up and, you know, 'talked' to him?"

"Not lately."

"Why not?"

"Manpower," Wills answered simply. "Funny thing about employees, they all expect to be paid. We're not that big."

"So why doesn't CIA ask the local cops to pick him up? Bahrain's a friendly country."

"Friendly, but not a vassal. They have their ideas about civil rights, too, just not the same as ours. Also, you can't pick a guy up for what he knows and what he thinks. Only for what he's done. As you can see, we don't know that he's actually done anything."

"So, put a tail on his ass."

"And how can CIA do that with only two field spooks?" Wills asked.

"Jesus!"

"Welcome to the real world, Junior." The Agency ought to have recruited some agents, maybe cops in Bahrain, to help out with such tasks, but that hadn't happened yet. The Station Chief could also have requested more people, of course, but Arabic-speaking and -looking field officers were a little thin over at Langley, and those they had went to more obviously troublesome postings.

THE RENDEZVOUS took place as planned. There were three vehicles, each with a driver who spoke scarcely a word, and that in Spanish. The drive was pleasant, and distantly reminiscent of home. The driver was cautious; he didn't speed or do anything else to attract attention, but they moved right along in any case. Nearly all of the Arabs smoked cigarettes, and exclusively American brands, like Marlboro. Mustafa did as well, and wondered—as had Mohammed before him—what the Prophet would have said about cigarettes. Probably nothing good, but he *hadn't* said anything, had he? And so, Mustafa could smoke as much as he wished. The issue of dangers to his health was a distant concern now, after all. He expected to live another four or five days, but little more than that, if things went according to plan.

He'd expected some excited chattering from his people, but there was none. Hardly anyone spoke a word. They just looked blankly out at the passing countryside, speeding past a culture about which they knew little, and they would not learn more.

"OKAY, BRIAN, here's your carry permit." Pete Alexander handed it over.

It might as well have been a second driver's license, and it went into his wallet. "So, I'm street-legal now?"

"As a practical matter, no cop is going to hassle a Marine officer for carrying a pistol, concealed or not, but better to dot the I's and cross the T's. You going to carry the Beretta?"

"It's what I'm used to, and the fifteen rounds make for security. What am I supposed to carry it in?"

"Use one of these, Aldo," Dominic said, holding up his fanny pack. It looked like a money belt, or the kind of pouch used more often by women than by men. A pull on the string ripped it open, and revealed the pistol and two extra magazines. "A lot of agents use this. More comfortable than a hip holster. Those can dig into your kidneys on a long car ride."

For the moment, Brian would tuck his into his belt. "Where to today, Pete?"

"Back to the mall. More tracking drills."

"Great," Brian responded. "Why don't you have invisibility pills?"

"H. G. Wells took the formula with him."

CHAPTER 9

GOING WITH GOD

JACK'S DRIVE to The Campus took about thirty-five minutes, listening to NPR's *Morning Edition* all the way because, like his father, he didn't listen to contemporary music. The similarities with his dad had both vexed and fascinated John Patrick Ryan, Jr., throughout his life. Through most of his teenage years, he'd fought them off, trying to establish his own identity in contrast to his button-down father, but then in college he had somehow drifted back, hardly even noticing the process. He'd thought he was just doing the sensible thing, for instance, to date girls who might be good wife candidates, though he'd never quite found the perfect one. This he unconsciously judged by his mom. He'd been annoyed by teachers at George-town who said he was a chip off the old block, and at first taken some offense at it, then reminded himself that his father wasn't all that bad a guy. He could have done worse. He'd seen a lot of rebellion even at a university as conser-vative as G-Town, with its Jesuit traditions and rigorous scholarship. Some of his classmates had even made a show of rejecting their parents, but what asshole would do something like that? However staid and old-fashioned his father surely was, he'd been a pretty good dad, as dads went. He'd never been overbearing and let him go his own way and choose his own path...in confidence that he'd turn out okay? Jack wondered. But, no. If his father had been that conspiratorial, Jack would have noticed, surely.

He thought about conspiracy. There had been a lot of that in the newspapers and pulp-book media. His father had even joked more than once about having the Marine Corps paint his "personal" helicopter black. That would have been a hoot, Jack thought. Instead, his surrogate father had been Mike Brennan, whom he'd regularly bombarded with questions, many of them about conspiracy. He'd been hugely disappointed to learn that the United States Secret Service was one hundred percent confident that Lee Harvey Oswald had assassinated Jack Kennedy, and all by himself. At their academy at Beltsville, outside Washington, Jack had held, and even shot, a replica of the 6.5mm Mannlicher-Carcano rifle that had taken the former President's life, and been fully briefed on the case—to his own satisfaction, if not that of the conspiracy industry that so fervently and commercially believed otherwise. The latter had even proposed that his father, as a former CIA official, had been the final beneficiary of a conspiracy that had gone on for at least fifty years for the express purpose of giving CIA the reins of government. Yeah, sure. Like the Trilateral Commission, and the World Order of Freemasons, and whoever else the fiction writers could make up. From both his father and Mike Brennan, he'd heard a lot of CIA stories, few of which bragged on the competence of that federal agency. It was pretty good, but nowhere near as competent as Hollywood proposed. But Hollywood probably believed that Roger Rabbit was real—after all, his picture had made money, right? No, the CIA had a couple of profound shortcomings...

...and was The Campus a means of correcting them...? That was a question. *Damn,* Junior thought, turning onto Route 29, *maybe the conspiracy theorists might be right after all...?* His own internal answer was a snort and a grimace.

No, The Campus wasn't like that at all, not like the SPECTRE of the old James Bond movies, or the THRUSH of *The Man from U.N.C.L.E.* reruns on Nick at Nite. Conspiracy theory depended on the ability of large numbers of people to keep their mouths shut, and as Mike had told him so many times, Bad Guys couldn't keep their mouths shut. There were no deaf-and-dumb people in federal prisons, Mike had told him many times, but criminals never quite figured that one out, the idiots.

Even the people he was tracking had that problem, and they were, supposedly, smart and highly motivated. Or so they thought. But, no, not even they were the Bad Guys of the movies. They needed to talk, and talking would be their downfall. He wondered which it was: Did people who did evil things need to brag, or did they need others to tell them they were doing good in some perverse way upon which they all agreed? The guys he was looking at were Muslims, but there were other Muslims. He and his father both knew Prince Ali of Saudi Arabia, and he was a good guy, the guy who'd given his dad the sword from which he'd gotten his Secret Service code name, and he still stopped by the house at least once a year, because the Saudis, once you made friends with them, were the most loyal people in the world. Of course, it helped if you were an ex-President. Or, in his case, the son of a former President, now making his own way in the "black" world...

Damn, how will Dad react to this*?* Jack wondered. *He's going to have a cow. And Mom? A real hissy fit.* That was good for a laugh as he turned left. But Mom didn't need to find out. The cover story would work for her—and Grandpa—but not for Dad. Dad had helped set this place up. Maybe he needed one of those black helicopters after all. He slid into his own parking place, number 127. The Campus couldn't be all that big and powerful, could it? Not with less than a hundred fifty employees. He locked his car and headed in, remarking to himself that this every-morning-to-work thing sucked. But everybody had to start somewhere.

He walked in the back entrance, like most of the others. There was a reception/security desk. The guy there was Ernie Chambers, formerly a sergeant first class in the 1st Infantry Division. His blue uniform blazer had a miniature of the Combat Infantryman's Badge, just in case you didn't notice the shoulders and the hard black eyes. After the first Persian Gulf War, he'd changed jobs from grunt to MP. He'd probably enforced the law and directed traffic pretty well, Jack thought, waving good-morning at him.

"Hey, Mr. Ryan."

"'Morning, Ernie."

"You have a good one, sir." To the ex-soldier, everybody was named "sir."

IT WAS two hours earlier outside Ciudad Juárez. There, the van pulled into a vehicle-service plaza and stopped by a cluster of four other vehicles. Behind them were the other minivans who'd followed them all the way to the American border. The men roused from their sleep and stumbled into the chill morning air to stretch.

"Here I leave you, *señor*," the driver said to Mustafa. "You will join the man by the tan Ford Explorer. *Vaya con Dios, amigos*," he said in that most charming of dismissals: Go with God.

Mustafa walked over and found a tallish man wearing a cowboy-type hat. He didn't appear very clean, and his mustache needed trimming. "*Buenos dias,* I am Pedro. I will be taking you the rest of the way. There are four of you for my vehicle, yes?"

Mustafa nodded. "That is correct."

"There are water bottles in the truck. You may wish to have something to eat. You can buy anything you like from the shop." He waved to the building. Mustafa did, his colleagues did much the same, and after ten minutes they all boarded the vehicles and headed out.

They went west, mostly along Route 2. Immediately, the vehicles broke up, no longer "flying formation," as it were. There were four of them, all large American-made SUV-type vehicles, all of them coated with a thick coating of dirt and grit so that they did not appear new. The sun had climbed above the horizon to their rear, casting its shadows onto the khaki-colored ground.

Pedro appeared to have spoken his piece back at the plaza. Now he said nothing, except an occasional belch, and chain-smoked his cigarettes. He had the radio on to an AM station, and hummed along with the Spanish music. The Arabs sat in silence.

"HEY, TONY," Jack said in greeting. His workmate was already on his workstation.

"Howdy," Wills responded.

"Anything hot this morning?"

"Not after yesterday, but Langley is talking about putting some coverage on our friend Fa'ad—again."

"Will they really do it?"

"Your guess is as good as mine. The Station Chief in Bahrain is saying that he needs more personnel to make it happen, and the personnel weenies at Langley are probably batting that back and forth right now."

"My dad liked to say that the government is really run by accountants and lawyers."

"He ain't far wrong on that one, buddy. God knows where Ed Kealty fits in that, though. What does your dad think of him?"

"Can't stand the son of a bitch. He won't talk in public about the new administration because he says that's wrong, but if you say something about the guy over dinner, you might end up wearing your wine home. It's funny. Dad hates politics, and he really tries hard to keep his cool, but that guy is definitely not on the Christmas card list. But he keeps it quiet, won't talk to any reporters about it. Mike Brennan tells me the Service doesn't like the new guy, either. And they *have* to like him."

"There are penalties for being a professional," Wills agreed.

And then Junior lit up his computer and looked at the night traffic between Langley and Fort Meade. It was a lot more impressive in its volume than its content. It seemed that his new friend, Uda, had—

"Our pal Sali had lunch with somebody yesterday," Jack announced.

"Who with?" Wills asked.

"The Brits don't know. Appears Middle Eastern, age about twenty-eight, one of those thin—well, narrow—beards around the jawline, and mustache, but no ident on the guy. They spoke in Arabic, but nobody got close enough to overhear anything."

"Where'd they eat?"

"Pub on Tower Hill called 'Hung, Drawn and Quartered.' It's on the edge of the financial district. Uda drank Perrier. His pal had a beer. And they had a British ploughman's lunch. They sat in a corner booth, made it hard for whoever was watching to get close and listen in."

"So, they wanted privacy. It doesn't necessarily make them bad guys. Did the Brits tail him?"

"No. That probably means a single-man tail on Uda?"

"Probably," Wills agreed.

"But it says they got a photo of the new guy. Not included in the report."

"It was probably someone from the Security Service—MI5—doing the surveillance. And probably a junior guy. Uda isn't regarded as very important, not enough for full coverage. None of those agencies have all the manpower they want. Anything else?"

"Some money trades that afternoon. Looks pretty routine," Jack said, scrolling through the transactions. *I'm looking for something small and harmless,* he reminded himself. But small, harmless things were, for the most part, small and harmless. Uda moved money around every day, in large and small amounts. Since he was in the wealth-preservation business, he rarely speculated, dealing mostly in real-estate transactions. London—and Britain in general—was a good place to preserve cash. Real-estate prices were fairly high but very stable. If you bought something, it might not go up very much, but it sure as hell wasn't going to have the bottom drop out. So, Uda's daddy was letting the kid stretch his legs some, but not letting him run out and play in the traffic. How much personal liquidity did Uda have? Since he paid off his whores in cash and expensive handbags, he must have his own cash supply. Maybe modest, but "modest" by Saudi standards wasn't exactly modest by many others. The kid *did* drive an Aston Martin, after all, and his dwelling was not in a trailer park . . . so—

"How do I differentiate between Sali's trading his family money and trading his own?"

"You don't. We think he keeps the two accounts close, in the sense both of being covert and near to each other. Your best bet on that is to see how he sets up his quarterly statements to the family."

Jack groaned. "Oh, great, it'll take me a couple of days to add up all the transactions, and then to analyze them."

"Now you know why you're not a real CPA, Jack." Wills managed a chuckle.

Jack nearly snarled, but there was only one way to accomplish this task, and it *was* his job, wasn't it? First, he tried to see if his program could shortcut the process. Nope. Fourth-grade arithmetic with a nose attached. What fun. At least by the time he finished, he'd probably be better at entering numbers into the numeric keypad on the right side of the keyboard. *There* was something to look forward to! Why didn't The Campus employ some forensic accountants?

THEY TURNED off Route 2 onto a dirt road that wound its way north. The road had seen a good deal of use, some of it recent, judging by the tracks. The general area was somewhat mountainous. The real peaks of the Rocky Mountain chain were off to the west, far enough away that he couldn't see them, but the air was thinner here than he was accustomed to, and it would be warm walking. He wondered how far that would be, and how close they were to the U.S. border. He'd heard that the American-Mexican border was guarded, but not well guarded. The Americans could be lethally competent in some areas, but utterly infantile in others. Mustafa and his people hoped to avoid the former and to make use of the latter. About eleven in the morning, he saw a large, boxy truck in the distance, and their SUV headed toward it. The truck, he saw as they came closer, was empty, its large red doors wide open. The Ford Explorer came to within a hundred meters and stopped. Pedro switched off the engine and got out.

"We are here, my friends," he announced. "I hope you are ready to walk."

All four of them got out, and as before they stretched their legs and looked around. A new man walked in their direction, as the other three SUVs parked and disgorged their passengers.

"Hello, Pedro," the new Mexican greeted the lead driver, evidently an old friend.

"*Buenos dias,* Ricardo. Here are the people who want to go to America."

"Hello." He shook hands with the first four. "My name is Ricardo, and I am your *coyote.*"

"What?" Mustafa asked.

"It is just a term. I take people across the border, for a fee. In your case, of course, I have already been paid."

"How far?"

"Ten kilometers. A modest walk," he said comfortably. "The country will mostly be like this. If you see a snake, just walk away from it. It will not chase you. But if you get within a meter, it can strike you and kill you. Aside from that, there is nothing to fear. If you see a helicopter, you must fall to the ground and not move. The Americans do not guard their border well, and, oddly enough, not as well in daylight as at night. We have also taken some precautions."

"What is that?"

"There were thirty people in that van," he said, pointing to the large truck they'd seen coming in. "They will walk in ahead of and to the west of us. If anyone is caught, it will be them."

"How long will it take?"

"Three hours. Less, if you are fit. Do you have water?"

"We know the desert," Mustafa assured him.

"As you say. Let us be off, then. Follow me, *amigo*." And with that, Ricardo started walking north. His clothes were all khaki, he wore a military-style web belt with three canteens attached, and he carried military-style binoculars, plus an Army-style floppy hat. His boots were well worn. His stride was purposeful and efficient, not overly fast for show, just to cover ground efficiently. They fell in behind him, forming a single file to conceal their numbers from any possible trackers, with Mustafa in the lead, about five meters behind their coyote.

THERE WAS a pistol range about three hundred yards from the plantation house. It was outdoors, and had steel targets, a set just like those at the FBI Academy, with head-plates, circular and roughly the size of a human head. They made an agreeable *clang* when hit, and then they fell down, as a human target would do if hit there. Enzo turned out to be better at this. Aldo explained that the Marine Corps didn't emphasize pistol shooting too much, whereas the FBI paid particular attention to it, figuring that anybody could shoot a shoulder weapon accurately. The FBI brother used the two-handed Weaver stance, while the Marine tended to stand up straight and shoot one-handed, the way the services taught their people.

"Hey, Aldo, that just makes you a better target," Dominic warned.

"Oh yeah?" Brian rippled off three rounds and got three satisfying *clang*s as a result. "Hard to shoot after you take one between the running lights, bro."

"And what's this one-shot/one-kill crap? Anything worth shooting is worth shooting twice."

"How many did you give that mutt in Alabama?" Brian asked.

"Three. I didn't feel like taking any chances," Dominic explained.

"You say so, bro. Hey, let me try that Smith of yours."

Dominic cleared his weapon before handing it over. The magazine went separately. Brian dry-fired it a few times to get used to the feel, then loaded and cycled the action. His first shot *clanged* a headplate. So did his second. The third one missed, though number four did not, a third of a second later. Brian handed the weapon back. "Feels different in the hand," he explained.

"You get used to it," Dominic promised.

"Thanks, but I like the extra six rounds in the magazine."

"Well, it's what you like."

"What's with all the head-shot stuff, anyway?" Brian wondered. "Okay, shooting sniper rifle, it's the surest one-shot stopper, but not with a pistol."

"When you can do a guy in the head from fifteen yards," Pete Alexander answered, "it's just a nice talent to have. It's the best way of ending an argument I know."

"Where did you come from?" Dominic asked.

"You didn't scan, Agent Caruso. Remember that even Adolf Hitler had friends. Don't they teach that at Quantico?"

"Well, yes," Dominic admitted, somewhat crestfallen.

"When your primary target is down, you scan the area for any friends he might have had. Or you get the hell out of town. Or both."

"You mean run away?" Brian asked.

"Not unless you're on a track. You make your way clear in such a way as to be inconspicuous. That can mean walking into a bookstore and making a purchase, getting a coffee, whatever. You have to make your decision based on circumstances, but keep your objective in mind. Your objective is *always* to get clear of the immediate area as quickly as circumstances allow. Move too fast and people will notice. Move too slow and they might remember seeing you and your subject close together. They will never report the person they didn't notice. So, you want to be one of those. What you wear out on a job, the way you act out in the field, the way you walk, the way you think—all of that must be designed to make you invisible," Alexander told them.

"In other words, Pete, you're saying that when we kill these people we're training for," Brian observed quietly, "you want us to be able to do it and walk away so that we can get away with it."

"Would you prefer to be caught?" Alexander asked.

"No, but the best way to kill somebody is to pop him in the head with a good rifle from a couple of hundred meters away. That works every time."

"But what if we want him dead in such a way that nobody knows he was killed?" the training officer asked.

"How the hell do you manage that?" This was Dominic.

"Patience, lads. One thing at a time."

THERE WERE the remains of some sort of fence. Ricardo just walked through it, using a hole that did not look recent. The fence posts had been painted a rich green, but that had mainly rusted off. The fencing material was in even worse shape. Getting through was the least of their problems. The coyote went a further fifty meters or so, and selected a large rock, then sat down, lit a smoke, and took a drink from his canteen. It was his first stop. The walk had not been difficult at all, and clearly he'd done this many times. Mustafa and his friends did not know that he'd brought several hundred groups across the border along this very route, and had only been arrested once—and that had not amounted to very much, except for stinging his pride. He'd also forfeited his fee, because he was an honorable coyote. Mustafa went over to him.

"Are your friends okay?" Ricardo asked.

"It has not been strenuous," Mustafa replied, "and I have seen no snakes."

"Not too many along here. People usually shoot them, or throw rocks. No one cares much for snakes."

"Are they dangerous—truly, I mean?"

"Only if you are a fool, and even then you are unlikely to die. You will be ill for a few days. No more than that, but it can make walking rather painful. We will wait here for a few minutes. We are ahead of schedule. Oh, yes, welcome to America, *amigo.*"

"That fence is all there is?" Mustafa asked in amazement.

"The *norteamericano* is rich, yes, and clever, yes, but he is also lazy. My people would not go there except that there is work the gringo is too lazy to do on his own."

"How many people do you smuggle into America, then?"

"I, you mean? Thousands. Many thousands. For this, I am well paid. I have a fine house, and six other coyotes work for me. The gringos worry more about people smuggling drugs across the border, and I avoid doing that. It is not worth the trouble. I let two of my men do that for me. The pay for that is very high, you see."

"What kind of drugs?" Mustafa asked.

"The kind for which I am paid." He grinned and took another swig from his canteen.

Mustafa turned as Abdullah came up.

"I thought this would be a difficult walk," his number two observed.

"Only for city dwellers," Ricardo replied. "This is my country. I was born of the desert."

"As was I," Abdullah observed. "It is a pleasant day." Better than sitting in the back of a truck, he didn't have to add.

Ricardo lit up another Newport. He liked menthol cigarettes, easier on the throat. "It does not get hot for another month, perhaps two. But then it can be truly hot, and the wise man takes a good water supply. People have died out here without water in the August heat. But none of mine. I make sure everyone has water. The Mother Nature, she has no love and no pity," the coyote observed. At the end of his walk, he knew a place where he could get a few *cervezas* before driving east to El Paso. From there, it was back to his comfortable home in Ascensión, too far from the border to be bothered with would-be emigrants, who had a bad habit of stealing things they might need for the crossing. He wondered how much stealing they did on the gringo side of the line, but it was not his problem, was it? He finished his cigarette and stood. "Three more kilometers to go, my friends."

Mustafa and his friends fell in and restarted the trudge north. Only three kilometers more? At home, they walked farther to a bus stop.

PUNCHING NUMBERS into a keypad was about as much fun as running naked in a garden of cactus. Jack was the sort to need intellectual stimulation, and while some men might find that in investigative accounting, he was not one of them.

"Bored, eh?" Tony Wills asked.

"Mightily," Jack confirmed.

"Well, that's the reality of gathering and processing intelligence information. Even when it's exciting, it's pretty dull—well, unless you're really on the scent of a particularly elusive fox. Then it can be kinda fun, though it's not like watching your subject out in the field. I've never done that."

"Neither did Dad," Jack observed.

"Depends on which stories you read. Your pop occasionally found his way to the sharp end. I don't imagine he liked it much. He ever talk about it?"

"Not ever. Not even once. I don't even think Mom knows much about that. Well, except the submarine thing, but most of what I know about that comes from books and stuff. I asked Dad once, and all he said was, 'You believe everything you see in the papers?' Even when that Russian guy, Gerasimov, got on TV, all Dad did was grunt."

"The word on him at Langley was that he was a king spook. Kept all the secrets like he was supposed to. But he mostly worked up in the Seventh Floor. I never made it that high myself."

"Maybe you can tell me something."

"Like what?"

"Gerasimov, Nikolay Borissovich Gerasimov. Was he really the head of KGB? Did my dad really drag his ass out of Moscow?"

Wills hesitated for a moment, but there was no avoiding it. "Yeah. He was the KGB chairman, and, yes, your dad did arrange his defection."

"No shit? How the hell did Dad arrange that one?"

"That is a very long story and you are not cleared for it."

"Then why did he rat Dad out?"

"Because he was an unwilling defector. Your father forced him to bug out. He wanted to get even after your dad became President. But, you know, Nikolay Borissovich sang—maybe not like a canary, but he sang anyway. He's in the Witness Protection Program right now. They still bring him in every so often to get him to sing some more. The people you bag, they never give you everything all at once, and so you go back to them periodically. It makes them feel important—enough that they sing some more, usually. He's still not a happy camper. He can't go home. They'd shoot his ass. The Russians have never been real forgiving on state treason. Well, neither are we. So, he lives here with federal protection. Last I heard, he took up golf. His daughter got married to some old-money aristocrat asshole in Virginia. She's a real American now, but her dad will die an unhappy man. He wanted to take the Soviet Union over, by which I mean he *really* wanted that job, but your father screwed that one up for all time, and Nick still carries the grudge."

"I'll be damned."

"Anything new with Sali?" Wills asked, bringing things back to reality.

"There's some little stuff. You know, fifty thousand here, eighty thousand there—pounds, not dollars. Into accounts I don't know much about. He goes through anywhere from two to eight thousand pounds a week in what he probably considers petty cash."

"Where does that cash originate?" Wills asked.

"Not entirely clear, Tony. I figure he skims some off his family account, maybe two percent that he can write off as expenses. Not quite enough to alert his father that's he stealing from Mom and Pop. I wonder how they'd react to that?" Jack speculated.

"They wouldn't cut his hand off, but they could do something worse—cut his money off. You see this guy working for a living?"

"You mean real work?" Jack had himself a brief laugh. "Somehow I don't see that happening. He's been on the gravy train too long to like driving spikes into the ties. I've been to London a lot. Hard to figure how a working stiff survives there."

Wills began humming. "'How you gonna keep 'em down on the farm after they seen Paree?'"

Jack flushed. "Look, Tony, yeah, I know I grew up rich, but Dad always made sure I had a summer job. I even worked construction for two months. Made life hard for

Mike Brennan and his pals. But Dad wanted me to know what it was like to do real work. I hated it at first, but, looking back, it was probably a good thing, I guess. Mr. Sali here has never done that. I mean, I could survive in a real-world entry-level job if I had to. It'd be a lot harder adjustment for this guy."

"Okay, how much unexplained money, total?"

"Maybe two hundred thousand pounds—three hundred thousand bucks, call it. But I haven't really pinned it down yet, and it's not all that much money."

"How much longer to narrow it down?"

"At this rate? Hell, maybe a week if I'm lucky. This is like tracking a single car during New York rush hour, y'know?"

"Keep it up. Isn't supposed to be easy, or fun."

"Aye, aye, sir." It was something he'd picked up from the Marines at the White House. They'd even said that to *him* once in a while, until his father had noticed and put an immediate end to it. Jack turned back to his computer. He kept his real notes on a pad of white lined paper, just because it was easier for him that way, then transferred them to a separate computer file every afternoon. As he wrote, he noted that Tony was leaving their little room for a trip upstairs.

"THIS KID'S got the eye," Wills told Rick Bell on the top floor.

"Oh?" It was a little early for any results from the rookie, regardless who his father was, Bell thought.

"I put him on a young Saudi living in London, name of Uda bin Sali—money changer for his family's interests. The Brits have a loose tail on him because he called somebody they found interesting once."

"And?"

"And Junior has found a couple of hundred thousand pounds that can't be accounted for."

"How solid is that?" Bell asked.

"We'll have to put a regular on it, but, you know . . . this kid's got the right sort of nose."

"Dave Cunningham, maybe?" A forensic accountant, he'd joined The Campus out of the Department of Justice, Organized Crime Division. Pushing sixty, Dave had a legendary nose for numbers. The trading department at The Campus mainly used him for "conventional" duties. He could have done very well on Wall Street, but he'd just loved bagging bad guys for a living. At The Campus, he could pursue that avocation well past government retirement rules.

"Dave'd be my pick," Tony agreed.

"Okay, let's cross-load Jack's computer files to Dave and see what he turns over."

"Works for me, Rick. You see the take-report from NSA yesterday?"

"Yeah. Got my attention," Bell answered, looking up. Three days before, message traffic from sources that the government intelligence services found interesting had dropped by seventeen percent and two *particularly* interesting sources had almost completely stopped. When radio traffic in a military unit did that, it often meant a standdown prior to real operations. The sort of thing that made signals-intelligence people nervous. The majority of the time, it meant nothing at all, just random chance in operation, but it had developed into something real often enough that the signal-spooks frequently went into a tizzy about it.

"Any ideas?" Wills asked.

Bell shook his head. "I stopped being superstitious about ten years ago."

Clearly, Tony Wills had not: "Rick, we're due. We've been due for a long time."

"I know what you're saying, but we can't run this place on that sort of stuff."

"Rick, this is like sitting at a ball game—dugout seats, maybe, but you still can't go on the field when you want."

"To do what, kill the umpire?" Bell asked.

"No, just the guy planning to throw a beanball."

"Patience, Tony, patience."

"Son of a bitch of a virtue to acquire, isn't it?" Wills had never quite learned it, despite all his experience.

"Think you have it bad? What about Gerry?"

"Yeah, Rick, I know." He stood. "Later, man."

THEY'D SEEN not another human being, not a car, not a helicopter. Clearly, there was nothing of value out here. No oil, no gold, not even copper. Nothing worth guarding or protecting. The walk had just been enough to be healthy. Some scrubby bushes, even some stunted trees. A few tire tracks, but none of them recent. This part of America might as well have been Saudi Arabia's Empty Quarter, the Rub' al-Khali, where even a hardy desert camel would have found it grim going.

But clearly the walk was over. As they crested a small rise, they saw five more vehicles sitting all alone, with men standing by them talking among themselves.

"Ah," Ricardo said, "they are early, too. Excellent." He could dump these morose foreigners and get on with his business. He stopped and let his clients catch up.

"This is our destination?" Mustafa asked, with hope in his voice. It had been an easy walk, far easier than he'd expected.

"My friends there will take you to Las Cruces. There you can make your travel plans for the future."

"And you?" Mustafa asked.

"I go home to my family," Ricardo answered. Wasn't that simple enough? Maybe this guy didn't have a family?

The remaining walk took only ten minutes. Ricardo got in the lead SUV after shaking hands with his party. They were friendly enough, albeit in a guarded fashion. It could have been harder to get them here, but illegal-immigrant traffic was far thicker in Arizona and California, and that was where the U.S. Border Patrol had most of its personnel. The gringos tended to grease the squeaky wheel—like everyone else in the world, perhaps, but still it was not terribly farsighted of them. Sooner or later, they'd realize that there was cross-border traffic here, too. Just not the dramatic sort. Then he might have to find a new way to make a living. He'd done well the past seven years, however—enough to set up a little business and raise his children into a more legitimate line of work.

He watched his party board their transport and motor off. He also headed in the general direction of Las Cruces, then turned south on I-10 toward El Paso. He'd long since stopped wondering what his clients planned to do in America. Probably not tending gardens or doing construction work, he judged, but he'd been paid ten thousand dollars in American cash. So, they were important to someone...but not to him.

|||||||||||||||||||||||||||||||||||||||||||||||||||||||||

CHAPTER 10

DESTINATIONS

FOR MUSTAFA and his friends, the ride to Las Cruces was a surprisingly welcome break, and though they didn't show it, there was obvious excitement now. They were in America. Here were the people they proposed to kill. The mission was now somehow closer to fulfillment, not by a mere handful of kilometers, but by a magical, invisible line. They were in the home of the Great Satan. Here were the people who had rained death upon their homeland, and upon the Faithful throughout the Muslim world, the people who so fawningly supported Israel.

At Deming, they turned east for Las Cruces. Sixty-two miles—a hundred kilometers—to their next intermediate stop, along I-10. There were billboards advertising road hotels and places to eat, tourist attractions of types routine and inconceivable, and more rolling land, and horizons which seemed far even as the car ate up the distances at a steady seventy miles per hour.

Their driver, as before, looked Mexican, and said nothing. Probably another mercenary. Nobody said anything, the driver because he didn't care, his passengers because their English was accented, and the driver might take note of it. This way he'd only remember that he'd picked up some people on a dirt road in southern New Mexico and driven them someplace else.

It was probably harder for the others in his party, Mustafa thought. They had to trust him to know what he was doing. He was the mission commander, the leader of a warrior band about to divide into four parts that would never reunite. The mission had been painstakingly planned. The only future communications would be via computer, and few enough of those. They'd function independently, but to a simple timetable and toward a single strategic objective. This plan would shake America as no other plan had ever done, Mustafa told himself, looking into a station wagon as it passed them. Two parents, and what appeared to be two little ones, a boy about four, and a smaller one perhaps a year and a half. Infidels, all of them. Targets.

His operational plan was all written down, of course, in fourteen-point Geneva type on sheets of plain white paper. Four copies. One for each team leader. The other data was in files on the personal computers that all of the men had in their small carry-bags, along with spare shirts and clean underwear and little else. They would not need much, and the plan was to leave very little behind in order to further befuddle the Americans.

It was enough to generate a thin smile at the passing countryside. Mustafa lit up a cigarette—he only had three left—and took a deep breath of tobacco smoke, and the air-conditioning blew cold air on him. Behind them, the sun was declining in the sky. They'd make their next—and last—stop in the darkness, which, he considered, was good tactical planning. He knew it was only an accident, but, if so, it meant that Allah Himself was smiling on their plan. As He ought to do, of course. They were all doing His work.

* * *

ANOTHER DULL day's work done, Jack told himself on the way to his car. One bad thing about The Campus was that he couldn't discuss it with anybody. *Nobody* was cleared for this stuff, though it was not yet evident why. He could, surely, kick this around with his dad—the President was by definition cleared for anything, and ex-Presidents had the same access to information, if not by law, then by the rules of practicality. But, no, he couldn't do that. Dad would not be pleased by his new job. Dad could make a phone call and screw all of that up, and Jack had had enough of a taste to keep himself hungry for a few months at least. Even so, the ability to kick a few things around with *somebody* who knew what was going on would have been a blessing of sorts. Just someone to say, yes, it really *is* important, and, yes, you really *are* contributing to Truth, Justice, and the American Way.

Could he really make a difference? The world worked the way it worked, and he couldn't change it much. Even his father, for all the power that had come to him, had been unable to do that. How much less could he, a junior prince of sorts, be able to accomplish? But if the broken parts of the world were ever to be fixed, it would have to be at the hands of someone who didn't care if it were impossible or not. Probably someone too young and dumb to know that impossible things were . . . impossible. But neither his mother nor his father believed in that word, and that's the way they had raised him. Sally was graduating medical school soon, and she was going into oncology—the one thing their mother had regretted not doing with her own medical career—and she told everyone who asked that she was going to be there when the cancer dragon was finally slain once and for all. So, believing in impossibility was not part of the Ryan creed. He just didn't know how yet, but the world was full of things to learn, wasn't it? And he was smart and well educated, and having a sizable trust fund meant that he could go forward without fear of starving if he offended the wrong person. That was the most important freedom his father had bequeathed him, and John Patrick Ryan, Jr., was smart enough to know just how important it was—if not to grasp the responsibility that such freedom carried with it.

INSTEAD OF cooking their own dinner, they decided to go to a local steak house that night. It was full of college kids from the University of Virginia. You could tell—they all looked bright, but not as bright as they thought they were, and they were all a little too loud, a little too confident in themselves. That was one of the advantages of being children—much as they would have detested that appellation—kids whose needs were still looked after by loving parents, albeit at a comfortable distance. To the two Caruso boys, it was a humorous look at what they'd themselves been only a few short years ago, before harsh training and experience in the real world had turned them into something else. Exactly what, they were not yet sure. What had seemed so simple in school had become infinitely complex after leaving the academic womb. The world was not digital, after all—it was an analog reality, always untidy, always with loose ends that could never be tied up neatly like shoelaces, and so it was possible to trip and fall with every incautious step. And caution only came with experience—with a few trip-and-falls that brought pain, only the worst of which taught remembered lessons. Those lessons had come early to the brothers. Not as early as they'd come to other generations, but still soon enough for them to realize the consequences of errors in a world that had never learned to forgive.

"Not a bad place," Brian judged, halfway through his filet mignon.

"Hard to mess up a decent piece of beef, no matter how dumb the cook is." This place obviously had a cook, not a chef, but the steak fries were pretty good for nearly raw carbohydrates, and the broccoli was fresh out of the freezer bag, Dominic thought.

"I really ought to eat better than this," the Marine major observed.

"Enjoy it while you can. We're not thirty yet, are we?"

That was good for a laugh. "Used to seem like an awfully big number, didn't it?"

"Where old age starts? Oh yeah. Well, you're pretty young for a major, right?"

Aldo shrugged. "I suppose. My boss liked me, and I had some good people working for me. I never did take a liking to MREs, though. They keep you going, but that's about all I can say for them. My gunny loved the things, said they were better than what he'd grown up in the Corps with."

"In the Bureau, you tend to live on Dunkin' Donuts and—well, they make about the best industrial coffee in America. It's hard to keep your belt loose on that kind of diet."

"You're in decent shape for a deskbound warrior, Enzo," Brian observed rather generously. At the end of the morning run, his brother occasionally looked as though he was about to drop. But a three-mile run was just like morning coffee for a Marine, something to open the eyes. "I still wish I knew exactly what we're training for," Aldo said after another bite.

"Bro, we're training to kill people, that's all we need to know. Sneak up without being seen, and then get the hell away without being noticed."

"With pistols?" Brian responded dubiously. "Kinda noisy, and not as sure as a rifle. I had a sniper with my team in Afghanistan. He did some bad guys at damned near a mile. Used a Barrett .50 rifle, big mother, like an old BAR on steroids. Shoots the .50 round from the Ma Deuce machine gun. Accurate as hell, and it makes for a definitive hit, y'know? Kinda hard to walk away with a half-inch hole in you." Especially since his sniper, Corporal Alan Roberts, a black kid from Detroit, had preferred head shots, and the .50 *really* did the job on heads.

".Well, maybe suppressed ones. You can silence a hand-gun fairly well."

"I've seen those. We trained with them at Recon School, but they're awful bulky for carrying under a business suit, and you still have to take them out and stand still and aim them at the target's head. Unless they send us to James Bond School to get courses in magic, we're not going to be killing many people with handguns, Enzo."

"Well, maybe we'll be using something else."

"So you don't know, either?"

"Hey, man, my checks still come from the Bureau. All I know is that Gus Werner sent me here, and that makes it most-of-the-way kosher . . . I think," he concluded.

"You mentioned him before. Who is he, exactly?"

"Assistant Director, head of the new Counter-Terrorism Division. You don't fuck with Gus. He was head of the Hostage Rescue Team, got all his other tickets punched, too. Smart guy, and tough as hell. I don't think he faints at the sight of blood. But he's also got a real head on his shoulders. Terrorism is the new thing at the Bureau, and Dan Murray didn't pick him for the job just because he can shoot a gun. He and Murray are tight, they go back twenty-plus years. Murray ain't no dummy, either. Anyway, if he sent me here, it's gotta be okay with somebody. So, I'll play along until they tell me to break the law."

"Me, too, but I'm still a little nervous."

LAS CRUCES had a regional airport for short hauls and puddle jumpers. Along with that came rent-a-car out-lets. They pulled in, and it was time for Mustafa to get ner-vous. He and one of his colleagues would hire cars here. Two more would make use of a similar business in the town itself.

"It is all prepared for you," the driver told them. He handed over two sheets of paper. "Here are the reservation numbers. You'll be driving Ford Crown Victoria four-door sedans. We could not get you station wagons as requested without going to El Paso, and that was not desirable. Use your Visa card in there. Your name is Tomas Salazar. Your friend is Hector Santos. Show them the reservation numbers and just do what they tell you to do. It is very easy." Neither man struck the driver as overly Latin in appearance, but the people at this rental office were both ignorant paddies who spoke little Spanish beyond "*taco*" and "*cerveza*."

Mustafa got out of the car and walked in, waving for his friend to follow.

Immediately, he knew it would be easy. Whoever owned this business, he hadn't troubled himself with recruiting intelligent people. The boy running the desk was hunched over it, reading a comic book with attention that looked a little too rapt.

"Hello," Mustafa said, with false confidence. "I have reservation." He wrote the number down on a pad and handed it to him.

"Okay." The attendant didn't show his annoyance at being diverted from the newest Batman adventure. He knew how to work the office computer. Sure enough, the computer spat out a rental form already filled out in most details.

Mustafa handed over his international driver's license, which the employee Xeroxed, and then he stapled the photocopy to his copy of the rental form. He was delighted that Mr. Salazar took all of the insurance options—he got extra money for encouraging people to do that.

"Okay, your car is the white Ford in slot number four. Just go out that door and turn right. The keys are in the ignition, sir."

"Thank you," Mustafa said in accented English. *Was it really* this *easy?*

Evidently, it was. He'd just got the seat in his Ford adjusted when Saeed showed up at slot number five for a light green twin to his sedan. Both had maps of the state of New Mexico, but they didn't need them, really. Both men started their cars and eased out of their parking slots and headed off to the street, where the SUVs were waiting. It was simple enough to follow them. The town of Las Cruces had traffic, but not all that much at the dinner hour.

There was another rental car agency just eight blocks north on what appeared to be the main street of Las Cruces. This one was called Hertz, which struck Mustafa as vaguely Jewish in character. His two comrades walked in, and, ten minutes later, walked back out and got in their leased cars. Again, they were Fords of the same make as his and Saeed's. With that done, perhaps the most hazardous mission they had to accomplish, it was time to follow the SUVs north for a few kilometers—about twenty, as it turned out—then off this road onto another dirt one. There seemed to be a lot of those here . . . just like home, in fact. Another kilometer or so, and there was a house standing alone, with only a truck parked nearby to suggest residency. There, all the vehicles parked and the occupants got out for what would be, Mustafa realized, their last proper meeting.

"We have your weapons here," Juan told them. He pointed to Mustafa. "Come with me, please."

The inside of this ordinary-looking wood-frame structure appeared to be a virtual arsenal. A total of sixteen cardboard boxes held sixteen MAC-10 sub-machine guns. Not an elegant firearm, the MAC is made of machine-steel stampings, with a generally poor finish on the metal. With each weapon were twelve magazines, apparently all loaded, and taped together end-to-end with black electrician's tape.

"The weapons are virgins. They have not been fired," Juan told them. "We also have suppressors for each of them. They are not efficient silencers, but they improve balance and accuracy. This gun is not as easily handled as the Uzi—but those are also more difficult to obtain here. For this weapon, its effective range is about ten meters. It is easily loaded and unloaded. It fires from an open bolt, of course, and the rate of fire is quite high." It would, in fact, empty a thirty-round magazine in less than three seconds, which was a little *too* fast for sensible use, but these people didn't seem overly particular to Juan.

They weren't. Each of the sixteen Arabs lifted a weapon and hefted it, as though to say hello to a new friend. Then one lifted a magazine pair—

"Stop! *Halto!*" Juan snapped at once. "You will not load these weapons inside. If you wish to test-fire them, we have targets outside."

"Will this not be too noisy?" Mustafa asked.

"The nearest house is four kilometers away," Juan answered dismissively. The bullets could not travel that far, and he assumed the noise could not either. In this, he was mistaken.

But his guests assumed he knew everything about the area, and they were always willing to shoot guns off, especially the rock-and-roll kind. Twenty meters from the house was a sand berm with some crates and cardboard boxes scattered about. One by one, they inserted the magazines into their SMGs and pulled back the bolts. There was no official command to fire. Instead, they took their lead from Mustafa, who grasped the strap dangling from the muzzle and pulled his trigger back.

The immediate results were agreeable. The MAC-10 made the appropriate noise, jumping up and right as all such weapons did, but since this was his first time and this was just range shooting, he managed to walk his rounds into a cardboard box about six meters to his left front. In seemingly no time at all, the bolt slammed shut on an empty chamber, having fired and ejected thirty Remington 9mm pistol cartridges. He thought of extracting the magazine and reversing it to enjoy another two or three seconds of blazing bliss, but he managed to control himself. There would be another time for that, in the not-too-distant future.

"The silencers?" he asked Juan.

"Inside. They screw on the muzzle, and it's better to screw them on—easier to control how they spray their bullets, you see." Juan spoke with some authority. He'd used the MAC-10 to eliminate business competitors and other unpleasant people in Dallas and Santa Fe over the years. Despite that, he looked on his guests with a certain unease. They grinned too much. They were not as he was, Juan Sandoval told himself, and the sooner they went on their way, the better. It would not be so for the people at their destinations, but that was not his concern. His orders came from on high. *Very* on high, his immediate superior had made clear to him the week before. And the money had been commensurate. Juan had no particular complaint, but, as a good reader of people, he had a red light flashing behind his eyes.

Mustafa followed him back in and picked up the suppressor. It was perhaps ten centimeters in diameter, and half a meter or so long. As promised, it screwed onto the thread on the gun's muzzle, and on the whole, it did improve the weapon's balance. He hefted it briefly and decided that he'd prefer to use it this way. Better to reduce muzzle climb, and make for more accurate shooting. The reduction in noise had little bearing on his mission, but accuracy did. But the suppressor made an easily concealed weapon unacceptably bulky. So, he unscrewed it for now, and replaced the silencer in its carry-bag. Then he went outside to gather his people. Juan followed him back out.

"Some things you need to know," he told the team leaders. Juan went on in a slow, measured voice: "The American police are efficient, but they are not all-powerful. If, during your driving, one pulls you over, all you need to do is to speak politely. If he asks you to get out of the car, then get out as he says. He is allowed by American laws to see if you have a weapon on your person—to search you with his hands—but if he asks you to search your car, simply say no, I do not wish you to do that—and by their laws he may *not* search your car. I will say this again: If an American policeman asks to search your car, you need only say no, and then he may not do it. Then drive away. When you drive, do not go faster than the number on the highway signs. If you do that, you will probably not be disturbed in any way. If you go faster than the speed limit, all you do is to give the police a reason to pull you over. So, *do not do that.* Exercise patience at all times. Do you have any questions?"

"What if a policeman is too aggressive, can we—"

Juan knew that question was coming. "Kill one? Yes, it is possible to do so, but then you will have many more police chasing you. When a police officer pulls you over, the very first thing he will do is radio his location, and the license number of your car, and a description, to his headquarters. So, even if you kill him, his comrades will look for you in a matter of minutes—and in large numbers. It is not worth the satisfaction of killing the policeman. You will only invite more trouble on yourselves. American police forces have many cars, and even aircraft. Once they start looking for you, they *will* find you. So, your only defense against that is to escape notice. Do not speed. Do not break their traffic laws. Do that and you will be safe. Violate those laws, and you will be caught, guns or not. Do you understand this?"

"We understand," Mustafa assured him. "Thank you for your assistance."

"We have maps for all of you. They are good maps, from the American Automobile Association. You all have cover stories, yes?" Juan asked, hoping to get this over as quickly as he could.

Mustafa looked at his friends for additional inquiries, but they were too eager to get on with their business to be sidetracked now. Satisfied, he turned to Juan. "Thank you for your help, my friend."

Friend be damned, Juan thought, but he took the man's hand and walked them around to the front of the building. Bags were quickly transferred from the SUVs to the sedans, and then he watched them pull off, heading back to State Route 185. It was only a few miles to Radium Springs, and the entrance onto I-25 North. The foreigners gathered one last time, to shake hands—and even share a few kisses, Juan was surprised to see. Then they split up into four teams of four men each and entered their rental cars.

Mustafa settled in his car. He set his cigarette packs on the seat next to him, made sure that the mirrors were properly aligned for his eyes, and buckled his seat belt—he'd been told that not buckling was as likely as speeding to get himself pulled over. Above all things, he didn't want to be pulled over by a policeman. Despite the briefing instructions he'd received from Juan, it was a risk he felt no desire to run. Passing by, a cop might not recognize them for what they were, but face-to-face was something else again, and he had no illusions about how Americans thought of Arabs. For that reason, all copies of the Holy Koran were tucked away in the trunk.

It would be a long time, Abdullah would spell him at the wheel, but the first stint would be his. North on I-25 to Albuquerque, then east on I-40 almost all the way to their target. Over three thousand kilometers. He'd have to start thinking in miles now, Mustafa told himself. One point six kilometers to a mile. He'd have to multiply every number by that constant, or just disregard metric altogether as far as his car was concerned. Whatever, he drove north on Route 185 until he saw the leaf-green sign and the arrow for I-25 North. He settled back in his seat, checked traffic as he merged, and increased speed to sixty-five miles per hour, setting the Ford's cruise control right on that number. After that, it was just a matter of steering, and watching all of the anonymous traffic which, like him and his friends, was headed north to Albuquerque...

JACK DIDN'T know why it was hard to go to sleep. It was past eleven in the evening, he'd seen his nightly take of TV, and had his two or three—tonight it had been three—drinks. He should have been sleepy. He *was* sleepy, as a matter of fact, but sleep wasn't coming. And he didn't know why. Just close your eyes and think happy thoughts, his mom had told him as a little boy. But thinking happy thoughts was the hard part now that he wasn't a kid anymore. He'd entered into a new world that had few enough of those in it. His job was to examine the known and suspected facts concerning people he'd probably never meet, try to decide if they wanted to kill other people he'd never meet, then pass the information on to other people who might or might not try to do something about it. Exactly *what* they would try to do he did not know, though he had his suspicions ... and ugly suspicions they were. Roll over, refluff the pillow, try to find a cool spot in the pillowcase, head back down, get some sleep ...

... it wasn't happening. It would, eventually. It always did, seemingly half a second before the clock radio went off.

God damn *it!* he raged at the ceiling.

He was hunting terrorists. Most of them believed something good—no, something heroic—about themselves as they went about their crimes. To them it wasn't a crime at all. For Muslim terrorists, it was the illusion that they were doing God's work. Except the Holy Koran didn't really say that. It particularly disapproved of killing innocent people, noncombatants. How did that really work? Did Allah greet suicide bombers with a smile, or something else? In Catholicism, personal conscience was sovereign. If you truly believed you were doing the right thing, then God couldn't slam you for it. Was Islam the same in its rules? Besides, since there was only *one* God, maybe the rules *were* the same for everybody. Problem was, which set of religious rules came closest to what God really thought? And how the hell did you tell which was which? The Crusades had done some pretty vile things. But that was a classic case of someone giving a religious title for a war that was really about economics and simple ambition. A nobleman just didn't want to appear to be fighting for money—

and with God on your side, there was nothing you couldn't do. Swing the sword, and whatever neck you severed was okay. The bishop said so.

Right. The real problem was that religion and political power made a shitty mix, though one easily adopted by the young and enthusiastic, for whom adventure was something that just pulled at your sleeve. His father had talked about that, sometimes, over dinner on the Residence Level of the White House, explaining that one of the things you had to tell young soldier and Marine recruits was that even war had rules, and that breaking them carried stiff penalties. American soldiers learned that pretty easily, Jack Sr. had told his son, because they came from a society in which undisciplined violence was harshly punished, which was better than abstract principle for teaching right and wrong. After a smack or two, you kinda picked up the message.

He sighed, and rolled over again. He was really too young to think about such Great Questions of Life, even though his degree from Georgetown suggested otherwise. Colleges typically did not tell you that ninety percent of your education came after you hung the parchment on the wall. People might ask for a rebate.

IT WAS past closing time at The Campus. Gerry Hendley was in his top-floor office, going over data that he hadn't been able to fit into the normal working day. It was the same for Tom Davis, who had reports from Pete Alexander.

"Trouble?" Hendley asked.

"The twins are still thinking a little too much, Gerry. We should have anticipated it. They're both smart, and they're both people who play within the rules, for the most part, so when they see themselves being trained to violate those rules it worries them. The funny part, Pete says, is that the Marine's the one who's worrying so much. The FBI one is playing along much better."

"I would have expected it to go the other way."

"So did I. And Pete." Davis reached for his ice water. He

never drank coffee this late at night. "Anyway, Pete says he's unsure how it's going to play out, but he has no choice other than to continue the training. Gerry, I should have warned you more about this. I figured we'd have this problem. Hell, it's our first time. The sort of people we want—like I said, they're not psychopaths. They *will* ask questions. They *will* want to know why. They *will* have second thoughts. We can't recruit robots, can we?"

"Like when they tried to whack Castro," Hendley observed. He'd read into the classified files on that mad, failed adventure. Bobby Kennedy had ramrodded Operation MONGOOSE. They'd probably decided over drinks, or maybe after some touch football, to play that game. After all, Eisenhower had used CIA for similar purposes during his presidency, so why shouldn't they? Except that a former lieutenant in the Navy who'd lost his command to ramming, and a lawyer who'd never practiced law, did not instinctively know all the things that a career soldier who'd gone to five stars fully understood from the very beginning. And besides, they'd had the power. The Constitution itself had made Jack Kennedy Commander in Chief, and with that sort of power invariably came the urge to make use of it, and so reshape the world into something more amenable to his personal outlook. And so, CIA had been ordered to make Castro go away. But CIA had never had an assassination department, and had never trained people to perform such missions. And so, the Agency had gone to the Mafia, whose commission members had little reason to admire Fidel Castro—who had shut down what had been about to become their most profitable venture ever. It'd been so sure a thing that some of the organized-crime big shots had invested their own, personal, money in the Havana casinos, only to have them closed down by the communist dictator.

And did not the Mafia know how to kill people?

Well, in fact, no, they had never been very efficient at it—especially at killing people able to fight back—Hollywood movies to the contrary. And even so, the government of the United States of America had tried to use them as contractors for the assassination of a foreign chief of state—because CIA didn't know how to make such a thing happen. It was, in retrospect, somewhat ludicrous. Somewhat? Gerry Hendley asked himself. It had come within an inch of exposure as a government-engineered train wreck. Enough to force President Gerry Ford into drafting his executive order that made such action illegal, and *that* order had lasted until President Ryan had decided to take out the religious dictator of Iran with two smart bombs. Remarkably, the time and circumstances had disabled the news media from commenting on the killing. It had been done, after all, by the United States Air Force, with properly marked—albeit stealthy—bomber aircraft in a time of an undeclared but very real war in which weapons of mass destruction had been used against American citizens. Those factors had combined to make the entire operation not only legitimate but laudable, as ratified by the American people at the following election. Only George Washington had garnered a larger plurality at the polls, a fact which still made the senior Jack Ryan uneasy. But Jack had known the import of the killing of Mahmoud Haji Daryaei, and so, before leaving office, had talked Gerry into establishing The Campus.

But Jack didn't tell me how hard this would be, Hendley reminded himself. That was how Jack Ryan had always operated: Pick good people, give them a mission and the tools to accomplish it, then let them do it with minimal guidance from on high. It was what had made him a good boss, and a pretty good president, Gerry thought. But it didn't make life much easier on his subordinates. Why the *hell* had he taken the assignment? Hendley asked himself. But then came a smile. How would Jack react when he found out his own son was part of The Campus? Would he see the humor of it?

Probably not.

"So, Pete says just to play it out?"

"What else can he say?" Davis asked in reply.

"Tom, ever wish you were back on your dad's farm in Nebraska?"

"It's awful hard work, and kind of dull out there." And there was no way you were going to keep Davis down on the farm after he'd been a CIA field officer. He might be a pretty good bond trader now in his "white" life, but Davis was no more white in his true avocation than he was in his skin color. He liked the action in the "black" world too much.

"What do you think of the Fort Meade stuff?"

"My gut tells me we're due for something. We've stung them. They'll want to sting us back."

"You think they can recover? Haven't our troops in Afghanistan bit into them pretty hard?"

"Gerry, some people are too dumb, or too dedicated, to notice being hurt. Religion is a powerful motivator. And even if their shooters are too dumb to know the import of what they're doing—"

"—they're smart enough to carry out missions," Hendley agreed.

"And isn't that why we're here?" Davis asked.

CHAPTER 11

CROSSING THE RIVER

THE SUN rose promptly at dawn. Mustafa was startled awake by the combination of bright light and a bump in the road. He shook his head clear and turned to see Abdullah smiling at the wheel.

"Where are we?" the team leader asked his principal subordinate.

"We are half an hour east of Amarillo. It has been a pleasant drive for the past three hundred and fifty miles, but I will soon need petrol."

"Why didn't you wake me hours ago?"

"Why? You were sleeping pleasantly, and the road has been almost completely clear all night, except for those damned big trucks. These Americans must all sleep at night. I do not think I have seen more than thirty real automobiles in the past several hours."

Mustafa checked the speedometer. The car was only doing sixty-five. So, Abdullah was not speeding. They hadn't been stopped by any policemen. There was nothing to be upset about—except that Abdullah had not followed his orders as precisely as Mustafa would have preferred.

"There." The driver pointed at a blue service sign. "We can get petrol and some food. I was planning to wake you up here anyway, Mustafa. Be at ease, my friend." The fuel gauge was almost on the "E," Mustafa saw. Abdullah had been foolish to let it get that low, but there was no sense in berating him for it.

They pulled into a sizable travel plaza. The gas pumps were labeled Chevron and were automated. Mustafa took out his wallet and inserted his Visa card in the slot, then filled up the Ford with over twenty gallons of premium gasoline.

By that time, the other three had cycled through the plaza's men's room and were examining the food options. Looked like doughnuts again. Ten minutes after pulling the car off the interstate highway, they were back onto it, heading east for Oklahoma. In another twenty minutes, they'd entered it.

In the back of the car, Rafi and Zuhayr were awake and talking, and, as he drove, Mustafa listened in without joining the conversation.

The land was flat, similar to home in its topography, though far greener. The horizon was surprisingly far away, enough so that estimating distance seemed impossible on first glance. The sun was above the horizon, and it burned into his eyes until he remembered the sunglasses in his shirt pocket. They helped somewhat.

Mustafa remarked to himself on his current state of mind. He found the driving pleasant, the passing terrain pleasing to the eye, and the work, such as it was, easy. Every ninety minutes or so, he saw a marked police car, usually passing his Ford at a good clip, too fast for the policeman inside to eyeball him and his friends. It had been good advice to cruise right on the speed limit. They moved along nicely, but people regularly passed them, even the big trucks. Not breaking the law even a little made them invisible to the police whose main business was to punish those in too great a hurry. He was confident that their mission security was solid. Had it not been the case, they'd have been followed, or pulled over on a particularly deserted stretch of highway into a trap with guns and many, many enemies. But that hadn't happened. An additional advantage of driving right on the speed limit was that anyone tailing them would stand out. It was just a matter of checking his mirror. No one lingered there for more than a few minutes. Any police shadow would be a man—it would have to be a man—in his twenties or thirties. Maybe two of them, one to drive and one to look. The men would be physically fit looking, with conservative haircuts. They'd tail for a few minutes before breaking contact, as someone else took the surveillance job over. They'd be clever, of course, but the nature of the mission made their procedures predictable. Some cars would disappear and reappear. But Mustafa was fully alert, and no car had appeared more than once. They might be tailed by aircraft, of course, but helicopters were easy to spot. The only real danger was a small fixed-wing aircraft, but he could not worry about everything. If it were written, then written it was, and there was no defense against that. For the moment, the road was clear and the coffee was excellent. It would be a fine day. OKLAHOMA CITY 36 MILES, the green road sign proclaimed.

NPR ANNOUNCED that it was Barbra Streisand's birthday, a vital piece of information with which to begin the day, John Patrick Ryan, Jr., told himself as he rolled out of bed and headed for the bathroom. A few minutes later, he saw that his clock-controlled coffeemaker had functioned properly and dripped two cups into the white plastic pot. He decided to hit McDonald's this morning and get an Egg McMuffin and hash browns on the way to work. It wasn't exactly a healthy breakfast, but it was filling, and at twenty-three he wasn't overly worried about cholesterol and fat, as his father was, courtesy of his mother. Mom would already be dressed and ready to be driven to Hopkins (by her principal agent of the Secret Service) for her morning's work, without coffee if she was operating today, because she worried that caffeine might give her hand a slight tremor—and drive her little knife into the poor bastard's brain after skewering the eyeball like the olive in a martini (that was his father's joke, which usually resulted in a playful slap from Mom). Dad would go to work on his memoirs, assisted by a ghostwriter (which he detested— but the publisher had insisted). Sally was in the pretend-doc stage of medical school; he didn't know what she was doing at this moment. Katie and Kyle would be dressing for school. But Little Jack had to go to work. It had recently occurred to him that college had been his last real vacation. Oh, sure, every little boy and girl wants nothing more than to grow up and take proper charge of his or her life, but then you get there—and it's too late to go back. This work-every-day thing was a drag. Okay, fine, you got paid for it—but he was *already* rich, the scion of a distinguished family. The money, in his case, was already *made,* and he wasn't the kind of wastrel likely to piss it all away and become a self-unmade man, was he? He set his empty coffee cup in the dishwasher and went to the bathroom to shave.

That was *another* drag. Damn, a teenybopper was so pleased to see the first bunch of peach fuzz turn dark and bristly, and then you got to shave once or twice a week, usually before a date. But every damned morning—what a pain in the ass that was! He remembered watching his father do it, as young boys often do, and thinking how neat it was to be a grown man. Yeah, sure. Growing up just wasn't worth the hassle. It was better to have a mom and dad to take care of all the administrative bullshit. And yet...

And yet, he was doing important stuff now, and that did have its satisfactions, sort of. Once you got past all the housekeeping that accompanied it. Well. Clean shirt. Pick a tie and tie tack. Slide the jacket on. Out the door. At least he had a fun car to drive. He might get himself another. A ragtop, maybe. Summer was coming, and it would be cool to have the wind blowing in your hair. Until some pervert with a knife slashed the canvas top, and you had to call the insurance company and the car vanished into the shop for three days. When you got down to it, growing up was like going to the shopping mall to buy underwear. Everyone needed it, but there wasn't much you could do with it except take it off.

The drive to work was about as routine as driving to school, except he didn't have to worry about an exam anymore. Except that if he screwed up, he'd lose the job, and *that* black mark would follow him a lot longer than an "F" in sociology would. So, he didn't want to screw up. The problem with this job was that every day was spent in learning, not in applying knowledge. The whole big lie about college was that it taught you what you needed to know for life. Yeah, right. It probably hadn't done that for his dad—and for Mom, hell, she *never* stopped reading her medical journals to learn about new stuff. Not just American journals, either, English and French, too, because she spoke pretty good French and she said that French docs were good. Better than their politicians were, but, then again, anyone who judged America by its political leaders probably thought the U.S. of A. was a nation of fuckups. At least since his dad had checked out of the White House.

He was listening to NPR again. It was his favorite news station, and it beat listening to the current brand of popular music. He'd grown up listening to his mom on the piano, mostly Bach and his peers—maybe a little John Williams in a gesture toward modernity, though he wrote more for brass than the ivories.

Another suicide bomber in Israel. Damn, his dad had tried awfully hard to settle that one down, but despite some earnest efforts, even by the Israelis, it had all come undone. The Jews and Muslims just could not seem to get along. His dad and Prince Ali bin Sultan talked about it whenever they got together, and the frustration they displayed was painful to see. The prince hadn't been screened for the kingship of his country—which was possibly good luck,

Jack thought, since being a king had to be even worse than being President—but he remained an important figure whose words the current king listened to most of the time... which brought him to...

Uda bin Sali. There'd be more news on him this morning. Yesterday's take from the British SIS, courtesy of the CIA pukes at Langley. CIA pukes? Jack asked himself. His own father had worked there, had served with distinction before moving up in the world, and had told his kids many times not to believe anything they saw in the movies about the intelligence business. Jack Jr. had asked him questions and mainly gotten unsatisfactory answers, and now he was learning what the business was really like. Mostly boring. Too much like accounting, like chasing after mice in Jurassic Park, though at least you had the advantage of being invisible to the raptors. Nobody knew that The Campus existed, and so long as that remained true everyone there was safe. That made for a comfortable feeling, but again, boring. Junior was still young enough to think excitement was fun.

Left off U.S. Route 29 and on to The Campus. The usual parking place. Smile and a wave at the security guard and up to his office. It was then that Junior realized he'd driven right past McDonald's, and so he picked two Danish off the treat tray, and made a cup of coffee on his way to his cubbyhole. Light up the computer and go to work.

"Good morning, Uda," Jack Jr. said to the computer screen. "What have you been up to?" The clock window on the computer said 8:25 AM. That translated to early afternoon in London's financial district. Bin Sali had an office in the Lloyd's insurance building, which, Junior remembered from previous hops across the pond, looked like a glassed-in oil refinery. Upscale neighborhood and some very wealthy neighbors. The report didn't say which floor, but Jack had never been in the building anyway. Insurance. Had to be the most boring job in the world, waiting for a building to burn down. So, yesterday Uda had made some phone calls, one of them to . . . aha! "I know that name from somewhere," the young Ryan told the screen. It was the name of a very rich Middle Eastern fellow who also had been known to play in the wrong playground on occasion, and who was also under surveillance by the Brit Security Service. So, what had they talked about?

There was even a transcript. The conversation had been in Arabic, and the translation . . . might as well have been instructions from the wife to buy a quart of milk on the way home from work. About that exciting and revealing—except that Uda had replied to a totally innocuous statement with "Are you sure?" *Not* the sort of thing you said to the wife when she said to get a quart of skim milk on the way home.

"The tone of voice suggests hidden meaning," the Brit analyst had opined gently at the bottom of the report.

Then, later in the day, Uda had left his office early and entered another pub and met with the same guy he'd been talking to on the phone. So, the conversation hadn't been innocuous after all? But, though they hadn't managed to overhear the conversation in a pub booth, neither had the phone chat specified a meeting or a meeting place . . . and Uda didn't spend much time in that particular pub.

"'Morning, Jack," Wills greeted as he came in and hung up his suit jacket. "What's happening?"

"Our friend Uda is wiggling like a live fish." Jack punched the PRINT command and handed the printout across to his roomie even before he'd had a chance to sit down.

"It seems to suggest that possibility, doesn't it?"

"Tony, this guy is a player," Jack said with some conviction in his voice.

"What did he do after the phone conversation? Any unusual transactions?"

"I haven't checked yet, but if there is, then he was ordered to do it by his friend, and then they met so that he could confirm it over a pint of John Smith's Bitter."

"You're making a leap of imagination. We try to avoid that here," Wills cautioned.

"I know," Junior growled. It was time to check out the previous day's money-moving.

"Oh, you're to be meeting somebody new today."

"Who's that?"

"Dave Cunningham. Forensic accountant, used to work for Justice—organized-crime stuff. He's pretty good at spotting financial irregularities."

"Does he think I found something interesting?" Jack asked with hope in his voice.

"We'll see when he gets here—after lunch. He's probably looking over your stuff right now."

"Okay," Jack responded. Maybe he'd caught the scent of something. Maybe this job really did have an element of excitement to it. Maybe they'd give him some purple ribbon for his adding machine. Sure.

THE DAYS were down to a routine. Morning run and PT, followed by breakfast and a talk. In substance, no different from Dominic's time at the FBI Academy, or Brian's at the Basic School. It was this similarity that distantly troubled the Marine. Marine Corps training was directed at killing people and breaking things. So was this.

Dominic was somewhat better at the surveillance part of it, because the FBI Academy taught it out of a book the Marines didn't have. Enzo was also pretty good with his pistol, though Aldo preferred his Beretta to his brother's Smith & Wesson. His brother had whacked a bad guy with his Smith, whereas Brian had done his job with an M16A2 rifle at a decently long range—fifty meters, close enough to see the looks on their faces when the bullets struck home, and far enough that a returning snapshot would not be close enough to be a serious worry. His gunny had chided him on not grabbing some dirt when the AKs had been turned in his direction, but Brian had learned an important lesson in his only exposure to combat. He'd found that, in that moment, his mind and his thinking went into hyperdrive, the world around him seemed to slow down, and his thinking had become extraordinarily clear. In retrospect, it had surprised him that he hadn't seen bullets in flight, his mind had been operating so fast—well, the last five rounds in the AK-47 magazine were usually tracers, and he *had* seen those in flight, though never in his immediate direction. His mind often went back to that busy five or six minutes, critiquing himself for things he might have done better, and promising that he would not repeat those errors of thinking and command, though Gunny Sullivan had been very respectful to his captain later during Caruso's after-action review with his Marines at their firebase.

"How was the run today, fellas?" Pete Alexander asked.

"Delightful," Dominic answered. "Maybe we should try it wearing fifty-pound backpacks."

"That could be arranged," Alexander replied.

"Hey, Pete, we used to do that in Force Recon. It ain't fun," Brian objected at once. "Turn down the sense of humor, bro," he added for his brother.

"Well, it's good to see you're still in shape," Pete observed comfortably. *He* didn't have to do the morning runs, after all. "So what's up?"

"I still wish I knew more about our goal here, Pete," Brian said, looking up from his coffee.

"You're not the most patient guy in the world, are you?" the training officer shot back.

"Look, in the Marine Corps we train every day, but even when it isn't clear exactly what we're training for, we know we're Marines, and we aren't getting set up to sell Girl Scout cookies in front of the Wal-Mart."

"What do you think you're getting set up for now?"

"To kill people without warning, with no rules of engagement that I can recognize. It looks a lot like murder." Okay, Brian thought, he'd said it out loud. What would happen next? Probably a drive back to Camp Lejeune and the resumption of his career in the Green Machine. Well, it could be worse.

"Okay, well, I guess it's time," Alexander conceded. "What if you had orders to terminate somebody's life?"

"If the orders are legitimate, I carry them out, but the law—the system—allows me to think about how legit the orders are."

"Okay, a hypothetical. Let's say you are ordered to terminate the life of a known terrorist. How do you react?" Pete asked.

"That's easy. You waste him," Brian answered immediately.

"Why?"

"Terrorists are criminals, but you can't always arrest them. These people make war on my country, and if I'm ordered to make war back, fine. That's what I signed on to do, Pete."

"The system doesn't always allow us to do that," Dominic observed.

"But the system does allow us to waste criminals on the spot, *in flagrante delicto,* like. You did it, and I haven't heard about any regrets, bro."

"And you won't. It's the same for you. If the President says to do somebody, and you're in uniform, he's the Commander in Chief, Aldo. You have the legal right—hell, the duty—to kill anybody he says."

"Didn't some Germans make that argument back in 1946?" Brian asked.

"I wouldn't worry too much about that. We'd have to lose a war for that to be a concern. I don't see that happening anytime soon."

"Enzo, if what you just said is true, then if the Germans had won World War Two, nobody'd need to care about those six million dead Jews. Is that what you're saying?"

"People," Alexander interrupted, "this isn't a class in legal theory."

"Enzo's the lawyer here," Brian pointed out.

Dominic took the bait: "If the President breaks the law, then the House of Representatives impeaches him and the Senate convicts him, and he's out on the street, and *then* he's subject to criminal sanctions."

"Okay. But what about the guys who carry out his orders?" Brian responded.

"That all depends," Pete told them both. "If the outgoing President has given them presidential pardons, what liability do they have?"

That answer jerked Dominic's head back. "None, I suppose. The President has sovereign power to pardon under the Constitution, the way a king did back in the old days. Theoretically, a president could pardon himself, but that would be a real legal can of worms. The Constitution is the supreme law of the land. In effect, the Constitution is God, and there is no appeal from that. You know, except when Ford pardoned Nixon, it's an area that has never really been looked into. But the Constitution is designed to be reasonably applied by reasonable men. That may be its only weakness. Lawyers are advocates, and that means they're not always reasonable."

"So, theoretically speaking, if the President gives you a pardon for killing somebody, you cannot be punished for the crime, right?"

"Correct." Dominic's face screwed in on itself somewhat. "What are you telling me?"

"Just a hypothetical," Alexander answered, backing up perceptibly. In any case, it ended the class on legal theory, and Alexander congratulated himself for telling them an awful lot and nothing at all at the same time.

THE CITY names were so alien to him, Mustafa remarked quietly to himself. Shawnee. Okemah. Weleetka. Pharaoh. That was strangest of all. They were not in Egypt, after all. That was a Muslim nation, albeit a confused one, with politics that didn't recognize the importance of the

Faith. But that would be turned around sooner or later. Mustafa stretched in his seat and reached for a smoke. Half a tank of gas still. This Ford surely had a capacious fuel tank in which to burn Muslim oil. They were such ungrateful bastards, the Americans. Islamic countries sold them oil, and what did America give in return? Weapons to the Israelis to kill Arabs with, damned little else. Dirty magazines, alcohol, and other corruption to afflict even the Faithful. But which was worse, to corrupt, or to be corrupted, to be a victim of unbelievers? Someday all would be put right, when the Rule of Allah spanned the world. It *would* come, someday, and he and his fellow warriors were even now on the leading wave of Allah's Will. Theirs would be martyrs' deaths, and that was a proud thing. In due course their families would learn of their fates—they could probably depend on Americans for that—and mourn their deaths, but celebrate their faithfulness. The American police agencies loved to show their efficiency after the battle was already lost. It was enough to make him smile.

DAVE CUNNINGHAM looked his age. He was pushing sixty pretty hard, Jack judged. Thinning gray hair. Bad skin. He'd quit smoking, but not soon enough. But his gray eyes sparkled with the curiosity of a weasel in the Dakotas, seeking after prairie dogs to eat.

"You're Jack Junior?" he asked on coming in.

"Guilty," Jack admitted. "What did you make of my numbers?"

"Not bad for an amateur," Cunningham allowed. "Your subject appears to be warehousing and laundering money—for himself, and for somebody else."

"Who is somebody else?" Wills asked.

"Not sure, but he's Middle Eastern, and he's rich, and he's tight with a buck. Funny. Everybody thinks they throw money around like drunken sailors. Some do," the accountant observed. "But some are misers. When they let go of the nickel, the buffalo screams." That showed his age. Buffalo nickels were a thing so far in the past that Jack didn't even get the joke. Then Cunningham laid some paper on the desk between Ryan and Wills. Three transactions were circled in red.

"He's a little sloppy. All his questionable transfers are done in ten-thousand-pound slugs. It makes them easy to spot. He disguises them as personal expenses—it goes into that account, probably to hide it from his parents. Saudi accountants tend to be sloppy. I guess it takes over a million of something to get them upset. They probably figure a kid like this can cut loose ten thousand pounds for a particularly nice night with the ladies, or at a casino. Young rich kids like to gamble, though they're not very good at it. If they live closer to Vegas or Atlantic City, it would do wonders for our balance of trade."

"Maybe they like European hookers better than ours?" Jack wondered aloud.

"Sonny, in Vegas you can order up a blond, blue-eyed Cambodian donkey and it'll be at your door half an hour after you set the phone down." Mafia kingpins had their favorite activities as well, Cunningham had learned over the years. It had originally offended the Methodist grandfather, but with the realization that it was just one more way to track criminals, he'd learned to welcome such expenditures. Corrupt people did corrupt things. Cunningham had also been part of Operation ELEGANT SERPENTS, which had sent six members of Congress to the federal country-club prison at Eglin Air Force Base in Florida, using methods just like this one to track his quarry. He figured it made for high-class caddies for the young fighter pilots who flew out of there, and probably good exercise for the former representatives of the people.

"Dave, is our friend Uda a player?" Jack asked.

Cunningham looked up from his papers. "He surely does wiggle like one, son."

Jack sat back in his chair with a great feeling of satisfaction. He'd actually accomplished something...maybe something important?

THE LAND got a little hilly as they entered Arkansas. Mustafa found that his reactions were a little slow after driving four hundred miles, and so he pulled off at a service plaza and, after filling the car, let Abdullah take the wheel. It was good to stretch. Then it was back onto the highway. Abdullah drove conservatively. They passed only elderly people, and stayed in the right lane to avoid being crushed by the passing truck traffic. In addition to their desire to avoid police notice, there was no real hurry. They had two more days to identify their objective and accomplish their mission. And that was plenty. He wondered what the other three teams were doing. They'd all had shorter distances to cover. One of them was probably already in its target city. Their orders were to select a decent but not opulent hotel less than an hour's drive from the objective, to conduct a reconnaissance of the objective, and then to confirm their readiness via e-mail, and sit tight until released by Mustafa to accomplish their missions. The simpler the orders, the better, of course, less chance for confusion and mistakes. They were good men, fully briefed. He knew them all. Saeed and Mehdi were, like himself, Saudi in origin, like himself children of wealthy families who'd come to despise their parents for their habit of bootlicking Americans and others like them. Sabawi was Iraqi in origin. Not born to wealth, he had come to be a true believer. A Sunni like the rest, he wanted to be remembered even by the Shi'a majority in his country as a faithful follower of the Prophet. The Shi'a in Iraq, so recently liberated—by *unbelievers*!—from Sunni rule paraded about their country as though they alone were the Faithful. Sabawi wanted to show the error in that false belief. Mustafa hardly ever concerned himself with such trivia. For him, Islam was a large tent, with room for nearly all...

"My ass is tired," Rafi said from the backseat.

"That cannot be helped, my brother," Abdullah replied from the driver's seat. As driver, he deemed himself to be in temporary command.

"I know that, but my ass is still tired," Rafi observed.

"We could have taken horses, but they would be too slow, and they can also be hard on the ass, my friend," Mustafa observed. This pronouncement was greeted by laughter, and Rafi went back to his copy of *Playboy*.

The map showed easy going until they reached the city of Small Stone. They'd have to be fully awake for that. But for now, the road wound through pleasant hills covered with green trees. It was quite a change from northern Mexico, which had been so much like the sandy hills of home . . . to which they would never return . . .

For Abdullah, the driving was a pleasure. The car was not so fine as the Mercedes his father drove, but it sufficed for the moment, and the feel of the wheel was sweet in his hands, as he leaned back and smoked his Winston with a contented smile on his lips. There were people in America who raced cars like this on great oval tracks, and what a pleasure that must be! To drive as fast as you could, to be in competition with others—and to defeat them! That must be better than having a woman . . . well, almost . . . or just different, he corrected himself. Now, to have a woman *after* winning a race, *that* would be pleasurable indeed. He wondered if there were cars in Paradise. Good, fast ones, like the Formula One cars favored in Europe, hugging the corners, then really letting it go on the straightaways, to drive as fast as car and road allowed. He could try that here. The car was probably good for two hundred kilometers per hour—but, no, their mission was more important.

He flipped his cigarette butt out the window. Just then a white police car went zipping by, with blue stripes on the side. Arkansas State Police. Now *that* looked like a fast car, and the man inside had a splendid cowboy hat, Abdullah thought. Like every human being on the planet, he'd seen his share of American movies, including the cowboy sort, men on horseback herding cattle, or just shooting it out with handguns in their drinking saloons, settling issues of honor. The imagery appealed to him—but that was what it was supposed to do, he reminded himself. One more attempt by the infidel to seduce the Faithful. To be fair, though, American movies were made mainly for the American audience. How many Arab movies had he seen showing the forces of Salah ad-Din—a Kurd, of all things—crushing the invading Christian Crusaders? They were there to teach history, and to encourage manhood in Arab men, the better to crush the Israelis, which, alas, had not yet happened. So it was, probably, with American Westerns. Their concept of manhood was not all that different from the Arabs', except that they used revolvers instead of the manlier sword. The pistol did, of course, have superior reach, and so Americans were practical fighters, in addition to being very clever at it. No braver than Arabs, of course, just cleverer.

He'd have to be careful of Americans and their handguns, Abdullah told himself. If any of them shot like movie cowboys, their mission could come to a premature end, and that wouldn't do.

He wondered what the policeman in the passing white car carried on his belt—and was he a proficient shot? They could find out, of course, but there was only one way to do that and it would endanger their mission. So, Abdullah watched the police car pull ahead until it faded from view, and he settled down to watching tractor-trailers whiz past while he cruised eastward at a steady sixty-five miles and three cigarettes per hour, plus a grumbling stomach. SMALL STONE 30 MILES.

"THEY'RE GETTING excited over at Langley again," Davis told Hendley.

"What did you hear?" Gerry asked.

"A field officer got something strange from a source-agent over in Saudi. Something about how some suspected players were out of town, so to speak, location unknown, but he thinks Western Hemisphere, like ten or so of them."

"How solid is that?" Hendley asked.

"A 'three' in terms of reliability, though the source is ordinarily well regarded. Some headquarters puke decided to downgrade it, reason unknown." That was one of the problems at The Campus. They were dependent on others for most of their analysis. Though they had some particularly fine people in their own analysis offices, the real work was done on the other side of the Potomac River, and CIA had blown its share of calls in the past few years—make that decades, Gerry reminded himself. Nobody hit 1.000 in this league, and a lot of CIA bureaucrats were overpaid even with meager government salaries. But as long as their filing was properly done, nobody really cared or even noticed. What was significant was that the Saudis had a way of deporting their own potential troublemakers by allowing them to go elsewhere and do their crimes, and if they suffered for it, the Saudi government would be cooperative as hell, thus covering all of its bases quite easily.

"What do you think?" he asked Tom Davis.

"Hell, Gerry, I'm not a gypsy. No crystal ball, no Delphic Oracle." Davis let out a frustrated breath. "Homeland Security has been notified, and so that means FBI and the rest of their analytical team, but this is 'soft' intelligence, y'know? Nothing to hang a hat on. Three names, but no photos, and any bonehead can get ID in a new name." Even popular novels told people how to do it. You didn't even need all that much patience, because no state in the union cross-referenced birth and death certificates, which would have been an easy thing, even for government bureaucrats to accomplish.

"So, what happens?"

Davis shrugged. "The usual. Airport security people will get another notice to stay awake, and so, they'll hassle more innocent people to make sure nobody tries to hijack an airliner. Cops all over will look for suspicious cars, but that'll mostly mean that people driving erratically get pulled over. There's been too much wolf-crying. Even the police have trouble taking it seriously, Gerry, and who can blame them?"

"So, all of our defenses are neutralized—by us?"

"For all practical purposes, yes. Until CIA has a lot more field assets to identify them before they get here, we're in a reactive mode, not a proactive one. What the hell," he grimaced, "my bond trading has been going great the last two weeks." Tom Davis had found the money business to be rather to his liking—or, at least, easily mastered. Maybe going into CIA right out of the University of Nebraska had been a mistake? he asked himself every so often.

"Any follow-up on the CIA report?"

"Well, somebody over there has suggested another talk with our asset, but it hasn't cleared the Seventh Floor yet."

"Jesus!" Hendley swore.

"Hey, Jerry, why are you surprised? You never worked there like I did, but down on The Hill, you must have seen this sort of thing before."

"Why the *fuck* didn't Kealty keep Foley as DCI?"

"He has a lawyer friend he likes better, remember? And Foley was a professional spook, and therefore unreliable. Look, let's face it—Ed Foley helped some, but a real fix will take a decade. That's one of the reasons we're here, right?" Davis added with a smile. "How are our two hit-men trainees doing down at Charlottesville?"

"The Marine is still having a conscience attack."

"Chesty Puller must be rolling over in his crypt," Davis opined.

"Well, we can't hire mad dogs. Better to ask questions now than out in the field on an assignment."

"I suppose. What about the hardware?"

"Next week."

"It's taken long enough. Testing phase?"

"In Iowa. Pigs. They have a similar cardiovascular system, so our friend tells us."

How appropriate, Davis thought.

SMALL STONE turned out to be not much of a navigation problem, and after dipping southwest on I-40, now they were going northeast. Mustafa was now back at the wheel, and the two in back were dozing after filling up on roast beef sandwiches and Coca-Cola.

It was mostly boring now. Nothing can remain captivating for more than twenty hours, and even dreams of their mission a day and a half in the future could scarcely keep their eyes open, and so Rafi and Zuhayr were sleeping like exhausted children. He motored northeast with the sun behind his left shoulder and started to see signs indicating the distance to Memphis, Tennessee. He thought for a moment—it was hard to think very clearly after being in a car so long—and realized that he had only two more states to go. Their progress was steady, if slow. It would have been better to take a plane, but getting their machine guns through the airports would probably have been difficult, he thought with a smile. And as overall mission commander he had more than one team to worry about. That was why he'd selected the most difficult and distant target of the four, to set the example to the others. But sometimes leadership was just a pain in the ass, Mustafa told himself, as he adjusted himself in the seat.

The next half hour passed quickly. Then came a bridge of considerable size and height, and a sign that announced the Mississippi River, followed by a sign that welcomed them to TENNESSEE, THE VOLUNTEER STATE. His mind wandering from so much driving, Mustafa started to wonder what that might mean, but the thought died aborning. Whatever it meant, he had to cross Tennessee on the way to Virginia. Rest would not come for at least fifteen more hours. He'd drive about a hundred kilometers east of Memphis, then turn the car over to Abdullah.

He'd just crossed a great river. His entire country had no permanent rivers, just wadis that flooded briefly with a rare passing shower and soon went dry again. America was such a rich country. That was probably the source of their arrogance, but his mission, and that of his three colleagues, was to take that arrogance down a few pegs. And that, *Insh'Allah,* they would do, in less than two more days.

Two days to Paradise, was the thought that lingered in his mind.

CHAPTER 12

ARRIVING

TENNESSEE PASSED quickly for those in the back, only because Mustafa and Abdullah shared the wheel for the three hundred fifty kilometers from Memphis to Nashville, during which Rafi and Zuhayr mainly slept. One and three quarters kilometers per minute, he calculated. It translated to another... what? Twenty more hours or so. He thought about speeding up, to make the trip go faster—but, no, that was foolish. Taking unnecessary chances was always foolish. Hadn't they learned that from the Israelis? The enemy was always waiting, like a sleeping tiger. Waking one up unnecessarily was very foolish indeed. You only woke up the tiger when your rifle was already aimed, and only then so that the tiger could know that he'd been outsmarted, and unable to take action. Just to be awake long enough to appreciate his own foolishness, enough to know fear. America would know fear. For all their weapons and their cleverness, all these arrogant people would tremble.

He found himself smiling into the darkness now. The

sun had set again, and his car's headlights bored white cones into the darkness, illuminating the white lines on the highway that dashed in and out of his vision as he drove eastward at a steady sixty-five miles per hour.

THE TWINS were now rising at 0600 and going out to do their daily dozen exercises without Pete Alexander's supervision, which, they'd decided, they really didn't need. The run was getting easier for both of them, and the rest of the exercises had also mutated into a routine. By 7:15, they were done and heading in for breakfast and the first skull-session with their training officer.

"Those shoes need some work, bro," Dominic observed.

"Yeah," Brian agreed, taking a sad look at his aging Nike sneaks. "They've served me well for a few years, but it looks like they need to go off to shoe heaven."

"Foot Locker in the mall." He referred to the Fashion Square shopping mall down the hill in Charlottesville.

"Hmm, maybe a Philly cheesesteak for lunch tomorrow?"

"Works for me, bro," Dominic agreed. "Nothing like grease, fat, and cholesterol for lunch, especially with cheese fries on the side. Assuming your shoes will last another day."

"Hey, Enzo, I like the smell. These sneaks and me been around the block a few times."

"Like those dirty T-shirts. God damn it, Aldo, can't you ever dress properly?"

"Just let me wear my utilities again, buddy. I *like* being a Marine. You always know where you stand."

"Yeah, in the middle of the shit," Dominic observed.

"Maybe so, but you work with a better class of guys there." And, he didn't add, they were all on your side, and they all carried automatic weapons. It made for a feeling of security rarely found in civilian life.

"Going out to lunch, eh?" Alexander said.

"Tomorrow, maybe," Dominic answered. "Then we need to arrange a proper burial for Aldo's running shoes. We got a can of Lysol around here, Pete?"

Alexander had himself a good laugh. "I thought you'd never ask."

"You know, Dominic," Brian said, looking up from his eggs, "if you weren't my brother, I wouldn't take this crap off of you."

"Really?" The FBI Caruso tossed him an English muffin. "I swear, you Marines are all talk. I always used to whip him when we were kids," he added for Pete's benefit.

Brian's eyes nearly popped out of his head: "My ass!"

And another training day got started.

AN HOUR later, Jack was back on his workstation. Uda bin Sali had enjoyed another athletic night, with Rosalie Parker again. He must like her a lot. Ryan wondered how the Saudi would react if he knew that after every session she gave a play-by-play to the British Security Service. But for her, business was business, which would have deflated a lot of male egos in the British capital. Sali surely had one of those, Junior thought. Wills came in at quarter to nine with a bag of Dunkin' Donuts.

"Hey, Anthony. What's shakin'?"

"You tell me," Wills shot back. "Doughnut?"

"Thanks, buddy. Well, Uda had some more exercise last night."

"Ah, youth, a wonderful thing, but wasted on the young."

"George Bernard Shaw, right?"

"I knew you were literate. Sali discovered a new toy a few years back, and I guess he's going to play with it till it breaks—or falls off. Must be tough duty for his shadow team, standing out in the cold rain and knowing he's getting his weasel greased upstairs." It was a line from the *Sopranos* on HBO, which Wills admired.

"You suppose they're the ones who debrief her?"

"No, that's a job for the guys over at Thames House. Must get old after a while. Pity they don't send us all the transcripts, though," he added with a chuckle. "Might be good for getting the blood flowing in the morning."

"Thanks, I can always buy a *Hustler* at the magazine store if I feel scuzzy some night."

"It's not a clean business we're in, Jack. The kind of people we look at, they aren't the kind you invite over for dinner."

"Hey, White House, remember? Half the people we hosted for a State Dinner—Dad could hardly shake hands with them. But Secretary Adler told him it was business, and so Dad had to be nice to the sunzabitches. Politics attracts some really scummy people, too."

"Amen. So, anything else new on Sali?"

"I haven't gone over yesterday's money moves yet. Hey, if Cunningham stumbles over anything significant, what happens next?"

"That's up to Gerry and the senior staff." *You're way too junior to get your panties in a wad about that,* he didn't add, though the young Ryan got the message anyway.

"WELL, DAVE?" Gerry Hendley was asking upstairs.

"He's laundering money and sending some of it off to persons unknown. Liechtenstein bank. If I had to guess, it's to cover credit card accounts. You can get a Visa or MasterCard through that particular bank, and so it could well be to cover credit card accounts for persons unknown. Could be a mistress or a close friend, or somebody in whom we might have direct interest."

"Any way to find out?" Tom Davis asked.

"They use the same accounting program most banks do," Cunningham answered, meaning that with a little patience, The Campus could crack their way inside and learn more. There were firewalls in the way, of course. It was a job better left to the National Security Agency, and so the trick was to get NSA to task one of its computer weenies to do the cracking. That would mean faking a request by CIA to do the job, and that, the accountant figured, was a little harder to accomplish than just typing a note into a computer terminal. He also suspected that The Campus had someone inside both intelligence agencies who could do the faking so that no discernible paper trail would be left behind.

"Is it strictly necessary?"

"Maybe in a week or so, I can find more data. This Sali guy might just be a rich kid playing stickball out in the traffic, but . . . but my nose tells me he's a player of some sort," Cunningham admitted. He'd developed good instincts over the years, as a result of which two former Mafia kingpins were now living in solitary cells at Marion, Illinois. But he didn't trust his own instincts as well as his former and current superiors did. A career accountant with a foxhound's nose, he was also very conservative in talking about it.

"A week, you think?"

Dave nodded. "About that."

"How's the Ryan kid?"

"Good instincts. He found something most people would have missed. Maybe his youth works for him. Young target, young bloodhound. Usually, it doesn't work. This time . . . looks like maybe it did. You know, when his dad appointed Pat Martin to be Attorney General, I heard some things about Big Jack. Pat really liked him, and I worked with Mr. Martin enough to respect him a lot. This kid may be going places. It'll take about ten years to be sure of that, of course."

"We're not supposed to believe in breeding over here, Dave," Tom Davis observed.

"Numbers is numbers, Mr. Davis. Some people have a good nose, some don't. He doesn't yet, not really, but he's sure heading that way." Cunningham had helped start the Justice Department's Special Accounting Unit, which specialized in tracking terrorist money. Everyone needed money to operate, and money always left a trail somewhere, but it was often found after the fact more easily than before. Good for investigations, but not as good for active defense.

"Thanks, Dave," Hendley said in dismissal. "Keep us posted, if you would."

"Yes, sir." Cunningham gathered his papers and made his way out.

"You know, he'd be a little more effective if he had a personality," Davis said fifteen seconds after the door closed.

"Nobody's perfect, Tom. He's the best guy they ever had at Justice for this sort of thing. I bet when he fishes, there's nothing left in the lake after he leaves."

"No argument here, Gerry."

"So, this Sali gent might be a banker for the bad guys?"

"It looks like a possibility. Langley and Fort Meade are still in a dither over the current situation," Hendley went on.

"I've seen the paperwork. It's a whole lot of paper for not much hard data." In the business of intelligence analysis, you got into the speculation phase too rapidly, the point when experienced analysts started applying fear to existing data, following it to God knew where, trying to read the minds of people who didn't speak all that much, even to each other. Might there be people out there with anthrax or smallpox in little bottles in their shaving kits? How the hell could you tell? That had been done once to America, but when you got down to it *everything* had been done once to America, and while it had given the country the confidence that her people could deal with damned near anything, it had also given Americans the realization that bad things could indeed happen here and that those responsible might not always be identifiable. The new President did not convey any assurance that we'd be able to stop or punish such people. That was a major problem in and of itself.

"You know, we're a victim of our own success," the former senator said quietly. "We've managed to handle every nation-state that ever crossed us, but these invisible bas-

tards who work for their vision of God are harder to identify and track. God is omnipresent. So are His perverted
agents."

"Gerry, my boy, if it was easy, we wouldn't be here."

"Tom, thank God I can always count on you for moral
support."

"We live in an imperfect world, you know. There isn't
always enough rain to make the corn grow, and, if there is,
sometimes the rivers flood. My father taught me that."

"I always meant to ask you—how the hell did your family ever end up in goddamned Nebraska?"

"My great-grandfather was a soldier—cavalryman,
Ninth Cavalry, black regiment. He didn't feel like moving
back to Georgia when his hitch ran out. He'd spent some
time at Fort Crook outside of Omaha, and the dumbass
didn't mind the winters. So, he bought a spread near
Seneca and farmed corn. That's how history started for us
Davises."

"Wasn't any Ku Klux Klan in Nebraska?"

"No, they stayed in Indiana. Smaller farms there, anyway. My great-grandfather shot himself some buffalo
when he got started. There's the biggest damned head over
the fireplace at home. Damned thing still smells. Dad and
my brother mainly hunt longhorn antelope now, the
'speed-goat,' they call it at home. Never got to like the
taste."

"What's your nose say on this new intel, Tom?" Hendley asked.

"I'm not planning to go to New York anytime soon,
buddy."

EAST OF Knoxville, the road divided. I-40 went east. I-
81 went north, and the rented Ford took the latter through
the mountains explored by Daniel Boone when the western
frontier of America had scarcely stretched out of sight of
the Atlantic Ocean. A road sign showed the exit for the
home of someone named Davy Crockett. Whoever that

was, Abdullah thought, driving downhill through a pretty mountain pass. Finally, at a town named Bristol, they were in Virginia, their final major territorial boundary. About six more hours, he calculated. The land here, in the sunlight, was lush in its greenness, with horse and dairy farms on both sides of the road. Even churches, usually white-painted wooden buildings with crosses atop the steeples. Christians. The country was clearly dominated by them.

Unbelievers.

Enemies.

Targets.

They had their guns in the trunk to deal with them. First, I-81 north to I-64. They'd long since memorized their routing. The other three teams were surely in place now. Des Moines, Colorado Springs, and Sacramento. Each a city large enough to have at least one good shopping mall. Two were provincial capitals. None were major cities, however. All were what they called "Middle America," where the "good" people lived, where the "ordinary," "hardworking" Americans made their homes, where they felt safe, far from the great centers of power and corruption. Few, if any, Jews to be found in those cities. Oh, maybe a few. Jews like to run jewelry stores. Maybe even in the shopping malls. That would be an added bonus, but only something to be scooped up if it accidentally offered itself. Their real objective was to kill ordinary Americans, the ones who considered themselves safe in the womb of ordinary America. They would soon learn that safety in this world was an illusion. They'd learn that the thunderbolt of Allah reached everywhere.

"SO, THIS is it?" Tom Davis asked.

"Yes, it is," Dr. Pasternak replied. "Be careful. It's fully loaded. The red tag, you see. The blue one is not charged."

"What does it deliver?"

"Succinylcholine, a muscle relaxant, essentially a synthetic and more potent form of curare. It shuts down all the muscles, including the diaphragm. You can't breath, speak, or move. You're fully awake. It'll be a miserable death," the physician added in a cold, distant voice.

"Why is that?" Hendley asked.

"You can't breathe. Your heart rapidly goes into anoxia, essentially a massive induced heart attack. It won't feel very good at all."

"Then what?"

"Well, the onset of symptoms would take about sixty seconds. Thirty seconds more for the full effects of the drug to present themselves. The victim would collapse then, say, ninety seconds after the injection. Breathing stops completely about the same time. The heart is starved for oxygen. It will try to beat, but it's not delivering any oxygen to the body, or to itself. Heart tissue will die in about two or three minutes—and will be extremely painful as it does so. Unconsciousness will happen at about the three-minute mark unless the victim had been exercising beforehand—in that case, the brain will be highly infused with oxygen. Ordinarily, the brain has about three minutes' worth of oxygen in it to function without additional oxygen infusion, but at about the three-minute mark—after onset of symptoms, that is; four and a half minutes after being stuck—the victim will lose consciousness. Complete brain death will take another three minutes or so. After that, the succinylcholine will metabolize in the body, even after death. Not entirely, but enough so that only a really sharp pathologist will pick it up on a toxicology scan, and then only if he's prepped to look for it. The only real trick is to get your test subject in the buttocks."

"Why there?" Davis asked.

"The drug works just fine with an IM—intramuscular—injection. When people are posted, it's always faceup so that you can see and remove the organs. They rarely turn the body over. Now, this injection system does leave a mark, but it's hard to spot under the best of circumstances, and then only if you're looking at the right area. Even drug addicts—that will be one of the things they check for—don't inject themselves in the rump. It will appear to be an unexplained heart attack. Those happen every day. Rare, but not at all unknown. Tachycardia can make it happen, for example. The injector pen is a modified insulin pen like the kind Type I diabetics use. Your mechanics did a great job of disguising it. You can even write with it, but if you rotate the barrel, it swaps out the pen part for the insulin part. A gas charge in the back of the barrel injects the transfer agent. The victim will probably notice it, like a bee sting but less painful, but inside a minute and a half, he won't be telling anybody about it. His most likely reaction will be a minor 'Ouch' and then rub the spot—if that much. Like a mosquito bite on the neck. You might slap at it, but you don't call the police."

Davis held the safe "blue" pen. It was a little bulky, like a third-grader might use on his first official introduction to a ballpoint pen after using thick-barrel pencils and crayons for a couple of years. So, as you approached your subject, you took it out of your coat pocket, and swung it in a reverse stabbing motion, and just kept going. Your backup hitter would watch the subject fall to the sidewalk, maybe even stop to render assistance, then watch the bastard die, and get up and go on his way—well, maybe call an ambulance so that his body could get sent to the hospital and be properly dismantled under medical supervision.

"Tom?"

"I like it, Gerry," Davis replied. "Doc, how confident are you about this stuff dissipating after the subject goes down for the count?"

"Confident," Dr. Pasternak answered, and both of his hosts remembered that he was professor of anesthesiology at the Columbia University College of Physicians and Surgeons. He probably knew his stuff. Besides, they'd trusted him enough to let him in on the secrets of The Campus. It was a little late to stop trusting him now. "It's just basic biochemistry. Succinylcholine is made up of two acetylcholine molecules. Esterases in the body break the chemical down into acetylcholine fairly rapidly, so it is very likely to be undetectable, even by someone up at Columbia-Presbyterian. The only hard part: to have it done covertly. If you could bring him into a doctor's office, for example, it would just be a matter of infusing potassium chloride. That would put the heart into fibrillation. When cells die, they give off potassium anyway, and so the relative increase would not be noticed, but the IV mark would be hard to hide. There are a lot of ways to do this. I just had to pick one that is applied relatively conveniently by fairly unskilled people. As a practical matter, a really good pathologist might not be able to determine the exact cause of death—and he would know that he didn't know, and that would bother him—but that's only if the body is examined by a really talented guy. Not too many of them around. I mean, the best guy up at Columbia is Rich Richards. He really hates not knowing something. He's a real intellectual, a problem solver, and genius biochemist in addition to being a superb physician. I asked him about this, and he told me it would be extremely difficult to detect even if he had a heads-up on what to look for. Ordinarily, extraneous factors come into play, the specific biochemistry of the victim's body, what he's had to eat or drink, ambient temperature would be a huge factor. On a cold winter day, outside, the esterases might not be able to break down the succinylcholine because of a diminution of chemical processes."

"So, don't do a guy in Moscow in January?" Hendley asked. This deep science stuff was troublesome for him, but Pasternak knew his stuff.

The professor smiled. Cruelly. "Correct. Also Minneapolis."

"Miserable death?" Davis asked.

He nodded. "Decidedly unpleasant."

"Reversible?"

Pasternak shook his head. "Once the succinylcholine is in the bloodstream, there's nothing you can do about it . . .

well, theoretically you could put the guy on a ventilator and breathe for him until the drug metabolizes—I've seen that done with Pavulon in an OR—but that would be a stretch. Theoretically possible to survive, but very, very unlikely. People have survived being shot right between the eyes, gentlemen, but it's not exactly common."

"How hard do you have to hit your target?" Davis asked.

"Not very, just a good poke. Enough to penetrate his clothing. A thick coat might be a problem because of the length of the needle. But ordinary business wear, no problem."

"Is anyone immune to the drug?" Hendley asked.

"Not to this one, no. That would be one in a billion."

"No chance he'd make noise?"

"As I explained, it's like a bee sting at most—more than a mosquito, but not enough to make a man cry out in pain. At most, you'd expect for the victim to be puzzled, maybe to turn around and see what caused it, but your agent will be walking away normally, not running. Under those conditions, without a target to yell at, and since the initial discomfort is transitory, the most likely reaction is to rub the spot and walk on . . . for about, oh, ten yards or so."

"So, rapid-acting, lethal, and undetectable, right?"

"All of the above," Dr. Pasternak agreed.

"How do you reload it?" Davis required. *Damn, how has CIA not developed something this good?* he wondered. Or KGB, for that matter.

"You unscrew the barrel, like this"—he demonstrated—"and take it apart. You use an ordinary syringe to inject a new supply of the drug, and swap out the gas charge. These little gas capsules are the only hard part to manufacture. You toss the used one into a trash can or the gutter— they're only four millimeters long and two millimeters wide—and reinsert the fresh one. When you screw in the replacement, a little spike in the back of the barrel punctures it and recharges the system. The gas capsules are coated with sticky stuff to make them harder to drop." And just that fast, the blue one was "hot" except for the absence of succinylcholine. "You want to be careful with the syringe, of course, but you'd have to be pretty stupid to stick yourself. If you cover your man as a diabetic, you can explain away the presence of syringes. There's an ID card to get insulin refills that works just about anywhere in the world, and diabetes has no outward symptoms."

"Damn, Doc," Tom Davis observed. "Anything else you could deliver this way?"

"Botulism toxin is similarly lethal. It's a neurotoxin; it blocks nerve transmissions, and it causes death by asphyxia, also fairly rapidly, but it's readily detectable in the blood during a post-, and kind of hard to explain away. It's available fairly readily around the world, but in microgram doses, because of its use in cosmetic surgery."

"Docs shoot women in the face with that, don't they?"

"Only the dumb ones," Pasternak replied. "It takes wrinkles away, sure, but since it kills the nerves in the face, it also takes away your ability to smile much. That's not my field, exactly. There are a lot of toxic and lethal chemicals. It's the combination of rapid action and difficult detectability that made this a problem. Another quick way to kill someone is to use a small knife at the back of the skull, where the spinal cord enters the base of the brain. The trick is getting right behind your victim and then hitting a fairly small target with the knife, and not having the knife jam between the vertebrae—at that range, why not a silenced .22 pistol? It's fast enough, but it leaves something behind. This method can easily be misdiagnosed as a heart attack. It's just about perfect," the physician concluded, in a voice sufficiently cold as to sprinkle snow on the carpet.

"Richard," Hendley said, "you have earned your fee on this one."

The professor of anesthesiology stood, checking his watch. "No fee, Senator. This one's for my little brother. Let me know if you need me for anything else. I have a train to catch back to New York."

"Jesus," Tom Davis said, after he left. "I always knew docs had to have evil thoughts."

Hendley picked up a package on his desk. There were a total of ten "pens" in it, with computer-printed instructions for this use, a plastic bag full of gas capsules, and twenty large vials of succinylcholine, plus a bunch of throwaway syringes. "He and his brother must have been pretty close."

"Know him?" Davis asked.

"Yeah, I did. Good guy, wife and three kids. Name was Bernard, Harvard Business School graduate, smart guy, very astute trader. Worked on the ninety-seventh floor of Tower One. Left a lot of money behind—anyway, his family's well taken care of. That's something."

"Rich is a nice guy to have on our side," Davis thought aloud, suppressing the shiver that came along with the opinion.

"That he is," Gerry agreed.

THE DRIVE ought to have been pleasant. The weather was fair and clear, the road not at all crowded and mostly straight northeast. But it was not pleasant. Mustafa kept getting "How far now?" and "Are we there yet?" from Rafi and Zuhayr in the backseat, to the point that more than once he considered pulling the car over and strangling them. Maybe it was hard sitting in the backseat, but he had to *drive this Goddamned car!!!* Tension. He was feeling it, and they probably were, too, and so he took a deep breath and commanded himself to be calm. The end of their journey was hardly four hours away, and what was that compared to their transcontinental trek? Certainly it was farther than the Holy Prophet ever walked or rode from Mecca to Medina and back—but he stopped that thought at once. He had no standing to compare himself with Mohammed, did he? *No, you do not.* One thing he was sure of. On getting to his destination, he was going to bathe and *sleep* just as long as he could. *Four hours to rest* was what he kept saying to himself, as Abdullah slept in the right-front seat.

THE CAMPUS had its own cafeteria, whose food was catered from a variety of outside sources. Today it was from a Baltimore deli called Atman's whose corned beef was pretty good, if not quite New York class—saying that might result in a fistfight, he thought, as he picked up a corned beef on a kaiser roll. What to drink? If he was having a New York lunch, then cream soda, but Utz, the local potato chips, of course, because they'd even had them in the White House—at his father's insistence. They probably had something from Boston there now. It was not exactly a renowned restaurant town, but every city has at least one good eatery, even Washington, D.C.

Tony Wills, his normal luncheon mate, was nowhere to be seen. So, he looked around and spotted Dave Cunningham, not surprisingly eating alone. Jack headed that way.

"Hey, Dave, mind if I sit down?" he asked.

"Take a seat," Cunningham said, cordially enough.

"How's the numbers business?"

"Exciting," was the implausible reply. Then he elaborated. "You know, the access we have into those European banks is amazing. If the Department of Justice had this sort of access, they'd really clean up—except you can't introduce this kind of evidence into a court of law."

"Yeah, Dave, the Constitution can really be a drag. And all those damned civil-rights laws."

Cunningham nearly choked on his egg salad on white. "Don't you start. The FBI runs a lot of operations that are a little shady—usually because some informant lays stuff on us, maybe because somebody asked, or maybe not, and they spin that off—but within the rules of criminal procedure. Usually it's part of a plea bargain. There are not enough crooked lawyers to handle all of their needs. The Mafia guys, I mean."

"I know Pat Martin. Dad thinks a lot of him."

"He's honest and very, very smart. He really ought to be a judge. That's where honest lawyers belong."

"Doesn't pay very much." Jack's official salary at The Campus was well above anything any federal employee made. Not bad for entry level.

"That *is* a problem, but—"

"But there's nothing all that admirable about poverty, my dad says. He toyed with the idea of zeroing out salaries for elected officials so that they'd have to know what real work was, but he eventually decided that it would make them even more susceptible to bribery."

The accountant picked up on that: "You know, Jack, it's amazing how little you need to bribe a member of Congress. Makes the bribes hard to identify," the CPA groused. "Like being down in the weeds for an aircraft."

"What about our terrorist friends?"

"Some of them like a comfortable life. A lot of them come from moneyed families, and they like their luxuries."

"Like Sali."

Dave nodded. "He has expensive tastes. His car costs a *lot* of money. Very impractical. The mileage it gets must be awful, especially in a city like London. The gas prices over there are pretty steep."

"But mainly he takes cabs."

"He can afford it. It probably makes sense. Parking a car in the financial district must be costly, too, and the cabs in London are good." He looked up. "You know that. You've been to London a lot."

"Some," Jack agreed. "Nice city, nice people." He didn't have to add that a protective detail of Secret Service agents and local cops didn't hurt much. "Any further thoughts on our friend Sali?"

"I need to go over the data more closely, but like I said, he sure acts like a player. If he was a New York Mafia subject, I'd figure him for an apprentice consiglieri."

Jack nearly gagged on his cream soda. "That high up?"

"Golden Rule, Jack. He who has the gold makes the

rules. Sali has access to a ton of money. His family's richer than you appreciate. We're talking four or five billion dollars here."

"That much?" Ryan was surprised.

"Take another look at the money accounts he's learning to manage. He hasn't played with as much as fifteen percent of it. His father probably limits what he's allowed to do. He's in the capital-preservation business, remember. The guy who owns the money, his father, won't hand him the whole pile to play with, regardless of his educational background. In the money business, it's what you learn *after* you hang your degrees on the wall that really matters. The boy shows promise, but he's still following his zipper everywhere he goes. That's not an unusual thing for a rich young kid, but if you have a few gigabucks in your wallet, you want to keep your boy on a leash. Besides, what he appears to be funding—well, what we suspect he's funding— isn't really capital-intensive. You spotted some trades on the margins. That was pretty smart. Did you notice that when he flies home to Saudi, he charters a G-V?"

"Uh, no," Jack admitted. "I didn't look into that. I just figured he flies first-class everywhere."

"He does, same way you and your father used to. *Real* first class. Jack, nothing is too small to check out."

"What do you think of his credit card usage?"

"Entirely routine, but that's noteworthy even so. He could charge *anything* if he wanted to, but he seems to pay cash for a lot of expenditures—and he spends *less* cash than he converts to his own use. Like with those hookers. The Saudis don't care about that, so he's paying cash there because he *wants* to, not because he *has* to. He's trying to keep some parts of his life covert for reasons not immediately apparent. Maybe just practice. I would not be surprised to find out that he's got more credit cards than the ones we know about—unused accounts. I'll be riffling through his bank accounts later today. He doesn't really know about how to be covert yet. Too young, too inexperienced, no formal training. But, yes, I think he's a player, hoping to move into the big leagues pretty soon. The young and rich are not known for their patience," Cunningham concluded.

I should have guessed that myself, Junior told himself. *I need to think this stuff through better. Another important lesson. Nothing too small to be checked out. What sort of guy are we dealing with? How does he see the world? How does he want to change the world?* His father had always told him how important it was to look at the world through the eyes of your adversary, to crawl inside his brain and *then* look out at the world.

Sali is a guy driven by his passions in women—but was there more to it? Was he hiring the hookers because they were good screws or because he was screwing the enemy? The Islamic world thought of America and the U.K. as essentially the same enemy. Same language, same arrogance, damned sure the same military, since the Brits and Americans cooperated so closely on so many things. That was worth considering. *Make no assumptions without looking out through his eyeballs.* Not a bad lesson for one lunchtime.

ROANOKE SLID off to their right. Both sides of I-81 were composed of rolling green hills, mostly farms, many of them dairy farms, judging from all the cows. Green highway signs telling of roads that, for his purpose, led nowhere. And more of the white-painted boxy churches. They passed school buses, but no police cars. He'd heard that some American states put highway police in ordinary-looking cars, ones not very different from his own, but probably with additional radio antennas. He wondered if the drivers wore cowboy hats here. That'd be decidedly out of place, even in an area with so many cows. "The Cow," the Second Sura of the Koran, he thought. If Allah tells you to slaughter a cow, you must slaughter it without asking too many questions. Not an old cow, nor a young one, just a cow pleasing to the Lord. Were not all sacrifices pleasing to Allah, so long as they were not sacrifices founded in conceit? Surely they were, if offered in the humility of the Faithful, for Allah welcomed and was pleased by the offerings of the truly Faithful.

Yes.

And he and his friends would make more sacrifices by slaughtering the unbelievers.

Yes.

Then he saw a sign for INTERSTATE HIGHWAY 64—but it was to the west, the wrong one. They had to go east, to cross the eastern mountains. Mustafa closed his eyes and remembered the map he'd looked at so many times. North for about an hour, then east. Yes.

"BRIAN, THOSE shoes are going to come apart in the next few days."

"Hey, Dom, I ran my first four-and-a-half-minute mile in these," the Marine objected. You remembered and treasured such moments.

"Maybe so, but next time you try that, they're going to come apart and beat the shit out of your ankle."

"Think so? Bet you a buck you're wrong."

"You're on," Dominic said at once. They shook hands formally on the wager.

"They look pretty scruffy to me, too," Alexander observed.

"You want me to buy new T-shirts, too, Mom?"

"They'll self-destruct in another month," Dominic thought aloud.

"Oh, yeah! Well, I outshot your ass with my Beretta this morning."

"Luck happens," Enzo sniffed. "See if you can make it two in a row."

"I'll put five bucks on that."

"Deal." Another handshake. "I could get rich this way," Dominic said. Then it was time to think about dinner. Veal

Piccata tonight. He had a thing for good veal, and the local stores had nice stuff. Pity about the calf, but he hadn't been the one to cut its throat.

THERE: I-84, next exit. Mustafa was tired enough that he might have given the driving over to Abdullah, but he wanted to finish himself, and he figured he could handle another hour. They were heading for a pass in the next range of mountains. Traffic was heavy, but in the other direction. They climbed up the highway toward . . . yes, there it was, a shallow mountain pass with a hotel on the south side—and then out onto a vista of a most pleasant valley to the south. A sign proclaimed its name, but the letters were too confusing for him to get them into his head as a coherent word. He did take in the view, off to his right. Paradise itself could scarcely have been more lovely—there was even a place to pull over, get out and take in the sight. But, of course, they had not the time. It was fitting that the drive was gently downhill, and it changed his mood entirely. Less than an hour to go. One more smoke to celebrate the timing. In the back, Rafi and Zuhayr were awake again, taking in the scenery. It would be their last such opportunity.

One day of rest and reconnaissance—time to coordinate via e-mail with their three other teams—and then they could accomplish their mission. That would be followed by Allah's Own Embrace. A very happy thought.

CHAPTER 13

MEETING PLACE

AFTER TWO thousand–plus miles of driving, the arrival was entirely anticlimactic. Not a kilometer off Interstate 64 was a Holiday Inn Express, which looked satisfactory, especially since there was a Roy Rogers immediately next door and a Dunkin' Donuts not a hundred meters uphill. Mustafa walked in and took two connecting rooms, paying with his Visa card out of the Liechtenstein bank. Tomorrow they'd go exploring, but for now all that beckoned was sleep. Even food was not important at this moment. He moved the car to the first-floor rooms he'd just leased, and switched off the engine. Rafi and Zuhayr unlocked the doors, then came back to open the trunk. They took their few bags in, and under them the four submachine guns still wrapped in thick, cheap blankets.

"We are here, comrades," Mustafa announced, entering the room. It was an entirely ordinary motel, not the more luxurious hotels they'd become accustomed to. They had one bathroom and a small TV each. The connecting door was opened. Mustafa allowed himself to fall backward on his bed, a double, but all for him. Some things were left to be done, however.

"Comrades, the guns must always be hidden, and the shades drawn *at all times*. We've come too far for foolish risks," he warned them. "This city has a police force, and do not think they are fools. We journey to Paradise at a time of our choosing, not at a time determined by an error. Remember that." And then he sat up, and removed his shoes. He thought about a shower, but he was too tired for that, and tomorrow would come soon enough.

"Which way to Mecca?" Rafi asked.

Mustafa had to think about that for a second, divining the direct line to Mecca and to the city's centerpiece, the Kaaba stone, the very center of the Islamic universe, to which they directed the Salat, verses from the Holy Koran said five times per day, recited from the knees.

"That way," he said, pointing southeast, on a line that transected northern Africa on its way to that holiest of Holy Places.

Rafi unrolled his prayer rug, and went to his knees. He was late in his prayers, but he had not forgotten his religious duty.

For his own part, Mustafa whispered to himself, "lest it be forgotten," in the hope that Allah would forgive him in his current state of fatigue. But was not Allah infinitely merciful? And besides, this was hardly a great sin. Mustafa removed his socks, and lay back in the bed, where sleep found him in less than a minute.

In the next room over, Abdullah finished his own Salat, and then plugged his computer into the side of the telephone. He dialed up an 800 number and heard the warbling screech as his computer linked up with the network. In another few seconds, he learned that he had mail. Three letters, plus the usual trash. The e-mails he downloaded and saved, and then he logged off, having been online a mere fifteen seconds, another security measure they'd all been briefed on.

* * *

WHAT ABDULLAH didn't know was that one of the four accounts had been intercepted and partially decrypted by the National Security Agency. When his account—identified only by a partial word and some numbers—tapped into Saeed's, it was also identified, but only as a recipient, not an originator.

Saeed's team had been the first to arrive at its destination of Colorado Springs, Colorado—the city was identified only by a code name—and was comfortably camped out in a motel ten kilometers from its objective. Sabawi, the Iraqi, was in Des Moines, Iowa, and Mehdi in Provo, Utah. Both of those teams were also in place and ready for the operation to commence. Less than thirty-six hours to execute their mission.

He'd let Mustafa do the replies. The reply was, in fact, already programmed: "190, 2" designating the 190th verse of the Second Sura. Not exactly a battle cry, but rather an affirmation of the Faith that had brought them here. The meaning was: *Proceed with your mission.*

BRIAN AND Dominic were watching the History Channel on their cable system, something about Hitler and the Holocaust. It had been studied so much you'd think it'd defy efforts to find something new, yet somehow historians managed every so often. Some of it was probably because of the voluminous records the Germans had left behind in the Hartz Mountain caves, which would probably be the subject of scholarly study for the next few centuries, as people continued to try to discern the thought processes of the human monsters who'd first envisioned and then committed such crimes.

"Brian," Dominic asked, "what do you make of this stuff?"

"One pistol shot could have prevented it, I suppose. Problem is, nobody can see that far into the future—not even gypsy fortune-tellers. Hell, Adolf whacked a bunch of them, too. Why didn't *they* get the hell out of town?"

"You know, Hitler lived most of his life with only one bodyguard. In Berlin, he lived in a second-floor apartment, with a downstairs entrance, right? He had one SS troop, probably not even a sergeant, guarding the door. Pop him, open the door, go upstairs, and waste the motherfucker. Would have saved a lot of lives, bro," Dominic concluded, reaching for his white wine.

"Damn. You sure about that?"

"The Secret Service teaches that. They send one of their instructors down to Quantico to lecture every class on security issues. The fact surprised us, too. A lot of questions on it. The guy said you could walk right past the SS guard on your way to the liquor store, like. *Easy* hit, man. Easier'n hell. The thinking is that Adolf thought he was immortal, that there wasn't a bullet anywhere with his name on it. Hey, we had a President whacked on a train platform waiting for his train to arrive. Which one was it? Chester Arthur, I think. McKinley got shot by a guy who walked right up to him with a bandage around his hand. I guess people were a little careless back then."

"Damn. It'd make our job a lot easier, but I'd still prefer a rifle from five hundred meters or so."

"No sense of adventure, Aldo?"

"Ain't nobody paying me enough money to play kamikaze, Enzo. No future in that, y'know?"

"What about those suicide bombers over in the Mideast?"

"Different culture, man. Don't you remember from second grade? You can't commit suicide because it's a mortal sin and you can't go to confession after. Sister Frances Mary made that pretty clear, I thought."

Dominic laughed. "Damn, haven't thought of her in a while, but she always thought you were the cat's ass."

"That's 'cause I didn't screw around in class like you did."

"What about in the Marines?"

"Screwing around? The sergeants took care of that before it came to my attention. *Nobody* messed with Gunny Sullivan, not even Colonel Winston." He looked at the TV for another minute or so. "You know, Enzo, maybe there are times when one bullet can prevent a lot of grief. That Hitler needed his ticket punched. But even trained military officers couldn't bring it off."

"The guy who placed the bomb just assumed that everybody in the building had to be dead, without going back inside to make sure. They say it every day in the FBI Academy, bro—assumptions are the mother of all fuckups."

"You want to make sure, yeah. Anything worth shooting is worth shooting twice."

"Amen," Dominic agreed.

IT HAD gotten to the point that Jack Ryan, Jr., woke up to the morning news on NPR expecting to hear about something dreadful. He guessed that came from seeing so much raw intelligence information, but without the judgment to know what was hot and what was not.

But though he did not know all that much, what he did know was more than a little worrying. He'd become fixated by Uda bin Sali—probably because Sali was the only "player" he knew much about. And that had to be because Sali was his personal case study. He had to figure this bird out, because if he didn't he'd be...encouraged to seek other employment...? He hadn't seen that possibility until now, which by itself did not speak well for his future in the spook business. Of course, his father had taken a long time to find something he was good at—nine years, in fact, after graduating Boston College—and he himself had not yet lived one whole year past his Georgetown sheepskin. So, would he make the grade at The Campus? He was about the youngest person there. Even the secretary pool was composed of women older than he was. Damn, *that* was an entirely new thought.

Sali *was* a test for him, and probably a very important

one. Did that mean that Tony Wills already had Sali figured out, and he was off chasing data already fully analyzed? Or did it mean that he had to make his case and sell it after he'd reached his own conclusions? It was a big thought for standing in front of the bathroom mirror with his Norelco. This wasn't school anymore. A failing grade here meant failing—life? No, not that bad, but not good, either. Something to think about with coffee and CNN in the kitchen.

FOR BREAKFAST, Zuhayr walked up the hill, where he purchased two dozen doughnuts and four large coffees. America was such a crazy country. So many natural riches—trees, rivers, magnificent roads, incredible prosperity—but all in the service of idolaters. And here he was, drinking their coffee and eating their doughnuts. Truly, the world was mad, and if it ran on any plan at all, it was Allah's Own Plan, and not something even for the Faithful to understand. They just had to obey that which was written. On returning to the motel, he found both TVs tuned in to the news—CNN, the global news network—the Jewish-oriented one, that is. Such a pity that no Americans watched Al-Jazeera, which at least tried to speak to Arabs, though to his eyes it had already caught the American disease.

"Food," Zuhayr announced. "And drink." One box of doughnuts went into his room, and the other to Mustafa, still rubbing the sleep from his eyes after eleven hours of snoring slumber.

"How did you sleep, my brother?" Abdullah asked the team leader.

"It was a blessed experience, but my legs are still stiff." His hand shot out for the large cup of coffee, and he snatched a maple-frosted doughnut from the box, downing half of it in one monstrous bite. He rubbed his eyes and looked at the TV to see what was happening in the world this day. The Israeli police had shot and killed another holy martyr before he'd been able to trigger his bodysuit of Semtex.

"DUMB FUCK," Brian observed. "How hard can it be to pull a string?"

"I wonder how the Israelis twigged to him. You gotta figure they have paid informants inside that Hamas bunch. This has got to be a code-worded Major Case for their police, lots of resources assigned, plus help from their spook shops."

"They torture people, too, don't they?"

Dominic nodded after a second's consideration. "Yeah, supposedly it's controlled by their court system and all that, but they interrogate a little more vigorously than we do."

"Does it work?"

"We talked that one around at the Academy. You put a bowie knife to somebody's dick, chances are he'll see the wisdom of singing, but it's not something anybody wanted to think much about. I mean, yeah, in the abstract it can even seem funny, but doing it yourself—probably not very palatable, y'know? The other question is, how much good information does it really generate? The guy's just as likely to say anything to get the knife away from his little friend, make the pain stop, whatever. Crooks can be really good liars unless you know more than they do. Anyway, we can't do it. You know, the Constitution and all that. You can threaten them with bad jail time, and scream at them, but even then there're lines you can't cross."

"They sing anyway?"

"Mostly. Interrogation's an art form. Some guys are really good at it. I never really had much of a chance to learn it, but I did see some guys play the game. The real trick is to develop a rapport with the mutt, saying stuff like, yeah, that nasty little girl really asked for it, didn't she? Makes you want to puke afterward, but the name of the game is getting the bastard to fess up. After he gets into the joint, his neighbors will hassle him a lot worse than I ever would. One thing you don't want to be in a prison is a child abuser."

"I believe it, Enzo. That friend of yours in Alabama, maybe you did him a favor."

"Depends on if you believe in hell or not," Dominic responded. He had his own thoughts about that.

WILLS WAS early this morning. Jack saw him on his workstation when he came in. "You beat me in, for once."

"My wife's car came back from the shop. Now she can take the kids to school for a change," he explained. "Check the feed from Meade," he directed.

Jack lit up his computer, sat through the start-up procedures, and typed in his personal encryption code to access the interagency traffic download file from the downstairs computer room.

The top of the electronic pile was a FLASH-priority dispatch from NSA Fort Meade to CIA, *and* FBI, *and* Homeland Security, one of whom would have surely briefed the President on it this morning. Strangely, there was almost nothing to it, just a numeric message, a set of numbers.

"So?" Junior asked.

"So, it might be a passage from the Koran. The Koran has a hundred fourteen suras—chapters—with a variable number of verses. If this is such a reference, it's a verse with nothing particularly dramatic in it. Scroll down and see for yourself."

Jack clicked his mouse. "That's all?"

Woods nodded. "That's all, but the thinking at Meade is that such a dull message is likely to denote something else—something important. Spooks tend to use a lot of reverse English when they hit the cue ball."

"Well, *duh*! You're telling me that because it appears to have no importance to it, it may be important? Hell, Tony, you can make that observation about anything! What else do they know? The network, where the guy logged on from, that sort of thing?"

"It's a European network, privately owned, with 800 numbers all over the world, and we know some bad guys have used it. You can't tell where the members log in from."

"Okay, so, first, we do not know if the message has any significance. Second, we do not know where the message originated. Third, we do not have any way of knowing who's read it or where the hell they are. The short version is that we don't know shit, but everybody's getting in a flutter about it. What else? The originator, what do we know about him?"

"He—or she, for all we know—is thought to be a possible player."

"What team?"

"Guess. The NSA profilers say that this guy's syntax seems to indicate Arabic as a first language—based on previous traffic. The shrinks at CIA agree. They've copied messages from this bird before. He says nasty things to nasty people on occasion, and they're time-linked with some other very bad things."

"Is it possible that he's making some signal related to the bomber the Israeli police bagged earlier today?"

"Possible, yes, but not terribly likely. The originator isn't linked to Hamas, as far as we know."

"But we don't really know, do we?"

"With these guys you can't be totally sure about anything."

"So, we're back to where we started. Some people are running around over something they don't really know shit about."

"That's the problem. In these bureaucracies it's better to cry wolf and be wrong than to have your mouth shut when the big gray critter runs off with a sheep in his mouth."

Ryan sat back in his chair. "Tony, how many years were you at Langley?"

"A few," Wills answered.

"How the hell did you stand it?"

The senior analyst shrugged. "Sometimes I wonder."

Jack turned back to his computer to scan the rest of the morning's message traffic. He decided to see if Sali had been doing anything unusual over the last few days, just to cover his own ass, and in thinking that, John Patrick Ryan, Jr., started thinking like a bureaucrat, without even knowing it.

"TOMORROW IT'S going to be a little different," Pete told the twins. "Michelle is your target, but this time she'll be disguised. Your mission is to ID her and track her to her destination. Oh, did I tell you, she's really good at disguises."

"She's going to take an invisible pill, right?" Brian asked.

"That's *her* mission," Alexander elucidated.

"You going to issue us magic glasses to see through the makeup?"

"Not even if we had any—which we don't."

"Some pal you are," Dominic observed coldly.

BY ELEVEN that morning, it was time to scout the objective.

Conveniently located just a quarter mile north on U.S. Route 29, the Charlottesville Fashion Square Mall was a medium-sized shopping mall that catered to a largely upscale clientele of local gentry and students at the nearby University of Virginia. It was anchored by a JCPenney at one end and a Sears at the other, with Belk's men's and women's stores in the middle. Unexpectedly, there was no food court per se—whoever had done the reconnaissance had been sloppy. A disappointment, but not all that uncommon. The advance teams the organization employed were often mere stringers, for whom missions of this sort were something of a lark. But, Mustafa saw on going in, it would do little harm.

A central courtyard opened into all four of the mall's

main corridors. An information stand even supplied diagrams of the mall, showing store locations. Mustafa looked one over. A six-pointed Star of David leaped off the page at his eyes. A synagogue, here? Was *that* possible? He walked down to see, halfway hoping that it was indeed possible.

But it wasn't. It was, rather, the mall's security office, where sat a male employee in a uniform of light blue shirt and dark blue pants. On inspection, the man did not have a gun belt. And that was good. He *did* have a phone, which would undoubtedly call the local police. So, this black man would have to be the first. With that decided, Mustafa reversed directions, walked past the restrooms and the Coke machine, and turned right, away from the men's store.

This was a fine target place, he saw. Only three main entrances, and a clear field of fire from the Central Court. The individual stores were mainly rectangular, with open access from the corridors. On the following day, at about this time, it would be even more crowded. He estimated two hundred people in his immediate sight, and though he'd hoped all the way into this city that they'd have the chance to kill perhaps a thousand, anything over two hundred would be a victory of no small dimension. There were all manner of stores here, and unlike Saudi malls, men and women shopped on the same floor. Many children, too. There were four stores listed as specialty children's goods—and even a Disney Store! That he had not expected, and to attack one of America's most treasured icons would be sweet indeed.

Rafi appeared at his side. "Well?"

"It could be a larger target, but the arrangement is nearly perfect for us. All on one level," Mustafa replied quietly.

"Allah is beneficent as always, my friend," Rafi said, unable to conceal his enthusiasm.

People circulated about. Many young women were pushing their little ones about in strollers—he saw that you could rent them from a stand just by the hair salon.

There was one purchase he had to make. He accomplished it in the Radio Shack next to a Zales Jewelers. Four portable radios and batteries, for which he paid in cash, and for which he got a brief lecture on how the radios worked.

All in all, it could have been better, in a theoretical sense, but it wasn't supposed to be a busy city street. Besides, there would be policemen on the street with guns who would interfere with their mission. So, as always in life, you measured the bitter against the sweet, and here there was much of the sweet for all of them to taste. The four of them all got pretzels from Auntie Anne's and headed out past the JCPenney back to their car. Formal planning would take place at their motel rooms, with more doughnuts and coffee.

JERRY ROUNDS'S official job was as head of strategic planning for The Campus's white side. This job he performed fairly well—he might have been the very Wolf of Wall Street had he not chosen to become an Air Force intelligence officer on leaving the University of Pennsylvania. The service had even paid for his master's degree from the Wharton School of Business before he'd made full-bull colonel. This had given him an unexpected master's degree to hang on the wall, which also gave him a superb excuse to be in the trading business. It was even a fun diversion for the former chief USAF analyst at the Defense Intelligence Agency's headquarters building at Bolling AFB in Washington. But along the way he'd found that being an "unrated weenie"—he'd never worn the silver wings of a USAF aviator—didn't compensate for being a second-class citizen in a service completely run by those who did poke holes in the sky, even if he were smarter than twenty of them in the same room. Coming to The Campus had seriously broadened his horizons in a lot of ways.

"What is it, Jerry?" Hendley asked.

"The folks at Meade and over across the river just got

excited about something," Rounds replied, handing some papers across.

The former senator read the traffic for a minute or so and handed it all back. In a moment, he knew he'd seen most of it before. "So?"

"So, this time they may be right, boss. I've been keeping an eye on the background stuff. The thing is, we have a combination of reduced message traffic from known players, and then this flies over the transom. I spent my life in DIA looking at coincidences. This here's one of them."

"Okay, what are they doing about it?"

"Airport security is going to be a little tighter starting today. The FBI is going to set people at some departure gates."

"Nothing on TV about it?"

"Well, the boys and girls at Homeland Security may have gotten a little smarter about advertising. It's counterproductive. You don't catch a rat by shouting at him. You do it by showing him what he wants to see, and then breaking his goddamned neck."

Or maybe by having a cat spring on him unexpectedly, Hendley didn't say. But that was a harder mission.

"Any ideas for us?" he asked instead.

"Not at the moment. It's like seeing a front move in. There may be heavy rain and hail in it, but there's no convenient way to stop it."

"Jerry, how good is our data on the planning guys, the ones who give the orders?"

"Some of it's pretty good. But it's the people who convey the orders, not the ones who originate them."

"And if they drop off the table?"

Rounds nodded immediate agreement. "Now you're talking, boss. Then the real big shots might poke their heads up out of their holes. Especially if they don't know that storm's coming in."

"For now, what's the biggest threat?"

"The FBI is thinking car bombs, or maybe somebody with a C-4 overcoat, like in Israel. It's possible, but from an operational point of view, I'm not so sure." Round sat down in the offered chair. "It's one thing to give the guy his explosives package and put him on a city bus for the ride to his objective, but, as applied to us, it's more complicated. Bring the bomber here, get him outfitted—which means having the explosives in place, which is a further complication—*then* getting him familiar with the objective, *then* getting him there. The bomber is *then* expected to maintain his motivation a long way from his support network. A lot of things can go wrong, and that's why black operations are kept as simple as possible. Why go out of your way to purchase trouble?"

"Jerry, how many hard targets do we have?" Hendley asked.

"Total? Six or so. Of those, four are real, no-shit targets."

"Can you get me locations and profiles?"

"Any time you say."

"Monday." No sense thinking about it over the weekend. He had two days of riding all planned out. He was entitled to a couple of days off once in a while.

"Roger that, boss." Rounds stood and headed out. Then he stopped at the door. "Oh, there's a guy at Morgan and Steel, bond department. He's a crook. He's playing fast and very loose with some client money, about one-fifty worth." By which he meant a hundred and fifty million dollars of other people's money.

"Anybody on to him?"

"Nope, I ID'd this guy on my own. Met him two months ago up in New York, and he didn't sound quite right, and so I put a watch on his personal computer. Want to see his notes?"

"Not our job, Jerry."

"I know, I shorted our business with him to make sure he didn't dick with our funds, but I think he knows it's time to leave town, like maybe a trip overseas, one-way ticket. Somebody ought to have a look. Maybe Gus Werner?"

"I'll have to think about that. Thanks for the heads-up."

"Roger that." And Rounds disappeared out the door.

"**SO, WE** just try to sneak up on her without being noticed, right?" Brian asked.

"That's the mission," Pete agreed.

"How close?"

"Close as you can get."

"You mean close enough to put one in the back of her head?" the Marine asked.

"Close enough to see her earrings," Alexander decided was the most polite way of putting it. It was even accurate, since Mrs. Peters wore her hair fairly long.

"So, not to shoot her in the head, but to cut her throat?" Brian pressed the question.

"Look, Brian, you can put it any way you want. Close enough to touch her, okay?"

"Okay, just so's I understand," Brian said. "We have to wear our fanny packs?"

"Yes," Alexander replied, though it wasn't true. Brian was being a pain in the ass again. Who'd ever heard of a Marine with conscience attacks?

"It'll make us easier to spot," Dominic objected.

"So, disguise it somehow. Be creative," the training officer suggested a little testily.

"When do we find out what all of this is for, exactly?" Brian asked.

"Soon."

"You keep saying that, man."

"Look, you can drive back to North Carolina whenever you want."

"I've thought about it," Brian told him.

"Tomorrow's Friday. Think about it over this weekend, okay?"

"Fair enough." Brian backed off. The tone of the interplay had gotten a little uglier than he'd actually wanted. It was time to back down. He didn't dislike Pete at all. It was the not knowing, and his distaste for what it *looked* like. Especially with a woman as the target. Hurting women was not part of his creed. Or children, which was what had set his brother off—not that Brian disapproved. He wondered briefly if he might have done the same thing, and told himself, sure, for a kid, but without being quite sure. When dinner was finished, the twins handled the cleanup, then settled in front of the downstairs TV for some drinks and the History Channel.

IT WAS much the same the next state up, with Jack Ryan, Jr., drinking a rum and Coke and flipping back and forth between History and History International, with an occasional sojourn to Biography, which was showing a two-hour look at Joseph Stalin. *That guy,* Junior thought, *was one seriously cold motherfucker.* Forcing one of his own confidants to sign the imprisonment order for his own wife. Damn. But how did that physically unprepossessing man exercise such control over people who were his own peers? What was the power he'd wielded over others? Where had it come from? How had he maintained it? Jack's own father had been a man of considerable power, but he had *never* dominated people in anything like that way. Probably never even thought about it, much less killing people for what amounted to the fun of it. Who were these people? Did they still exist?

Well, they had to. The one thing that never changed in the world was human nature. The cruel and the brutal still existed. Perhaps society no longer encouraged them as they had in, say, the Roman Empire. The gladiatorial games had trained people to accept and even to be entertained by violent death. And the dark truth of the matter was that if Jack had been given access to a time machine, he might—he *would*—have journeyed back to the Flavian Amphitheater to see it, just once. But that was human curiosity, not blood lust. Just a chance to gain historical knowledge, to see and *read* a culture connected to, yet different from, his own. He might even toss his cookies watching... or maybe not. Maybe his curiosity was that strong. But for damned sure, if he ever went back, he'd take a friend along for the ride. Like the Beretta .45 he'd learned to shoot with Mike Brennan. He wondered how many others might have taken the trip. Probably quite a few. Men. Not women. Women would have needed a lot of societal conditioning to want to look at that. But men? Men grew up on movies like *Silverado* and *Saving Private Ryan.* Men wanted to know how well they might have handled such things. So, no, human nature didn't really change. Society tended to stomp on the cruel ones, and since man was a creature of reason, most people shied away from behavior that could put them in prison or the death chamber. So, man *could* learn over time, but the basic drives probably did not, and so you fed the nasty little beast with fantasies, books and movies, and dreams, thoughts that walked through your consciousness while waiting for sleep to come. Maybe cops had a better time. *They* could exercise the little critter by handling those who stepped over the line. There was probably satisfaction in that, because you got both to feed the critter and to protect the society.

But if the beast still lived in the hearts of men, somewhere there would be men who would use whatever talents they had to—not so much control it as harness it to their own will, to use it as a tool in their personal quest for power. Such men were called Bad Guys. The unsuccessful ones were called sociopaths. The successful ones were called... Presidents.

Where did all this leave him? Jack Jr. wondered. He was still a kid, after all, even though he denied it and as a matter of law he was a grown man. Did a grown man stop growing? Stop wondering and asking questions? Stop seeking after information—or, as he thought of it, *truth*?

But once you had *truth,* what in hell did you do with it?

He didn't know that one yet. Maybe it was just one more thing to learn. Surely he had the same drive to learn as his father, else why was he watching this program instead of some mindless sitcom? Maybe he'd buy a book on Stalin and Hitler. Historians were always digging into old records. Problem was, then they applied their own personal ideas to what they found. He probably really needed a shrink to look things over. They had their ideological prejudices, too, but at least there was a patina of professionalism to their thought processes. It annoyed Junior that he went to sleep every night with thoughts unresolved and truths unfound. But that, he figured, was the whole point to this thing called life.

THEY WERE all praying. All quietly. Abdullah was murmuring through the words of his Koran. Mustafa was running through the same book in the sanctity of his own mind—not all of it, of course, just the parts that supported his mission for the coming day. To be brave, to remember their Holy Mission, to accomplish it without mercy. Mercy was Allah's business.

What if we survive? he asked himself, and was surprised at the thought.

They had a plan for this, of course. They'd drive back west and try to find their way back to Mexico, and then fly back home—to be welcomed with great rejoicing by their other comrades. In truth, he didn't expect this to happen, but hope was something no man sets completely aside, and however Paradise might beckon, life on earth was all that he actually knew.

That thought startled him, too. Did he just express doubt in his Faith? No, not that. Not that, exactly. Just a random thought. *There is no God but Allah and Mohammed is His messenger,* he chanted in his own mind, expressing the *Shahada,* which was the very foundation of Islam. No, he couldn't deny his Faith now. His Faith had brought him across the world, to the very location of his martyrdom.

His Faith had raised and nurtured his life, through childhood, through the anger of his father, into the very home of the infidels who spat upon Islam and nurtured the Israelis, there to affirm his Faith with his life. And his death, probably. Almost certainly, unless Allah Himself desired otherwise. Because all things in life were written by Allah's Own Hand . . .

THE ALARM went off just before six. Brian knocked on his brother's door.

"Wake up, G-man. We're wasting sunlight."

"Is that a fact?" Dominic observed from the far end of the corridor. "Beat ya, Aldo!" Which was a first.

"Then let's get it done, Enzo," Brian responded, and together they headed outside. An hour and a quarter later, they were back and at the breakfast table.

"It's a good day to be alive," Brian observed with his first sip of coffee.

"The Marine Corps must brainwash your ass, bro," Dominic observed, with a sip of his own.

"No, the endorphins just kick in. That's how the human body lies to itself."

"You grow out of it," Alexander told them. "All ready for your little field exercise?"

"Yes, Sergeant Major," Brian replied with a smile. "We get to whack Michelle for lunch."

"Only if you can track her without being spotted."

"It would be easier in the woods, you know. I'm trained in that particular skill."

"Brian, what do you think we've been doing here?" Pete inquired gently.

"Oh, is that what it is?"

"First get new shoes," Dominic advised.

"Yeah, I know. These are just about dead." The canvas uppers were separating from the rubber bottoms, and the bottoms were pretty shot, too. He hated doing it. He'd put a lot of miles in his running shoes, and a man can be senti mental about such things, which was frequently a matter of annoyance to his spouse.

"We'll hit the mall early. Foot Locker right next to the place they rent strollers," Dom reminded his brother.

"Yeah, I know. Okay, Pete, any advice on Michelle?" Brian asked. "You know, if we're out on a mission, we usually get a mission brief."

"That's a fair question, Captain. I'd suggest you look for her at Victoria's Secret, just across from The Gap. If you get close enough without being spotted, you win. If she says your name when you're more than ten feet away, you lose."

"This isn't strictly fair," Dominic pointed out. "She knows what we look like—especially height and weight. A real bad guy wouldn't have that information in his pocket. You can fake being taller, but not being shorter."

"And my ankles can't take high heels, y'know?" Brian added.

"You don't have the legs for it anyway, Aldo," Alexander needled. "Who ever said this job was easy?"

Except we still don't know what the fucking job is, Brian didn't respond. "Fair enough, we improvise, adapt, and overcome."

"Who are you now, Dirty Harry?" Dominic asked, finishing off his McMuffin.

"In the Corps, he's our favorite civilian, bro. Probably would have made a pretty good gunny."

"Especially with his .44 Smith."

"Kinda noisy for a handgun. Kinda tough on the hand, too. Except maybe the Auto-Mag. Ever shot one of those?"

"No, but I handled the one in the gun locker at Quantico. Damned thing ought to come with a trailer to haul it around with, but I bet it makes nice holes."

"Yeah, but if you want to conceal it, you better be Hulk Hogan."

"I hear that, Aldo." As a practical matter, the fanny packs they used didn't so much conceal a pistol as make it more convenient to carry. Any cop knew what it was on first sight, though few civilians recognized it. Both brothers carried a loaded pistol and a spare magazine in their packs, when they wore them. Pete wanted them to do so today just to make it harder to track Michelle Peters without being spotted. Well, you expected such things of training officers, didn't you?

THE SAME day began five miles away at Holiday Inn Express, and on this day, unlike the others, they all unrolled their prayer rugs and, as one man, said their morning Salat for what they all expected to be the last time. It took but a few minutes and then they all washed, to purify themselves for their task. Zuhayr even took the time to shave around his new beard, neatly trimming the part he wanted to wear into eternity, until, when satisfied, he dressed.

It wasn't until they were completely ready that they realized it was hours short of the proper time. Abdullah walked up the hill to Dunkin' Donuts for breakfast and coffee, this time even returning with a newspaper, which circulated its way around both rooms while the men drank their coffee and smoked their cigarettes.

Fanatics they might seem to their enemies, but they remained human, and the tension of the moment was unpleasant, and getting only worse by the minute. The coffee only pumped more caffeine into their systems, making hands shake and eyes narrow on the TV news. They checked their watches every few seconds, willing unsuccessfully for the hands to turn faster around the dials, then drank more of the coffee.

"NOW WE'RE getting excited, too?" Jack asked Tony at The Campus. He gestured at his workstation. "What's here that I don't see, buddy?"

Wills rocked back in his chair. "It's a combination of things. Maybe it's real. Maybe it's just a coincidence.

Maybe it's just a construct in the minds of professional analysts. You know how you tell what it really is?"

"Wait a week, look back, and see if anything actually happened?"

That was enough to make Tony Wills laugh. "Junior, you *are* learning the spook business. Jesus, I've seen more predictions go wrong in the intelligence business than they have on Preakness day at Pimlico. You see, unless you do know, you just *don't* know, but people in the business don't like to think that way."

"I remember when I was a kid, Dad used to get in shitty moods sometimes—"

"He was in CIA during the Cold War. The big shots were always asking for predictions that nobody could really give—at least not that meant anything. Your father was usually the guy who said, 'Wait awhile and you'll see for yourselves,' and that *really* pissed them off, but, you know, he was usually right, and there weren't any disasters on his watch."

"Will I ever be that good?"

"It's a lot to hope for, kid, but you never know. You're lucky to be here. At least the Senator knows what 'don't know' means. It means his people are honest, and they know they're not God."

"Yeah, I remember that from the White House. It always amazed me how many people in D.C. thought they really were."

DOMINIC DID the driving. It was a pleasant three or four miles down the hillside into town.

"Victoria's Secret? Suppose we'll bag her buying a nightie?" Brian wondered.

"We can only dream," Dominic said, turning left onto Rio Road. "We're early. Get your shoes first?"

"Makes sense. Park by the Belk's men's store."

"Roger that, Skipper."

* * *

"IS IT time?" Rafi asked. He'd done so three times in the past thirty minutes.

Mustafa checked his watch: 11:48. Close enough. He nodded.

"My friends, pack your things."

Their weapons were not loaded, but placed inside shopping bags. Assembled, they were too bulky and too obvious. Each man had twelve loaded magazines, with thirty rounds each, taped together in six pairs. Every weapon had a large sound suppressor tapped to screw onto the barrel. The purpose of these wasn't so much silence as control. He remembered what Juan had told him back in New Mexico. These weapons tended to jerk off target, climbing high and right. But he'd already gone over the weapons issues with his friends, and they all knew how to shoot, had all shot these things when they'd gotten them, and so they should know what to expect. Besides, they were going to what American soldiers called a target-rich environment.

Zuhayr and Abdullah carried out their travel things, locking them into the trunk of their rented Ford. On reflection, Mustafa decided to put the guns there, too, and so all four of them, each carrying his shopping bag, walked out to the car and set the bags standing up on the floor of the trunk. With that done, Mustafa got into the car, unthinkingly bringing the room key in his pocket. The drive was not a long one. The objective was already in sight.

The parking lot had the usual entrance points. He chose the northwest entrance, next to the Belk's men's store, where they could park close in. There, he switched off the engine and said his last prayer of the morning. The other three did much the same, getting out and walking to the back of the car. Mustafa popped the trunk. They were less than fifty meters from the door. Strictly speaking, there was little point in concealment, but Mustafa remembered the security desk. To delay police response, it had to begin there. So, he told them to keep their weapons in the shopping bags, and, bags dangling from their left hands, they walked to the door.

It was a Friday, not so busy a shopping day as Saturday, but close enough for their purposes. They came inside, passing the LensCrafters, which was busy—most of these people would probably escape unhurt, which was regrettable, but the main shopping area was still before them.

BRIAN AND Dominic were in the Foot Locker store, but Brian didn't see anything he liked. The Stride Rite next door was only for kids, so the twins proceeded forward, turning right. American Eagle Outfitters would doubtless have something, maybe in leather, with high tops that would be easier on the ankles.

TURNING LEFT, Mustafa passed a toy store and various clothing businesses on his way to the Center Court. His eyes were sweeping the area rapidly. Perhaps a hundred people in his immediate sight, and judging by K*B Toys, the retail stores would all be well peopled. He passed the Sunglass Hut and turned right for the security office. It was conveniently located, just a few steps from the restrooms. All four went into the men's room together.

A few people had noted their presence—four men of identically exotic appearance was unusual—but an American shopping mall is the nearest thing to a zoo for humans, and it took a lot for people to take much note of anything unusual, much less dangerous.

In the men's room, they all took their weapons from the shopping bags and assembled them. Bolts were pulled back. Magazines were inserted in the pistol grips. Each man slipped the five magazine pairs into pants pockets. Two screwed the lengthy suppressors onto their weapons. Mustafa and Rafi did not, deciding after rapid reflection that they preferred to hear the noise.

"Are we ready?" the leader asked. The replies were only nods.

"Then we shall eat lamb together in Paradise. To your places. When I shoot first, you will all begin."

BRIAN WAS trying on some low-top leather boots. Not quite the same as the boots he wore in the Marine Corps, but they looked and felt comfortable, and they fitted his feet as though custom designed. "Not bad."

"Want me to box them up?" the clerk—a girl—asked.

Aldo thought for a moment and decided: "No, I'll break them in right away." He handed her his disreputable Nikes, which she put in the box for the boots, and led him to the cash register.

MUSTAFA WAS looking at his watch. He figured two minutes for his friends to get in place.

Rafi, Zuhayr, and Abdullah were walking into the main concourse of the mall now, holding their weapons low, and, amazingly, largely escaping notice from the shoppers who bustled along and minded their own business. When the sweep hand reached twelve, Mustafa took a deep breath and walked out of the men's room, and to the left.

The security guard was at his chest-high desk, reading a magazine, when he saw a shadow on the desktop. He looked up to see a man of olive complexion.

"Can I help you, sir?" he asked politely. He had no time to react after that.

"Allahu Ackbar!" was the shouted reply. Then the Ingram came up.

Mustafa held the trigger for but a second, but in that second, a total of nine bullets entered the black man's chest. The impact of nine bullets pushed him backward half a step, and he fell, dead, to the tiled floor.

"WHAT THE hell was that?" Brian instantly asked his brother—the only person nearby—as all heads turned to the left.

* * *

RAFI WAS only twenty-five feet to their right-front when he heard the gunfire, and it was time for him to start. He dropped into a half crouch and brought his Ingram up. He turned right toward the Victoria's Secret store. The customers there all had to be women of no morals even to look at such whorish clothing, and perhaps, he thought, some would serve him in Paradise. He just pointed and held the trigger down.

The sound was deafening, like a colossal zipper of explosions. Three women were immediately hit and went down at once. Others just stood still for a second, their eyes wide with shock and disbelief, not taking any action at all.

For his part, Rafi was disagreeably surprised by the fact that more than half of his rounds had not hit anything. The poorly balanced weapon had jerked in his hand, spraying the ceiling. The bolt closed on an empty chamber. He looked down at it in surprise, then ejected the first magazine and reversed it, slapping it back into the port and looking for more targets. They'd started to run now, and so he brought the Ingram to his shoulder.

"FUCK!" Brian said. *What the hell is going on?* his mind shouted.

"Fuckin' right, Aldo." Dominic swiveled his fanny pack to the front of his belly and jerked at the string that opened the two-zipper closure. A second later, his Smith & Wesson was in his hands. "Cover my ass!" he commanded his brother. The shooter with the SMG was a bare twenty feet away, on the other side of a jewelry kiosk, facing away, but this wasn't Dodge City, there were no rules about facing down a criminal.

Dominic fell to one knee, and bringing the automatic up in both hands, he loosed two ten-millimeter hollow points into the center of the man's back, and then one more into the center of the back of his head. His target dropped straight down, and judging by the red explosion from the third shot, wouldn't be doing much else. The FBI agent jumped to the prostrate body and kicked the gun away. He noted immediately what it was, and then he saw that the body had extra magazines in its pockets. The immediate thought was *Oh, shit!* Then he heard the crackling roar of more gunfire to his left.

"More of 'em, Enzo!" Brian said, right at his brother's side, his Beretta in his right hand. "This one's all gone. Any ideas?"

"Follow me, cover my ass!"

MUSTAFA FOUND himself in a low-end jewelry store. There were six women in view, in front of and behind the counter. He lowered his weapon to his hip and fired, emptying his first magazine into them and feeling the momentary satisfaction of seeing them fall. When the gun stopped shooting, he ejected the empty magazine and reversed it to reload, cocking the bolt as he did so.

BOTH TWINS came to their feet and started moving west, not fast, but not slow either, with Dominic in the lead and Brian two steps back, their eyes mainly going to where the noise was. All Brian's training came flooding back into his consciousness. *Use cover and concealment wherever possible. Locate and engage the enemy.*

Just then a figure came left to right from Kay Jewelers, holding an SMG and spraying to his left into another jewelry store. The mall was a cacophony of screams and gunfire now, with people running blindly toward exits instead of first looking for where the danger was. A lot of those went down, mostly women. Some children.

Somehow this all passed the brothers by. They scarcely even saw the victims. There just wasn't time for that, and what training they'd had took over completely. The first target in view was the one standing there hosing the jewelry store.

"Going right," Brian said, darting that way with his head down but looking in the direction of his target.

* * *

BRIAN ALMOST died that way. Zuhayr was standing at Claire's Boutique, having just turned away from dumping a full magazine into it. Suddenly unsure of which way to go next, he turned left and saw a man with a pistol in his hand. He carefully shouldered his weapon and squeezed the trigger—

—two rounds fired off uselessly, then nothing. His first magazine had been expended, and it took two or three seconds for him to realize it. Then he ejected and reversed it, ramming it back into the bottom of his machine gun and looking back up—

—but the man was gone. Where? Without targets, he reversed direction and walked with a measured pace into the Belk's women's store.

BRIAN CROUCHED by the Sunglass Hut, peeking around the right side.

There, moving to the left. He brought his Beretta into his right hand and squeezed off one round—

—but it missed the head by a whisker when the man ducked.

"Fuck!" Brian then stood and put both hands on the pistol, leading just a hair and firing off four rounds. All four went into the thorax, below the shoulders.

MUSTAFA HEARD the noise but didn't feel the impacts. His body was full of adrenaline, and, under such circumstances, the body simply does not feel pain. Just a second later, he coughed up blood, which came as quite a surprise. More so, when he tried to turn to his left, his body didn't do what his mind commanded. The puzzlement lasted just another second or two when—

—DOMINIC WAS facing the second one, gun up and aimed. Again, he fired, as trained, for center-of-mass, and the Smith was on single-action, barking twice.

So good was his aim that the first round hit the target's weapon—

—THE INGRAM jumped in Mustafa's hands. He barely held on to it, but then he saw who'd attacked him and took careful aim and squeezed—but nothing happened. On looking down, he saw a bullet hole in the steel side of the Ingram, just where the bolt was. He took another second or two to realize that he was now disarmed. But his enemy was still before him and he raced toward him, hoping to use his gun as a club if nothing else.

DOMINIC WAS amazed. He'd seen at least one of his rounds take him in the chest—and the other one had broken his weapon. For some reason, he did not fire again. Instead he clubbed the bastard in the face with his Smith and headed forward, where there was more gunfire.

MUSTAFA FELT his legs weaken. The blow in the face did hurt, even though the five bullets had not. He tried to turn again, but his left leg would bear no weight, and he fell, turning to land on his back, where, suddenly, breathing came very hard indeed. He tried to sit up, even to roll, but as his legs had failed him, so the left side of his body was useless.

"THAT'S TWO down," Brian said. "Now what?"

The screaming had abated, but not by much. But the gunfire was still there, and it had changed character . . .

ABDULLAH blessed fate for putting the suppressor on his weapon. His shooting was more accurate than he'd ever hoped.

He was in the Sam Goody music store, which was filled with students. It was also a store with no rear exit, because it was so close to the westernmost entrance. Abdullah's face was grinning broadly as he walked into the store, firing as he went. The faces he saw were full of disbelief—and for an amused moment he told himself that *dis*belief was the reason he was killing them. He emptied his first magazine quickly, and indeed the suppressor allowed him to hit with half his shots. Men and women—boys and girls—screamed, stood still and staring for a few precious, deadly seconds, and then started running away. But at less than ten meters, it was just as easy to hit them in the back, and they really had nowhere to run. He just stood there, hosing the room, letting the targets select themselves. Some ran up the other side of the CD racks, trying to escape out the main door. These he shot as they passed, hardly two meters away. In seconds, he'd emptied his first magazine pair, and dumped it, pulling another from his pants pocket and slamming it home and cocking the bolt. But there was a mirror on the store's back wall, and in it he saw—

"JESUS, another one!" Dominic said.

"Okay." Brian darted to the other side of the entrance and took position against the wall, bringing his Beretta up. This put him on the same pseudo-corridor as the terrorist, but the setup didn't benefit a right-handed shooter worth a damn. He had to choose between shooting weak-hand—something he didn't practice as much as he should have done—or exposing his body to return fire. But something in his Marine mind just said *Fuck it* and he stepped to his left, pistol up in both hands.

Abdullah saw him and smiled, bringing his weapon to his shoulder—or trying to.

Aldo fired off two aimed shots into the target's chest, saw no effect, and then emptied his magazine. More than twelve rounds entered the man's body—

—ABDULLAH FELT them all, and he felt his body jerk with each impact. He tried firing his own weapon, but he missed with all of his shots, and then his body was no longer under his control. He fell forward, trying to recover his balance.

BRIAN EJECTED his empty magazine and pulled the other one from his fanny pack, slapping it in and dropping the slide-release lever. He was going on autopilot now. The bastard was still moving! Time to fix that. He walked over to the prone body, kicked the gun aside, and fired one round right into the back of his head. The skull split open—blood and brains exploded out onto the floor.

"JESUS, ALDO!" Dominic said, coming to his brother's side.

"Fuck that! We got at least one more out there. I'm down to one clip, Enzo."

"Me, too, bro."

Amazingly, most of the people on the floor, including the shot ones, were still alive. The blood on the floor could have been rain in a thunderstorm. But both brothers were too wired to be sickened by what they saw. They moved back out into the mall and headed east.

The carnage was just as bad here. The floor was defiled by numerous pools of blood. There were screams and whimpers. Brian passed a little girl, perhaps three years old, standing over the body of her mother, her arms fluttering like a baby bird's. No time, no damned time to do anything about it. He wished Pete Randall were close. He was a good corpsman. But even Petty Officer Randall would be overwhelmed by this mess.

There was still more chatter from a suppressed submachine gun. It was in the Belk's women's store, off to their left. Not all that far off by the sound of it. The sound of automatic-weapons fire is distinctive. Nothing else sounds quite the same. They split up, each taking one side of the short corridor leading past the Coffee Beanery and Bostonian Shoes into the next combat area.

The first floor of Belk's started off with perfumes and makeup. As before, they ran to the sound of the guns. There were six women down at perfume, and three more in makeup. Some were obviously dead. Others were just as obviously alive. Some called out for help, but there was no time for that. The twins split up again. The noise had just stopped. It had been off to their left front, but it wasn't there now. Had the terrorist run away? Was he just out of ammo?

There were expended cartridge cases all over the floor—nine-millimeter brass, they both saw. He'd had himself a good old time here, Dominic saw. The mirrors affixed to the building's internal pillars were nearly all shattered by gunfire. To his trained eye, it seemed as though the terrorist had walked in the front, sprayed the first people he'd seen—all women—and then worked his way back and to the left, probably going to wherever he saw the most potential targets. Probably just one guy, Brian's mind told him.

Okay, what are we up against? Dominic wondered. *How's he going to react? How does he think?*

For Brian it was simpler: *Where are you, you motherfucker?* For the Marine, he was an armed enemy, and nothing else. Not a person, not a human being, not even a thinking brain, just a target holding a weapon.

ZUHAYR EXPERIENCED a sudden diminution of excitement. He'd been more excited than at any moment in his life. He'd had only a few women in his life, and surely he'd killed more women here today than he'd ever fucked . . . but to him, here and now, somehow it felt just the same.

And all that struck him as very satisfying. He hadn't heard the shooting from before, none of it. He'd scarcely heard his own gunfire, so focused was he on his business. And good business it had been. The look on their faces when they saw him and his machine gun . . . and the look when the bullets struck . . . *that* was a pleasing sight. But he was down to his last two magazine pairs now. One was in his gun, and the other in his pocket.

Strange, he thought, that he could hear the relative silence now. There were no live women in his immediate area. Well . . . no unwounded women. Some of those he'd shot were making noise. Some were even trying to crawl away . . .

He couldn't have that, Zuhayr knew. He started walking toward one of them, a dark-haired woman wearing whorish red pants.

BRIAN WHISTLED to his brother and pointed. There he was, about five-eight, wearing khaki pants and a similarly colored bush jacket, fifty yards away. A playground shot for a rifle, something for a boot at Parris Island to do, but not quite so easy for his Beretta, however good a marksman he was.

Dominic nodded and started heading that way, but swiveling his head in all directions.

"TOO BAD, woman," Zuhayr said in English. "But do not be afraid, I send you to see Allah. You will serve me in Paradise." And he tried to fire a single round into her back. But the Ingram doesn't allow that easily. Instead he rippled off three rounds from a range of one meter.

BRIAN SAW the whole thing, and something just came loose. The Marine stood up and aimed with both hands. *"You motherfucker!"* he screamed, and fired as rapidly as accuracy allowed, from a range of perhaps a hundred feet. He fired a total of fourteen shots, almost emptying his weapon. And some of them, remarkably, hit the target.

Three, in fact, one of which got the target right in the belly, and another in center chest.

* * *

THE FIRST one *hurt*. Zuhayr felt the impact as he might have felt a kick in the testicles. It caused his arms to drop as though to cover up and protect from another injury. His weapon was still in his hands, and he fought through the pain to bring it back up as he watched the man approach.

BRIAN DIDN'T forget everything. In fact, a lot came flooding back into his consciousness. He had to remember the lessons of Quantico—and Afghanistan—if he wanted to sleep in his own bed that night. And so he took an indirect path forward, dodging around the rectangular goods tables, keeping his eyes on his target and trusting Enzo to look around. But he did that, too. His target didn't have command of his weapon. He was looking straight at the Marine, his face strangely fearful . . . but smiling? *What the hell?*

He walked right in now, straight at the bastard.

FOR HIS part, Zuhayr stopped fighting the suddenly massive weight on his weapon, and stood as straight as he could, looking in the eyes of his killer. *"Allahu Ackbar,"* he said.

"THAT'S NICE," Brian replied, and fired right into his forehead. "I hope you like it in hell." Then he bent down and picked up the Ingram, slinging it over his back.

"Clear it and leave it, Aldo," Dominic commanded. Brian did just that.

"Jesus, I hope somebody called 911," he observed.

"Okay, follow me upstairs," Dominic said next.

"What—why?"

"What if there's more'n four of 'em?" The reply-question was like a punch in Brian's mouth.

"Okay, I got your six, bro."

It struck both of them as incredible that the escalator was

still working, but they rode it up, both crouching and scanning all around. There were women all over the place—all over meaning as far from the escalator as possible—

"FBI!" Dominic called. "Is everybody okay here?"

"Yes," came multiple, separate, and equivocal replies from around the second floor.

Enzo's professional identity came back into full command: "Okay, we have it under control. The police will be here shortly. Until they get here, just sit tight."

The twins walked from the top of the "up" escalator to the top of the "down" one. It was immediately clear that the shooters hadn't come up here.

The ride down was dreadful beyond words. Again, there were pools of blood on a straight line from perfume to handbags, and now the lucky ones who were merely wounded were crying out for help. And, again, the twins had more important things to do. Dominic led his brother out into the main concourse. He turned left to check the first one he'd shot. This one was dead beyond question. His last ten-millimeter bullet had exploded out through his right eye.

On reflection, that left only one, if he was still alive.

HE WAS, despite all of his hits. Mustafa was trying to move, but his muscles were drained of blood and oxygen, and were not listening to the commands that came through the central nervous system. He found himself looking up, somewhat dreamily it seemed, even to him.

"You have a name?" one of them asked.

Dominic had only halfway expected an answer. The man was clearly dying, and not slowly, either. He turned to look for his brother—not there. "Hey, Aldo!" he called, to no immediate response.

BRIAN WAS in Legends, a sporting-goods shop, taking a quick look. His initiative was rewarded, and he took it back to the mall corridor.

Dominic was there, talking to his "suspect," but without getting much of a response.

"Hey, raghead," Brian said, returning. Then he knelt down in the blood beside the dying terrorist. "I got something for you."

Mustafa looked up in some puzzlement. He knew that death was close, and while he didn't exactly welcome it, he was content in his own mind that he'd done his duty to his Faith, and to Allah's Law.

Brian grabbed the terrorist's hands and crossed them on his bleeding chest. "I want you to carry this to hell with you. It's a pigskin, asshole, made from the skin of a real Iowa pig." And Brian held his hands on the football as he looked into the bastard's eyes.

The eyes went wide with recognition—and horror at the moment's transgression. He willed his arms to move away, but the infidel's hands overpowered his efforts.

"Yeah, that's right. I am Iblis himself, and you're going to my place." Brian smiled until the eyes went lifeless.

"What's that about?"

"Save it," Brian responded. "Come on."

They headed for where it had all started. A lot of women were on the floor, most of them moving some. All of them bleeding, and some quite a lot— "Find a drugstore. I need bandages, and make sure somebody called 911."

"Right." Dominic ran off, looking, while Brian knelt next to a woman of about thirty, shot in the chest. Like most Marines, and all marine officers, he knew rudimentary first aid. First he checked her airway. Okay, she was breathing. She was bleeding from two bullet holes in her upper left chest. There was a little pink froth on her lips. Lung shot, but not a bad one. "Can you hear me?"

A nod, and a rasp: "Yes."

"Okay, you're going to be okay. I know it hurts, but you are going to be okay."

"Who are you?"

"Brian Caruso, ma'am, United States Marines. You're going to be fine. Now I have to try'n help some others."

"No, no—I—" She grasped his arm.

"Ma'am, there's other people here hurt worse than you. You *will* be fine." And with that he pulled away.

The next one was pretty bad. A child, maybe, five years old, a boy, with three hits in his back, and bleeding like an overturned bucket. Brian turned him over. The eyes were open.

"What's your name, kid?"

"David," came the reply, surprisingly coherent.

"Okay, David, we're going to get you fixed up. Where's your mom?"

"I don't know." He was worried about his mother, more fearful for her than for himself, as any child would be.

"Okay, I'll take care of her, but let me look after you first, okay?" He looked up to see Dominic running toward him.

"There ain't no drugstore!" Dominic half shouted.

"Get something, T-shirts, anything!" he ordered his cop brother. And Dominic raced into the outfitters store where Brian had gotten his boots. He came out a few seconds later with an arm full of sweatshirts with various logos on the front.

And just then the first cop arrived, his service automatic out in both hands.

"Police!" the cop shouted.

"Over here, God damn it!" Brian roared in return. It took perhaps ten seconds for the officer to make it over. "Leather that pistol, trooper. The bad guys are all down," Brian told him in a more measured voice. "We need every damned ambulance you have in this town, and tell the hospital that they got a shitload of casualties coming. You got a first-aid kit in your car?"

"Who are you?" the cop demanded, without holstering his pistol.

"FBI," Dominic answered from behind the cop, holding his credentials up in his left hand. "The shooting part is over, but we got a lot of people down here. Call everybody. Call the local FBI office and everybody else. Now get on that radio, Officer, and right the hell now!"

Like most American cops, Officer Steve Barlow had a portable Motorola radio, with a microphone/speaker clipped to the epaulet of his uniform shirt, and he made a frantic call for backup and medical assistance.

Brian turned his attention to the little boy in his arms. At this moment, David Prentiss was the entire world for Captain Brian Caruso. But all the damage was internal. The kid had more than one sucking chest wound, and this was not good.

"Okay, David, let's take it real easy. How bad does it hurt?"

"Bad," the little boy replied after half a breath. His face was going pale.

Brian set him on the countertop of the Piercing Pagoda, then realized there might be *something* there to help—but he found nothing more than cotton balls. He crammed two of them into each of the three holes in the child's back, then rolled him back over. But the little boy was bleeding on the inside. He was bleeding so much internally that his lungs would collapse, and he'd go to sleep and die from asphyxiation in minutes unless somebody sucked his chest out, and there was not a single thing that Brian could do about it.

"Christ!" Of all people, it was Michelle Peters, holding the hand of a ten-year-old girl whose face was as aghast as a child could manage.

"Michelle, if you know anything about first aid, pick somebody and get your ass to work," Brian ordered.

But she didn't, really. She took a handful of cotton balls from the ear-piercing place and wandered off.

"Hey, David, you know what I am?" Brian asked.

"No," the child answered, with some curiosity peering past the pain he was feeling in his chest.

"I'm a Marine. You know what that is?"

"Like a soldier?"

The boy was dying right in his arms, Brian realized. *Please, God, not this one, not this little boy.*

"No, we're a lot better than soldiers. A Marine's about the best thing a man can be. Maybe someday when you grow up, maybe you can be a Marine like me. What do you think?"

"Shoot bad guys?" David Prentiss asked.

"You bet, Dave," Brian assured him.

"Cool," David thought, and then his eyes closed.

"David? Stay with me, David. Come on, Dave, open those eyes back up. We need to talk some more." He gently set the body back on the counter and felt for a carotid pulse.

But there wasn't any.

"Oh, shit. Oh, shit, man," Brian whispered. With that, all the adrenaline evaporated from his bloodstream. His body became a vacuum, and his muscles slack.

The first firefighters raced in, wearing khaki turnout coats and carrying boxes of what had to be medical gear. One of them took command, directing his people into various directions. Two headed to where Brian was. The first of them took the body from his arms and looked at it briefly, then set it on the floor, and then he moved away without a word to anyone, leaving Brian standing there, with a dead child's blood on his shirt.

Enzo was nearby, just standing and looking, now that professionals—mainly volunteer firefighters, actually, but proficient for all that—were assuming control of the area. Together they walked out the nearest exit into the clear noontime air. The entire engagement had lasted less than ten minutes.

Just like real combat, Brian realized. A lifetime—no, many lifetimes had come to their premature ends in what was relatively a blink of time. His pistol was back in his fanny pack. The expended magazine was probably back in Sam Goody. What he'd just experienced was the nearest thing to being Dorothy, sucked into a Kansas tornado. But he hadn't emerged into the Land of Oz. It was still central Virginia, and a bunch of people were dead and wounded behind them.

"Who are you guys?" It was a police captain.

Dominic held up his FBI ID, and that was enough for the moment.

"What happened?"

"Looks like terrorists, four of them, came in and shot up the place. They're all dead. We got 'em, all four of them," Dominic told him.

"You hurt?" the captain asked Brian, gesturing to the blood on his shirt.

Aldo shook his head. "Not a scratch. Cap'n, you got a lot of hurt civilians in there."

"What were you guys doing here?" the captain asked next.

"Buying shoes," Brian answered, a bitter edge on his voice.

"No shit..." the police captain observed, looking at the mall entrance, and standing still only because he was afraid of what he was going to see inside. "Any ideas?"

"Get your perimeter set up," Dominic said. "Check every license plate. Check the dead bad guys for ID. You know the drill, right? Who's the local SAC?"

"Just a Resident Agent here. Nearest real office is Richmond. Called there already. The SAC's a guy named Mills."

"Jimmy Mills? I know him. Well, the Bureau ought to send a lot of troops here. Your best move is to secure the crime scene and stand by, get the wounded people clear. It's a fucking mess in there, Cap'n."

"I believe it. Well, I'll be back."

Dominic waited for the police captain to walk inside, then he elbowed his brother and together they walked to his Mercedes. The police car at the parking lot entrance—two uniforms, one of which held a shotgun—saw the FBI ID and waved them past. Ten minutes later, they were back at the plantation house.

"What's going on?" Alexander asked in the kitchen. "The radio said—"

"Pete, you know about the second thoughts I've been having?" Brian asked.

"Yeah, but what—"

"You can forget about them, Pete. Forever and always," Brian announced.

||||||||||||||||||||||||||||||||||||||||||||||||||||||||||||||||||

CHAPTER 14

PARADISE

THE NEWS crews flocked to Charlottesville like vultures on a fallen carcass—or started to until things got more complex.

The next news flash came from a place called Citadel Mall in Colorado Springs, Colorado, then came one from Provo, Utah, and finally Des Moines, Iowa. *That* made it a colossal story. The Colorado mall hit involved six dead cadets from the U.S. Air Force Academy—several more had been pulled outside to safety by their classmates—and twenty-six civilian deaths.

But word of Colorado Springs had gotten quickly to Provo, Utah, and there the local police chief, with a good cop's instinct, had dispatched radio cars to every shopping center in town. At Provo Towne Center, they scored. Each car carried the mandatory police shotgun, and an epic shoot-out developed between four armed terrorists and six cops—all of whom knew how to shoot. That produced two badly wounded cops, three dead civilians—a total of eleven local citizens had joined in the pitched battle—and four very dead terrorists in what the FBI would later term a bungled attack. Des Moines might have turned out the same, except that the local city police were slow to react, and the final score there was four terrorists dead, but thirty-one citizens to keep them company.

In Colorado, two surviving terrorists were holed up in a retail store with a police SWAT team just fifty yards away, and a company of National Guard riflemen—activated with alacrity by the state's governor—on the way and champing at the bit to live out every soldier's fantasy: to use fire and maneuver to immolate the invaders and set their remains out for cougar bait. It took over an hour for this to come to pass, but aided by smoke grenades, the weekend warriors used enough firepower to destroy an invading army and ended the lives of two criminals—Arabs, as it turned out, to no one's surprise—in spectacular fashion.

By this time, all of America was watching TV, with reporters in New York and Atlanta telling America what they knew, which was little, and trying to explain the events of the day, which they did with the accuracy of grammar-school children. They endlessly repeated the hard facts they had managed to gather, and hauled in "experts" who knew little but said a lot. It was good for filling airtime, at least, if not to inform the public.

THERE WERE TVs at The Campus, too, and most work stopped as the troops watched them.

"Holy Jesus," Jack Jr. observed. Others had murmured or thought much the same, but it was somewhat worse for them, since they were technically members of the intelligence community, which had not provided strategic warning against this attack on their home country.

"It's pretty simple," Tony Wills observed. "If we do not have human-intelligence assets in the field, then it's hard for us to get any kind of warning, unless the bad guys are really loose on how they use their cell phones. But the news media likes to tell people how we track the bad guys, and the bad guys learn from that. The White House staffers, too—they like to tell reporters how smart they are, and they leak data on signals intelligence. You sometimes wonder if they're stringers for the terrorists, the way they give away code-word-sensitive information." In reality, the staff pukes were just showing off to the reporters, of course, which was about the only thing they knew how to do.

"So, the rest of the day the newsies will be screaming about 'another intelligence failure,' right?"

"Bet on it," Wills responded. "The same people who trash the intelligence community will now complain that it can't do the job—but without acknowledging their own role in crippling it every chance they get. Same thing from Congress, of course. Anyway, let's get back to work. NSA will be looking for a little cheering on the part of the opposition—they're human, too, right? They like to thump their chests some when they pull off an operation. Let's see if our friend Sali is one of them."

"But who's the big kahuna who ordered this one?" Jack asked.

"Let's see if we can find out." More important, Wills didn't add at the moment, was determining *where* the bastard was. A face with a location attached to it was a lot more valuable than a face without one.

UPSTAIRS, Hendley had his senior people together in front of *his* TV set.

"Thoughts?"

"Pete called up from Charlottesville. Care to guess where our two trainees were?" Jerry Rounds asked.

"You're kidding," Tom Davis responded.

"No, I'm not. They whacked the bad guys for fair, without outside assistance, and they're back at the house now. Bonus: Brian—the Marine—had been having second thoughts about his function. That, Pete reports, is a thing of the past. He can't wait to go out on some real missions. Pete thinks they're just about ready, too."

"So, we just need some solid targets?" Hendley asked.

"My people will be checking the feed from NSA. You gotta assume that the bad guys will be talking back and forth now. Their downtime in chatting back and forth should be coming to an end even now," Rick Bell thought aloud. "If we're ready to go active, then we can go active, and soon."

That was Sam Granger's department. He'd kept quiet to this point, but now it was time to speak.

"Well, guys, we have two kids ready to go out and service some targets," he said, using a phrase the Army had invented twenty years before. "They are good kids, Pete tells me, and from what happened today I think they will be properly motivated."

"What is the opposition thinking?" Hendley asked. It wasn't hard to figure out, but he wanted additional opinions.

"They wanted to sting us cleverly. The objective here manifestly is to strike at Middle America," Rounds led off. "They think they can strike fear in our hearts by showing us they can attack us anywhere, not just at obvious targets like New York. That was the element of cleverness in this operation. Probably fifteen to twenty total terrorists, plus some support personnel, maybe. That's a fairly large number, but not unprecedented—they maintained good operational security. Their people were well motivated. I would not say that they were particularly well trained, though, they just decided to toss a mad dog in the backyard to bite some of the kids, as it were. They've demonstrated their political willingness to do some very bad things, but that's not a surprise; also to throw dedicated personnel away, but that's not a surprise either. The attack was low-tech in nature, just some bad guys with light automatic weapons. They have demonstrated viciousness, but not real professionalism. In less than two days, the FBI will have them tracked down to their point of origin, probably, and maybe their routes of entry. They did not learn to fly or anything like that, so they probably have not been in-country all that long. I'd be interested in learning who scouted out their objectives. The element of timing suggests some preplanning, but not much, I'd guess—it's not hard to read the time off a wristwatch. They didn't plan on getting away after doing their shooting. They probably came in with their objectives already identified. At this point, I'd bet a few bucks that they've only been inside our borders for a week or two—even less, depending on their method of ingress. The Bureau will have that one nailed down pretty soon."

"Pete reports the weapons were Ingram submachine guns. They look pretty—that's why they show up in TV and the movies," Granger explained. "But they are not really efficient weapons."

"How did they get them?" Tom Davis asked.

"Good question. Figure the FBI already has the ones from Virginia, and is busy tracking them down by serial number. They're good at it. We should have the information by tonight. That will give them leads on how the weapons got into the terrorists' hands, and then the investigation will get going."

"WHAT'S THE Bureau going to do, Enzo?" Brian asked.

"It's a major case. It'll have a code word assigned, and every agent in the country can be called in to work on it. Right now, first thing they're looking for is the car the bad guys used. Maybe it's stolen. More likely it's rented. You have to sign for those, leave a copy of your driver's license, credit card, all the normal stuff you do in order to exist in America. It can all be followed. It all leads somewhere, bro. That's why you chase them all down."

"How are you guys doing?" Pete asked, entering the room.

"A drink helps," Brian answered. He'd already cleaned his Beretta, as Dominic had done with his Smith & Wesson. "It wasn't fun, Pete."

"It isn't supposed to be. Okay, I just talked with the home office. They want to see you guys in a day or so.

Brian, you had some qualms before, and you say that's changed. That still true?"

"You've trained us to identify, close on, and kill people, Pete. And I can live with that—just so's we're not doing something completely off the reservation."

Dominic just nodded agreement, but his eyes didn't leave Alexander.

"Okay, good. There's an old joke in Texas about why the lawyers are so good down there. The answer is, there's more men who need killin' than horses that need stealin'. Well, those who need killing, maybe you two can help them along some."

"Are you finally going to tell us who we're working for, exactly?" Brian asked.

"You will find that out in due course—just a day or so."

"Okay, I can wait that long," Brian said. He was doing some quick analysis of his own. General Terry Broughton might know something. For damned sure that Werner guy in FBI did, but this former tobacco plantation they'd been training on didn't belong to any part of the government he knew about. CIA had "The Farm" near Yorktown, Virginia, but that was about a hundred fifty miles away. This place didn't feel like "Agency," at least not in accordance with his assumptions, wrong though they could be. In fact, this place didn't smell "government" at all, not to his nose. But one way or another, in a couple of days he'd know something substantive, and he could wait that long.

"What do we know about the guys we whacked today?"

"Nothing much. That'll have to wait awhile. Dominic, how long before they start finding stuff out?"

"By noon tomorrow they'll have a lot of information, but we don't have a pipeline into the Bureau, unless you want me to—"

"No, I don't. We might have to let them know that you and Brian aren't the new version of the Lone Ranger, but it ought not to go very far."

"You mean I'll have to talk to Gus Werner?"

"Probably. He has enough juice in the Bureau to say you're on 'special assignment' and make it stick. I imagine he'll be patting himself on the back for talent-scouting you for us. You two did pretty damned well, by the way."

"All we did," the Marine said, "was what we've been trained to do. We had just enough time to get our shit together, and after that it was all automatic. They taught me at the Basic School that the difference between making it and not making it is usually just a few seconds' worth of thinking. If we'd been in the Sam Goody when it all started instead of a few minutes later, it might have been different in the final outcome. One other thing—two men are about four times as effective as one man. There's actually a study about it. 'Non-Linear Tactical Factors In Small-Unit Engagements,' I think the title is. It's part of the syllabus at Recon School."

"Marines really do know how to read, eh?" Dominic asked, reaching for a bottle of bourbon. He poured two stiff ones, handing one to his brother and taking a pull on his own.

"The guy in the Sam Goody—he smiled at me," Brian said in reflective amazement. "I didn't think about it at the time. I guess he wasn't afraid to die."

"It's called martyrdom, and some people really do think that way," Pete told them both. "So, what did you do?"

"I shot him, close range, maybe six or seven times—"

"Far side of ten times, bro," Dominic corrected him. "Plus the last one in the back of his head."

"He was still moving," Brian explained. "And I didn't have any cuffs to slap on him. And, you know, I'm not really all that worried about it." And besides, he would have bled out anyway. The way things had worked out, his trip into the next dimension had just happened sooner.

"B-3 AND bingo! We have a bingo," Jack announced from his workstation. "Sali is a player, Tony. Look here," he said, pointing to his computer screen.

Wills punched up his "take" from NSA, and there it was. "You know, chickens are supposed to cackle after they lay an egg, just to let the world know how good they are. Works with these birds, too. Okay, Jack, it's official. Uda bin Sali is a player. Who is this addressed to?"

"It's a guy he chats on the 'Net with. He mainly talks to him about money moves."

"Finally!" Wills observed, checking the document on his own workstation. "They want photos of the guy, a whole spread. Maybe Langley is finally going to put some coverage on him. Praise the Lord!" He paused. "Got a list of the people he e-mails to?"

"Yep. Want it?" Jack keyed it up and hit the PRINT command. In just fifteen seconds, he handed the sheet over to his roomie. "Numbers and dates of e-mails. I can print up all the interesting ones, and the reasons I find them interesting, if you want."

"We'll let that sit for the moment. I'll get this up to Rick Bell."

"I'll hold the fort."

DID YOU SEE THE NEWS ON TV, Sali had written to a semiregular correspondent. THIS OUGHT TO GIVE THE AMERICANS A STOMACHACHE!

"Yeah, it sure will," Jack told the screen. "But you just tipped your hand, Uda. Oops."

SIXTEEN MORE martyrs, Mohammed thought, watching a TV in Vienna's Bristol Hotel. It was only painful in the abstract. Such people were, really, expendable assets. They were less important than he, and that was the truth, because of his value to the organization. He had the looks and the language skills to travel anywhere, and the brainpower to plan his missions well.

The Bristol was an especially fine hotel, just across the street from the even more ornate Imperial, and the minibar had some good cognac, and he liked good cognac. The mission had not gone all that well... he'd hoped for hundreds of dead Americans, instead of several dozen, but with all the armed police and even some armed citizens, the high end of his expectations had been overly optimistic. But the strategic objective had been achieved. All Americans now knew that they were not safe. No matter where they might live, they could be struck by his Holy Warriors, who were willing to trade their lives for the Americans' sense of security. Mustafa, Saeed, Sabawi, and Mehdi were now in Paradise—if that place really existed. He sometimes thought it was a tale told to impressionable children, or to the simpleminded who actually listened to the preaching of the imams. You had to choose your preachers carefully, since not all the imams saw Islam the way Mohammed did. But they did not want to rule all of it. He did—or maybe just a piece of it, just so long as it included the Holy Places.

He couldn't talk aloud about matters like this. Some senior members of the organization really did believe, they were more to the conservative—reactionary—side of the Faith than were those such as the Wahabis of Saudi Arabia. To his eyes the latter were just the corrupt rich of that hideously corrupt country, people who mouthed the words while indulging their vices at home and abroad, spending their money. And money was easily spent. You could not take it to the afterlife, after all. Paradise, if it truly existed, had no need of money. And if it did not exist, then there was no use for money, either. What *he* wanted, what he hoped to—no, what he *would* have in his lifetime—was power, the ability to direct people, to bend others to his will. For him, religion was the matrix that set the shape of the world that he would be controlling. He even prayed on occasion, lest he forget that shape—more so when he met with his "superiors." But as the chief of operations, it was he and not they who determined their organization's course through the obstacles placed in their path by the idolaters of the West. And in choosing the path, he also chose the nature of their strategy, which came from their religious beliefs, which were easily guided by the political world in which they operated. Your enemy shaped your strategy, after all, since his strategy was that which had to be thwarted.

So, now, the Americans would know fear as they'd not known it before. It was not their political capital or their financial capital that was at risk. It was all of their lives. The mission had been designed from the beginning mainly to kill women and children, the most precious and most vulnerable parts of any society.

And with that done, he twisted the top off another small bottle of cognac.

Later, he'd light up his laptop and get reports from his underlings in the field. He'd have to tell one of his bankers to put some more currency into his Liechtenstein account. It wouldn't do to tap that account dry. Then the Visa accounts would be eliminated, and vanish forever into the ether-world. Otherwise, the police would come after him, with a name and perhaps with photos. That would not do. He'd be in Vienna another few days, then back home for a week to meet with his seniors and plan future operations. With such a success under his belt, they'd listen more closely now. His alliance with the Colombians had paid off, despite their misgivings, and he was riding the crest of the wave. A few nights more of celebration and he'd be ready to return to the rather less lively nightlife of his home, which was mostly coffee or tea—and talk, endless talk. Not action. Only through action could he achieve the goals set for him . . . by his seniors . . . and himself.

"MY GOD, Pablo," Ernesto said, turning his own TV off.

"Come now, it's not that much of a surprise," Pablo responded. "You didn't expect them to set up a table to sell Girl Scout cookies."

"No, but this?"

"That is why they are called terrorists, Ernesto. They kill without warning and attack people unable to defend themselves." There had been a lot of TV coverage from

Colorado Springs, where the presence of National Guard trucks made such a dramatic backdrop. There the uniformed civilians had even dragged the two terrorist bodies out—ostensibly to clear the area where the smoke grenades had started some fires, but really to display the bodies, of course. The local military in Colombia liked to do similar things. Soldiers showing off. Well, the Cartel's own *sicarios* often did the same, didn't they? But it wasn't something he'd point out in this setting. It was important to Ernesto that his identity be that of a "businessman," and not a drug dealer or terrorist. In his mirror, he saw a man who provided a valuable product and service to the public, for which he was paid, and to protect which he had to deal with his competitors.

"But how will the *norteamericanos* react?" Ernesto asked the air.

"They will bluster and investigate it like any street murder, and some things they will find out, but most things they will not—and we have a new distribution network in Europe, which," he reminded his boss, "is *our* objective."

"I did not expect so spectacular a crime, Pablo."

"But we discussed all this," Pablo said in the calmest of voices. "Their hope was to commit some spectacular demonstration"—he did not say *crime,* of course—"which would strike fear into their hearts. Such rubbish is important to them, as we all knew beforehand. The important thing to us is that it will direct their troublesome activities away from our interests.

Sometimes he had to be patient explaining things to his boss. The important thing was the money. With money, you could buy power. With money, you could buy people and protection, and not only safeguard your own life and the life of your family, but also control your country. Sooner or later, they would arrange the election of someone who would say the words the *norteamericanos* wanted to hear, but who would do little, except maybe deal with the Cali group, which suited them fine. Their only real concern was that they might buy the protection of a turncoat, one who would take their money and then turn on them like a disloyal dog. Politicians were all made of the same cloth, after all. But he'd have informers inside the camp of such people, backup security of his own. They would "avenge" the assassination of the false friend whose life he'd have to take in such circumstances. All in all, it was a complex game, but a playable one. And he knew how to maneuver the people and the government—even the North American one, if it came to that. His hands reached far, even into the minds and souls of those who had no idea whose hand was pulling their strings. This was especially true of those who spoke against legalizing his product. Should *that* happen, then his profit margin would evaporate, and, along with it, his power. He couldn't have that. No. For him and his organization, the status quo was a perfectly fine *modus vivendi* with the world as a whole. It was not perfection—but perfection was something he could not hope to achieve in the real world.

THE FBI had worked fast. Picking out the Ford with New Mexico tags had not been taxing, though every single tag number in the parking lot had been "run" and tracked down to its owner, and in many cases the owner had been interviewed by a sworn, gun-toting agent. In New Mexico, it had been discovered that the National car rental agency had security cameras, and the tape for the day in question was available, and, remarkably, it showed another rental that was of direct interest to the Des Moines, Iowa, field office. Less than an hour later, the FBI had the same agents back to check out the Hertz office just half a mile away, and that, too, had TV cameras inside. Between printed records and the TV tapes, they had false names (Tomas Salazar, Hector Santos, Antonio Quinones, and Carlos Oliva) to play with, images of their equally false driver's licenses, and cover names for four subjects. The documentation was also important. The international driver's licenses had been obtained in Mexico City, and telexes were fired off to the Mexican Federal Police, where cooperation was immediate and efficient.

In Richmond, Des Moines, Salt Lake City, and Denver, Visa card numbers were queried. The chief of security at Visa was a former senior FBI agent, and here computers not only identified the bank of origin for the credit accounts, but also tracked four cards through a total of sixteen gas stations, showing the paths taken and the speed of advance for all four terrorist vehicles. Serial numbers off the Ingram machine guns were processed through the FBI's sister agency, the Treasury Department's Bureau of Alcohol, Tobacco, Firearms and Explosives. There it was determined that all sixteen weapons had been part of a shipment hijacked eleven years earlier in Texas. Some of their sisters had turned up in drug-related shootings all across the country, and *that* piece of information opened a whole new line of investigation for the Bureau to run down. At the four major crime scenes, fingerprints were taken of the dead terrorists, plus blood for DNA identification.

The cars, of course, were removed to the FBI offices and thoroughly dusted for fingerprints and also sampled for DNA evidence to see if perhaps additional persons had been in them. The management and staff of each hotel were interviewed, and also the employees of the various fast-food establishments, as were employees of local bars and other restaurants. The phone records of the motels were obtained to check out what, if any, telephone calls had been made. These turned up mainly Internet Service Providers, and the laptop computers of the terrorists were seized, dusted for prints, and then analyzed by the Bureau's in-house techno-weenies. A total of seven hundred agents were assigned exclusively to the case, code-named ISLAMTERR.

The victims were mostly in local hospitals, and those who could speak were interviewed that evening to ascertain what they knew or could remember. Bullets from their bodies were taken for evidence and would be matched with the weapons seized and taken to northern Virginia, site of the brand-new FBI Laboratory, for testing and analysis. All of this information went to the Department of Homeland Security, which, of course, forwarded every bit of it to CIA, NSA, and the rest of the American intelligence community, whose field intelligence officers were already pinging their agents for any relevant information. The spooks also queried those foreign intelligence services thought to be friendly—this was an exaggeration in most cases, of course—for feedback and information relating to the case. All of the information thus gleaned came to The Campus via the CIA/NSA link. All of the data intercepted found its way to The Campus's enormous central computer room in the basement, where it was classified as to type and set up for the analysts who'd arrive in the morning.

UPSTAIRS, everyone had gone home for the night, except for the security staff and those who cleaned up after every day. The workstations used by the analysis staff were protected in several ways to make sure they could not be turned on without authorization. Security was tight there, but it was kept low-key, the better to maintain it, and monitored by closed-circuit television cameras whose "take" was always under electronic and human scrutiny.

IN HIS apartment, Jack thought about calling his father, but decided not to. He was probably getting bombarded by TV and print newsies, despite his well-known practice of saying nothing about anything in order to give the sitting President, Edward Kealty, free rein. There *was* a secure and very private line that only the kids knew about, but Jack decided to leave that one to Sally, who was a little more excitable than he was. Jack let it go with sending his dad an e-mail that essentially said *What the hell* and *I sure wish you were still in the White House.* But he knew that Jack Sr. was most likely thanking God that he wasn't, maybe even hoping that Kealty would listen to his advisers for a change—what good ones he had—and think before acting. His father probably *had* called some friends abroad to find out what they knew and thought, and maybe passed on some high-level opinions, since foreign governments mostly listened to what he had to say, quietly, in private rooms. Big Jack was still somewhat inside the system. He could call friends left over from his presidency to find out what was really going on. But Jack didn't think that one all the way through.

HENDLEY HAD a secure telephone in his office and at his home, called an STU-5, a brand-new product of AT&T and NSA. It had come to him through irregular means.

He was on it at that moment.

"Yes, that's right. We'll have the feed tomorrow morning. Not much point in sitting in the office and staring at a mostly blank screen right now," the former senator said reasonably, sipping at his bourbon and soda. Then he listened to the following inquiry.

"Probably," he responded to a rather obvious question. "But nothing 'hard' yet . . . about what you'd expect at this point, yes."

Another lengthy question.

"We have two guys right now, just about ready . . . Yes, we do—about four of them. We're taking a close look at them right now—tomorrow, that is. Jerry Rounds is thinking hard on the subject, along with Tom Davis—that's right, you don't know him, do you? Black guy, from other side of the river, both parts of the building. He's pretty smart, has a good feel for financial stuff, and also the operational side. Surprising that you never crossed paths with him. Sam? He's hot to trot—believe it. The trick is picking the right targets . . . I know, you can't be a part of that. Please pardon my calling them 'targets.'"

A lengthy monologue, plus a tag question.

"Yes, I know. That's why we're here. Soon, Jack.

Soon . . . Thanks, buddy. You, too. See ya sometime." And he hung up, knowing that he wouldn't actually be seeing his friend anytime soon . . . maybe never again in person. And that was a goddamned shame. There weren't many people who understood things like this, and more was the pity. One more call to make, and this on a regular phone.

CALLER ID told Granger who it was before he picked up.

"Yeah, Gerry?"

"Sam, those two recruits. You sure they're ready to play in the bigs?"

"Ready as they need to be," the chief of operations assured his boss.

"Get 'em up here for lunch. You, me, them, and Jerry Rounds."

"I'll call Pete first thing in the morning." No sense doing it right away. It was barely a two-hour drive, after all.

"Good. You have any misgivings?"

"Gerry, the proof of the pudding, you know? We have to see sooner or later."

"Yeah, right. See you tomorrow."

"'Night, Gerry." Granger hung the phone back up and went back to his book.

THE MORNING news was particularly sensational all over America—all over the world, for that matter. The satellite feeds from CNN, FOX, MSNBC, and every other agency that owned TV cameras and an uplink truck provided the world with a lead story that could not be buried by anything less than a nuclear detonation. The European papers expressed ritual sympathy with America for its newest travail—soon to be forgotten and retracted, in effect if not in particulars. The American news media talked about how frightened American citizens were. Not with any poll numbers to back it up, of course, but across the country citizens were suddenly buying firearms for their

own personal protection, which purpose would not be
served well, or at all. Police knew without being told to
take a close look at anyone who might have come from a
country east of Israel, and if some dumbass lawyers called
that ethnic profiling, then to hell with him. The crimes of
the previous day had not been committed by a tour group
from Norway.

Church attendance was up, a little.

All across America, people went to work and did their
jobs, with a "What do you think of all this?" aimed at co-
workers, who invariably shook their heads and went back
to the business of making steel, automobiles, or delivering
the mail. They were not terribly fearful, in fact, because
even with four such incidents, it had all happened far from
where most of them lived, and such events happened very
rarely, and not enough to be a seriously personal threat. But
all the working men in the country knew in their hearts that
somebody, somewhere, really needed to have his ass
kicked.

Twelve miles away, Gerry Hendley saw his papers—the
New York Times was delivered by special messenger, while
the *Washington Post* had arrived by a normal pickup truck.
In both cases, the editorials could have been written by the
same clone, urging calm and circumspection, noting that
the country had a President to react to these dreadful
events, and calmly instructing the President to think before
acting. The Op-Ed pieces were somewhat more interesting.
Some columnists actually reflected the average citizen.
There would be a national cry for vengeance on this day,
and for Hendley the good news was that he might just be
able to respond to it. The bad news was that no one would
ever know, if he did it right.

All in all, this Saturday would not be a slow news day.

And The Campus's parking lot would be full, which
would escape the notice of those who drove past the place.
The cover story, if one were needed, was that the four mas-
sacres of the previous day had caused some instability in

the financial markets—which, it turned out later in the day, was true.

Jack Jr. correctly assumed it would be a casual-dress day, and drove his Hummer 2 into work wearing jeans, a pullover shirt, and sneaks. The security people were fully uniformed, of course, and as stone-faced as ever.

Tony Wills was just lighting up his computer when Jack came in at 8:14.

"Hey, Tony," the young Ryan said in greeting. "What's the traffic like?"

"See for yourself. They're not asleep," Wills told his trainee.

"Roger that." He set down his coffee on the desk and slid into his comfortable swivel chair before lighting up his computer and getting through the security systems that protected what was on it. The morning "take" from NSA— that outfit *never* slept. And it was immediately clear that the people he kept track of paid attention to the news.

It was to be expected that the people in whom NSA had so much interest were not friends of the United States of America, but, even so, Jack Jr. was surprised—even shocked—by the content of some of the e-mails he read. He remembered his own feelings when the United States Army had charged into Saudi Arabia after the forces of the now defunct United Islamic Republic, and the *rush* of satisfaction when he'd seen a tank explode from direct fire. He hadn't thought for a moment about the three men who'd just perished within their steel tomb, rationalizing that they had taken up arms against America, and that was something that bore a price, a wager of sorts, and if the coin came up tails, well, that was why they called it gambling. Partly that had been his youth, since for a child everything seems directed to him as the center of the known universe, an illusion that takes time to discard. But for the most part the people killed the day before had been innocent civilians, noncombatants, mostly women and children, and to take pleasure in their deaths was just plain barbarism. But here it was. Twice now, America had expended blood to save the mother country of Islam, and some Saudis were talking like *this*?

"Damn," he whispered. Prince Ali wasn't like this. He and Jack's father were *friends*. They were *pals*. They'd visited each other's homes. He himself had spoken with the guy, picked his brain, listened closely to what he'd had to say. Okay, sure, he'd mostly been a kid then, but Ali wasn't this sort of guy. But neither had his own father ever been Ted Bundy, and Bundy had been an American citizen, had probably even voted. So, living in a country did not make you a roving ambassador.

"Not everybody loves us, kid," Wills said, looking over at his face.

"What have we ever done to hurt them?" Junior asked.

"We're the biggest, richest kid on the block. What we say goes, even when we don't tell people what to do. Our culture is overpowering, whether it's Coca-Cola or *Playboy* magazine. That sort of thing can offend people's religious beliefs, and in some parts of the world religious beliefs define how they think. They do not recognize our principle of religious freedom, and if we allow something that offends their closely held beliefs, then in their mind it's our fault."

"Are you defending these birds?" Jack Jr. demanded.

"No, I am explaining how they think. To understand something does not mean approval of it." Commander Spock had said that once, but evidently Jack had missed that episode. "Your job, remember, is to understand how they think."

"Fine. They think fucked-up. I understand that. Now I have numbers to check out," and Jack set the e-mail transcripts aside and started looking into money moves. "Hey, Uda is working today. Hmm, he does some of this from his home, doesn't he?"

"That's right. Nice thing about computers," Wills said. "He doesn't have the lash-up at home he has at the office, though. Any interesting moves?"

"Just two, into the Liechtenstein bank. Let me run this account..." Ryan did some mouse work and came up with an ID on the account. It wasn't an especially big one. In fact, by Sali's standards it was downright tiny. Just half a million Euros, used mostly for credit card expenditures, his own and...others...

"Hey, this account supports a bunch of Visa cards," he said to Wills.

"Really?"

"Yeah, like a dozen or so. No, it's...sixteen, aside from the ones he uses..."

"Tell me about the account," Wills ordered. Sixteen suddenly seemed a very important number.

"It's a numbered one. NSA got it because of the trapdoor in the bank's accounting program. It's not big enough to be very important, but it is covert."

"Can you pull up the Visa numbers?"

"The account numbers? Sure." Jack selected the account numbers, cut-and-pasted them to a new document, and printed it. Then he handed it across.

"No, you look at this," Wills said, handing across a sheet of his own.

Jack took it, and instantly the account numbers looked familiar. "What's your list about?"

"Those bad boys in Richmond all had Visa cards, used 'em to buy gas across the country—looks like their trip originated in New Mexico, by the way. Jack, you tied Uda bin Sali to yesterday. It looks like he's the guy who bankrolled their expense accounts."

Jack looked at the sheets again, comparing one list of numbers with the others. Then he looked up.

"Fuck," he breathed.

And Wills thought about the miracle of computers and modern communications. The shooters from Charlottesville had used the Visa cards to purchase gas and food, all right, and their little friend Sali had just pumped some money into the bank account that paid the bills. He'd probably act Monday to kill off the accounts, to drop them off the face of the earth. But he'd be too late.

"Jack, who told Sali to drop money into the bank account?" *We got us a target,* Wills did not say. *Maybe more than one.*

CHAPTER 15

RED COATS AND BLACK HATS

THEY LET Jack do the computer work, cross-referencing the e-mails to and from Uda bin Sali that day. It was actually fairly miserable work, since Jack had the skills but not yet the soul of an accountant. But he soon learned that the notice to fund the account came from someone named 56MoHa@eurocom.net, who'd logged in over an 800 line from Austria.

They couldn't track him down any more closely than that, but now they had a new name on the Internet to keep track of. It was the cyber identity of somebody who gave orders to a suspected—*known*—banker for terrorists, and that made 56MoHa@eurocom.net very interesting indeed. It was up to Wills to twig NSA to keep track of that one, in case they had not already made it a "handle of interest," as such identities were known. It was widely believed in the computer community that such handles were largely anonymous, and largely they were, but once they became known to the proper agencies they could be pursued. It was usually by illegal means, but if the line between legal and illegal conduct on the Internet could operate in favor of teenaged pranksters, the same was true for the intelligence community, whose computers were difficult to locate, much less to hack. The most immediate problem was that Eurocom.net did not maintain any long-term storage of its message traffic, and once they fell off the server RAM—by being read by the intended recipient—they were essentially gone forever. Maybe NSA would note that this mutt had written to Uda bin Sali, but lots of people did, for money-changing purposes, and even NSA didn't have the manpower to read and analyze every single e-mail that crossed its computerized path.

THE TWINS arrived just before 11:00 A.M., guided by their in-car GPS computers. The identical C-class Mercedes sedans were directed to the small visitors' parking lot located directly behind the building. There Sam Granger met them, shook hands, and walked them inside. They were immediately issued lapel passes to get them past the security personnel, whom Brian immediately typed as former military NCOs.

"Nice place," Brian observed as they headed for the elevators.

Bell smiled. "Yeah, in private industry we can hire better decorators." It also helped if you happened to like the decorator's taste in art, which, fortunately, he did.

"You said 'private industry,'" Dominic observed at once. This was not, he thought, a time to enjoy the subtlety of the moment. This was the agency he worked for, and *everything* here was important.

"You'll get fully briefed today," Bell said, wondering how much truth he had just relayed to his guests.

The Muzak in the elevators was no more offensive than usual, and the lobby on the top floor—where the boss always was—was pretty vanilla, though it was Breyers vanilla instead of the Safeway house brand.

* * *

"**SO, YOU** tumbled to this today?" Hendley was asking. This new kid, he thought, really did have his father's nose.

"It just jumped off the screen at me," Jack replied. About what one would expect him to say, except that it had not leaped off anyone else's screen.

The boss's eyes went to Wills, whose analytical ability he knew well. "Jack's been looking at this Sali guy for a couple of weeks. We thought he might be a minor-league player, but today he moved up to triple-A status, maybe more," Tony speculated. "He's indirectly tied to yesterday."

"NSA twig to this yet?" Hendley asked.

Wills shook his head. "No, and I don't think they will. It's too indirect. They and Langley are keeping an eye on his guy, but as a barometer, not a principal." *Unless somebody at one place or the other has a lightbulb moment,* he didn't have to add. They happened, just not very often. In both bureaucracies, an off-the-reservation insight often got lost in the system, or was buried by those to whom it did not immediately occur. Every place in the world had its own orthodoxy, and woe betide the apostates who worked there.

Hendley's eyes swept over the two-page document. "Sure wiggles like a fish, doesn't he?" Then his phone buzzed, and he picked up the receiver. "Okay, Helen, send them in . . . Rick Bell is bringing in those two guys we talked about," he explained to Wills.

The door opened, and Jack Jr.'s eyes popped somewhat. So did Brian's. "Jack? What are you doing here?"

Dominic's face changed a moment later. "Hey, Jack! What's happening?" he exclaimed.

For his part, Hendley's eyes twisted into a hurt expression. He hadn't thought this all the way through, a rare error on his part. But the room had only one door, unless you counted the private washroom.

The three cousins shook hands, momentarily ignoring the boss, until Rick Bell took control of the moment.

"Brian, Dominic, this is the big boss, Gerry Hendley." Handshakes were exchanged in front of the two analysts.

"Rick, thanks for bringing that up. Well done to both of you," Hendley said in dismissal.

"I guess it's back to the workstation. See you, guys," Jack said to his cousins.

The surprise of the moment didn't fade immediately, but Brian and Dominic settled into their chairs and filed the happenstance away for the moment.

"Welcome," Hendley said to them, leaning back in his chair. Well, sooner or later they'd find out, wouldn't they? "Pete Alexander tells me that you've done very well down at the country house."

"Aside from the boredom," Brian responded.

"Training is like that," Bell said in polite sympathy.

"What about yesterday?" Hendley asked.

"It wasn't fun," Brian said first. "It was a lot like that ambush in Afghanistan. Ka-boom, it started, and then we had to deal with it. Good news, the bad guys weren't all that bright. They acted like free agents instead of a team. If they'd been trained properly—if they'd acted like a team with proper security—it would have gone different. As it was, it was just a matter of taking out one at a time. Any idea on who they were?"

"What the FBI knows to this point, they seem to have come into the country through Mexico. Your cousin ID'd the source of their funding for us. He's a Saudi expatriate living in London, and he may be one of their backers. They were all Arabian in origin. They've positively ID'd five of them as Saudi citizens. The guns were stolen about ten years ago. They rented the cars—all four groups—in Las Cruces, New Mexico, and probably drove independently to their objectives. Their routes have been tracked by gas purchases."

"Motivation was strictly ideological?" Dominic asked.

Hendley nodded. "Religious—their version of it, yes. So it would seem."

"Is the Bureau looking for me?" Dominic asked next.

"You'll have to call Gus Werner later today so he can fill out his paperwork, but don't expect any hassles. They have a cover story all cooked up already."

"Okay."

This was Brian: "I assume that this is what we've been training for? To hunt down some of these people before they can do any more bad things over here?"

"That's about right," Hendley confirmed.

"Okay," Brian said. "I can live with that."

"You will go into the field together, covered as people in the banking and trading business. We'll brief you in on the stuff you need to know to maintain that cover. You'll operate mainly out of a virtual office via laptop computer."

"Security?" Dominic wondered.

"That will not be a problem," Bell assured him. "The computers are as secure as we can make them, and they can double as Internet phones for times when voice communications are required. The encryption systems are highly secure," he emphasized.

"Okay," Dominic said dubiously. Pete had told them much the same, but he'd never trusted any encryption system. The FBI's radio systems, secure as they were supposed to be, *had* been cracked once or twice by clever bad guys or by computer geeks, the kind who liked to call the local FBI field office to tell them how smart they were. "What about our legal cover?"

"This is the best we can do," Hendley said, handing a folder across. Dominic took it and flipped it open. His eyeballs widened immediately.

"Damn! How the hell did you get this?" he asked. The only presidential pardon he'd ever seen had been in a legal textbook. This one was effectively blank, except that it was signed. A blank pardon? Damn.

"You tell me," Hendley suggested.

The signature gave him the answer, and his legal education came back. This pardon was bulletproof. Even the Supreme Court couldn't toss this one out, because the

President's sovereign authority to pardon was as explicit as freedom of speech. But it would not be very helpful outside American borders. "So, we'll be doing people here at home?"

"Possibly," Hendley confirmed.

"We're the first shooters on the team?" Brian asked.

"Also correct," the former senator answered.

"How will we be doing it?"

"That will depend on the mission," Bell answered. "For most of them, we have a new weapon that is one hundred percent effective, and very covert. You'll be learning about that, probably tomorrow."

"We in a hurry?" Brian asked further.

"The gloves are all the way off now," Bell told them both. "Your targets will be people who have done, are planning to do, or who support missions aimed at causing serious harm to our country and her citizens. We are not talking about political assassinations. We will only target people who are directly involved in criminal acts."

"There's more to it than that. We're not the official executioners for the state of Texas, are we?" This was Dominic.

"No, you are not. This is outside the legal system. We're going to try to neutralize enemy forces by the elimination of their important personnel. That should at the least disrupt their ability to do business, and we hope it will also force their senior people to show themselves, so that they can be addressed, too."

"So this"—Dominic closed the folder and passed it back to his host—"is a hunting license, with no bag limit and an open season."

"Correct, but within reasonable limits."

"Suits me," Brian observed. Only twenty-four hours earlier, he remembered, he'd been holding a dying little boy in his arms. "When do we go to work?"

Hendley handled the reply.

"Soon."

* * *

"UH, TONY, what are they doing here?"

"Jack, I didn't know they'd be in today."

"Nonresponsive." Jack's blue eyes were unusually hard. "You've figured out why this place was set up, right?"

And that was enough of an answer. Damn. His own cousins? Well, one was a Marine, and the FBI one—the lawyer one, as Jack had thought of him once—had well and truly whacked some pervert down in Alabama. It had made the papers, and he'd even discussed it briefly with his father. It was hard to disapprove of it, assuming the circumstances had been within the law, but Dominic had always been the sort to play by the rules—that was almost the Ryan family motto. And Brian had probably done something in the Marines to get noticed. Brian had been the football type in his high school, while his brother had been the family debater. But Dominic wasn't a pussy. At least one bad guy had found that out the hard way. Maybe some people needed to learn that you didn't mess with a big country that had real men in its employ. Every tiger had teeth and claws...

...and America grew large tigers.

With that settled, he decided to go back looking for 56MoHa@eurocom.net. Maybe the tigers would go looking for more food. That made him a bird dog. But that was okay. Some birds needed their flying rights revoked. He'd arrange to query that "handle" via NSA's taps into the world's cybercommunications jungle. Every animal left a trail somewhere, and he'd go sniffing for it. Damn, Jack thought, this job had its diversions after all, now that he saw what the real objective was.

MOHAMMED WAS at his computer. Behind him, the television was going on about the "intelligence failure," which made him smile. It could only have the effect of further diminishing American intelligence capabilities, especially with the operational distractions sure to come from the investigative hearings the American Congress would conduct. It was good to have such allies within the target country. They were not very different from the seniors in his own organization, trying to make the world coincide with their vision rather than with the realities of life. The difference was that his seniors at least listened to him, because he did achieve real results, which, fortunately, coincided with their ethereal visions of death and fear. Even more fortunately, there were people out there willing to cast away their lives to make those visions real. That they were fools mattered not to Mohammed. One used such tools as one had, and, in this case, he had hammers to strike down the nails he saw across the world.

He checked his e-mails to see that Uda had complied with his instructions on the banking business. Strictly speaking, he could have just let the Visa accounts die, but then some officious bank employee might have poked around to see why the last set of bills had not been paid. Better, he thought, to leave some surplus cash in the account and to leave the account active but dormant, because a bank would not mind having surplus cash in its electronic vault, and if *that* account went dormant, no bank employee would do any investigation into it. Such things happened all the time. He made sure that the account number and access code remained hidden on his computer in a document only he knew about.

He considered sending a letter of thanks to his Colombian contacts, but nonessential messages were a waste of time and an invitation to vulnerability. You didn't send messages for fun or for good manners. Only what was strictly necessary, and as brief as possible. He knew enough to fear the American ability to gather electronic intelligence. The Western news media often talked about "intercepts," and so his organization had sworn completely off the satellite telephones they'd used for convenience. Instead they most often used messengers, who relayed information they'd carefully memorized. It was inconveniently slow, but it had the virtue of being completely secure...

unless the messenger was corrupted somehow. Nothing was totally secure. Every system had its weaknesses. But the Internet was the best thing going. Individual accounts were beautifully anonymous, since they could be set up by anonymous third parties, and their identities relayed to the real end users, and therefore they existed only as electrons or photons—as alike as grains of sand in the Empty Quarter, as secure and anonymous as anything could be. And there were literally billions of Internet messages every day. Perhaps Allah could keep track of them, but only because Allah knew the mind and heart of every man, a capability He had not granted even to the Faithful. And so Mohammed, who rarely stayed in the same location for more than three days, felt free to use his computer at will.

THE BRITISH Security Service, its headquarters located at Thames House, upriver from the Palace of Westminster, maintained literally hundreds of thousands of wiretaps—the privacy laws of the United Kingdom were a lot more liberal than those of the United States ... for the agencies of the state, that is—four of which applied to Uda bin Sali. One of those was for his cellular phone, and rarely developed much of anything valuable. His electronic accounts at work in the financial district and at home were the most valuable, since he distrusted voice communications and preferred electronic mail for all of his important contacts with the outside world. This included letters to and from home, mostly to reassure his father that the family money was secure. Strangely, he didn't even trouble himself to use an encryption program, assuming that the sheer volume of message traffic on the 'Net would preclude official surveillance. Besides, there were many people in the capital-preservation business in London—a lot of the city's valuable real estate was actually titled to foreigners—and money-trafficking was something that even most of the players found boring. The money alphabet had only a few elements, after all, and its poetry did little to move the soul.

But his e-mail line never chirped without an echo chirp at Thames House, and those fragments of signals went to GCHQ—Government Communications Headquarters at Cheltenham, north and west of London, from which they were relayed via satellite to Fort Belvoir, Virginia, and from there to Fort Meade, Maryland, via fiber-optic cable, for inspection mainly by one of the supercomputers in the headquarters buildings' enormous and strangely dungeon-like basement. From there, material regarded as important went to CIA's Langley, Virginia, headquarters, after transiting a certain building's flat roof, after which the signals were digested by yet another set of computers.

"Something new here, from Mr. Fifty-six," Junior said almost to himself, meaning 56MoHa@eurocom.net. He had to think for a few seconds. It was mostly numbers. But one of the numbers was the electronic address of a European commercial bank. Mr. 56 wanted some money, or so it appeared, and now that they knew that Mr. 56 was a "player," they had a new bank account to look at. That would happen the following day. It might even develop a name and a mailing address, depending on the individual bank's in-house procedures. But probably not. All the international banks were gravitating toward identical procedures, the better to maintain their competitive advantages, one over the other, until the playing field was as flat as a football pitch, as everyone adopted the most depositor-friendly procedures possible. Every person had his own version of reality, but everyone's money was equally green—or orange in the case of the Euro, decorated as it was with buildings never built and bridges never crossed. Jack made appropriate notes and shut his machine down. He'd be having dinner tonight with Brian and Dominic, just to catch up with family stuff. There was a new seafood restaurant on U.S. 29 that he wanted to check out. And his working day was done. Jack made a few notes for the next Monday morning—he didn't expect to be in on Sunday, national emergency or not. Uda bin Sali merited a very close examination. Exactly how close, he wasn't sure, though he'd begun to suspect that Sali would be meeting one or two people he knew well.

"HOW SOON?" It had been a bad question from Brian Caruso, but coming from Hendley's mouth it had rather more immediacy.

"Well, we have to put a plan of some sort together," Sam Granger replied. For everyone here, it was the same. What had been a slam dunk in the abstract became more complex when you had to face the reality of it. "First, we need a set of targets who make sense, and then a plan for servicing them in a way that also makes some sort of sense."

"Operational concept?" Tom Davis wondered aloud.

"The idea is to move logically—from our point of view, but to an outsider it should appear random—from target to target, making people stick their heads up like prairie dogs so's we can take them one at a time. It's simple enough in concept, but more difficult in the practical world." It was a lot easier to move chess pieces around a board than it was to manage people to move, on command, to the squares desired, a fact often lost on movie directors. Something as prosaic as a missed bus connection or a traffic accident, or the need to take a piss, could play hell with the most elegant theoretical plan. The world, one had to remember, was analog, not digital, in the way it operated. And "analog" actually meant "sloppy."

"So, you saying we need a psychiatrist?"

Sam shook his head. "They have some of those at Langley. It hasn't helped them very much."

"Ain't that the truth." Davis laughed. But this was not a time for humor. "Speed," he observed.

"Yes, the faster the better," Granger agreed. "Deny them the time to react and think."

"Also, better to deny them the ability to know anything's going on," said Hendley.

"Make people disappear?"

"Too many people have apparent heart attacks, and somebody'll get suspicious."

"You suppose they have any of our agencies penetrated?" the former senator wondered aloud. The other two in the room winced at the suggestion.

"Depends on what you mean." Davis took the question. "A penetration agent? That would be hard to arrange, absent a really juicy bribe, and even then it would be hard to set up, unless the Agency had a guy who went to them looking for a bankroll. Maybe that is a possibility," he added after a moment's reflection. "The Russians were always niggardly with money—they didn't have that much hard currency to toss around. These people, hell, they have more than they need. So . . . maybe . . ."

"But that works for us," Hendley thought. "Not too many people at the Agency know we exist. So, if they start thinking CIA is offing people, they can use their penetration agent, if any, to tell them it's not happening?"

"So then their expertise is counterproductive to them?" Granger speculated.

"They'd think 'Mossad,' wouldn't they?"

"Who else?" Davis asked in return. "Their own ideology works against them." It had been a ploy rarely—but sometimes successfully—used against KGB. Nothing like making the other guy feel clever. And if it made it tough for the Israelis, nobody in the American intelligence community would lose much sleep over it. "Ally" or not, the Israelis were not entirely beloved by their American counterparts. Even the Saudi spooks played with them, because national interests often overlapped in the most unlikely of ways. And for this series of plays, Americans would be looking out only for the mother country, and doing so completely off the books.

"The targets we have identified, where are they?" Hendley asked.

"All in Europe. They tend to be bankers or communications people. They move money around, or they handle messages, do briefings. One seems to gather intelligence. He travels a lot. Maybe he scouted locations for yesterday, but we haven't been on him long enough to know. We have some targets who do comms, but we want to leave those alone. They're too valuable. The other concern is to avoid targets whose demise will tell the opposition how we twigged to them. It has to appear random. I think for some we set it up in such a way that the opposition think they've gone over the hill. Took the money and bugged out— grabbed a piece of the good life and dropped off the earth. We can even leave e-mail messages like that behind."

"And if they have a code to show it's their messages, and not somebody who's taken charge of their computers?" Davis asked.

"That works for us as much as it works against us. It's a natural play, to arrange your disappearance in such a way as to suggest you've been whacked. Nobody's going to come looking for a dead man, right? They must have that kind of concern. They hate us for corrupting their society, and so they must know that their people can be corrupted. They will have brave ones, and they'll have cowardly ones. These people are not unified in their outlook. They're not robots. Some will be true believers, sure, but others are in it for the ride, the fun, the glamour of what they're doing, but when it comes to the nut-crunching time, life will be more attractive to them than death." Granger knew people and motivations, and, no, they were not robots. In fact, the smarter they were, the less likely they were to be motivated by the simple. Most of the Muslim extremists, interestingly enough, were either in Europe or had been educated there. In a comfortable womb, they'd been isolated by their ethnic background—but also liberated from the repressive societies from which they'd sprung. Revolution had always been a creature of rising expectations—not a product of oppression, but of proto-liberation. It was a time of personal confusion and a time for seeking after identity, a period of psychological vulnerability when an anchor was needed and grasped at, whatever the anchor happened to be. It was sad to have to kill people who were more lost than anything else, but they'd chosen their path freely, if not intelligently, and if that path led to the wrong place, that was not the fault of their victims, was it?

THE FISH was pretty good. Jack tried the rockfish, the striped bass of the Chesapeake Bay. Brian opted for the salmon, and Dominic the crusted sea perch. Brian had chosen the wine, a French white from the Loire Valley.

"So, how the hell did you get here?" Dominic asked his cousin.

"I looked around, and this place interested me. So, I looked into it, and the more I found out, the less I could figure out. So, I came over and talked to Gerry, and I talked my way into a job."

"Doing what?"

"They call it analysis. It's more like mind reading. One guy in particular. Arabian name, plays with money in London. Mainly family money, dicks around with it, mainly trying to protect his father's pile—it's a nice pile," Jack assured his companions. "He trades real estate. Nice way to preserve capital. The London market isn't going down anytime soon. The Duke of Westminster is one of the richest guys in the world. He owns most of central London. Our little friend is emulating His Grace."

"What else?"

"What else is that he's fed money into a certain bank account that's the source of payment for a bunch of Visa cards, four of whose owners you guys met yesterday." It wasn't a completed circle yet, but that wouldn't take the

FBI much longer to close it up tight. "He also talked in his e-mails about the 'wonderful events' of yesterday."

"How did you get access to his e-mails?" Dominic asked.

"I can't say. You'll have to get that from somebody else."

"About ten miles that way, I bet," Dominic said, pointing northeast. The spook community tended to work on lines that were ordinarily forbidden to the Federal Bureau of Investigation. In any case, Cousin Jack just maintained a fairly blank look that would not have won him any money at a high-stakes poker table.

"So, he funds bad guys?" Brian asked.

"Correct."

"That does not make him a good guy," Brian developed the thought a little further.

"Probably not," Junior agreed.

"Maybe we'll meet him. What else can you tell us?" Brian continued.

"Expensive place, a town house on Berkeley Square—nice part of London, couple of blocks from the U.S. Embassy. Likes to use whores for his sexual recreation. He especially likes one girl named Rosalie Parker. The British Security Service keeps an eye on him, and they regularly debrief his main squeeze—the Parker girl. He pays her top dollar, in cash. Miss Parker is supposed to be popular with rich people. I suppose she slings it pretty good," Jack added with distaste. "There's a new photo on the computer file. He's about our age, olive complexion, a sort of beard—the kind a guy might have to look sexy, you know? Drives an Aston Martin. Hot car. Usually goes around London in cabs, though. He doesn't have a place in the country, but he takes country trips on weekends to getaway hotels, mostly with Miss Parker or another rent-a-broad. Works downtown in the financial district. Has an office in the Lloyd's of London building—third floor, I think. He makes three or four trades per week. Mainly, I think he just sits there and watches the TV and stock tickers, reads the papers, stuff like that."

"So, he's a spoiled rich kid who wants some excitement in his life?" Dominic summarized.

"Correct. Except maybe he likes to go out and play in the traffic."

"That's dangerous, Jack," Brian pointed out. "It could even get somebody Excedrin Headache number three-five-six." Brian was wearing his game face, in anticipation of meeting the guy who had financed the death of David Prentiss.

And suddenly Jack thought that Miss Rosalie Parker of London might not be getting all that many more Louis Vuitton bags. Well, she probably had a nice retirement plan already arranged if she was as smart as the Security Service and Special Branch thought she was.

"How's your dad doing?" Dominic asked.

"Writing his memoirs," Jack answered. "I wonder how much he'll be able to put in? You know, even Mom doesn't know much about what he did at CIA, and the little bit I know—well, there's a lot of stuff he can't write about. Even the things that are sort of out in the public eye, he can't confirm they really happened."

"Like getting the head of the KGB to defect. That's gotta be some story. That guy's been on TV. I guess he's still pissed at your dad for keeping him from taking the Soviet Union over. Probably thinks he could have saved it."

"Maybe so. Dad has a lot of secrets, all right. So do some of his pals from the Agency. One guy in particular, named Clark. Scary guy, but him and Dad are pretty tight. I think he's in England now, boss of that new secret counterterrorism bunch that the press talks about every year or so, the 'men of black,' they call 'em."

"They're real," Brian said. "Out at Hereford in Wales. They're not that secret. The senior guys from Force Recon have been out there to train with 'em. Never been there myself, but I know two guys who have. Them and the Brit SAS. They're serious troops."

"How far inside were you, Aldo?" his brother asked.

"Hey, the special-operations community is pretty tight. We cross-train, share new equipment and stuff. Most important part is when we sit down with beers and share war stories. Everybody has a different way of looking at problems, and, you know, sometimes the other guy has a better idea than you have. The Rainbow team—that's the 'men of black' the newsies talk about—they're very smart, but they've learned a thing or two from us over the years. Thing is, they're smart enough to listen to new ideas. The boss man, this Clark guy, he's supposed to be very smart."

"He is. I've met him. Dad thinks he's the cat's ass." He paused before going on. "Hendley knows him, too. Why he isn't here, I don't know. I asked the first day I came here. Maybe because he's too old."

"He's a shooter?"

"I asked Dad once. Dad said he couldn't say. That's how he says yes. I guess I caught him at a weak moment. Funny thing about Dad, he can't lie worth a damn."

"I guess that's why he loved being President so much."

"Yeah, I think that's the main reason he quit. He figured Uncle Robby could handle it better than he did."

"Until that cracker bastard wasted his ass," Dominic observed. The shooter, one Duane Farmer, was currently sitting on death row in Mississippi. "The last of the Klan," the newspapers called him, and so he was, at age sixty-eight, just a damned-by-everybody bigot who could not abide the thought of a black President, and had used his grandfather's World War One revolver to make it so.

"That was bad," John Patrick Ryan, Jr., agreed. "You know, except for him, I wouldn't have been born. It's a big family story. Uncle Robby's version of it was pretty good. He loved telling stories. Him and Dad were pretty tight. After Robby got wasted, the political pukes were running around in circles, some of them wanted Dad to pick up the flag again, like, but he didn't do it, and so, I guess, he helped that Kealty guy get elected. Dad can't stand him. That's the other thing he never learned, how to be nice to people he hates. He just didn't like living at the White House very much."

He was good at it, being President, Dominic thought.

"You tell him that. Mom didn't mind leaving, either. That First Lady stuff wrecked her doctor work, and she *really* hated what it did with Kyle and Katie. You know that old saying, the most dangerous place in the world is between a mom and her kids? It's for real, guys. Only time I ever saw her lose her temper—Dad does that a lot more than Mom does—was when somebody told her that her official duties required her not to go to Kyle's pageant at his day-care center. Jeez, she really came unglued. Anyway, the nannies helped—and the newspeople hammered her about that, how it wasn't American and all that. You know, if anybody had ever taken a picture of Dad taking a piss, I bet someone would have said he wasn't doing it right."

"That's what critics are for, to tell you how much smarter they are than the person they're criticizing."

"In the Bureau, Aldo, they're called lawyers, or the Office of Professional Responsibility," Dominic informed the table. "They have their sense of humor surgically removed before they join up."

"The Marines have reporters, too—and I bet not one of them ever went through boot camp." At least the guys who worked in the IG had been through the Basic School.

"I guess we should cheer up," Dominic announced, holding up his wineglass. "Ain't nobody going to criticize us."

"And live," Jack added with a chuckle. *Damn,* he thought, *what the hell is Dad going to say when he finds out about me?*

CHAPTER 16

AND THE PURSUING HORSES

SUNDAY WAS a day of rest for most people, and at The Campus it was much the same, except for the security people. Gerry Hendley believed that maybe God had had a point, that seven-day schedules accomplished a lot less than adding 16.67 percent to a man's weekly productivity. It also dulled the brain by denying it free-form exercise, or just the luxury of doing nothing at all.

But today it was different, of course. Today they'd be planning real black operations for the first time. The Campus had been active just over nineteen months, and that time had mostly been spent in establishing their cover as a trading and arbitrage business. His department heads had taken the Acela trains back and forth to New York many times to meet their white-world counterparts, and though it had seemed slow at the time, in retrospect it had been very quickly indeed that they'd made their reputation in the money-management community. They'd hardly ever shown the world their real results, of course, from speculating on currencies and a few very carefully chosen stock issues, sometimes even insider trades on companies which themselves didn't know the business that was coming their way. Staying covert had been the overall objective, but since The Campus had to be self-supporting, it also had to generate real income. In World War II, the Americans had peopled its black-operations establishments with lawyers, while the Brits had used bankers. Both had proven to be good for screwing people... and killing them. It had to be something about the way they looked at the world, Hendley thought over his coffee.

He gazed at the others: Jerry Rounds, his head of Strategic Planning; Sam Granger, his chief of Operations. Even before the building had been completed, the three of them had been thinking about the shape of the world, and how a few of the corners could best be rounded off. Rick Bell was here, too, his chief of Analysis, the one who spent his working days sorting through the "take" from NSA and CIA, and trying to find meaning in the flood of unrelated information—aided, of course, by the thirty-five thousand analysts at Langley, Fort Meade, and other such places. Like all senior analysts, he also liked to frolic in the operations playground, and here that was actually possible, since The Campus was too small to have been overtaken by its own bureaucracy. He and Hendley worried that it might not always be so, and both made sure that no empires were being built.

To the best of their knowledge, theirs was the only institution in all the world like this. And it had been set up in such a way that it could be erased from the landscape in a matter of two or three months. Since Hendley Associates did not invite outside investors, their public profile was low enough that the radar never spotted their machinations, and, in any case, the community they were in did not advertise. It was easy to hide in a field in which everyone did the same, and nobody ratted on anyone else, unless very badly stung. And The Campus didn't sting. At least not with money.

"So," Hendley began, "are we ready?"

"Yes," Rounds said for Granger. Sam nodded soberly and smiled.

"We're ready," Granger announced officially. "Our two boys have earned their spurs in a way we never anticipated."

"They earned 'em, all right," Bell agreed. "And the Ryan boy has identified a good first target, this Sali fellow. The events of Friday have generated a lot of message traffic. They turn out a lot of cheerleaders. A lot of them are stringers and wanna-bes, but even if we pop one of them by mistake it's no great loss. I have the first four all lined up. So, Sam, do you have a plan for dealing with them?"

That was Davis's cue. "We're going to do reconnaissance by fire. After we whack one or two, we'll see what reaction, if any, results, and we will take our guidance from there. I agree that Mr. Sali looks like a profitable first target. Question is, is his elimination going to be overt or covert?"

"Explain," Hendley ordered.

"Well, if he's found dead on the street, that's one thing. If he disappears with his daddy's money and leaves behind a note saying that he wants to stop what he's doing and just retire, that's something else," Sam explained.

"Kidnapping? It's dangerous." The Metropolitan Police in London had a closure rate on kidnappings that nibbled at one hundred percent. That was a dangerous game to play, especially on their first move.

"Well, we can hire an actor, dress him up right, fly him to New York Kennedy, and then just have him disappear. In fact, we dispose of the body and keep the money. How much does he have access to, Rick?"

"Direct access? Hell, it's over three hundred million bucks."

"Might look good in the corporate exchequer," Sam speculated. "And it wouldn't hurt his dad much, would it?"

"His father's money—all of it? Try the sunny side of three billion," Bell answered. "He'll miss it, but it wouldn't break him. And given his opinion of his son, it might even develop as good cover for our operation," he hypothesized.

"I am not recommending this as a course of action, but it is an alternative," Granger concluded.

It had been talked about before, of course. It was too obvious a play to escape notice. And three hundred million dollars would have looked just fine in a Campus account, say in the Bahamas or Liechtenstein. You could hide money anywhere that had telephone lines. It was just electrons anyway, not gold bricks.

Hendley was surprised that Sam had brought this up so soon. Maybe he wanted to get a read on his colleagues. They were clearly not overcome with emotion at the thought of ending this Sali's life, but to steal from him in the process pushed some very different buttons. A man's conscience could be a funny thing, Gerry concluded.

"Let's set that aside for the moment. How hard will the hit be?" Hendley asked.

"With what Rick Pasternak gave us? It's child's play, so long as our people don't make a complete hash of it. Even then the worst thing that can happen is that it'll look like a mugging that went wrong," Granger told them.

"What if our guy drops the pen?" Rounds worried.

"It's a pen. You can write with it. It'll pass inspection with any cop in the world," Granger replied confidently. He reached in his pocket and passed his sample around the table. "This one's cold," he assured them.

They'd all been briefed in. To all appearances, it was an expensive ballpoint, gold-plated, with obsidian on the clip. By depressing the clip and turning the nib cover, you switched the point from a real pen to a hypodermic with a lethal transfer agent. It would paralyze the victim in fifteen to twenty seconds, and kill him in three minutes, with no cure, and a very transient signature in the body. As the pen went around the conference table, the executives invariably felt the hypo point, and then experimented with using it for a simulated hit, mostly as an ice-pick strike, though Rounds handled it like a diminutive sword.

"It would be nice to try it on a dry run," he observed quietly.

"Anyone here want to volunteer as the victim?" Granger asked the table. No heads nodded. The mood of the room didn't surprise him much. It was time for a sober pause, the sort of thing that comes over a man when he signs his application for life insurance, a product that is valuable only if you are dead, which rather takes the fun out of the moment.

"Fly them to London together?" Hendley asked.

"Correct." Granger nodded, and turned back to his business voice. "We have them scout out the target, pick their moment, and make their hit."

"And wait to see the results?" Rounds asked, rhetorically.

"Correct. Then they can fly off to the next target. The whole operation should not take more than a week. Then we fly them home and await developments. If somebody taps into his money pile after his demise, we'll probably know, right?"

"We ought to," Bell confirmed. "And if anyone purloins it, we'll know where it goes."

"Excellent," Granger observed. After all, that was what "reconnaissance-by-fire" meant.

THEY WOULDN'T be here long, the twins both thought. They were quartered in adjoining rooms at the local Holiday Inn, and this Sunday afternoon they were both watching TV with one guest.

"How's your mom?" Jack asked.

"Fine, doing a lot of stuff with the local schools— parochial ones. A little more than a teacher's aide, but not actually teaching. Dad's working some new project—supposedly Boeing is back looking at an SST, supersonic airliner. Dad says they'll probably never build it, unless Washington coughs up a lot of money, but with the Concorde retired people are thinking about it again, and Boeing likes to keep their engineers busy. They're a little nervous about the Airbus people, and they don't want to be caught with their pants down if the French start getting ambitious."

"How was the Corps?" Jack asked Brian.

"The Corps is the Corps, cuz. It just rolls along, keeping busy for the next war that'll come along."

"Dad was worried when you went to Afghanistan."

"It was a little exciting. The people there, they're tough, and they're not dumb, but they're not trained that well, either. So, when we bumped heads with 'em, we came out ahead. If we saw something that looked hinky, we called air in on it, and that usually took care of things."

"How many?"

"How many did we take out? Some. Not enough, but some. The Green Berets went in first, and the Afghans learned from that that a stand-up fight was not in their interest. Mostly, we did pursuit and reconnaissance, bird-dogging for the airedales. We had a CIA guy with us, and a signals-intelligence detachment. The bad guys used their radios a little too much. When we got a hit, we'd move in to about a mile or so and give it a look-see, and if it was interesting enough we'd call in air and scramble the hell out of it. Scary to watch," Brian summarized.

"I bet." Jack popped open a can of beer.

"So this Sali guy, the one with the girlfriend, Rosalie Parker?" Dominic asked. Like most cops, he had a good memory for names. "You said that he was jumpin' up and down about the shootings?"

"Yup," Jack said. "Thought they were just swell."

"So who was the cheerleading with?"

"Pals he e-mails to. The Brits have his phones tapped, and the e-mails—well, as I said, I can't tell you about the e-mails. Those European phone systems aren't anywhere near as secure as people think—I mean, everybody knows about intercepting cell phones and stuff, but the cops over there pull stuff we can't do here. The Brits especially, they use intercepts to track the IRA guys. I heard that the rest of the European countries are even freer to act."

"They are," Dominic assured him. "At the Academy, we had some in the national Academy program—that's like a doctoral course for cops. They'd talk about that sort of thing after you got a few drinks into them. So, this Sali guy liked what those mutts did, eh?"

"Like his team won the Super Bowl," Jack replied at once.

"And he bankrolls them?" Brian asked.

"That's right."

"Interesting," was all Brian had to say after getting that question answered.

HE COULD have stayed another night, but he had things to do in the morning, and so he was driving back to London in his Aston Martin Vanquish, Bowland black. Its interior was charcoal, and its handmade twelve-cylinder engine was pushing out most of its 460 horsepower as he headed east on the M4 at a hundred miles per hour. In its way, the car was better than sex. It was a pity Rosalie wasn't with him, but—he looked over at his companion—Mandy was an agreeable bed warmer, if a little too skinny for his usual tastes. If only she could put some meat on her bones, but European fashion did not encourage that. The fools who determined the rules of women's bodies were probably pederasts who wished them all to look like young boys. Madness, Sali thought. Pure madness.

But Mandy enjoyed riding in this car, more than Rosalie did. Rosalie, sadly, was fearful of driving fast, not as trusting of his skills as she should have been. He hoped he could take this car home—he'd fly it there, of course. His brother had a fast car of his own, but the dealer had told him that this four-wheeled rocket topped out at over three hundred kilometers per hour—that was 196 miles per hour—and the Kingdom had some fine, flat, straight roads.

Okay, so he had a cousin who flew Tornado fighters for the Royal Saudi Air Force, but this car was *his,* and that made all the difference. Unfortunately, the police here in England would not allow him to exercise it properly—one more traffic ticket and he might lose his driver's license, the spoilsports—but at home there would be no such problems. And after seeing what it could *really* do, he'd fly it back to Gatwick and use it to excite women, which was almost as good as just driving it. Certainly Mandy was properly excited by it. He'd have to get her a nice Vuitton bag and have it messengered to her flat tomorrow. It didn't hurt to be generous with women, and Rosalie needed to learn that she had some competition.

Racing into town as rapidly as the traffic and the police allowed, he zoomed past Harrods, through the vehicle tunnel, and past the Duke of Wellington's house before turning right onto Curzon Street and then left onto Berkeley Square. A flash of his lights told the man he paid to guard his parking place to move his car, and he was able to park just in front of his three-story brownstone town house. With continental manners, he got out of the car and raced around to open Mandy's door and gallantly escorted her up the steps to the huge oak front door, and, smiling, held it open for her. In a few minutes, she'd be opening an even nicer door for him, after all.

"THE LITTLE bugger's back," Ernest observed, making the proper note of the time on his clipboard. The two Security Service officers were in a British Telecom van parked fifty yards away. They'd been there for about two hours. This young Saudi madman drove as though he were the reincarnation of Jimmy Clark.

"I suppose he had a better weekend than we did," Peter agreed. Then he turned to punch the buttons to activate various wiretap systems in the Georgian town house. These included three cameras whose tapes were collected every third day by a penetration team. "He is a vigorous little bastard."

"Probably uses Viagra," Ernest thought aloud, and somewhat enviously.

"One must be a good sport, Ernie, my lad. It will cost him two weeks of our pay. And for what she is about to receive, she will surely be truly grateful."

"Bugger," Ernest observed sourly.

"She's thin, but not *that* thin, boyo." Peter had himself a good laugh. They knew what Mandy Davis charged her "tricks," and, like men everywhere, they wondered what special things she might do to earn it, all while holding her in contempt. As counterintelligence officers, they did not quite have the degree of sympathy a seasoned police constable might have had for relatively unskilled women trying to earn their way. Seven hundred fifty pounds for an evening's visit, and two thousand pounds for a complete night. Exactly what her custom was for a full weekend, no one had asked.

They both picked up the earphones to make sure the microphones worked, switching channels to track them through the house.

"He's an impatient sod," Ernest observed. "Suppose she'll stay the night?"

"I'll wager she doesn't, Ernie. Then maybe he'll get on the bloody phone and we can get something useful off the bastard."

"Bloody wog," Ernest muttered, to his partner's agreement. They both thought Mandy was prettier than Rosalie. Fit for a government minister.

THEY WERE correct in their judgment. Mandy Davis left at 10:23 A.M., stopping at the door for one last kiss, and a smile certain to break any man's heart, and then she walked downhill on Berkeley Street heading toward Piccadilly, where she did not turn right at the Boots drugstore for the Underground station on the corner of Piccadilly and

Stratton, but rather caught a cab that took her downtown, to New Scotland Yard. There, she'd be debriefed by a friendly young detective whom she rather fancied, though she was too skilled in her profession to mix business of the business sort with business of the pleasure sort. Uda was a vigorous john, and a generous one, but whatever illusions existed in their relationship were his, not hers.

THE NUMBERS came up on the LED register, and were saved and time-stamped in their laptop computers—there were two of them, and at least one more at Thames House. On each of Sali's phones was a pin register that noted the destination of every call he made. A similar device did the same for all incoming calls, while three tape machines recorded every word. This one was an overseas call, to a mobile phone.

"He's calling his friend Mohammed," Peter observed. "I wonder what they'll be talking about."

"At least ten minutes of his adventure this weekend, I'll wager."

"Yes, he does like to talk," Peter agreed.

"SHE'S TOO skinny, but she is an accomplished harlot, my friend. There is something to be said for unbelieving women," Sali assured his colleague. She and Rosalie really liked him. He could always tell.

"I am glad to hear that, Uda," Mohammed said patiently from Paris. "Now, to business."

"As you wish, my friend."

"The American operation went well."

"Yes, I saw. How many in total?"

"Eighty-three dead and a hundred forty-three wounded. It could have been more, but one of the teams made an error. More importantly, the news reports were everywhere. All they had on TV today was coverage of our holy martyrs and their attacks."

"That is truly wonderful. A great blow for Allah."

"Oh, yes. Now, I need some money transferred into my account."

"How much?"

"A hundred thousand British pounds should do for now."

"I can have that done by ten in the morning." In fact, he could have done it an hour or two faster, but he planned on sleeping in the following morning. Mandy had tired him out. Now he was lying in bed, drinking French wine and smoking a cigarette, watching the TV without getting too involved. He wanted to catch Sky News at the top of the hour. "Is that all?"

"Yes, for now."

"It shall be done," he told Mohammed.

"Excellent. Good night, Uda."

"Wait, I have a question—"

"Not now. We must be cautious," Mohammed warned. Using a mobile phone had its dangers. He heard a sigh in reply.

"As you wish. Good night." And both killed their respective phones.

"THE PUB out in Somerset was rather nice—the Blue Boar, it was," said Mandy. "The food was decent. Uda had turkey and two pints on Friday night. Last night we dined at a restaurant across from the hotel, The Orchard. He had Chateaubriand and I had the Dover Sole. We went out to shop briefly on Saturday afternoon. He really didn't want to go out much, mostly just wanted to stay in bed." The cute detective was taping it all, plus making notes, as was another policeman. They both were being as clinical as she was.

"Did he talk about anything? The news on TV or in the papers?"

"He watched the news on TV. But he didn't speak a word. I said that it was appalling, all that killing, but all he did was grunt. He can be the most heartless chap, though he's always nice to me. We've still not had a cross word," she told them, caressing both with her blue eyes.

It was hard for the cops to regard her with professionalism. She had the looks of a fashion model, though at five foot one she was too short for it. There was also a sweetness about her that must have stood her in good stead. But inside was a heart of pure ice. It was sad, but not really their concern.

"Did he make any telephone calls?"

She shook her head. "None at all. He didn't bring his mobile phone this weekend. He told me that he was all mine and I wouldn't have to share him with anyone else this weekend. That was a first. Other than that, it was the usual." She thought of something else: "He does bathe more now. I had him shower both days, and he didn't even complain. Well, I helped. I went into the shower with him." She gave them a coquettish smile. That pretty much ended the interview.

"Thank you, Miss Davis. As always, you've been very helpful."

"Just doing my bit. You think he's a terrorist or something?" she had to ask.

"No. If you were in any danger, we'd give you fair warning."

Mandy reached into her Louis Vuitton purse and pulled out a knife with a five-inch blade. It wasn't legal for her to carry such a thing concealed, but in her line of work she needed one sure friend to accompany her, and the detectives understood. She probably knew how to make proper use of it, they surmised. "I can look after myself," she assured them both. "But Uda isn't like that. He's actually rather a gentle man. That's one thing you get to know in my business, reading men. Unless he's a bloody fine actor, he's not a dangerous sort. He plays with money, not guns."

Both cops took that pronouncement seriously. She was right—if there was anything a hooker was good at, it was reading men. Those who couldn't often died before reaching twenty.

After Mandy took a cab home, the two Special Branch detectives wrote up what she'd told them, and then e-mailed it to Thames House, where it became another entry in the Security Service files on the young Arab.

BRIAN AND Dominic arrived at The Campus at 8:00 A.M. on the dot. Their newly issued security passes allowed them to take the elevator up to the top floor, where they sat and drank coffee for half an hour until Gerry Hendley showed up. Both of the twins sprang to attention, especially Brian.

"Good morning," the former senator said on his way past, then he stopped. "You want to talk to Sam Granger first, I think. Rick Pasternak will be here at around nine-fifteen. Sam should be in any time now. I have to see to my desk right now, okay?"

"Yes, sir," Brian assured him. What the hell, the coffee wasn't bad.

Granger came out of the elevator just two minutes later. "Hey, guys. Follow me." And they did.

Granger's office was not as large as Hendley's, but it wasn't a trainee's cubbyhole, either. He pointed to the two visitors' chairs and hung up his coat.

"How soon will you be ready for an assignment?"

"How does today grab you?" Dominic asked in reply.

Granger smiled at the reply, but overly eager people could worry him. On the other hand, three days before . . . maybe eagerness was not so bad a thing after all.

"Is there a plan?" Brian asked.

"Yeah. We worked on it over the weekend." Granger started with the operational concept: reconnaissance by fire.

"Makes sense," Brian observed. "Where do we do it?"

"On the street, probably. I'm not going to tell you how to perform a mission. I will tell you what we want done.

How you do it is going to be up to you. Now, for your first target we have a good crib sheet on his location and habits. It will just be a matter of identifying the right target and deciding how to do the job."

Do the job, Dominic thought. Like something from *The Godfather.*

"Who is he and why?"

"His name is Uda bin Sali, he's twenty-six, he lives in London."

The twins exchanged amused looks. "I should have known," Dominic said. "Jack told us about him. He's the money puke who likes hookers right?"

Granger opened the manila file he'd picked up on the way in and handed it across. "Photos of Sali and his two girlfriends. Location and photos of his house in London. Here's one of him in his car."

"Aston Martin," Dominic observed. "Nice wheels."

"He works in the financial district, has an office at the Lloyd's insurance building." More photos. "One complication. He usually has a tail. The Security Service—MI5— keeps an eye on him, but the troop they have assigned seems to be a rookie, and there's only one. So, when you make your hit, keep that in mind."

"Not using a gun, are we?" Brian asked.

"No, we have something better. No noise, nice and covert. You'll see when Rick Pasternak gets here. No firearms for this mission. European countries don't like guns much, and hand-to-hand is too dangerous. The idea is that it looks like he just had a heart attack."

"Residue?" Dominic asked.

"You can ask Rick about that. He'll give you chapter and verse."

"What are we using to deliver the drug?"

"One of these." Granger opened his desk drawer and took out the "safe" blue pen. He handed it across and told them how it worked.

"Sweet," Brian observed. "Just stab him in the ass, like?"

"Exactly right. It transfers seven milligrams of the drug—it's called succinylcholine—and that pretty much takes care of business. The subject collapses, is brain-dead in a few minutes, and all-the-way dead in less than ten."

"What about medical attention? What if there's an ambulance just across the street?"

"Rick says it won't matter unless he's in an operating room with doctors standing right at his side."

"Fair enough." Brian picked up the photo of their first target, looking at it, but really seeing young David Prentiss. "Tough luck, buddy."

"I SEE our friend had a nice weekend," Jack was saying to his computer. This day's report included a photo of a Miss Mandy Davis, along with a transcript of her interview with the Metropolitan Police Special Branch. "She's a looker."

"Not cheap, either," Wills observed from his workstation.

"How much longer has Sali got?" Jack asked him.

"Jack, it's better not to speculate on that," Wills warned.

"Because the two hitters—hell, Tony, they're cousins of mine."

"I do not know much about that, and I do not want to find out. The less we know, the less problems we can have. Period," he emphasized.

"You say so, man," Jack responded. "But whatever sympathy I might have had for this prick died when he started cheerleading and funding people with guns. There are lines you can't cross."

"Yeah, Jack, there are. Be careful that you don't step too far yourself."

Jack Ryan, Jr., thought about that for a second. Did he want to be an assassin? Probably not, but there were people who needed killing, and Uda bin Sali had crossed over into that category. If his cousins were going to take him down, they were just doing the Lord's work—or his country's work, which, to the way he'd been brought up, was pretty much the same thing.

"THAT FAST, Doc?" Dominic asked.

Pasternak nodded. "That fast."

"That reliable?" Brian inquired next.

"Five milligrams is enough. This pen delivers seven. If anyone survives, it would have to be a miracle. Unfortunately, it will be a very unpleasant death, but that can't be helped. I mean, we could use botulism toxin—it's a very fast-acting neurotoxin—but that leaves residue in the blood that would come out in a postmortem toxicology scan. Succinylcholine metabolizes very nicely. Detecting it would take another miracle, unless the pathologist knows exactly what to look for, and that is unlikely."

"How fast again?"

"Twenty to thirty seconds, depending on how close you get to a major blood vessel, then the agent will cause total paralysis. Won't even be able to blink his eyes. He will not be able to move his diaphragm, so no breathing, no oxygen through the lungs. His heart will continue to beat, but since it will be the organ using the most oxygen, the heart will go ischemic in a matter of seconds—that means that without oxygen, the heart tissue will start to die from lack of oxygen. The pain will be massive. Ordinarily, the body has a reserve supply of oxygen. How much depends on physical condition—the obese have less oxygen reserves than the slender among us. Anyway, the heart will be the first. It will try to continue beating, but that only makes the pain worse. Brain death will occur in three to six minutes. Until then, he'll be able to hear but not see—"

"Why not?" Brian asked.

"The eyelids probably will close. We're talking total paralysis here. So, he'll be lying there, in enormous pain, unable to move at all, with his heart trying to pump unoxygenated blood until his brain cells expire from anoxia. After that, it's theoretically possible to keep the body alive—muscle cells last the longest without oxygen—but the brain will be gone. Okay, it's not as sure as a bullet in the brain, but it makes no noise, and leaves virtually no evidence. When the heart cells die, they generate enzymes that we look for in a probable heart attack. So, whatever pathologist gets the body to post will think 'heart attack,' or 'neurological seizure'—a brain tumor can cause that—and maybe he'll carve the brain up to look for one. But as soon as the blood work comes back, the enzyme test will say 'heart attack,' and that should settle matters right then and there. The blood work will not show the succinylcholine because it metabolizes even after death. They will have an unexpected massive heart attack on their hands, and those happen every day. They'll run his blood for cholesterol and some other risk factors, but nothing will change the fact that he's dead from a cause they'll never figure out."

"Jesus," Dominic breathed. "Doc, how the hell did you get into this business?"

"My little brother was a vice president at Cantor Fitzgerald," was all he had to say.

"So we want to be careful with these pens, eh?" Brian asked. The doc's reason was good enough for him.

"I would," Pasternak advised them.

||||||||||||||||||||||||||||||||||||||||||||||||||||||||||||||||

CHAPTER 17

AND THE LITTLE RED FOX, AND THE FIRST FENCE

THEY FLEW out of Dulles International Airport on a British Airways flight, which turned out to be a 747 whose control surfaces their own father had designed twenty-seven years earlier. It occurred to Dominic that he'd been in diapers then, and that the world had turned over quite a few times from that day to this.

Both had brand-new passports in their own names. All other relevant documents were in their laptops, fully encrypted, along with modems and communications software, also fully encrypted. Aside from that, they were casually dressed, like most others in the first-class section. The stewardesses fluttered about efficiently, giving everyone munchies, along with white wine for both of the brothers. As they got to altitude, the food was decent—about the best thing that can be said about airline food—and so was the movie selection: Brian picked *Independence Day* while Dominic settled for *The Matrix*. Both had enjoyed science fiction since childhood. In the coat pockets of both were their gold pens. The reload cartridges were in their shaving kits, packed away in their regular luggage somewhere below. It would be about six hours to Heathrow, and both hoped to get some sleep on the way.

"Any second thoughts, Enzo?" Brian asked quietly.

"No," Dominic replied. "Just so it all works out." The prison cells in England lacked plumbing, he didn't add, and, no matter how embarrassing it might be for a Marine officer, it would be positively humiliating for a sworn special agent of the FBI.

"Fair enough. 'Night-night, bro."

"Roger that, jarhead." And both played with the complex seat controls to settle back to a nearly flat surface. And so the Atlantic passed beneath them for three thousand miles.

BACK IN his apartment, Jack Jr. knew that his cousins were gone overseas, and though he hadn't exactly been told why, their mission didn't require a spectacular leap of imagination. Surely Uda bin Sali would not live out the week. He'd learn about it from the morning message traffic out of Thames House, and he found himself wondering what the Brits would be saying, how excited and/or regretful they might be. Certainly, he'd learn a lot about how the job had been done. That excited his curiosity. He'd spent enough time in London to know that guns were not done over there, unless it was a government-sanctioned killing. In such a case—if the Special Air Service dispatched someone especially disliked by No. 10 Downing Street, for example—the police knew not to press too deeply into the case. Maybe just some pro forma interviews, enough to establish a case file before slipping it into the UNSOLVED cabinet to gather dust and little interest. You didn't have to be a rocket scientist to figure those things out.

But this would be an American hit on British soil, and *that,* he was sure, would not be pleasing to Her Majesty's Government. It was a matter of propriety. Besides, this was not an action by the American government. As a matter of law, it was a premeditated murder, upon which all governments frowned rather severely. So, whatever happened, he hoped they'd be careful. Even his father couldn't run much interference for this.

"OH, UDA, you are a *beast*!" Rosalie Parker exclaimed as he finally rolled off her body. She checked her watch. He'd gone late, and she had an appointment just after lunch the next day with an oil executive from Dubai. He was a rather dear old fellow, and a good tipper, even if he had told her once that she reminded him of one of his favorite daughters, the nasty old bugger.

"Stay the night," Uda urged.

"I can't, love. I have to pick up my mum for lunch and then take her shopping at Harrods. Good Lord, I must be off," she said with well-feigned excitement, springing to an upright position.

"No." Uda reached for her shoulder and pulled it back.

"Oh, you devil!" A chuckle and a warm smile.

"He is called *'Shahateen,'*" Uda corrected. "And he is not part of my family."

"Well, you can wear a girl out, Uda." Not that it was a bad thing, but she had things to do. So she stood and got her clothes off the floor, where he tended to throw them.

"Rosalie, my love, there is only you," he moaned. And she knew that was a lie. It was she who had introduced him to Mandy, after all.

"Is that so?" she asked.

"Oh, that one. She is far too skinny. She doesn't eat. She's not like you, my princess."

"You're so nice." Bend over, kiss, then put the bra on. "Uda, you are the best, the very best," she said. It was always good for the male ego to be stroked, and his ego was bigger than most.

"You just say that to make me feel good," Sali accused her.

"Do you think I'm an actress? Uda, you make my eyeballs pop out. But I have to go, love."

"As you say." He yawned. He'd buy her some shoes the next day, Uda decided. There was a new Jimmy Choo store close to his office that he'd been meaning to check out, and her feet were a spot-on size 6. He rather liked her feet, in fact.

Rosalie made a quick dart into the bathroom to check the mirror. Her hair was a fright—Uda kept messing it up, as though to mark his property. A few seconds with a brush made it almost presentable.

"I must be off, love." She bent down to kiss him again. "Don't get up. I know where the door is." And a final kiss, lingering and inviting . . . for the next time. Uda was as regular as regular could be. And she'd be back here. Mandy was good, and a friend, but she knew how to treat these wogs, and, best of all, she didn't have to starve herself like a bloody runway model. Mandy had too many American and European regulars to eat normally.

Outside, she hailed a cab.

"Where to, dear?" the cabby asked.

"New Scotland Yard, please."

IT'S ALWAYS disorienting to wake up on an airplane, even in good seats. The window shades went up and the cabin lights came on, and the earphones played news that might or might not be new—since it was British, it wasn't easy to tell. Breakfast was served—plenty of fat, along with no-shit Starbucks coffee that was about a six on a one-to-ten scale. Maybe a seven. Through the windows to his right, Brian saw the green fields of England instead of the slate black of the stormy ocean that had passed during his thankfully dreamless sleep. Both twins were afraid of dreams right now, for the past they contained, and the future they feared, despite their commitment to it. Twenty more minutes and the 747 touched down gently at Heathrow. Immigration was a gentle formality—the Brits did it much better than the Americans, Brian thought. Baggage was on the carousel quickly enough, and then they walked out to the cabs.

"Where to, gentlemen?"

"Mayfair Hotel on Stratton Street."

The driver took this information with a nod and headed off east toward the city. The drive took about thirty minutes with the start of the morning rush hour. It was the first time in England for Brian, though not for Dominic. The sights were pleasant for the latter, and both new and adventurous for the former. It seemed like home, Brian thought, except that people drove on the wrong side of the road. On first inspection, drivers also seemed more courteous, but that was hard to gauge. There was at least one golf course with emerald green grass, but aside from that, rush hour here wasn't all that different from the one in Seattle.

Half an hour later, they were looking at Green Park, which was, indeed, itself beautifully green, then the cab turned left, two more blocks, and right, and there was the hotel. Just on the other side of the street was a dealership for Aston Martin cars, looking as shiny as the diamonds in the window of Tiffany's in New York City. Clearly an upscale neighborhood. Though Dominic had been to London before, he hadn't stayed here. European hotels could teach lessons to any American establishment in terms of service and hospitality. Six more minutes had them in their connecting rooms. The bathtubs were large enough to exercise a shark, and the towels hung on a steam-heated rack. The minibar was generous in its selection, if not in its prices. Both twins took the time to shower. A check of the time made it a quarter to nine, and since Berkeley Square was only a hundred yards away, they took the moment to leave the hotel and head left for the landmark where nightingales sang.

Dominic elbowed his brother and pointed left. "Supposedly MI5 used to have a building that way, up Curzon Street. For the embassy, you go to the top of the hill, go left, two more blocks, then right, and left to Grosvenor Square. Ugly building, but that's the government for you. And our friend lives right about—there, on the other side of the park, half a block from the Westminster Bank. That's the one with the horse on the sign."

"Looks pricey here," Brian observed.

"Believe it," Dominic confirmed. "These houses go for a ton of money. Most of 'em are broken up into three apartments, but our friend Uda keeps the whole thing for himself, a Disneyland for sex and dissipation. Hmm," he observed, seeing a British Telecom van parked about twenty yards ahead of them. "I bet that's the surveillance team . . . kinda obvious." There were no people visible in the truck, but that was because the windows were plastic-treated to keep the light inside. It was the only inexpensive vehicle on the street—in this neighborhood, everything was at least a Jaguar. But the king of the hill, auto-wise, was the black Vanquish on the other side of the park.

"Damn, that's one bad-ass automobile," Brian observed. And indeed it looked as though it were doing a hundred miles per hour just sitting in front of the house.

"The real champ is the McLaren F1. Million bucks, but it only seats one up front, I think. Fast as a fighter plane. The one you're looking at is quarter-mil' worth of car, bro."

"Fuck . . ." Brian reacted. "That much?"

"They're handmade, Aldo, by guys who work on the Sistine Chapel in their off-hours. Yeah, it's a lot of wheels. Wish I could afford it. You could probably put the engine in a Spitfire and shoot down some Germans, y'know?"

"Probably gets lousy mileage," Brian observed.

"Oh, well . . . Everything has its little price—shit. There's our boy."

And just then the door to the house opened, and a young man walked out. The suit he wore was three-piece, and Johnny Reb gray in color. He stood in the middle of the four stone steps and looked at his watch. As though on cue, a black London cab came down the hill and he walked down the steps to hop in.

Five-ten, 155 to 160 pounds, Dominic thought. *Black beard down the line of his jaw, like from a pirate movie. Sucker ought to wear a sword... but he doesn't.*

"Younger than us," Brian observed, as they continued to walk. Then, on Dominic's initiative, they crossed over the park and headed back the other way, slowing for a covetous look at the Aston Martin before heading on their way. The hotel had a coffee shop, where they got some coffee and a light breakfast of croissants and marmalade.

"I don't like the idea of having coverage on our bird," Brian said.

"Can't be helped. The Brits must think he's a little hinky, too. But he's just going to have a heart attack, re-member. It's not like we're going to pop him, even with a suppressed weapon. No marks, no noise."

"Okay, fine, we check him out downtown, but if it doesn't look good we blow it off and step back to think it over, okay?"

"Agreed." Dominic nodded. They'd have to be clever about it. He'd probably take the lead, because it would be his job to spot the guy's police tail. But there was no sense in waiting too long, either. They'd looked at Berkeley Square just to get a feel for it, and hoping to eyeball the tar-get. It would not be a good place to make a hit, not with a surveillance team camped out thirty yards away. "The good news is that his tail is supposed to be a rookie. If I can ID the guy, then, when I get ready, you just bump into him and—hell, I'll ask directions to something or other. You'll only need a second to make the pop. Then we both keep on going like nothing happened. Even if people yell for an ambulance, nothing more than a casual turn, and you keep on going."

Brian thought his way through that. "We have to check out the neighborhood first."

"Agreed." They finished breakfast without another word.

* * *

SAM GRANGER was already in his office. It was 3:15
A.M. when he got in and lit up his own computer. The twins
had gotten to London at about 1:00 A.M. his time, and something in the back of his head told him that they would not
dally on their mission. This first mission would validate—
or not—The Campus's idea of a virtual office. If things
went according to plan, he'd get notification of the operation's progress even faster than Rick Bell's news over the
intelligence network's wire service. Now came the part he
always knew he'd hate: waiting for others to effect the mission he'd drawn up in his own mind, here at his own desk.
Coffee helped. A cigar would have helped even better, but
he didn't have a cigar. That's when his door opened.

It was Gerry Hendley.

"You, too?" Sam asked, with both surprise and amusement.

Hendley smiled. "Well, first time, right? I couldn't sleep
at home."

"I hear you. Got a deck of cards?" he wondered aloud.

"I wish." Hendley was actually pretty good with a deck
of cards. "Any word from the twins?"

"Not a peep. They got in on time, probably at the hotel
by now. I imagine they got in, freshened up, and went out
for a look-see. The hotel is only a block or so from Uda's
house. Hell, for all I know they might have popped him in
the ass already. The timing's about right. He'd be going to
work about now, if the locals have his routine figured out,
and I think we can depend on that."

"Yeah, unless he got an unexpected call, or he saw
something in the morning paper that caught his interest, or
his favorite shirt wasn't properly pressed. Reality is analog, Sam, not digital, remember?"

"Don't we know it," Granger agreed.

THE FINANCIAL district looked exactly like what it
was, though somewhat homier than New York's tower-

targets of steel and glass. There were some of those, too, of course, but they weren't as oppressive. Half a block from where they got out of the cab was a portion of the original Roman wall that had surrounded the legion town of Londinium, as the British capital had originally been known, a place selected for its good wells and large river. The people here were mostly well dressed, they noticed, and the shops all upscale in a city where few things were low scale. The bustle factor was high, with crowds of people moving about with speed and purpose. There was also a good supply of pubs, most of which had chalkboards near the doors to advertise their food. The twins picked one in easy sight of the Lloyd's building; agreeably, it had outside tables, as though it were a Roman restaurant near the Spanish Steps. The clear sky belied London's wet reputation. Both twins were sufficiently well dressed not to appear too obviously to be American tourists. Brian spotted an ATM machine and got some cash, which he split with his brother, and then they ordered coffee—they were too American to get tea—and waited.

IN HIS office, Sali was working on his computer. He had a chance to buy a town house in Belgravia—a neighborhood even more upscale than his own—for eight and a half million pounds, which wasn't quite a bargain, but neither was it excessive. Certainly he could rent it out for a good sum, and it was a freehold, meaning that in buying the house he'd also own the land, instead of paying ground rent to the Duke of Westminster. It wasn't excessive, either, but it did add up. He made a note to go look at it this week. Otherwise, the currency valuations were fairly stable. He'd played with currency arbitrage on and off for a few months, but he didn't really think he had the education to delve deeply into it. At least not yet. Maybe he would talk to a few people skilled in that game. Anything that could be done could also be learned, and with access to more than two hundred million pounds, he was able to play without doing his father's money too much damage. In fact, he was up this year by nine million pounds, which wasn't too bad. For the next hour, he sat at his computer and looked for trends—the trend is your friend—trying to make sense out of it. The real trick, he knew, was spotting them early—early enough to get in low before bailing out high—but, though he was closing in on it, he hadn't learned that particular skill yet. Had he done so, his trading account would have been up by thirty-one million pounds, instead of a mere nine. Patience, he thought, was a damnably hard virtue to acquire. How much better to be young and brilliant.

His office had a TV, too, of course, and he switched it to an American financial channel that spoke of a coming weakness in the pound against the dollar, though the reasons for it were not entirely convincing, and he thought better of buying thirty million dollars on speculation. His father had warned him about speculating before, and since it was his father's money he had listened attentively and granted the old bastard his wishes. Over the previous nineteen months, he was only down three million pounds, and most of those mistakes were a year behind him. The real-estate portfolio was doing very nicely. He was mostly buying property from older Englishmen and selling a few months later to his own countrymen, who usually paid cash or its electronic equivalent. All in all, he considered himself a real-estate speculator of great and growing talents. And, of course, a superb lover. It was approaching noon, and already his loins were aching for Rosalie. Might she be available this evening? For a thousand pounds, she ought to be, Uda thought. So, just before noon, he lifted his phone and hit the number 9 speed-dial button.

"My beloved Rosalie, this is Uda. If you can come over tonight, about seven-thirty, I will have something nice for you. You know my number, darling." And he set the phone down. He'd wait until four or so, and if she did not call him back, he'd call Mandy. It was a rare day indeed when both of them were unavailable. He preferred to believe they spent such time shopping or having dinner with friends. After all, who paid them better than he did? And he wanted to see Rosalie's face when she got the new shoes. English women really liked this Jimmy Choo fellow. To his eye, the designs looked grotesquely uncomfortable, but women were women, not men. For his fantasies, he drove his Aston Martin. Women preferred sore feet. There was no understanding them.

BRIAN GOT bored too easily to just sit and stare at the Lloyd's building. Besides, it hurt his eyes. It was more than undistinguished, it was positively grotesque, like a glassed-in DuPont plant for making nerve gas or some other noxious chemical. It was also probably bad field craft to stare at any one thing for any length of time. There was some shopping on this street, again none of it cheap. A men's tailor shop and similarly nice-looking places for women, and what appeared to be a very expensive shoe store. That was one item he didn't bother with much. He had good black leather dress shoes—he was wearing them now—a good pair of sneaks that he'd bought on a day best forgotten, and four pairs of combat boots, two black and two the buff color the Marine Corps was heading to, except for parades and other official stuff that did not often concern the snake-eating Marines of Force Recon. All Marines were supposed to be "pretty" troops, but the snake-eating ones were thought to be from the side of the family that you didn't talk much about. And he was still coming to terms with the shoot-out of the previous week. Even the people he'd gone after in Afghanistan hadn't made any overt attempts to kill women and kids, at least that he knew about. They were barbarians, sure, but even barbarians were supposed to have limits. Except for the bunch of people that this guy played with. It wasn't manly—even the beard wasn't manly. The Afghans' were, but this guy just looked like some sort of pimp. He was, in short, unworthy of the Marine's steel, not a man to be killed, but a cockroach to be eliminated. Even if he did drive a car worth more than a Marine captain made in ten years, *before* taxes. A Marine officer might save up for a Chevy Corvette, but, no, this POS had to have the grandson of James Bond's car, to go along with the whores he rented. You could call him a lot of things, but "man" was definitely not among them, the Marine thought, subconsciously working himself up for the mission.

"Tallyho, Aldo," Dominic said, putting cash down on the table to cover the bill. Both stood and walked *away* from the target at first. At the corner, both stopped and turned as though looking around for something. There was Sali...

...and there was Sali's tail. Dressed as a working man, expensively. He'd also appeared out of a pub, Dominic saw. He was indeed a rookie. His eyes were too obviously fixed on the subject, though he did stay back, fifty yards or so, clearly unconcerned about being spotted by his target. Sali was probably not the most alert of subjects, unschooled in countersurveillance. He doubtless thought himself perfectly safe. Probably thought himself pretty clever, too. All men had their illusions. This one's would prove to be more serious than normal.

The brothers scanned the street. Hundreds of people were in direct view. Lots of cars moving on the street. Visibility was good—a little too good—but Sali was presenting himself to them as though it were deliberate, and it was just too good to pass up...

"Plan A, Enzo?" Brian asked quickly. They had three plans thought out, plus the wave-off signal.

"Roger that, Aldo. Let's do it." They split up, heading in opposite directions in the hope that Sali would turn toward the pub where they'd endured the bad coffee. Both wore sunglasses to hide the direction of their gaze. In Aldo's case, this meant the spook who was tailing Sali. It was probably routine as hell for him, something he'd been doing for a few weeks, and you couldn't do anything that long without settling into a routine, anticipating what your subject was going to do, fixing on him and not scanning the street as you were supposed to do. But he was working in London, maybe his home turf, a place where he figured he knew all that was knowable and had nothing to fear. More dangerous illusions. His only job was to watch a not very intriguing subject in whom Thames House had some unexplained interest. The subject's habits were well established, and he was not a danger to anyone, at least not on this turf. A spoiled rich kid, that was all. Now he was turning left after crossing the street. Shopping today, it looked like. Shoes for one of his ladies, the Security Service officer surmised. Better presents than he could afford for *his* significant other, and he was *engaged,* the spook groused within his own mind.

THEY HAD a nice pair of shoes in the window, Sali saw, black leather and gold hardware. He hopped boyishly up onto the curb, then turned left toward the store entrance, smiling in anticipation of the look Rosalie would have in her eyes when she opened the box.

Dominic took out his Chichester map of central London, a small red book that he opened as he walked past the subject, without taking so much as a glance, letting his peripheral vision do the work. His eyes were fixed on the tail. Looked even younger than he and his brother were, probably his first job out of whatever academy the Security Service conducted, assigned to an easy target for that very reason. He'd probably be a little nervous, hence his fixed eyes and balled-fist hands. Dominic hadn't been all that different only a year or so before, in Newark, young and earnest. Dominic stopped and turned quickly, gauging the distance from Brian to Sali. Brian would be doing exactly the same thing, of course, and his job was to synchronize movement with his brother, who had the lead. Okay. Again his peripheral vision took over, until the last few steps.

Then his eyes fixed on the tail. The Brit's eyes noted

this, and his gaze shifted as well. He stopped almost automatically and heard the Yank tourist ask stupidly: "Excuse me, could you tell me where..." He held up his map book to illustrate how lost he was.

BRIAN REACHED into his coat pocket and pulled out the gold pen. He twisted the nib and the black point changed to an iridium tip when he pressed down on the obsidian clip. His eyes locked on the subject. At a range of three feet, he took half a step right as though to avoid someone who wasn't there at all, and bumped into Sali.

"THE TOWER of London. Why, you go right there," the MI5 guy said, turning to point.
Perfect.

"EXCUSE ME," Brian said, and let the man pass with a half step to his left, and the pen came down in a backward stabbing motion, and caught the subject square in the right ass cheek. The hollow syringe point penetrated perhaps as much as three millimeters. The CO_2 charge fired, injecting its seven milligrams of succinylcholine into the tissue of the largest muscle on Sali's anatomy. And Brian Caruso kept right on walking.

"OH, THANKS, buddy," Dominic said, tucking the Chichester's back into his pocket and taking a step in the proper direction. When he was clear of the tail, he stopped and turned—this was bad tradecraft, and he knew it—to see Brian putting the pen back into his coat pocket. His brother then rubbed his nose in the prearranged signal of MISSION ACCOMPLISHED.

SALI WINCED ever so slightly at the bump or stick— whatever it was—on his ass, but it was nothing serious. His right hand reached back to rub the spot, but the pain faded immediately, and he shrugged it off and kept heading for the shoe store. He took perhaps ten more steps and then he realized—

—his right hand was trembling ever so slightly. He stopped to look at it, reaching over with his left hand—

—that was trembling, too. Why was—

—his legs collapsed under him, and his body fell vertically down to the cement sidewalk. His kneecaps positively bounced on the surface, and they hurt, rather a lot in fact. He tried to take in a deep breath to ward off the pain and the embarrassment—

—but he *didn't* breathe. The succinylcholine had fully infused his body now, and had neutralized every nerve-muscle interface that existed in his body. The last to go were his eyelids, and Sali, his face now rapidly approaching the sidewalk, didn't see himself hit. Instead, he was enveloped by blackness—actually, redness from the low-frequency light that penetrated the thin tissue of his eyelids. Very rapidly, his brain was overwhelmed first by the confusion that had to come before panic.

What is this? his mind demanded of itself. He could *feel* what was happening. His forehead was against the rough surface of semifinished cement. He could hear the footsteps of people to his left and right. He tried to turn his head—no, first he had to open his eyes—

—but they did not open. *What* is *this?!!!*—

—he wasn't breathing—

—he commanded himself to breathe. As though in a swimming pool underwater, and coming to the surface after holding his breath for an uncomfortably long time, he told his mouth to open and his diaphragm to expand—

—*but nothing happened!*—

—*What is this?* his mind shouted at itself.

His body operated on its own programming. As carbon dioxide built up in his lungs, automatic commands went from there to his diaphragm to expand his lungs to take in more air to replace the poison in his lungs. But nothing happened, and, with that bit of information, his body went into panic all by itself. Adrenal glands flooded the blood-stream—the heart was still pumping—with adrenaline, and, with that natural stimulant, his awareness increased and his brain went into overdrive...

What is this? Sali asked himself urgently yet again, for now the panic was beginning to take over. His body was betraying him in ways that surpassed imagination. He was suffocating in the dark on a sidewalk in the middle of central London in broad daylight. The overload of CO_2 in his lungs did not really cause pain, but his body reported the fact to his mind as such. Something was going very wrong, and it made no sense, like being hit in the street by a lorry—no, like being run over by a lorry in his *living room.* It was happening too fast for him to grasp it all. It made no sense, and it was so—surprising, astonishing, astounding.

But neither could it be denied.

He continued to command himself to breathe. It had to happen. It had never *not* happened, and so it must. He felt his bladder emptying next, but the flash of shame was immediately overcome by the building panic. He could *feel* everything. He could *hear* everything. But he couldn't *do* anything, nothing at all. It was like being caught naked in the King's own court in Riyadh with a pig in his arms—

—and then the pain started. His heart was beating frantically, now at 160 beats per minute, but in doing so it was only sending unoxygenated blood out into his cardiovascular system, and in doing that the heart—the only really active organ in his body—had used up all of the free and reserve oxygen in his body—

—and denied of oxygen, the faithful heart cells, immune to the muscle relaxant that it had itself infused throughout its owner's body, started to die.

It was the greatest pain the body can know, as each separate cell started to die, starting at the heart, the danger to which was immediately reported to the body as a whole, and the cells were now dying by the thousands, each connected to a nerve that screamed into the brain that DEATH was happening, and happening now—

He couldn't even grimace. It was like a fiery dagger in his chest, twisting, pushing deeper and deeper. It was the feel of Death, something delivered by the hand by Iblis himself, by Lucifer's own hand...

And that was the instant Sali saw Death coming, riding across a field of fire to take his soul, to Perdition. Urgently, but in a state of internal panic, Uda bin Sali thought as loudly as he could the words of the Shahada: *There is no God but Allah and Mohammed is His messenger...There is no God but Allah and Mohammed is His messenger...There is no God but Allah and Mohammed is His messenger—*

—Thereisnogodbutallahandmohammedishismessenger.

His brain cells, too, were deprived of oxygen, and they, too, started to die, and in that process the data they contained was dumped into a diminishing awareness. He saw his father, his favorite horse, his mother before a table full with food—and Rosalie, Rosalie riding him from on top, her face full of delight, that somehow became more distant...fading...fading...fading...

...to black.

People had gathered around him. One bent down and said, "Hello, are you all right?" A stupid question, but that's what people asked in such circumstances. Then the person—he was a salesman of computer peripherals heading to the nearby pub for a pint and a British ploughman's lunch—shook his shoulder. There was no resistance at all, like turning over a piece of meat in the butcher's shop... And that frightened him more than a loaded pistol would have done. At once he rolled the body over and felt for a pulse. There *was* one. The heart was beating frantically—but the man wasn't breathing. Bloody hell...

Ten meters away, Sali's tail had his cell phone out and was dialing 999 for emergency services. There was a fire station only blocks away, and Guy's Hospital was just across Tower Bridge. Like many spooks, he had started to identify with his subject, even though detesting him, and the sight of the man crumpled on the sidewalk had shaken him deeply. What had happened? Heart attack? But he was a young man . . .

BRIAN AND Dominic rendezvoused at a pub, just uphill from the Tower of London. They picked a booth, and scarcely had they sat down when a waitress came to them and asked what they wanted.

"Two pints," Enzo told her.

"We have Tetley's Smooth and John Smith's, love."

"Which one do you drink?" Brian shot back.

"John Smith's, of course."

"Two of those," Dominic ordered. He took the lunch menu from her.

"Not sure I want anything to eat, but the beer's a good idea," Brian said, taking the menu, his hands shaking ever so slightly.

"And a cigarette, maybe." Dominic chuckled. Like most kids, they'd experimented with smoking in high school, but both had sworn off it before getting hooked. Besides, the cigarette machine in the corner was made of wood, and was probably too complex for a foreigner to operate.

"Yeah, right," Brian dismissed the thought.

Just as the beers arrived, they heard the dissonant note of a local ambulance three blocks away.

"How you feel?" Enzo asked his brother.

"Little shaky."

"Think about last Friday," the FBI agent suggested to the Marine.

"I didn't say I regretted it, dumbass. You just get a little worked up. You distract the tail?"

"Yeah, he was looking right into my eyes when you made the stick. Your subject walked maybe twenty feet before he collapsed. I didn't see any reaction from the stick. You?"

Brian shook his head. "Not even an 'ouch,' bro." He took a sip. "This is pretty good beer."

"Yeah, shaken, not stirred, Double-Oh-Seven."

In spite of himself, Brian laughed aloud. "You asshole!" he said.

"Well, that's the business we've fallen into, right?"

CHAPTER 18

‖‖‖

AND THE DEPARTING FOXHOUNDS

JACK JR. found out first. He was just starting his coffee and doughnuts, and had lit up his computer, navigating his way first to the message traffic from CIA to NSA, and at the very top of the electronic pile was a FLASH-priority alert for NSA to pay special attention to "known associates" of Uda bin Sali, who had, CIA said the Brits had reported, evidently dropped dead of a heart attack in central London. The Security Service FLASH traffic, included in the CIA-gram, said in terse English prose that he'd collapsed on the street before the eyes of their surveillance officer, and had been rushed by ambulance to Guy's Hospital, where he "had failed to revive." The body was now being posted, MI5 said.

IN LONDON, Special Branch Detective Bert Willow called Rosalie Parker's apartment.

"Hello." She had a charming, musical voice.

"Rosalie, this is Detective Willow. We need to see you as soon as possible here at the Yard."

"I'm afraid I am busy, Bert. I have a client coming any

minute. It will take two hours or so. I can come directly after that. Will that be okay?"

At the other end of the line, the detective took a deep breath, but, no, it really wasn't that urgent. If Sali had died of drugs—the most likely cause that had occurred to him and his colleagues—he hadn't gotten them from Rosalie, who was neither an addict nor a supplier. She wasn't stupid for a girl whose entire education had been in state schools. Her work was too lucrative to take that risk. The girl even attended church occasionally, her file read. "Very well," Bert told her. He was curious about how she'd take the news, but didn't expect anything important to develop there.

"Excellent. Bye-ee," she said before hanging up.

AT GUY'S Hospital, the body was already in the postmortem lab. It had been undressed and laid faceup on a stainless steel table by the time the senior duty pathologist came in. He was Sir Percival Nutter, a distinguished academic physician, and chairman of the hospital's Department of Pathology, sixty years of age. His technicians had already drawn 0.1 liter of blood for the lab to work on. It was quite a lot, but they'd be running every test known to man.

"Very well, he has the body of a male subject approximately twenty-five years of age—get his identification to get the proper dates, Maria," he told the microphone that hung down from the ceiling, which led to a tape recorder. "Weight?" This question was directed to a junior resident.

"Seventy-three point six kilograms. One hundred eighty-one centimeters in length," the brand-new physician responded.

"There are no distinguishing marks on the body, on visual inspection, suggesting a cardiovascular or neurological incident. What's the hurry on this, Richard? The body is still warm." No tattoos and so on. Lips were somewhat bluish. His nonofficial comments would be edited from the tape, of course, but a body still warm was quite unusual.

"Police request, sir. Seems he dropped dead on the street while being observed by a constable." It wasn't exactly the truth, but it was close enough.

"Did you see any needle marks?" Sir Percy asked.

"No, sir, not a hint of that."

"So, lad, what do you think?"

Richard Gregory, the new M.D. doing his first pathology rotation, shrugged in his surgical greens. "From what the police say, the way he went down, sounds like a possible massive heart attack or a seizure of some sort—unless it's drug-related. He looks healthy for that, and there are no needle-mark clusters to suggest drugs."

"Rather young for a fatal infarction," the senior man said. To him, the body might as easily have been a piece of meat in the market, or a dead deer in Scotland, not the remaining shell of a human being who'd been alive—what?—as little as two or three hours earlier. Bad bloody luck for the poor bastard. Looked vaguely Middle Eastern. The smooth, unmarked skin on the hands did not suggest manual labor, though he did appear reasonably fit. He lifted the eyelids. Eyes were brown enough to appear black at a distance. Good teeth, not much dental work. On the whole, a young man who appeared to have taken decent care of himself. This was odd. Congenital heart defect, perhaps? They'd have to crack his chest for that. Nutter didn't mind doing it—it was just a routine part of the job, and he'd long since learned to forget about the immense sadness associated with it—but on such a young body, it struck him as a waste of time, even though the cause of death was mysterious enough to be of intellectual interest, perhaps even something for an article in *The Lancet,* something he'd done many times in the preceding thirty-six years. Along the way, his dissection of the dead had saved hundreds, even thousands, of living people, which was why he'd chosen pathology. You also didn't have to talk to your patients much.

For the moment, they'd wait for the blood-toxicology

readings to come out of the serology lab. It would at least give him a direction for his investigation.

BRIAN AND Dominic took a cab back to their hotel. Once there, Brian lit up his laptop and logged on. The brief e-mail he sent was automatically encrypted and dispatched in a matter of four minutes. He figured an hour or so for The Campus to react, assuming nobody wet his pants, which was unlikely. Granger looked like a guy who could have done this job himself, fairly tough for an old guy. His time in the Corps had taught him that you read the tough ones from the eyes. John Wayne had played football for USC. Audie Murphy, rejected by a Marine recruiter—to the everlasting shame of the Corps—had looked like a street waif, but he'd killed more than three hundred men all by himself. He'd also had cold eyes when provoked.

It was suddenly and surprisingly lonely for both Carusos.

They'd just murdered a man they didn't know and to whom neither had spoken a single word. It had all seemed logical and sensible at The Campus, but that was now a place far away in both linear distance and spiritual vastness. But the man they'd killed had funded the creatures who'd shot up Charlottesville, killing women and children without mercy, and, in facilitating that act of barbarism, he'd made himself guilty as a matter of law and common morality. So, it wasn't as though they'd wasted Mother Teresa's little brother on his way to Mass.

Again, it was harder on Brian than on Dominic, who walked over to the minibar and took out a can of beer. This he threw to his brother.

"I know," Brian responded. "He had it coming. It's just that—well, it's not like Afghanistan, y'know?"

"Yeah, this time we got to do to him what they tried to do to you. It's not our fault he's a bad guy. It's not our fault he thought the mall shoot was almost as good as getting laid. He did have it coming. Maybe he didn't shoot anybody, but he damned sure bought the guns, okay?" Dominic asked as reasonably as circumstances allowed.

"I ain't going to light a candle for him. Just—damn it, this isn't what we're supposed to do in a civilized world."

"What civilized world is that, bro? We offed a guy who needed to meet God. If God wants to forgive him, that's His business. You know, there're people who think anybody in uniform is a mercenary killer. Baby-killers, that sort of thing."

"Well, that's just fucked up," Brian snarled back. "What I'm afraid of is, what if we turn into *them*?"

"Well, we can always back off a job, can't we? And they told us they'll always give us the reason for the hit. We won't turn into them, Aldo. I won't let it happen. Neither will you. So, we have things to do, right?"

"I suppose." Brian took a big pull on the beer and pulled the gold pen from his coat pocket. He had to recharge it. That took less than three minutes, and it was again ready to rock and roll. Then he twisted it back to a writing instrument and put it back in his coat pocket. "I'll be okay, Enzo. You're not supposed to feel good about killing a guy on the street. Though I still wonder if it doesn't make sense simply to pick the guy up and interrogate him."

"The Brits have civil-rights rules like ours. If he asks for a lawyer—you know he's been briefed to do that, right?— the cops can't even ask him the time, just like at home. All he has to do is smile and keep his trap shut. That's one of the drawbacks of civilization. It makes sense for criminals, I suppose, most of them, but these guys aren't criminals. It's a form of warfare, not street crime. That's the problem, and you can't hardly threaten a guy who wants to die in the performance of his duty. All you can do is stop him, and stopping a person like that means his heart has to discontinue beating."

Another pull on the beer. "Yeah, Enzo. I'm okay. I wonder who our next subject is."

"Give 'em an hour to chew on it. How about a walk?"

"Works for me." Brian stood, and in a minute they were back out on the street.

It was a little too obvious. The British Telecom van was just pulling away, but the Aston Martin was still in place. He wondered if the Brits would put a black-bag team into the house to toss it for interesting things, but that black sports car was right here, and it sure looked sexy.

"Wish you could get it in the estate sale?" Brian asked.

"Can't drive it at home. Wheel's on the wrong side," Dominic pointed out. But his brother was right. It was felonious for such a car to go to waste. Berkeley Square was pretty enough, but too small for anything except letting the infants crawl around on the grass and get some fresh air and sun. The house would probably be sold, too, and it would go for a large sum. Lawyers—"solicitors" over here—to tie things up, taking their cut before returning the residuary property to whatever family a snake left behind. "Hungry yet?"

"I could eat something," Brian allowed. So they walked some more. They headed toward Piccadilly and found a place called Pret A Manger, which served sandwiches and cold drinks. After a total of forty minutes away from the hotel, they headed back in and Brian lit up his computer again.

MISSION ACCOMPLISHED CONFIRMED BY LOCAL SOURCES. MISSION CLEAN, the message from The Campus read, and went on: SEATS CONFIRMED FLIGHT BA0943 DEPART HEATHROW TOMORROW 07:55 ARRIVE MUNICH 10:45. TICKETS AT COUNTER. There was a page of details, followed by ENDS.

"Okay," Brian observed. "We have another job."

"Already?" Dominic was surprised at the efficiency of The Campus.

Brian wasn't. "I guess they're not paying us to be tourists, bro."

"YOU KNOW, we need to get the twins out of Dodge quicker," Tom Davis remarked.

"If they're covert, it's not necessary," Hendley said.

"If somebody spots them somehow or other, better that they should not be around. You can't interview a ghost," Davis pointed out. "If the police have nothing to track, then they have less to think about. They can query the passenger list on a flight, but if the names they look for—assuming they have names—just go about normal business, then they have a blank wall with no evidence hanging on it. Better yet, if whatever face might or might not have been spotted just evaporates, then they have *gornischt,* and they're most likely to write it off as an eyewitness who couldn't be trusted anyway." It is not widely appreciated that police agencies trust eyewitnesses the least of all forms of criminal evidence. Their reports are too volatile, and too unreliable to be of much use in a court of law.

"AND?" SIR Percival asked.

"CPK-MB, and troponin are greatly elevated, and the lab says his cholesterol was two hundred thirteen," Dr. Gregory said. "High for one his age. No evidence whatever of drugs of any sort, not even aspirin. So, we have enzyme evidence of a coronary incident, and that's all at the moment."

"Well, we'll have to crack his chest," Dr. Nutter observed, "but that was in the cards anyway. Even with elevated cholesterol, he's young for a major cardiovascular obstruction, don't you think?"

"Were I to wager, sir, I think prolonged QT interval, or arrhythmia." Both of which left little postmortem evidence except in a negative sense, unfortunately, but both of which were uniformly fatal.

"Correct." Gregory seemed a bright young medical school graduate, and like most of them, exceedingly earnest. "In we go," Nutter said, reaching for the big skin knife. Then they'd use the rib cutters. But he was pretty sure what they'd find. The poor bastard had died of heart failure, probably caused by a sudden—and unexplained— onset of cardiac arrhythmia. But whatever caused it, it had been as lethal as a bullet in the brain. "Nothing else on the toxicology scan?"

"No, sir, nothing whatever." Gregory held up the computer printout. Except for reference marks on the paper, it was almost entirely blank. And that pretty much settled that.

IT WAS like listening to a World Series game on the radio, but without the color-commentary filler. Somebody at the Security Service was eager to let CIA know what was going on with the subject about which Langley clearly had some interest, and so whatever dribs and drabs of information came in were immediately dispatched to CIA, and thence to Fort Meade, which was scanning the ether waves for any resulting interest from the terrorist community around the world. The latter's news service, it appeared, was not as efficient as its enemies had hoped.

"HELLO, DETECTIVE Willow," Rosalie Parker said with her customary want-to-fuck-me smile. She made love for a living, but that didn't mean that she disliked it. She breezed in wearing her visitor's badge and took her seat opposite his desk. "So, what can I do for you this fine day?"

"Bad news, Miss Parker." Bert Willow was formal and polite, even with whores. "Your friend Uda bin Sali is dead."

"What?" Her eyes went wide with shock. "What happened?"

"We're not sure. He just dropped down on the street, just across the street from his office. It appears that he had a heart attack."

"Really?" Rosalie was surprised. "But he seemed so healthy. There was never a hint that anything was wrong with him. I mean, just last night . . ."

"Yes, I saw that in the file," Willow responded. "Do you know if he ever used drugs of any sort?"

"No, never. He occasionally drank, but even that not much."

To Willow's eyes, she was shocked and greatly surprised, but there wasn't a hint of tears in her eyes. No, for her, Uda had been a business client, a source of income, and little more. The poor bastard had probably thought otherwise. Doubly bad luck for him, then. But that wasn't really Willow's concern, was it?

"Anything unusual in your most recent meeting?" the cop asked.

"No, not really. He was quite randy, but, you know, some years ago I had a john die on me—I mean, he came and went, as they say. It was bloody awful, not the sort of thing you forget, and so I keep an eye on my clients for that. I mean, I'd never leave one to die. I'm not a barbarian, you know. I really do have a heart," she assured the cop.

Well, your friend Sali doesn't anymore, Willow thought, without saying it. "I see. So last night he was completely normal?"

"Entirely. Not a single sign that anything was amiss." She paused to work on her composure. Better to appear more regretful, lest he think her to be an uncaring robot. "This is terrible news. He was so generous, and always polite. How very sad for him."

"And for you," Willow said in sympathy. After all, she'd just lost a major source of income.

"Oh. Yes, oh yes, for me too, love," she said, catching up with the news finally. But she didn't even try to fool the detective with tears. Waste of time. He'd see right through it. Pity about Sali. She'd miss the presents. Well, surely she'd get some more referral business. Her world hadn't ended. Just his. And that was his bad luck—with some thrown in for her, but nothing she couldn't recover from.

"Miss Parker, did he ever give you any hints on his business activities?"

"Mostly, he talked about real estate, you know, buying and selling those posh houses. Once, he took me to a house he was buying in the West End, said he wanted my opinion on painting it, but I think he was just trying to show me how important he was."

"Ever meet any of his friends?"

"Not too many—three, maybe four, I think. All were Arabs, most about his age, perhaps five years older, but not more than that. They all looked me over closely, but no business resulted from it. That surprised me. Arabs can be horny buggers, but they are good at paying a girl. You think he might have been involved in illegal activity?" she asked delicately.

"It's a possibility," Willow allowed.

"Never saw a hint of it, love. If he played with bad boys, it was out of my sight entirely. Love to help you, but there's nothing to say." She seemed sincere to the detective, but he reminded himself that when it came to dissimulation, a whore of this class could probably have shamed Dame Judith Anderson.

"Well, thank you for coming in. If anything—anything at all—comes to mind, do give me a call."

"That I will, love." She stood and smiled her way out the door. He was a nice chap, this Detective Willow. Pity he couldn't afford her.

Bert Willow was already back on his computer, typing up his contact report. Miss Parker actually seemed a nice girl, literate and very charming. Part of that had been learned for her business persona, but maybe part of it was genuine. If so, he hoped she'd find a new line of work before her character was completely destroyed. He was a romantic, Willow was, and someday it might be his downfall. And he knew it, but he had no desire to change himself for his job as she had probably done. Fifteen minutes later, he e-mailed the report to Thames House, and then printed it up for the Sali file, which would in due course go to the closed files in Central Records, probably never to be heard from again.

* * *

"**TOLD YOU.**" Jack said to his roomie.

"Well, then you can pat yourself on the back," Wills responded. "So, what's the story, or do I have to call up the documents?"

"Uda bin Sali dropped dead of an apparent heart attack. His Security Service tail didn't see anything unusual, just the guy collapsing on the street. *Zap,* no more Uda to swap funds for the bad guys."

"How do you feel about it?" Wills asked.

"It's fine with me, Tony. He played with the wrong kids, on the wrong playground. End of story," Ryan the younger said coldly. *I wonder how they did it?* he wondered more quietly. "Was it our guys helping him along, you think?"

"Not our department. We provide information to others. What they do with it out of our sight is not for us to speculate upon."

"Aye, aye, sir." The remainder of the day looked as though it would be pretty dull after such a fast beginning.

MOHAMMED GOT the news over his computer—rather, he was told in code to call a cutout named Ayman Ghailani whose cell phone number he had committed to memory. For that purpose, he took a walk outside. You had to be careful using hotel phones. Once on the street, he walked to a park and sat down on a bench, with a pad and pen in his hand.

"Ayman, this is Mohammed. What is new?"

"Uda is dead," the cutout reported somewhat breathlessly.

"What happened?" Mohammed asked.

"We're not sure. He fell near his office and was taken to the nearest hospital. He died there," was the reply.

"He was not arrested, not killed by the Jews?"

"No, there is no report of that."

"So, it was a natural death?"

"So it appears at this time."

I wonder if he did the funds transfer before he left this

life? Mohammed thought. "I see..." He didn't, of course, but he had to fill the silence with some words. "So, there is no reason to suspect foul play?"

"Not at this time, no. But when one of our people dies, one always—"

"Yes, I know, Ayman. One always suspects. Does his father know?"

"That is how I found out."

His father will probably be glad to be rid of the wastrel, Mohammed thought. "Who do we have to make sure of the cause of death?"

"Ahmed Mohammed Hamed Ali lives in London. Perhaps through a solicitor...?"

"Good idea. See that it is done." A pause. "Has anyone told the Emir?"

"No, I don't think so."

"See to it." It was a minor matter, but, even so, he was supposed to know everything.

"I shall," Ayman promised.

"Very well. That is all, then." And Mohammed thumbed the kill button on his cell phone.

He was back in Vienna. He liked the city. For one thing, they'd handled the Jews here once, and many Viennese managed to control their regrets over it. For another, it was a good place to be a man with money. Fine restaurants staffed by people who knew the value of skilled service to their betters. The former imperial city had a lot of cultural history to appreciate when he was of a mind to be a tourist, which happened more often than one might imagine. Mohammed found that he often did his best thinking when looking at something of no importance to his work. Today, an art museum, perhaps. He'd let Ayman do the scut work for now. A London solicitor would root about for information surrounding Uda's death, and, being a good mercenary, he'd let them know of anything untoward. But sometimes people simply died. It was the hand of Allah, which was not something easily understood, and never predicted.

* * *

OR MAYBE not so dull. NSA cross-decked some new message traffic after lunch. Jack did some mental arithmetic and decided it was evening on the other side of the pond. The electronic weenies of the Italian Carabinieri—their federal police, who walked about in rather spiffy uniforms—had made some intercepts, which they'd forwarded to the U.S. Embassy in Rome, and which had gone right up on the satellite to Fort Belvoir—the main East Coast downlink. Somebody named Mohammed had called somebody named Ayman—they knew this from the recorded conversation, which had also mentioned the death of Uda bin Sali, which had caused an electronic "Bingo" on various computers, flagging it for a signals-intelligence analyst, and causing the embassy puke to squirt the bird.

"'Has anyone told the Emir?' Who the hell is the Emir?" Jack asked.

"That's a nobleman's title, like a duke or something," Wills answered. "What's the context?"

"Here." Jack handed a printed sheet across.

"That looks interesting." Wills turned and queried his computer for EMIR, and got only one reference. "According to this, it's a name or title that cropped up about a year ago in a tapped conversation, context uncertain, and nothing significant since. The Agency thinks it's probably shorthand for a medium-sized hitter in their organization."

"In this context, looks bigger than that to me," Jack thought aloud.

"Maybe," Tony conceded. "There's a lot about these guys that we don't know yet. Langley will probably write it off to somebody in a supervisory position. That's what I would do," he concluded, but not confidently.

"We have anybody on staff who knows Arabic?"

"Two guys who speak the language—from the Monterey school—but no experts on the culture, no."

"I think it's worth a look."

"Then write it up and we'll see what they think. Langley

has a bunch of mind readers, and some of them are pretty good."

"Mohammed is the most senior guy we know in this outfit. Here, he's referring to somebody senior to himself. That is something we need to check out," the younger Ryan pronounced with all the power he possessed.

For his part, Wills knew that his roomie was right. He'd also just implicitly identified the biggest problem in the intelligence business. Too much data, too little analytical time. The best play would be to fake an inquiry to CIA from NSA and to NSA from CIA, asking for some thoughts on this particular issue. But they had to be careful with that. Requests for data happened a million times a day, and, due to the volume, they were never, ever checked—the comm link was secure, after all, wasn't it? But asking for time from analysts could too easily result in a telephone call, which required both a number and a person to pick up the phone. *That* could lead to a leak, and leaks were the single thing The Campus could not afford. And so, inquiries of this kind went to the top floor. Maybe twice a year. The Campus was a parasite on the body of the intelligence community. Such creatures were not supposed to have a mouth for speaking, but only for sucking blood.

"Write your ideas up for Rick Bell, and he'll discuss it with the Senator," Wills advised.

"Great," Jack grumbled. He hadn't learned patience yet. More to the point, he hadn't learned much about bureaucracies. Even The Campus had one. The funny thing was that if he'd been a midlevel analyst at Langley, he could have picked up a phone, dialed a number, and talked to the right person for an expert opinion, or something close to it. But this wasn't Langley. CIA was actually pretty good about obtaining and processing information. It was doing something effective with it that constantly befuddled the government agency. Jack wrote up his request and the reasons for it, wondering what would result.

* * *

THE EMIR took the news calmly. Uda had been a useful underling, but not an important one. He had many sources of money for his operations. He was tall for his ethnicity, not particularly handsome, with a Semitic nose and olive skin. His family was distinguished and very wealthy, though his brothers—he had nine—controlled most of the family money. His home in Riyadh was large and comfortable, but not a palace. Those he left to the Royal Family, whose numerous princelings paraded about as though each of them were the king of this land and protector of the Holy Places. The Royal Family, whose members he knew well, were objects of silent contempt for him, but his emotions were something buried within his soul.

In his youth, he'd been more demonstrative. He'd come to Islam in his early teens, inspired by a very conservative imam whose preachings had eventually gotten him into trouble, but who had inspired a raft of followers and spiritual children. The Emir was merely the cleverest of the lot. He, too, had spoken his mind, and as a result been sent off to England for his education—really to get him out of the country—but in England, in addition to learning the ways of the world, he'd been exposed to something entirely alien. Freedom of speech and expression. In London, it is mostly celebrated at Hyde Park Corner, a tradition of spleen venting that dates back hundred of years, sort of a safety valve for the British population, and which, like a safety value, merely vents troublesome thoughts into the air without letting them take much hold anywhere. Had he gone to America, it would have been the radical press. But what had struck him as hard as the arrival of a spaceship from Mars was that people were able to challenge the government in any terms they pleased. He'd grown up in one of the world's last absolute monarchies, where the very soil of the nation *belonged* to the king, and the law was what the reigning monarch said it was—subject in name if not in substance to the Koran and the Shar'ia, the Islamic legal traditions which dated back to the Prophet himself.

These laws were fair—or at least consistent—but very stern indeed. The problem was that not everyone agreed about the words of the Koran, and therefore about how the Shar'ia applied to the physical world. Islam had no pope, no real philosophical hierarchy as other religions understood the concept, and therefore no cohesive standard of application to reality. The Shi'a and the Sunni were often—always—at each other's throats over that question, and even within Sunni Islam, the Wahabis—the principal sect of the Kingdom—adhered to a stern belief system indeed. But for the Emir this very apparent weakness of Islam was its most useful attribute. One only had to convert a few individual Muslims to his particular belief system, which was remarkably easy, since you didn't have to go looking for those people. They identified themselves virtually to the point of advertising their identities. And most of them were people educated in Europe or America, where their foreign origin forced them to cleave together just to maintain a comfortable intellectual place of self-identity, and so they built upon a foundation of outsiderness that had led many of them to a revolutionary ethos. That was particularly useful, since along the way they'd acquired a knowledge of the enemy's culture that was vital in targeting his weaknesses. The religious conversions of these people had largely been preinstalled, as it were. After that, it was just a matter of identifying their objects of hatred—that is, the people to be blamed for their youthful discontent—and then deciding how to do away with their self-generated enemies, one at a time, or as a grand coup de main, which appealed to their sense of drama, if not their scant understanding of reality.

And at the end of it, the Emir, as his associates had taken to calling him, would be the new Mahdi, the ultimate arbiter of all of the global Islamic movement. The intra-religious disputes (Sunnis and Shi'a, for example) he planned to handle through a sweeping fatwa, or religious pronouncement of tolerance—that would look admirable even to his enemies. And, after all, weren't there a hundred or more Christian sects who had largely ended their own internal strife? He could even reserve to himself tolerance of the Jews, though he would have to save that for later years, after he had settled into the seat of ultimate power, probably with a palace of suitable humility outside the city of Mecca. Humility was a useful virtue for the head of a religious movement, for as the pagan Thucydides had proclaimed, even before the Prophet, of all manifestations of power, that which most impresses men is restraint.

It was the tallest of orders, the thing he wanted to accomplish. It would require time and patience, and its success was hardly guaranteed. It was his misfortune that he had to depend upon zealots, each of whom had a brain, and the consequent strong opinions. Such people could, conceivably, turn on him and seek to replace him with religious outlooks of their own. They might even believe their own concepts—they might be *true* zealots, as the Prophet Mohammed had been, but Mohammed, blessings and peace be upon him, had been the most honorable of men, and had fought a good and honorable fight against pagan idolaters, while his own effort was mainly within the community of Faithful. Was he, then, an honorable man? A difficult question. But didn't Islam need to be brought into the current world, and not remain trapped in antiquity? Did Allah desire His Faithful to be prisoners of the seventh century? Certainly not. Islam had once been the center of human scholarship, a religion of advancement and learning that had, sadly, lost its way at the hands of the great Khan, and then been oppressed by the infidels of the West. The Emir *did* believe in the Holy Koran, and the teachings of the imans, but he was not blind to the world around him. Nor was he blind to the facts of human existence. Those who had power guarded it jealously, and religion had little to do with that, because power was a narcotic all its own. And people needed something—preferably *someone*—to follow if they were to advance. Freedom, as the Europeans

and Americans understood the concept, was too chaotic—
he'd learned *that* at Hyde Park Corner, too. There had to be
order. He was the man to provide it.

So, Uda bin Sali was dead, he thought, taking a sip of
juice. A great misfortune for Uda, but a minor irritation to
the Organization. The Organization had access to, if not a
sea of money, then a number of comfortably large lakes, a
small one of which Uda had managed. A glass of orange
juice had fallen off the table, but thankfully it had not
stained the carpet under it. It required no action on his part,
even at second hand.

"Ahmed, this is sad news, but not a matter of great importance to us. No action need be taken."

"It shall be as you say," Ahmed Musa Matwalli responded respectfully. He killed his phone. It was a cloned
phone, bought from a street thief for that one purpose, and
then he tossed it into the river Tevere—the Tiber—off the
Ponte Sant'Angelo. It was a standard security measure for
speaking with the great commander of the Organization,
whose identity was known to but a few, all of whom were
among the most faithful of the Believers. At the higher ech-
elons, security was tight. They all studied various manuals
for intelligence officers. The best had been bought from a
former KGB officer, who had died after the sale, for so it
had been written. Its rules were simple and clear, and they
did not deviate from them a dot. Others had been careless,
and they'd all paid for their foolishness. The former USSR
had been a hated enemy, but its minions had never been
fools. Only unbelievers. America, the Great Satan, had
done the entire world a favor by destroying that abortion
of a nation. They'd done it only for their own benefit, of
course, but that, too, must have been written by the Hand of
God, because it had also served the interests of the Faithful, for what man could plot better than Allah Himself?

CHAPTER 19

BEER AND HOMICIDE

THE FLIGHT into Munich was silky smooth. German customs were formal but efficient, and a Mercedes-Benz cab took them to the Hotel Bayerischer.

Their current subject was somebody named Anas Ali Atef, reportedly an Egyptian by nationality, and a civil engineer by education, if not by profession. Five feet nine inches or so, 145 pounds, clean-shaven. Black hair and dark brown eyes, supposed to be skilled at unarmed combat and a good man with a gun, if he had one. He was thought to be a courier for the opposition, and also worked to recruit talent—one of whom, for certain, had been shot dead in Des Moines, Iowa. They had an address and a photo on their laptops. He drove an Audi TT sports car, painted battleship gray. They even had the tag number. Problem: He was living with a German national named Trudl Heinz, and was supposedly in love with her. There was a photo of her, too. Not exactly a Victoria's Secret model, but not a skank, either—brown hair and blue eyes, five feet three inches, 120 pounds. Cute smile. Too bad, Dominic thought, that she had questionable taste in men, but that was not his problem.

Anas worshipped regularly at one of the few mosques in Munich, which was conveniently located a block from his apartment building. After checking in and changing their clothes, Dominic and Brian caught a cab to that location and found a very nice *Gasthaus*—a bar and grill—with outside tables from which to observe the area.

"Do all Europeans like to sit on the sidewalk and eat?" Brian wondered.

"Probably easier than going to the zoo," Dominic said.

The apartment house was four stories, proportioned like a cement block, painted white with a flat but strangely barnlike roof. There was a remarkably clean aspect to it, as though it was normal in Germany for everything to be as pristine as a Mayo Clinic operating room, but that was hardly cause for criticism. Even the cars here were not as dirty as they tended to be in America.

"*Was darf es sein?*" the waiter asked, appearing at the table.

"*Zwei Dunkelbieren, bitte,*" Dominic replied, using about a third of his remaining high-school German. Most of the rest was about finding the *Herrnzimmer,* always a useful word to know, in any language.

"American, yes?" the waiter went on.

"Is my accent that bad?" Dominic asked, with a limp smile.

"Your speech is not Bavarian, and your clothes look American," the waiter observed matter-of-factly, as though to say the sky was blue.

"Okay, then two glasses of dark beer, if you please, sir."

"Two Kulmbachers, *sofort,*" the man responded and hurried back inside.

"I think we just learned a little lesson, Enzo," Brian observed.

"Buy some local clothes, first chance we get. Everybody's got eyes," Dominic agreed. "Hungry?"

"I could eat something."

"We'll see if they have a menu in English."

"That must be the mosque our friend uses, down the road a block, see?" Brian pointed discreetly.

"So, figure he'll probably walk this way . . . ?"

"Seems likely, bro."

"And there's no clock on this, is there?"

"They don't tell us 'how,' they just tell us 'what,' the man said," Brian reminded his brother.

"Good," Enzo observed as the beer arrived. The waiter looked to be about as efficient as a reasonable man could ask. "*Danke sehr.* Do you have a menu in English?"

"Certainly, sir." And he produced one from an apron pocket as though by magic.

"Very good, and thank you, sir."

"He must have gone to Waiter University," Brian said as the man walked away again. "But wait till you see Italy. Those guys are artists. That time I went to Florence, I thought the bastard was reading my mind. Probably has a doctorate in waitering."

"No inside parking at that building. Probably around back," Dominic said, coming back to business.

"Is the Audi TT any good, Enzo?"

"It's a German car. They make decent machines over here, man. The Audi isn't a Mercedes, but it ain't no Yugo, either. I don't know that I've ever seen one outside of *Motor Trend.* But I know what they look like, kinda curvy, slick, like it goes fast. Probably does, with the autobahns they have here. Driving in Germany can be like running the Indy 500, or so they say. I don't really see a German driving a slow car."

"Makes sense." Brian scanned the menu. The names of the dishes were in German, of course, but with English subtitles. It looked as though the commentary was for Brits rather than Americans. They still had NATO bases here, maybe to guard against the French rather than the Russians, Dominic thought with a chuckle. Though, historically, the Germans didn't need much help from that direction.

"What do you wish to have, *mein Herrn*?" the waiter

asked, reappearing as though transported down by Scottie himself.

"First, what is your name?" Dominic asked.

"Emil. *Ich heisse Emil.*"

"Thank you. I'll have the sauerbraten and potato salad."

Then it was Brian's turn. "And I'll have the bratwurst. Mind if I ask a question?"

"Of course," Emil responded.

"Is that a mosque down the street?" Brian asked, pointing.

"Yes, it is."

"Isn't that unusual?" Brian pushed the issue.

"We have many Turkish guest workers in Germany, and they are also Mohammedans. They will not eat the sauerbraten or drink the beer. They do not get on well with us Germans, but what can one do about it?" The waiter shrugged, with only a hint of distaste.

"Thank you, Emil," Brian said, and Emil hurried back inside.

"What does that mean?" Dominic wondered.

"They don't like 'em very much, but they don't know what to do about it, and they're a democracy, just like we are, so they have to be polite to 'em. The average Fritz in the street isn't all that keen on their 'guest workers,' but there's not much real trouble about it, just scuffles and like that. Mainly bar fights, so I'm told. So, I guess the Turks have learned to drink the beer."

"How'd you learn that?" Dominic was surprised.

"There's a German contingent in Afghanistan. We were neighbors—our camps, like—and I talked some with the officers there."

"Any good?"

"They're Germans, bro, and this bunch was professionals, not draftees. Yeah, they're pretty good," Aldo assured him. "It was a reconnaissance group. Their physical routine is tough as ours, they know mountains pretty good, and they are well drilled at the fundamentals. The noncoms got along like thieves, swapped hats and badges a lot. They also brought beer along with their TO and E, so they were kinda popular with my people. You know, this beer is pretty damned good."

"Like in England. Beer is a kind of religion in Europe, and everybody goes to church."

Then Emil appeared with lunch—*Mittagessen*—and that, they both learned, was also okay. But both kept watching the apartment house.

"This potato salad is dynamite, Aldo," Dominic observed between bites. "I never had anything like it. Lots of vinegar and sugar, kinda crispy on the palate."

"Good food isn't all Italian."

"When we get home, gotta try to find a German restaurant."

"Roger that. Lookie, lookie, Enzo."

It wasn't their subject, but it was his squeeze, Trudl Heinz. Just like the photo on their computers, walking out of the apartment house. Pretty enough to turn a man's head briefly, but not a movie star. Her hair had been blond once, but that had changed in her midteens, by the look of her. Nice legs, better-than-average figure. A pity she'd linked up with a terrorist. Maybe he'd latched onto her as part of his cover, and so much the better for him that it had side benefits. Unless they were living platonically, which didn't seem likely. Both Americans wondered how he treated her, but you couldn't tell something like that from watching her walk. She went up the other side of the street, but passed the mosque. So, she wasn't heading there at the moment.

"I'm thinking . . . if he goes to church, we can poke him coming out. Lots of anonymous people around, y'know?" Brian thought aloud.

"Not a bad concept. We'll see how faithful this guy is this afternoon, and what the crowd's like."

"Call that a definite maybe," Dominic replied. "First, let's finish up here and then get some clothes that'll fit us in better."

"Roger that," Brian said. He checked the time: 14:00. Eight in the morning at home. Only one hour of jet lag from London, easily written off.

JACK CAME in earlier than usual, his interest piqued by what he took to be an ongoing operation in Europe, and wondering what today's message traffic would show.

It turned out to be fairly routine, with some additional traffic on Sali's death. Sure enough, MI5 had reported his death to Langley as having been the apparent result of a heart attack, probably caused by the onset of fatal arrhythmia. That's what the official autopsy read, and his body had been released to a solicitors' firm representing the family. Arrangements were being made to fly him home to Saudi Arabia. His apartment had been looked at by the London version of a black-bag team, which had not, however, turned up anything of particular interest. That included his office computer, whose hard drive had been copied and the data carted off. It was being examined bit by bit by their electronic weenies, details to follow. That could take a lot of time, Jack knew. Stuff hidden on a computer was technically discoverable, but, theoretically, you could also take the pyramids of Giza apart stone by stone to see what was hidden under them. If Sali had been really clever about burying things into slots only he knew about, or in a code to which only he knew the key...well, it would be tough. Had he been that clever? Probably not, Jack thought, but you could only tell by looking, and that was why people always looked. It'd take at least a week, to be sure. A month, if the little bastard was good with keys and codes. But just finding hidden stuff would tell them that he'd been a real player and not just a stringer, and the varsity at GCHQ would be assigned to it. Though none of them would be able to discover what he'd taken away to death with him inside his head.

"Hey, Jack," Wills said, coming in.

"'Morning, Tony."

"Nice to be eager. What have they turned on our departed friend?"

"Nothing much. They're airmailing the box home later today, probably, and the pathologist called it a heart attack. So, our guys are clean."

"Islam pretty much requires that the body be disposed of quickly, and in an unmarked grave. So, once the body's gone, it's all-the-way gone. No exhumation to check for drugs and stuff."

"So, we did do it? What did we use?" Ryan asked.

"Jack, I do not know, and I do not want to know what, if anything, we had to do with his untimely death. Nor do I have any desire to find out. Nor should you, okay?"

"Tony, how the hell can you be in this business and *not* be curious?" Jack Jr. demanded.

"You learn what is not good to know, and you learn not to speculate on such things," Wills explained.

"Uh-huh," Jack reacted dubiously. *Sure, but* I'm *too young for that shit,* he didn't say. Tony was good at what he did, but he lived inside a box. So did Sali right now, Jack thought, and it wasn't a good place to be. *And besides, we* did *waste his ass.* Exactly how, he didn't know. He could have asked his mom about what drugs or chemicals there might be that could accomplish this mission, but, no, he couldn't do that. She'd sure as hell tell his father, and Big Jack would sure as hell want to know why his son had asked such a question—and might even guess the answer. So, no, that was out of the question. All the way out.

With the official government traffic on Sali's death, Jack started looking for NSA and related intercepts from other interested sources.

There was no further reference to the Emir in the daily traffic. That had just come and gone, and previous references were limited to the one Tony had pulled up. Similarly, his request for a more global search of signals records at Fort Meade and Langley had not been approved by the people upstairs, disappointingly but not surprisingly. Even The Campus had its limits. He understood the unwillingness of the people upstairs to risk having somebody wonder who'd made such a request, and, not finding an answer, to make a deeper query. But there were *thousands* of such requests back and forth every day, and one more couldn't raise that much of a ruckus, could it? He decided not to ask, however. There was no sense in being identified as a boat rocker this early into his new career. But he did instruct his computer to scan all new traffic for the word "Emir," and, if it came up, he could log it and then have a firmer case for his special inquiry the next time, if there was a next time. Still, a title like that—to his mind, it was indicative of the ID for a specific person, even if the only reference CIA had about it was "probably an in-house joke." The judgment had come from a senior Langley analyst, which carried a lot of weight in that community, and therefore in this one as well. The Campus was supposed to be the outfit that corrected CIA's mistakes and/or inabilities, but since they had fewer people on staff, they had to accept a lot of ideas that came from the supposedly disabled agency. It did not make all that much logical sense, but he hadn't been consulted when Hendley had set the place up, and therefore he had to assume that the senior staff knew their business. But as Mike Brennan had told him about police work, assumption was the mother of all screwups. It was also a widely known adage of the FBI. Everybody made mistakes, and the size of any mistake was directly proportional to the seniority of the man making it. But such people didn't like to be reminded of that universal truth. Well, nobody really did.

THEY BOUGHT the clothes off the rack. They were generally like what one would buy in America, but the differences, while individually subtle, added up to an entirely different look. They also got shoes to match the outfits, and, after changing at their hotel, they went back out on the street.

The passing grade came when Brian was stopped on the street by a German citizen asking directions to the *Hauptbahnhoff,* at which time Brian had to respond in English that he was new here, and the German woman backed away with an embarrassed smile and buttonholed somebody else.

"It means the main train station," Dominic explained.

"So, why can't she catch a cab?" Brian demanded.

"We live in an imperfect world, Aldo, but now you must look like a good Kraut. If anyone else asks you, just say *Ich bin ein Aüslander.* It means 'I'm a foreigner,' and that'll get you out of it. Then they'll probably ask the question in better English than you'd hear in New York."

"Hey, look!" Brian pointed to the Golden Arches of a McDonald's, a more welcome sight than the Stars and Stripes over the U.S. Consulate, though neither felt like eating there. The local food was simply too good. By nightfall they were back at the Hotel Bayerischer, enjoying just that.

"WELL, THEY'RE in Munich, and they spotted the subject's building and mosque, but not him yet," Granger reported to Hendley. "They eyeballed his lady friend, though."

"Things going smoothly, then?" the Senator asked.

"No complaints to this point. Our friend is not being looked at by the German police. Their counterintelligence service knows who he is, but they're not running any sort of case on him. They've had some problems with domestic Muslims, and some of them are being covered, but this guy hasn't popped up on the radar screen yet. And Langley hasn't pressed the issue. Their relations with Germany aren't all that good at the moment."

"Good news and bad news?"

"Right." Granger nodded. "They can't feed us much information, but we don't have to worry about fooling a tail. The Germans are funny. If you keep your nose clean and everything's *in Ordnung,* you're reasonably safe. If you step over the line, they can make your life pretty miserable. Historically, their cops are very good, but their spooks are not. The Soviets and the Stasi both had their spook shop thoroughly penetrated, and they're still living that down today."

"They do black ops?"

"Not really. Their culture is too legalistic for that. They raise honest people who play by the rules, and that's a crippling influence on special operations—those they do try occasionally crater badly. You know, I bet the average German citizen even pays his taxes on time, and in full."

"Their bankers know how to play the international game," Hendley objected.

"Yeah, well, maybe that's because international bankers don't really recognize the concept of having a country to be loyal to," Granger responded, sticking the needle in slightly.

"Lenin once said the only country a capitalist knows is the ground he stands on when he makes a deal. There are some like that," Hendley allowed. "Oh, did you see this?" He handed over the request from downstairs to root around for somebody called "the Emir."

The director of operations scanned the page and handed it back. "He doesn't make much of a case for it."

Hendley nodded. "I know. That's why I denied it. But . . . but, you know, it caused his instincts to twitch, and he had the brains to ask a question."

"And the boy's smart."

"Yes, he is. That's why I had Rick set him up with Wills as a roommate and training officer. Tony is bright, but he doesn't reach outside very much. So, Jack can learn the business and also learn about its limitations. We'll see how much he chafes from that. If this kid stays with us, he just might go places."

"You think he has his father's potential?" Granger wondered. Big Jack had been a king spook before going on to bigger things.

"I think he might grow into it, yes. Anyway, this 'Emir'

business strikes me as a fundamentally good idea on his part. We don't know much about how the opposition operates. It's a Darwinian process out there, Sam. The bad guys learn from their antecedents, and they get smarter—on our nickel. They're not going to offer themselves up to get a smart bomb in the ass. They're not going to try to be TV stars. Good for the ego, maybe, but fatal. A herd of gazelles doesn't knowingly head toward the lion pride."

"True," Granger agreed, thinking back to how his own ancestor had handled obstreperous Indians in the Ninth U.S. Cavalry Regiment. Some things didn't change much. "Gerry, the problem is, all we can do about their organizational model is to speculate. And speculation is not knowledge."

"So, tell me what you think," Hendley ordered.

"Minimum two layers between the head of it all: Is it one man or a committee? We do not and cannot know right now. And the shooters: We can get all those we want, but that's like cutting grass. You cut it, it grows, you cut it, it grows, ad infinitum. You want to kill a snake, best move is to take off the head. Okay, fine, we all know that. Trick is finding the head, because it's a *virtual* head. Whoever it is, or are, they're operating a lot like we are, Gerry. That's why we're doing a recon-by-fire, to see what we can shake loose. And we have all of our analytical troops looking for that, here, and at Langley, and Meade."

A tired sigh. "Yeah, Sam, I know. And maybe something will shake loose. But patience is a mother to live by. The opposition is probably basking in the sun right now, feeling good about stinging us, killing all those women and kids—"

"Nobody likes that, Gerry, but even God took seven days to make the world, remember?"

"You turning preacher on me?" Hendley asked, with narrowed eyes.

"Well, the eye-for-an-eye part works for me, bud, but it takes time to find the eye. We have to be patient."

"You know, when Big Jack and I talked about the need

for a place like this, I was actually dumb enough to think we could solve problems more quickly if we had the authority to do so."

"We'll be quicker than the government ever will, but we're not *The Man from U.N.C.L.E.* Hey, look, the operational end just got under way. We've made only one hit. Three more to go before we can expect to see any real response from the other side. Patience, Gerry."

"Yeah, sure." He didn't add that time zones didn't help much, either.

"YOU KNOW, there's one other thing."

"What's that, Jack?" Wills asked.

"It would be better if we knew what operations were going on. It would enable us to focus our data hunt a little more efficiently."

"It's called 'compartmentalization.'"

"No, it's called horseshit," Jack shot back. "If we're on the team, we can help. Things that might look like non sequiturs appear different if you know the context that appears out of nowhere. Tony, this whole building is supposed to be a compartment, right? Subdividing it like they do at Langley doesn't help get the job done, or am I missing something?"

"I see your point, but that's not how the system works."

"Okay, I knew you'd say that, but how the hell do we fix what's broke at CIA if all we do is just to clone their operation?" Jack demanded.

And there wasn't a ready answer for that which would satisfy the questioner, was there? Wills asked himself. There simply wasn't, and this kid was catching on way too fast. What the hell had he learned in the White House? For damned sure, he'd asked a lot of questions. And he'd listened to all the answers. And even thought about them.

"I hate to say this, Jack, but I'm only your training officer, not the Big Boss of this outfit."

"Yeah, I know. Sorry about that. I guess I got used to my

dad having the ability to make things happen—well, it looked that way to me, at least. Not to him, I know, not all the time. Maybe impatience is a family characteristic." Doubly so, since his mom was a surgeon, accustomed to fixing things on her own schedule, which was generally *right the hell now.* It was hard to be decisive sitting at a workstation, a lesson his dad had probably had to learn in his time, back when America had lived in the gunsights of a really serious enemy. These terrorists could sting, but they couldn't do serious structural harm to America, though it *had* been tried in Denver once. These guys were like swarming insects rather than vampire bats...

But mosquitoes could transmit yellow fever, couldn't they?

SOUTH OF Munich, in the port city of Piraeus, a container was lifted off its ship by a gantry crane and lowered to a waiting truck trailer. Once secured, the trailer went off, behind the Volvo truck driving out of the port, bypassing Athens, and heading north into the mountains of Greece. The manifest said it was going to Vienna, a lengthy nonstop drive over decent highways, delivering a cargo of coffee from Colombia. It didn't occur to the port security people to conduct a search, since all the bills of lading were in good order and passed the bar-code scans properly. Already men were assembling to deal with the part of the cargo not intended to be mixed with hot water and cream. It took a lot of men to break down a metric ton of cocaine into dose-sized packets, but they had a single-story warehouse, recently acquired, in which to accomplish the task, and then they would be driving individually all over Europe, taking comfort in the lack of internal borders the continent had adopted since the formation of the European Union. With this cargo, the word of a business partner was being kept, and a psychological profit was being recompensed by a monetary one. The process went on through the night, while Europeans slept the sleep of the just, even those who would soon be making use of the illegal part of the cargo as soon as they found a street dealer.

THEY SAW the subject at 9:30 the following morning. They were having a leisurely breakfast at another *Gasthaus* half a block from the one that employed their friend Emil, and Anas Ali Atef was walking purposely up the street, and came within twenty feet of the twins, who were breakfasting on strudel and coffee, along with twenty or so German citizens. Atef didn't notice he was being watched; his eyes looked forward and did not discreetly scan the area as a trained spook would have done. Evidently, he felt safe here. And that was good.

"There's our boy," Brian said, spotting him first. As with Sali, there was no neon sign over his head to mark him, but he matched the photo perfectly, and he had come out of the right apartment building. His mustache made an error in identification unlikely. Reasonably well dressed. Except for his skin and mustache, he might have passed for a German. At the end of the block, he boarded a streetcar, destination unknown, but heading east.

"Speculate?" Dominic asked his brother.

"Off to have breakfast with a pal, or to plot the downfall of the Infidel West—we really can't say, man."

"Yeah, it'd be nice to have real coverage on him, but we're not conducting an investigation, are we? This mutt recruited at least one shooter. He's earned his way onto our shit list, Aldo."

"Roger that, bro," Brian agreed. His conversion was complete. Anas Ali Atef was just a face to him now, and an ass to be stuck with his magic pen. Beyond that, he was someone for God to talk to in due course, a jurisdiction that didn't directly concern either of them at the moment.

"If this was a Bureau op, we'd have a team in the apartment right now, at least to toss his computer."

Brian conceded the point. "Now what?"

"We see if he goes to church, and, if he does, we see how easy it might be to pop him on the way in or out."

"Does it strike you that this is going a little fast?" Brian wondered aloud.

"I suppose we could sit in the hotel room and jerk off, but that's hard on the wrist, y'know?"

"Yeah, I guess so."

Finishing breakfast, they left cash on the table but not a large tip. That would too surely mark them as Americans.

THE STREETCAR wasn't as comfortable as his car, but it was ultimately more convenient because of the necessity of finding a parking place. European cities had not been designed with automobiles in mind. Neither had Cairo, of course, and the traffic jams there could be incredible—even worse than they were here—but at least in Germany they had reliable mass transportation. The trains were glorious. The quality of the lines impressed the man who'd had engineering training a few—was it really just a few? he asked himself; it seemed like a complete lifetime—years before. The Germans were a curious people. Standoffish and formal, and oh so superior, they thought, to all the other races. They looked down on Arabs—and, indeed, on most other Europeans as well—and opened their doors to foreigners only because their internal laws—imposed upon them sixty years earlier by Americans after World War II—said that they must. But because they were compelled to do so, they did, mostly without open complaint, because these mad people obeyed the law as though it had been delivered to them by God's own hand. They were the most docile people he'd ever encountered, but underneath that docility was the capacity for violence—*organized* violence—such as the world hardly knew. Within living memory, they'd risen up to slaughter the Jews. They'd even converted their death camps into museums, but museums in which the pieces and machines undoubtedly still worked, as though standing ready. What a pity they could not summon the political will to make it so.

The Jews had humiliated his country four separate times, in the process killing his eldest brother, Ibrahim, in the Sinai while he'd been driving a Soviet T-62 tank. He didn't remember Ibrahim. He'd been far too young then, and only had photographs to give him an idea of what he'd looked like, though his mother still wept for his memory. He'd died trying to finish the job these Germans had started, only to fail, killed by a cannon shot from an American M60A1 main battle tank at the battle of the Chinese farm. It was the Americans who protected the Jews. America was ruled by its Jews. That was why they supplied his enemies with weapons, fed them with intelligence information, and loved killing Arabs.

But the Germans' failure at their task hadn't tamed their arrogance. Just redirected it. He could see it on the streetcar, the brief sideways looks, the way old women scuttled a few steps away from where he stood. Someone would probably wipe down the overhead bar with disinfectant after he got off, Anas grumbled to himself. By the Prophet, these were unpleasant people.

The ride took another seven minutes exactly, and it was time to get off, at Dom Strasse. From there, it was a one-block walk. Along the way, he saw more of the glances, the hostility in the eyes, or, even worse, the eyes that took note of his presence and just passed on, as though having seen a stray dog. It would have been satisfying to take some action here in Germany—right here in Munich!—but his orders were specific.

His destination was a coffee shop. Fa'ad Rahman Yasin was already there, dressed casually, like a working man. There were many like him in this café.

"*Salaam aleikum,*" Atef said in greeting. Peace be unto you.

"*Aleikum salaam,*" Fa'ad said in return. "The pastry here is excellent."

"Yes," Atef agreed, speaking softly in Arabic. "So, what is new, my friend?"

"Our people are pleased with last week. We have shaken the Americans badly," Fa'ad said.

"Not enough for them to disown the Israelis. They love the Jews more than their own children. Mark my words on this. And they will lash out at us."

"How?" Fa'ad demanded. "Lash out, yes, at whomever their spy agencies know about, but that will only inflame the faithful and drive more to our cause. No, our organization they do not know about. They do not even know our name." This was because their organization did not really have a name. "Organization" was merely a descriptive word for their association of the Faithful.

"I hope you are correct. So, do I have more orders?"

"You have done well—three of the men you recruited chose martyrdom in America."

"Three?" Atef was agreeably surprised. "They died well, I trust?"

"They died in Allah's Holy Name. That should be good enough. So, do you have any more recruits ready for us?"

Atef sipped his coffee. "Not quite, but I have two leaning in our direction. This is not easy, as you know. Even the most faithful wish to enjoy the fruits of a good life." As he was doing himself, of course.

"You have done well for us, Anas. Better to be sure than to be overly demanding of them. Take your time. We can be patient."

"How patient?" Atef wanted to know.

"We have additional plans for America, to sting them worse. This time we killed hundreds. The next time, we shall kill thousands," Fa'ad promised, with a sparkle in his eye.

"How, exactly?" Atef asked immediately. He could have been—*should* have been—a plans officer. His engineering education made him ideal for such things. Didn't they know that? There were people in the organization who thought with their balls instead of their brains.

"That I am not at liberty to say, my friend." Because he didn't know, Fa'ad Rahman Yasin did not say. He wasn't sufficiently trusted by those higher in the organization, which would have outraged him had he known it.

The son of a whore probably doesn't know himself, Atef thought at the same time.

"We approach the hour of prayer, my friend," Anas Ali Atef said, checking his watch. "Come with me. My mosque is only ten minutes away." It would soon be time for the Salat. It was a test for his colleague, to make sure that he was truly faithful.

"As you say." Both rose and walked to the streetcar, which fifteen minutes later stopped a block from the mosque.

"HEADS UP, Aldo," Dominic said. They'd been checking out the neighborhood, really just to get a feel for the area, but there was their friend, walking down the street with what had to be a friend of his own.

"Who's wog number two, I wonder?" Brian said.

"Nobody we know, and we can't freelance. You packin'?" Dominic asked.

"Bet your bippy, bro. You?"

"Hang a big roger on that," Dominic answered. Their target was about thirty yards off, walking right at them, probably heading to the mosque, which was half a block behind them. "What do you think?"

"Wave off, better to bag him on the way out."

"Okay." And both turned right to look into the window of a hat shop. They heard—they damned near *felt*—him pass by. "How long you suppose it'll take?"

"Damned if I know, man, I haven't been to church myself in a couple of months."

"Super," Brian growled. "My own brother's an apostate."

Dominic stifled a laugh. "You always were the altar boy in the family."

* * *

SURE ENOUGH. Atef and his friend walked in. It was time for daily prayers, the Salat, the second of Islam's Five Pillars. They would bend and kneel, facing Mecca, whispering favored phrases from the Holy Koran, affirming their faith as they did so. On entering the building, they removed their shoes, and, to Yasin's surprise, this mosque suffered from a German influence. There were individualized cubbyholes in the wall of the atrium for their shoes, all of them properly numbered, to prevent confusion ... or theft. That was a rare offense indeed in any Muslim country, because the Islamic penalty for thievery was very harsh, and to do so in Allah's Own House would have been a deliberate offense to God Himself. They then entered the mosque proper and made their obeisance to Allah.

It didn't take long, and with it came a kind of refreshment for Atef's soul, as he reaffirmed his religious beliefs. Then it was over. He and his friend made their way back to the atrium, collected their shoes, and walked outside.

They weren't the first out the large doors, and the others had served to alert the two Americans. It was really a question of which way they'd go. Dominic was watching the street, looking for a police or intelligence officer, but didn't see any. He was betting that their subject would head toward his apartment. Brian took the other direction. It looked as though forty or so people had gone in for prayers. Coming out, they scattered to the four winds, singly or in small groups. Two got into the fronts of taxicabs—presumably their own—and drove off to catch fares. That did not include any of their coreligionists, who were probably working-class schlubs who walked or took public transportation. It hardly made them seem villainous to the twins, both of whom closed in, but neither too fast nor two obviously. Then the subject and his pal came out.

They turned left, directly toward Dominic, thirty yards away.

From his perspective, Brian saw it all. Dominic removed the gold pen from the inside pocket of his not-quite-a-suit jacket, furtively twisting the tip to arm it, then holding it in his right hand like an ice pick. He was heading on a close reciprocal course to the subject . . .

It was, perversely, a thing of beauty to watch. Just six feet away, Dominic appeared to trip over something, and fell right into the Atef guy. Brian didn't even see the stick. Atef went down with his brother, and that would have covered the discomfort of the stab. Atef's pal helped both of them up. Dominic made his apology and headed on his way, with Brian following the target. He hadn't seen Sali check out, and so this was interesting in a grim sort of way. The subject walked about fifty feet, then stopped in his tracks. He must have said something, because his friend turned as though to ask a question, just in time to see Atef fall down. One arm came up to protect his face from the fall, but then the entire body went limp.

The second man was clearly dumbfounded by what he saw. He bent down to see what was wrong, first in puzzlement, then in concern, and then in panic, rolling the body over and speaking loudly to his fallen friend. Brian passed them about then. Atef's face was as composed and unmoving as a doll's. The guy's brain was active, but he couldn't even open his eyes. Brian stood there for a minute, then wandered off, without looking back, but he gestured to a German passerby to provide assistance, which the German did, reaching into his coat and pulling out a cell phone. He'd probably call for an ambulance. Brian walked to the next intersection and turned to observe, checking his watch. The ambulance was there in six and a half minutes. The Germans really were well organized. The responding fireman/paramedic checked the pulse, looked up in surprise, and then with alarm. His coworker on command pulled a box from inside the vehicle, and, as Brian watched, Atef was intubated and bagged. The two firemen were well trained, clearly going through a process they'd practiced in the station and had probably used on the street many times. In their urgency, they did not move Atef into the ambulance, but instead treated him as best they could on the spot.

Ten minutes since he'd gone down, Brian saw by his watch. Atef was already brain-dead, and that was the name of that tune. The Marine officer turned left and walked to the next corner, where he caught a taxi, fumbling through the name of the hotel, but the driver figured it out. Dominic was in the lobby when he got there. Together they headed for the bar.

The one good thing about wasting a guy right out of church was that they could be reasonably certain that he wasn't going to hell. At least, that was one less thing to trouble their consciences. The beer helped, too.

||||||||||||||||||||||||||||||||||||||||||||||||||||||||||||||

CHAPTER 20

THE SOUND OF
HUNTING

MUNICH AT 14:26 in the afternoon translated into 8:26
A.M. Eastern Standard Time at The Campus. Sam Granger
was in his office early, wondering if he'd see an e-mail..
The twins were working fast. Not recklessly so, but they
were certainly making use of the technology with which
they'd been provided, and they were not wasting The Campus's time or money along the way. He'd already set up
Subject No. 3, of course, encrypted and ready to go out on
the 'Net. Unlike with Sali in London, he could not expect
any "official" notice about the death from the German intelligence service, the *Bundesnachrichtendienst,* which had
taken scant notice of Anas Ali Atef. It would be, if anything, a matter for the city police in Munich, but more
likely a case for the local coroner's office—just one more
fatal heart attack for a country in which too many citizens
smoked and ate fatty foods.

The e-mail arrived at 8:43 from Dominic's computer,
reporting the successful hit in considerable detail, almost
like an official investigative report to the FBI. The fact that

Atef had had a friend close by was probably a bonus. That an enemy had witnessed the killing probably meant that no suspicion would be attached to the subject's demise. The Campus would do its best to get the official report on Atef's departure, however, just to make sure, though that would have its elements of difficulty.

DOWNSTAIRS, RYAN and Wills did not know anything about it, of course. Jack was going through his routine tasks of scanning message traffic within the American intelligence services—which took over an hour—and after that, a scan of Internet traffic to and from known or suspected terrorist addresses. The overwhelming majority of it was so routine it was like e-mails between a husband and wife over what to pick up at the Safeway on the way home from work. Some of those e-mails could easily be coded messages of significant import, but there was no telling that without a program or crib sheet. At least one terrorist had used "hot weather" to mean heavy security at a location of interest to his colleagues, but the message had been sent in July, when the weather was, indeed, warmer than was comfortable. And *that* message had been copied down by the FBI, and the Bureau hadn't taken particular notice of it at first. But one new message positively leaped off the screen at him this morning.

"Hey, Tony, you want to look at this one, buddy."

The addressee was their old friend 56MoHa@eurocom.net, and the content reconfirmed his identity as a nexus for bad-guy message traffic:

ATEF IS DEAD. HE DIED RIGHT BEFORE MY EYES HERE IN MUNICH. AN AMBULANCE WAS SUMMONED AND THEY TREATED HIM ON THE SIDEWALK BUT HE DIED IN THE HOSPITAL OF A HEART ATTACK. REQUIRE INSTRUCTIONS. FA'AD. And his address was Honeybear@ostercom.net, which was new to Jack's computer index.

"Honeybear?" Wills observed with a chuckle. "This guy must surf for women on the 'Net."

"So, he does cybersex, fine. Tony, if we just whacked a guy named Atef over in Germany, here's confirmation of the event, plus a new target for us to track." Ryan turned back to his workstation and used his mouse to check sources. "Here, NSA picked up on it, too. Maybe they think he's a possible player."

"You sure like making leaps of imagination," Wills observed tersely.

"My ass!" Jack was actually angry for once. He was beginning to understand why his father had often been so pissed off at intelligence information that arrived in the Oval Office. "God damn it, Tony, how much clearer do things have to be?"

Wills took a deep breath and spoke as calmly as usual. "Settle down, Jack. This is single-source, a single report on something that might or might not have taken place. You don't throw your hat over the barn about something until it's confirmed by a known source. This Honeybear identity could be a lot of things, few of which we can certify as a good guy or a bad guy."

For his part, Jack Jr. wondered if he was being tested—again!—by his training officer. "Okay, let's walk through it. MoHa Fifty-six is a source that we're highly confident is a player, probably an operations officer for the bad guys. We've been sweeping the 'Net for him since I've been here, okay? So, we sweep the ether and this letter turns up in his mailbox at the same time we believe we—us—have a kill team in the field. Unless you're going to tell me that Uda bin Sali really did have a myocardial infarction while he was daydreaming about his favorite whore in downtown London. And that the Brit Security Service found the event highly interesting only because it's not every day that a suspected terrorist banker drops dead on the street. Have I missed anything?"

Wills smiled. "Not a bad presentation. A little thin on the evidence, but your proposition was well organized. So, you think I should walk it upstairs?"

"No, Tony, I think you should run it upstairs," Ryan said, easing back on the obvious anger. *Take a deep breath and count to ten.*

"Then I guess I'll do it."

FIVE MINUTES later, Wills walked into Rick Bell's office. He handed over two sheets of paper.

"Rick, do we have a team at work in Germany?" Wills asked. The response was not the least bit surprising.

"Why do you ask?" Bell had a poker face that would have impressed a marble statue.

"Read," Wills suggested.

"Damn," the chief of analysis reacted. "Who pulled this fish out of the electronic ocean?"

"Take a guess," Tony suggested.

"Not bad, for the kid." Bell looked very closely at his guest. "How much does he suspect?"

"At Langley, he'd sure as hell be getting people nervous."

"Like you are?"

"You might say that," Wills replied. "He makes good leaps of imagination, Rick."

Bell made a face this time. "Well, it's not exactly the Olympic long-jump competition, is it?"

"Rick, Jack puts two and two together about as fast as a computer tells the difference between one and zero. He's right, isn't he?"

Bell took a second or two before replying. "What do you think?"

"I think they got that Sali character for sure, and this is probably mission number two. How are they doing it?"

"You really do not want to know. It's not as clean as it looks," Bell answered. "This Atef guy was a recruiter. He sent at least one guy to Des Moines."

"That's a good enough reason," Wills judged.

"Sam feels the same way. I'll turn this over to him. Follow-up?"

"This MoHa guy needs a closer look. Maybe we can track him down," Wills said.

"Any idea where he is?"

"Italy, looks like, but a lot of people live on the boot. Lots of big cities with lots of ratholes. But Italy is a good place for him. Centrally located. Air service everywhere. And the terrorists have let Italy alone lately, and so nobody's hunting down the dog that isn't barking."

"Same in Germany, France, and the rest of Central Europe?"

Wills nodded. "Looks that way. They're next, but I don't think they fully appreciate it. Heads in the sand–like, Rick."

"True," Bell agreed. "So, what do we do with your student?"

"Ryan? Good question. Sure as hell, he's a quick learner. He's particularly good at connecting things," Wills thought out loud. "He makes big leaps of imagination, sometimes too far, but, still, it's not a bad quality for an analyst to have."

"Grade to this point?"

"B-plus, maybe a low A, and that's only because he's new. He's not as good as I am, but I've been in the business since before he was born. He's a comer, Rick. He'll go far."

"That good?" Bell asked. Tony Wills was known as a careful conservative analyst, and one of the best Langley had ever turned out, despite the green eyeshade and the garters on the sleeves.

Wills nodded. "That good." He was also scrupulously honest. It was his natural character, but he could also afford to be. The Campus paid far better than any government agency. His kids were all grown—the last one was in his final year at the University of Maryland in physics, and, after that, he and Betty could think about the next big step in life, though Wills liked it here and had no immediate plans to leave. "But don't tell him I said so."

"Big head?"

"No, that wouldn't be fair. But I don't want him to start thinking he knows it all yet."

"Nobody with half a brain thinks that way," Bell said.

"Yeah." Wills stood. "But why take the chance?"

Wills headed out, but Bell still didn't know what to do with the Ryan kid. Well, something to talk with the Senator about.

"**NEXT STOP**, Vienna," Dominic informed his brother. "We got another subject."

"You wonder how steady this job will be?" Brian wondered aloud.

His brother laughed. "Man, there's enough mutts in America to keep us busy for the rest of our lives."

"Yeah, save money, fire all the judges and juries."

"My name ain't Dirty Harry Callahan, you jarhead."

"And I'm not Chesty Puller, either. How do we get there? Fly, train—maybe drive?"

"Driving might be fun," Dominic said. "I wonder if we can rent a Porsche . . . ?"

"Oh, great," Brian grunted. "Okay, log off so I can download the file, will ya?"

"Sure. I'll see what the concierge can set up for us." And he headed out of the room.

"**THIS IS** the only confirmation we have?" Hendley asked.

"Correct." Granger nodded. "But it tallies exactly with what our guys on the ground told us."

"They're going too fast. What if the other side thinks, 'Two heart attacks in less than a week' . . . ? Then what?"

"Gerry, the nature of this mission is recon-by-fire, remember? We halfway want the other side to get a little nervous, but soon their arrogance will set in and they'll write it off as random chance. If this were TV or the movies, they'd think CIA was playing hardball, but it isn't the movies, and they know that CIA doesn't play that kind of game. The Mossad, maybe, but they're already wary of the Israelis. Hey"—a lightbulb went off in Granger's brain— "what if they're the guys who offed the Mossad officer in Rome?"

"I don't pay you to speculate, Sam."

"It's a possibility," Granger persisted.

"It's also possible that the Mafia hit the poor bastard because they mistook him for a fellow mafioso who owed money to the mob. But I wouldn't bet the ranch on it."

"Yes, sir." Granger walked back to his office.

MOHAMMED HASSAN AL-DIN was in Rome at the moment, at the Hotel Excelsior, drinking his coffee and working on his computer. It was bad news about Atef. He was—he'd been—a good recruiter, with just the right mix of intelligence, plausibility, and commitment to persuade others to join the cause. He'd wanted to enter the field himself, to take lives and be a Holy Martyr, but though he might have been good at it, a man who could recruit was more valuable than a man willing to throw away his own life. It was simple arithmetic, something a graduate engineer like Atef should have understood. What was it with him? A brother, wasn't it, killed by the Israelis back in 1973? A long time to hold a grudge, even for men in his organization, but not without precedent. Atef was with his brother now, though, in Paradise. That was good fortune for him, but bad fortune for the organization. So it was written, Mohammed comforted himself, and so it would be, and so the struggle would go on until the last of their enemies were dead.

He had a pair of cloned phones on his bed, phones he could use without fear of interception. Should he call the Emir about this? It was worth thinking about. Anas Ali Atef was the second heart attack in less than a week, and in both cases they'd been young men, and that was odd, statistically very unusual. Fa'ad had been standing right next to Anas Ali at the time, though, and so he hadn't been shot or poisoned by an Israeli intelligence officer—a Jew would probably have killed *both* of them, Mohammed thought—and so with an eyewitness right there, there seemed little cause to suspect foul play. For the other, well, Uda had liked the life of a whoremonger, and he would hardly have been the first man to die of that weakness of the flesh. So, it just seemed like an unlikely coincidence and thus unworthy of an urgent call to the Emir himself. He made a note of the dual incidents on his computer, however, encrypted the file, and shut down. He felt like a walk. It was a pleasant day in Rome. Hot by most European standards, but the very breath of home for him. Just up the street was a pleasant sidewalk restaurant whose Italian food was only average, but the average here was better than in many fine restaurants across the world. You'd think that all Italian women would be obese, but, no, they suffered from the Western female disease of thinness, like West African children, some of them. Like young boys instead of mature, experienced women. So sad. But instead of eating, he crossed the Via Veneto to get a thousand Euros from the cash machine. The Euro had made European travel so much more convenient, praise Allah. It was not yet the equal of the American dollar in terms of stability, but, with luck, it might soon become so, which would ease his travel convenience even more.

Rome was a difficult city not to love. Conveniently located, international in character, awash with foreigners, and full of hospitable people who bowed and scraped for cash money like the peasants they all were. A good city for women, with shopping such as Riyadh could scarcely offer. His English mother had liked Rome, and the reasons were obvious. Good food and wine and a fine historical atmosphere that antedated even the Prophet himself, blessing and peace be upon him. Many had died here at the hands of the Caesars, butchered for public enjoyment in the Flavian Amphitheater, or killed because they had displeased the emperor in one way or another. The streets had probably been very peaceful here during the empire period. What better way to ensure it than to enforce the laws ruthlessly? Even the weak could recognize the price for bad behavior. So it was in his homeland, and so, he hoped, it would remain after the Royal Family had been done away with—either killed or chased abroad, perhaps to the safety of England or Switzerland, where people with money and noble status were treated well enough to live out their lives in indolent comfort. Either alternative would suit Mohammed and his colleagues. Just so that they would no longer rule his country, filled with corruption, kowtowing to the infidels and selling them oil for money, ruling the people as though they were the sons of Mohammed himself. That would come to an end. His distaste for America quailed before his hatred for the rulers of his own country. But America was his primary target because of its power, whether held to its own use or parceled out for others to use in America's own imperial interests. America threatened everything he held dear. America was an infidel country, patron and protector of the Jews. America had invaded his own country and stationed troops and weapons there, undoubtedly with the ultimate objective of subordinating all of Islam, and thus ruling a *billion* of the Faithful for its own narrow and parochial interests. Stinging America had become his obsession. Even the Israelis were not as attractive as targets. Vicious though they might be, the Jews were merely America's cat's-paws, vassals who did America's bidding in return for money and weapons, without even knowing how cynically they were being used. The Iranian Shiites had been correct. America was the Great Satan, Iblis himself, so great in power that it was hard to strike decisively at it, but still vulnerable in its evil before the righteous forces of Allah and the Faithful.

THE CONCIERGE at the Hotel Bayerischer had outdone himself, Dominic thought, securing a Porsche 911 whose forward-mounted trunk barely held their bags, and that only with a little squeezing. But it was enough, and better even than a rented small-engine Mercedes. The 911 had balls. Brian would get to fumble with the maps as they went southeast through the Alps to Vienna. That they were going south to kill someone was beside the point for the moment. They were serving their country, which was about as big as loyalty got.

"Do I need a crash helmet?" Brian asked, getting in, which in the case of this car almost meant sitting on the pavement.

"Not with me driving, Aldo. Come on, bro. It's time to rock and roll."

The car was a horrible shade of blue, but the tank was filled, and the six-cylinder engine was properly tuned. The Germans did like things *in Ordnung*. Brian navigated them out of Munich and onto the autobahn southeast to Vienna, and from there Enzo decided to see how fast this Porsche could really go.

"DO YOU think maybe they need some backup?" Hendley asked Granger, whom he'd just called into his office.

"What do you mean?" Sam responded. "They" had to be the Caruso brothers, of course.

"I mean they do not have much in the way of intelligence support," the former Senator pointed out.

"Well, we've never really thought about that, have we?"

"Exactly." Hendley leaned back in his chair. "In a sense, they're operating naked. Neither one has much in the way of intelligence experience. What if they hit the wrong guy? Okay, they probably won't get bagged doing it, but it won't help their morale, either. I remember a Mafia guy, in the Atlanta Federal Pen, I think. He killed some poor bastard he thought was trying to kill him, but it was the wrong guy, and he came unglued as a result. Sang like a canary. That's how we got our first big break on the Mafia and how it was organized, remember?"

"Oh, yeah, it was a Mafia soldier named Joe Valachi, yeah, but he was a criminal, remember?"

"And Brian and Dominic are good guys. So, guilt could hit them worse. Maybe some intel backup is a good idea."

Granger was surprised at the suggestion. "I can see the need for better intelligence evaluation, and this 'virtual office' stuff has its limitations, I admit. They can't ask questions, like, but if they have one, they can still e-mail us for advice—"

"Which they haven't done," Hendley pointed out.

"Gerry, they're only two steps into the mission. It's not time to panic yet, y'know? These are two very bright and very capable young officers. That's why we picked them. They know how to think on their own, and that's precisely what we want in our operations people."

"We're not just making assumptions, we're *launching* assumptions into the future. You think that's a good idea?" Hendley had learned how to pursue ideas on Capitol Hill, and he was deadly effective at it.

"Assumptions are always a bad thing. I know that, Gerry. But so are complications. How do we know we're sending the right guy? What if it just *adds* a level of uncertainty? Do we want to do that?" Hendley, thought Granger, was suffering from the deadliest congressional disease. It was too easy to oversight something to death.

"What I'm saying is that it's a good idea to have somebody out there who thinks a little different, who takes a different kind of approach to the data that goes out there. The Caruso boys are pretty good. I know that. But they are inexperienced. The important thing is to have a different brain out there to take a different view of the facts and the situation."

Granger felt himself being backed into a corner. "Okay, look, I can see the logic of that, but it's a level of complication that we don't need."

"Okay, so look at it this way—what if they see something for which they are not prepared? In that case, they need a second—whatever you call it—opinion of the data at hand. That will make them less likely to make a mistake in the field. The one thing that bothers me is that they make a mistake, and it's a fatal mistake for some poor schlub, and that the error affects the way they carry out their missions in the future. Guilt, remorse, and maybe then they start talking about it, okay? Can we completely discount that?"

"No, maybe not entirely, but it also means that we just add an additional element to the equation that can say no when a yes is the right way to go. Saying no is something anybody can do. It isn't necessarily right. You can take caution too far."

"I don't think so."

"Fine. So, who do you want to send?" Granger asked.

"Let's think about it. Ought to be—*has* to be somebody they know and trust..." His voice trailed off.

Hendley had made his operations chief nervous. He had an idea fixed in his head, and Hendley knew all too well that he was the head of The Campus, and that within this building his word was law, and there was nobody to appeal it to. So, if Granger was to select a name for this notional job, it had to be somebody who would not screw everything up.

THE AUTOBAHN was superbly, even brilliantly, engineered. Dominic found himself wondering who'd set it up. Then he thought that the road looked as though it had been there for a long time. And it linked Germany and Austria... maybe Hitler himself had ordered this road built? Wasn't that a hoot? In any case, there was no speed limit here, and the Porsche's six-cylinder engine was purring like a stalking tiger on the scent of some warm meat. And the German drivers were amazingly polite. All you had to do was flash your lights, and they hustled out of your way as though having received a divine edict. Definitely unlike America, where some little old lady in her overage Pinto was in the far-left lane because she was left-handed and *liked* holding up the maniacs in their Corvettes. The Bonneville Salt Flats could scarcely have been more fun.

For his part, Brian was doing his best not to cringe. He closed his eyes occasionally, thinking back to nap-of-the-earth flying in the Recon Marines through mountain passes in the Sierra Nevada, often enough in CH-46 helicopters older than he was. They hadn't killed him. This probably wouldn't either, and, as a Marine officer, he wasn't allowed to show fear or weakness. And it *was* exciting. Rather like riding in a roller coaster without the safety bar across the seat. But he saw that Enzo was having the time of his life, and he consoled himself with the fact that his seat belt *was* attached, and that this little German car was probably engineered by the same design crew that had done the Tiger tank. Getting through the mountains was the scariest part, and when they entered farm country, the land got flatter and the road straighter, thanks be to God.

"The hills are alive with the sound of myoosikkkk," Dominic sang, horribly.

"If you sing like that in church, God'll strike your ass dead," Brian warned, pulling out the city maps for the approach to Wien, as Vienna was known to its citizens.

And the city streets were a rat warren. The capital of Austria—Osterreich—predated the Roman legions, with no street straight for a longer distance than would be needed by a legion to parade past its *tribunus militaris* on the emperor's birthday. The map showed inner and outer ring roads, which probably marked the former site of medieval walls—the Turks had come here more than once hoping to add Austria to their empire, but that trinket of military history had not been part of the official Marine Corps reading list. A largely Catholic country, because the ruling House of Hapsburg had been so, it had not kept the Austrians from exterminating its prominent and prosperous Jewish minority after Hitler had subsumed Osterreich into the Greater German Reich. That had been after the *Anschluss* plebiscite of 1938. Hitler had been born here, not in Germany as widely believed, and the Austrians had repaid that loyalty with some of their own, becoming more Nazified than Hitler himself, or so objective history reported, not necessarily the Austrians' now. It was the one country in the world where *The Sound of Music* had fallen flat at the box office, maybe because the movie had been uncomplimentary toward the Nazi party.

For all that, Vienna looked like what it was, a former imperial city with wide, tree-lined boulevards and classical architecture, and remarkably well-turned-out citizens. Brian navigated them to the Hotel Imperial on Kartner Ring, a building that looked to be an adjunct to the well-known Schonbrunn Palace.

"You have to admit they put us up in nice places, Aldo," Dominic observed.

It was even more impressive inside, with gilt plaster and lacquered woodwork, every segment of which appeared to have been installed by master craftsmen imported from Renaissance Florence. The lobby was not spacious, but the reception desk was impossible to miss, manned as it was by people wearing clothing that marked them as hotel staff as surely as a Marine in dress blues.

"Good day," the concierge said in greeting. "Your name is Caruso?"

"Correct," Dominic said, surprised at the concierge's ESP. "You should have a reservation for my brother and myself?"

"Yes, sir," the concierge replied with enthusiastic subordination. His English might have been learned at Harvard. "Two connecting rooms overlooking the street."

"Excellent." Dominic fished out his American Express black card and handed it across.

"Thank you."

"Any messages for us?" Dominic asked.

"No, sir," the concierge assured him.

"Can you have the valet attend to our car? It's rented. We're not sure if we'll be keeping it or not."

"Of course, sir."

"Thank you. Can we see our rooms?"

"Yes. You are on the first floor—excuse me, the second floor, as you say in America. Franz," he called.

The bellman's English was just as good. "This way, if you please, gentlemen." No elevator, but rather a walk up a flight of red-carpeted steps directly toward a full-length portrait of somebody who looked very important indeed, in his white military uniform and beautifully combed-out chin whiskers.

"Who might that be?" Dominic asked the bellman.

"The Emperor Franz Josef, sir. He visited the hotel upon its opening in the nineteenth century."

"Ah." It explained the attitude of the staff here, but you couldn't knock the style of this place. Not by a long shot.

In another five minutes, they were settled into their accommodations. Brian came wandering into his brother's room. "God damn, the Residence Level at the White House isn't this good."

"Think so?" Dominic asked.

"Dude, I *know* so. Been there, done that. Uncle Jack had me up after I got my commission—no, actually it was after I came through the Basic School. Shit, this place is something. I wonder what it costs?"

"What the hell, it's on my card, and our friend is nearby at the Bristol. Kinda interesting to hunt rich bastards, isn't it?" That brought them back to business. Dominic pulled his laptop out of his bag. The Imperial was used to guests with computers, and the setup for it was very efficient indeed. For the moment, he opened the most recent file. He'd only scanned it before. Now he took his time with every single word.

*   *   *

GRANGER WAS thinking it through. Gerry wanted somebody to baby-sit the twins, and it seemed as though his mind was fixed on it. There were a lot of good people in the intelligence department under Rick Bell, but as former intelligence officers at CIA and elsewhere, they were all too old to be proper companions for the twins, young as the Caruso kids were. It wouldn't look right to have people in their late twenties chumming around Europe with somebody in his middle fifties. So, better somebody younger. There weren't many of those, but there was one...

He picked up his phone.

FA'AD WAS only two blocks away on the third floor of the Bristol Hotel, a famous and very upper-crust accommodation known particularly for its superior dining room and its nearness to the State Opera, which sat just across the street, consecrated to the memory of Wolfgang Amadeus Mozart, who had been the court musician for the House of Hapsburg before dying an early death, right here in Vienna. But Fa'ad wasn't the least bit interested in such history. Current events were his obsession. Watching Anas Ali Atef die right before his eyes had shaken him badly. That had not been the death of infidels, something you could watch on TV and smile quietly about. He'd been standing there, watching the life drain invisibly from his friend's body, watching the German paramedics fight vainly for his life—evidently doing their very best even for a person they must have despised. That was a surprise. And, yes, they were Germans just doing their job, but they'd *done* that job with obstinate determination, then they'd raced his comrade to the nearest hospital, where the German doctors had probably done the same, only to fail. A doctor had come to him in the waiting room and sadly told him the news, saying unnecessarily that they'd done everything that could have been done, and that it had looked like a massive heart attack, and that further laboratory work would be done to make certain that this indeed had been the cause of death, and finally asking for information on his family, if any, and who would see about the body after they were done picking it apart. Strange thing about the Germans, how precise they always were about everything. Fa'ad had made what arrangements he could, and then boarded a train for Vienna, sitting alone in a first-class seat and trying to come to terms with the dreadful event.

He was making his report to the organization. Mohammed Hassan al-Din was his gateway for that. He was probably in Rome at the moment, though Fa'ad Rahman Yasin was not quite sure. He didn't have to be sure. The Internet was a good enough address, formless as it was. It was just so very sad for a young and vigorous and valuable comrade to fall down dead on the street. If it served any purpose at all, only Allah Himself knew what it might be—but Allah had His Plan for everything, and it was not always something for men to know. Fa'ad took a minibottle of cognac from his minibar and drank it right out of the glass container instead of pouring it into one of the snifters on top of the cabinet. Sinful or not, it helped steady his nerves, and anyway he never did it in public. Damn such bad luck! He took another look at the minibar. Two more cognacs remained, and after that, several miniatures of Scotch whisky, the favorite drink of Saudi Arabia, Shar'ia or not.

"GOT YOUR passport?" Granger asked as soon as he'd sat down.

"Well, sure. Why?" Ryan asked.

"You're going to Austria. Plane leaves tonight from Dulles. Here's your ticket." The director of operations tossed the folder across the desk.

"What for?"

"You're booked into the Imperial Hotel. There you will link up with Dominic and Brian Caruso to keep them advised of intelligence developments. You can use your regular e-mail account, and your laptop is equipped with the proper encryption technology."

What the hell? Jack wondered. "Excuse me, Mr. Granger. Can we go back a couple of steps? Exactly what's going on here?"

"Your father asked that question once or twice, I bet." Granger managed a smile that would chill the ice in a highball. "Gerry thinks the twins need backup on the intelligence side. So, you are detailed to provide that backup, kind of a consultant to them while they're in the field. This does not mean that you'll actually be doing anything but keeping an eye on intel developments through the virtual office. You've done some pretty good work on that. You have a good nose for tracking things on the 'Net—damned sight better than Dom and Brian. Getting your eyes in the field might be useful. That's why. You can decline the job, but in your place, I'd take it. Okay?"

"When's the flight?"

"It's on your ticket folder."

Jack looked. "Damn, I'll have to hustle."

"So, hustle. There'll be a car to take you to Dulles. Get going."

"Yes, sir," Jack replied, coming to his feet. Just as well he had a car service heading his way. He didn't like the idea of leaving his Hummer in the Dulles parking lot. Thieves had fallen in love with the things. "Oh, who is cleared to know this?"

"Rick Bell will let Wills know. Aside from that, nobody, I repeat, *nobody*. Clear?"

"Clear, sir. Okay, I'm out of here." He looked in the ticket folder to find an American Express black card. At least the trip was on the company dime. How many of these things did The Campus have sitting around in its file drawers? he wondered. But for damned sure it was all he needed for this day.

* * *

"WHAT'S THIS?" Dominic asked his computer. "Aldo, we've got company coming over tomorrow morning."

"Who?" Brian asked.

"Doesn't say. It says to take no action until he links up with us, though."

"Jesus, who do they think we are, Louis the Fish? It's not our fault the last guy jumped right into our lap. Why fuck around?"

"These are government types. If you get too efficient, they get scared," Dominic thought aloud. "What about dinner, bro?"

"Fine, we can check their version of Vitello Milanese. You suppose they have any decent wines here?"

"Only one way to find out, Aldo." Dominic picked a tie out of his suitcase. The hotel dining room looked about as formal as Uncle Jack's old house.

CHAPTER 21

STREETCAR
NAME DESIRED

IT WAS a new adventure for Jack in two different ways. He'd never been to Austria before. He'd damned sure never gone into the field as a spook to join up with an assassination team, and while the idea of terminating the lives of people who liked killing Americans seemed quite a good thing at a desk in West Odenton, Maryland—in seat 3A of an Airbus 330, thirty-four thousand feet over the Atlantic Ocean, it was suddenly a dicey state of affairs. Well, Granger had told him he wouldn't really have to do anything. And that was fine with Jack. He still knew how to shoot a pistol—he regularly went shooting at the Secret Service's range in downtown D.C., or sometimes at their academy at Beltsville, Maryland, if Mike Brennan was around. But Brian and Dom weren't shooting people, were they? Not according to the MI5 report that had come to his computer. Heart attack—how the hell did you fake a heart attack well enough that a pathologist took the bait? He'd have to ask them about that. Presumably, he was cleared for it.

In any case, the food was better than average for airline slop, and even an airline can't ruin the booze when it is still in the bottle. With enough alcohol in him, sleep came fairly easily, and the first-class seat was the old-fashioned kind instead of the new gollywog with a hundred moving parts, none of which were comfortable. As usual, about half the people up front watched movies all night. Every person had his own way of dealing with travel shock, as his father invariably called it. Jack's was to sleep through it.

THE WIENER schnitzel was excellent, as were the local wines.

"Whoever does this needs to talk to Granddad," Dominic said, after the last bite. "He may know something that Pop-Pop can learn from."

"He's probably Italian, bro, or at least somewhere along the line." Brian finished off his glass of the excellent local white the waiter had recommended. About fifteen seconds later, the waiter took note of it and refilled the glass before vanishing again. "Damn, a man could get used to this eatery. Beats the hell out of MREs."

"With luck, you may never have to eat that crap again."

"Sure, if we just continue this line of work," Aldo responded dubiously. They were essentially alone in a corner booth. "So, what do we know about the new subject?"

"Courier, supposedly. He carries messages in his head—the ones they don't send via the 'Net. Would have been useful to pick his brain some, but that's not the mission. We have a physical description, but no photo this time. That's a little worrisome. He doesn't sound all that important. That's worrisome, too."

"Yeah, I hear you. He must have pissed the wrong people off. Tough luck." His pangs of conscience were a thing of the past, but he really wanted to bag one closer to the top of the food chain. The absence of a photo for ID was indeed worrisome. They'd have to be careful. You didn't want to hit the wrong guy.

"Well, he didn't get on the list by singing too loud at church, y'know?"

"And he ain't the Pope's nephew." Brian completed the litany. "I hear you, man." He checked his watch. "Time to hit the rack, bro. We have to see who's coming tomorrow. How are we supposed to meet him?"

"Message said he'd come to us. Hell, maybe he's going to stay here, too."

"The Campus has funny ideas about security, doesn't it?"

"Yeah, it's not like the movies." Dominic had himself a quiet laugh. He waved for the check. They'd pass on dessert. In a place like this, it could be lethal. Five more minutes and they were in their beds.

"THINK YOU'RE clever, eh?" Hendley asked Granger over the secure phones in both their homes.

"Gerry, you told me to send an intel weenie, right? Who else can we spare out of Rick's shop? Everybody's been telling me how sharp the kid is. Okay, let him prove it at the sharp end."

"But he's a rookie," Hendley protested.

"And the twins aren't?" Granger asked in reply. *Gotcha. From now on, you'll let me run my shop* my *way,* he thought just as loudly as he could. "Gerry, he's not going to get his hands wet, and this will probably make him a better analyst. He's related to them. They know him. He knows them. They will trust and believe what he has to say, and Tony Wills says he's the brightest young analyst he's seen since he left Langley. So, he's perfect for the assignment, isn't he?"

"He's too junior." But Hendley knew he was losing this one.

"Who isn't, Gerry? If we had any guys available with experience in this line of work, we would have put 'em on the payroll."

"If this blows up—"

"Then I go up in smoke. I know that. Can I watch some TV now?"

"See you tomorrow," Hendley said.

"'Night, buddy."

HONEYBEAR WAS surfing the 'Net, chatting with somebody named Elsa K 69, who said she was twenty-three years old, 160 centimeters in height, and fifty-four kilograms in weight, with decent but not exceptional measurements, brown hair, blue eyes, and a nasty, inventive mind. She also had good typing skills. In fact, though Fa'ad had no way of knowing it, it was a man, fifty years old, half drunk and rather lonely. They chatted in English. The "girl" on the other end said "she" was a secretary in London. It was a city the Austrian accountant knew well.

"She" was real enough for Fa'ad, who soon got deeply into the perverse fantasy. It wasn't as good as a real woman by a long shot, but Fa'ad was careful about indulging his passions in Europe. You never knew if the woman you rented might be someone from the Mossad, who'd be just as happy to cut it off as to take it inside. He didn't fear death much, but like all men he did fear pain. In any case, the fantasy lasted almost half an hour, which left him sated enough to take note of the "handle" in case "she" showed up again. He could not know that the Tyrolean accountant made a similar notation in his Buddy File before retiring to a cold and lonely bed.

WHEN JACK woke up, the window blinds were raised to reveal the purple-gray of mountains about twenty thousand feet below. His watch showed that he'd been aboard about eight hours, and had probably slept for six of them. Not too bad. He had a mild headache from the wine, but the wake-up coffee was good, as was the pastry, which combined to get him semi-awake as Flight 94 cruised in for landing.

The airport was hardly a large one, considering it was the flagship port of entry for a sovereign country, but Austria had about the same population as New York City, which had *three* airports. The aircraft thumped down, and the captain welcomed them all to his homeland, telling them that the local time was 9:05 A.M. So, he'd have one day of heavy jet lag to deal with, but with luck maybe he'd be approximately okay tomorrow.

He cleared immigration easily—the flight had only been about half full—recovered his bags and headed outside for a cab.

"Hotel Imperial, please."

"Where?" the driver asked.

"Hotel Imperial," Ryan repeated.

The driver thought for a moment. *"Ach so,* Hotel Imperial, *ja?"*

"Das ist richtig," Junior assured him, and sat back to enjoy the ride. He had a hundred Euros, and assumed that would be enough, unless this guy had attended the New York City school of taxi driving. In any case, there'd be ATM machines on the street.

The drive took half an hour, fighting the rush-hour traffic. A block or two from the hotel, he passed a Ferrari dealership, which was something new for him—he'd seen Ferraris only on TV before, and wondered, as all young men wonder, what it might be like to drive one.

The hotel staff greeted him like an arriving prince, and delivered him to a fourth-floor suite whose bed looked very inviting indeed. He immediately ordered breakfast and unpacked. Then he remembered why he was here, and picked up the phone, asking for a connection with Dominic Caruso's room.

"HELLO?" It was Brian. Dom was in the gold-encrusted shower.

"Hey, cuz, it's Jack," he heard.

"Jack who—wait a minute, *Jack?"*

"I'm upstairs, Marine. Just flew in an hour ago. Come on up, so we can talk."

"Right. Give me ten minutes," Brian said, and headed

into the bathroom. "Enzo, you ain't gonna believe who's upstairs."

"Who?" Dominic asked, toweling himself off.

"Let it be a surprise, man." Brian went back to the sitting room, not sure whether to laugh or barf as he read the *International Herald Tribune*.

"YOU GOTTA be fucking kidding," Dominic breathed as the door opened.

"You ought to see it from my side, Enzo," Jack answered. "Come on in."

"Food's good in Motel 6, isn't it?" Brian observed, following his brother.

"Actually, I prefer Holiday Inn Express. I need to pick up a Ph.D. for my curriculum vitae, y'know?" Jack laughed and waved them to the chairs. "I got extra coffee."

"They do it well here. I see you discovered the croissants." Dominic poured himself a cup and stole a pastry. "Why the hell did they send you?"

"I guess because you both know me." Junior buttered his second. "Tell you what. Let me finish breakfast and we can take a walk down to the Ferrari dealership and talk about it. How do you like Vienna?"

"Just got here yesterday afternoon, Jack," Dominic informed him.

"I didn't know that. I gather you had a productive time in London, though."

"Not bad," Brian answered. "Tell you about it later."

"Right." Jack continued his breakfast while Brian went back to his *International Trib.* "They're still excited at home about the shootings. Had to take my shoes off at the airport. Good thing I had clean socks. Looks like they're trying to see if anybody's trying to leave town in a hurry."

"Yeah, that was pretty damned bad, man," Dominic observed. "Anybody you know get clobbered?"

"No, thank God. Even Dad didn't, with all the people he knows in the investment crowd. What about you guys?"

Brian gave him a funny look. "Nobody we knew, no." He hoped that little David Prentiss's soul would not be offended.

Jack finished the last croissant. "Let me shower and you guys can show me around."

Brian finished the paper and turned the TV on to CNN—the only American station the Imperial had—to check on the news at 0500 in New York. The last of the victims had been buried the previous day, and the reporters were asking the bereaved how they felt about their loss. *What a dumbass question!* the Marine raged. You were supposed to leave twisting the knife to the bad guys. And politicians were ranting on about What America Has to Do.

Well, Brian thought, *we're doing it for you, guys.* But if they found out, they'd probably foul their silk drawers. But that just made him feel better about it. Somebody had to play a little catch-up ball, and that was his job now.

AT THE Bristol, Fa'ad was just waking up. He, too, had ordered coffee and pastry. He was scheduled to meet a fellow courier the next day to receive a message that he'd then pass on in due course. The Organization operated with great security for its important communications. The really serious messages were all passed exclusively by word of mouth. The couriers knew only their incoming and outgoing counterparts, so that they were organized in cells of three only, another lesson learned from the dead KGB officer. The inbound courier was Mahmoud Mohamed Fadhil, who'd be arriving from Pakistan. Such a system could be broken, but only through painstaking and lengthy police work, which was easily foiled if only one man removed himself from the ratline. The trouble was that the unexpected removal of a rat from the line could prevent a message from reaching its destination entirely, but that had not yet happened, and was not expected to. It was not a bad life for Fa'ad. He traveled a lot, always first-class, resided only in top-of-the-line hostelries, and, all in all, it was rather comfortable. He occasionally felt guilty for this. Others did what he thought were the dangerous and admirable things, but on taking the job he'd been briefed that the organization could not function without him and his eleven comrades, which was good for his morale. So was the knowledge that his function, while of great importance, was also quite safe. He received messages and passed them on, often to the operatives themselves, all of whom treated him with great respect, as though he had originated the mission instructions himself, of which he did not disabuse them. So, in two days, he'd receive more orders for transfer, whether to his nearest geographic colleague—Ibrahim Salih al-Adel, home-based in Paris—or to an operative currently unknown. Today he would find out, and make such communications as were necessary, and act upon developments. The job could be both boring and exciting at the same time, and with the comfortable hours and zero risk to his person, it was easy to be a hero of the movement, as he sometimes allowed himself to think of himself.

THEY WALKED east on Kartner Ring, which almost at once angled northeast and changed its name to Schubertring. On the north side of it was the Ferrari dealership.

"So, how are you guys doing?" Jack asked, out in the open, and with the traffic noise beyond the reach of any possible tapping device.

"Two down. One more to go, right here in Vienna, then off somewhere else, wherever it is. I kinda thought you would know," Dominic said.

Jack shook his head. "Nope. I haven't been briefed on that."

"Why did they send you?" This one came from Brian.

"I'm supposed to give you second guesses, I think. Back you up on the intel side and be some sort of consultant. That's what Granger told me, anyway. I know what happened in London. We got lots of inside stuff from the

Brits—indirectly, that is. It was written off as a heart attack. Munich I do not know much about. What can you tell me?"

Dominic answered. "I got him coming out of church. He went down on the sidewalk. Ambulance arrived. The paramedics worked him over and carted him off to the hospital. All I know."

"He's dead. We caught that on an intercept," Ryan told them. "He was accompanied by a guy named 'Honeybear' on the 'Net. Saw his buddy go down and reported it in to a guy with the handle Fifty-six MoHa, somewhere in Italy, we think. The Munich guy—his name was Atef—was a recruiter and courier. We know he recruited a shooter in the mess last week. So, you can be sure he earned his way onto the hit list."

"We know. They told us that," Brian said.

"How are you doing these people, exactly?"

"With this." Dominic pulled his gold pen from the suit jacket pocket. "You swap the point out by twisting the nib and stick them, preferably in the ass. It injects a drug called succinylcholine, and that ruins the subject's whole day. The drug metabolizes in the bloodstream even after death, and can't be detected easily unless the pathologist's a genius, and a lucky one at that."

"Paralyzes them?"

"Yep. They collapse, and then they can't breathe. Takes about thirty seconds for the drug to take hold, and then they drop down, and, after that, it's just a matter of mechanics. It *looks* like a heart attack afterward, and it tests out like that, too. Perfect for what we do."

"Damn," Jack said. "So, you guys were in Charlottesville, too, eh?"

"Yeah." This was Brian. "Not much fun. I had a little boy die in my arms, Jack. That was pretty tough."

"Well, nice shooting."

"They weren't very smart," Dominic evaluated them. "No smarter than street hoods. No training. They didn't check their backs. I guess they figured they didn't have to, with automatic weapons. But they learned different. Still, we were lucky—Son of a bitch!" he observed, as they got to the Ferraris.

"Damn. They are pretty," Jack agreed at once. Even Brian was impressed.

"That's the old one," Dominic told them. "575M, V-twelve, five hundred–plus horses, six-speed transmission, two hundred twenty big ones to drive it away. The really cool one's the Ferrari Enzo. That baby's the fucking bomb, guys. Six hundred sixty horses. They even named it after me. See, back in the far corner."

"How much?" Junior asked.

"The far side of six hundred thousand bucks. But if you want to get something hotter, you gotta call Lockheed Burbank." And sure enough, the car had twin openings on the front that looked like jet intakes. The entire machine looked like personal transportation for Luke Skywalker's rich uncle.

"Still knows his cars, eh?" Jack observed. A private jet probably got better mileage, too, but the car was sleekly pretty.

"He'd rather sleep with a Ferrari than with Grace Kelly," Brian snorted. His own priorities were rather more conventional, of course.

"You can ride a car longer than a girl, people." Which was one version of efficiency. "Damn, I bet that honey moves pretty fast."

"You could get a private pilot's license," Jack suggested.

Dominic shook his head. "Nah. Too dangerous."

"Son of a bitch." Jack almost laughed out loud. "As compared with what you've been doing?"

"Junior, I'm used to that, y'know?"

"You say so, man." Jack just shook his head. Damn, those were pretty cars. He liked his Hummer at home. In the snow he could drive anywhere, and he'd win any collision on the highway, and, if it wasn't exactly sporty, what the hell? But the little boy in him could understand the list on his cousin's face. If Maureen O'Hara had been born a car, maybe she'd be one of these. The red body color would have gone nicely with her hair. After ten minutes, Dominic figured he'd drooled enough, and they walked on.

"So, we know everything about the subject except for what he looks like?" Brian asked half a block up the street.

"Correct," Jack confirmed. "But how many Arabs do you expect there to be in the Bristol?"

"A lot of them in London. Trick is going to be to ID the subject. Doing the job right on the sidewalk ought not to be too hard." And, looking around, that seemed likely. Street traffic wasn't as thick as in New York or London, but it wasn't Kansas City after dark either, and doing the job in broad daylight had its own attractions. "I guess we stake out the hotel's main entrance, and whatever side entrance there is. Can you see if you can get more data from The Campus?"

Jack checked his watch and did the mental arithmetic. "They should be open for business in two hours or so."

"Then check your e-mail," Dominic told him. "We'll wander around and look for a likely subject."

"Right." They walked across the street and headed back to the Imperial. Once back in his room, Jack flopped onto the bed and grabbed a nap.

THERE WAS nothing he had to do right now, Fa'ad thought, so he might as well get some air. Vienna had plenty of things to look at, and he hadn't exhausted them all yet. So, he dressed properly, like a businessman, and walked outside.

"BINGO, ALDO." Dominic had a cop's memory for faces, and they had practically walked into this one.

"Isn't he—"

"Yep. Atef's pal from Munich. You wanna bet he's our boy?"

"Sucker bet, bro." Dominic cataloged the target. *Middle*

*Eastern as hell, medium height, five feet ten inches or so,
light build at about hundred fifty pounds, black and brown,
slightly Semitic nose, dresses well and expensively, like a
businessman, walks around with purpose and confidence.*
They walked within ten feet of him, careful not to stare,
even with their sunglasses. *Gotcha, sucker.* Whoever these
people were, they didn't know dick about hiding in plain
sight. They walked to the corner.

"Damn, that was easy enough," Brian observed. "Now
what?"

"We let Jack check it out with the home office and just
be cool, Aldo."

"Roger, copy that, bro." He unconsciously checked his
coat to make sure the gold pen was in place, as he might
have checked his holster for his M9 Beretta automatic in
uniform and in the field. It felt as though he were an invisible lion in a Kenyan field full of wildebeest. It didn't get
much better than that. He could pick out the one he wanted
to kill and eat, and the poor bastard didn't even know he
was being stalked. *Just like they do it.* He wondered if this
guy's colleagues would see the irony of having such tactics
used against them. It wasn't how Americans were conditioned to act, but then all that stuff about showdowns on
main street at high noon was something invented by Hollywood, anyway. A lion was not in the business of risking his
life, and as they'd told him in the Basic School, if you
found yourself in a fair fight, then you hadn't planned it
very well beforehand. Fighting fair was okay in the
Olympic Games, but this wasn't that. No big-game hunter
walked up to a lion making noise and holding a sword. Instead, he did the sensible thing: He took cover behind a log
and did it with a rifle from two hundred yards or so. Even
the Masai tribesmen of Kenya, for whom killing a lion was
the passage into manhood, had the good sense to do it in a
squad-sized unit of ten, and not all of them teenagers, to
make sure it was the lion's tail they took back to the kraal.

It wasn't about being brave. It was about being effective. Just being in this business was dangerous enough. You did your best to take every element of unnecessary risk out of the equation. It was business, not a sport. "Do him out here on the street?"

"Worked before, Aldo, didn't it? I don't figure we can hit him in the hotel saloon."

"Roge-o, Enzo. Now what do we do?"

"Play tourist, I suppose. The opera house looks impressive. Let's take a look.... The sign says they're doing Wagner's *The Valkyries*. I've never seen that one."

"I've never seen an opera in my life. I suppose I ought to someday—part of the Italian soul, ain't it?"

"Oh yeah, I got more soul than I can control, but I'm partial to Verdi."

"My ass. When you been to the opera?"

"I have some of the CDs," Dominic answered, with a smile. As it turned out, the State Opera House was a magnificent example of imperial architecture, built and executed as though for God Himself to attend a performance, and bedecked in scarlet and gold. Whatever its faults might have been, the House of Hapsburg had shown impressive taste. Dominic thought briefly about checking out the cathedrals in town, but decided it wasn't fitting, given the reason they were here. In all, they walked around for two hours, then headed back to the hotel and up to Jack's room.

"NO JOY from the home office," Jack told them.

"No problem. We saw the guy. He's an old friend from Munich," Brian reported. They walked into the bathroom and opened the faucets, which would put out enough white noise to annoy any microphones in the room. "He's a pal of Mr. Atef. He was there when we popped him in Munich."

"How can you be sure?"

"A hundred percent sure, we can't be—but what are the odds that he just happened to be in both cities, and the right hotel, man?" Brian asked reasonably.

"Hundred percent certainty is better," Jack objected.

"I agree, but when you're on the right side of thousand-to-one odds, you put the money down and toss the dice," Dominic responded. "By Bureau rules, he's at least a known associate, somebody we'd take aside to interview. So, he probably isn't out collecting for the Red Cross, y'know?" The agent paused. "Okay, it's not perfect, but it's the best we got, and I think it's worth going with."

It was gut-check time for Jack. Did he have the author-ity to give a go-no-go on this? Granger hadn't said so. He was intel backup for the twins. But what, exactly, did that mean? Great. He had a job without a job description, and no assigned authority. This did not make much sense. He remembered his father saying once that headquarters people weren't supposed to second-guess the troops out in the field, because the troops had eyes, and were supposed to be trained to think on their own. But in this case his training was probably at least as good as theirs. *But* he hadn't seen the face of the supposed subject and they had. If he said no, they could just as easily tell him where to stick his opinion, and, since he had no power to enforce it, they'd win the day and he'd just stand around with his dick in his hand, wondering who was right on the call. The spook business was suddenly very unpredictable, and he was stuck in the middle of a swamp without a helicopter to lift his ass out.

"Okay, guys, it's your call." This seemed a lot like taking the coward's way out to Jack, and even more so when he said, "I'd still feel better if we were a hundred percent sure."

"So would I. But like I said, man, a thousand to one con-stitutes betting odds. Aldo?"

Brian thought it over and nodded. "It works for me. He looked very concerned over his pal in Munich. If he's a good guy, he has funny friends. So, let's do him."

"Okay," Jack breathed, bowing to the inevitable. "When?"

"As soon as convenient," Brian responded. He and his

brother would discuss tactics later, but Jack didn't need to know about that.

HE WAS lucky, Fa'ad decided at 10:14 that night. He got an instant message from Elsa K 69, who evidently remembered him kindly.

WHAT SHALL WE DO TONIGHT? he asked "her."

I'VE BEEN THINKING. IMAGINE WE ARE IN ONE OF THE K-LAGERS. I AM A JEWESS, AND YOU ARE THE KOMMANDANT . . . I DO NOT WISH TO DIE WITH THE REST, AND I OFFER YOU PLEASURE IN RETURN FOR MY LIFE . . . "she" proposed.

It could scarcely have been a more pleasant fantasy for him. GO AHEAD AND BEGIN, he typed.

And so it went for a while, until: PLEASE, PLEASE, I AM NOT AN AUSTRIAN. I AM AN AMERICAN MUSIC STUDENT TRAPPED BY THE WAR . . .

Better and better. OH, YES? I HAVE HEARD MUCH ABOUT AMERICAN JEWS AND THEIR WHORISH WAYS . . .

And so it went for nearly an hour. At the end, he sent her to the gas anyway. After all, what were Jews good for, really?

PREDICTABLY, Ryan couldn't sleep. His body hadn't yet acclimated to the shift of six time zones, despite the decent amount of sleep he'd had on the plane. How flight crews did it was a mystery to him, though he suspected they simply stayed synchronized to wherever they lived, disregarding wherever they happened to be at the time. But you have to stay constantly mobile to do that, and he wasn't. So, he plugged in his computer and decided to Google his way into Islam. The only Muslim he knew was Prince Ali of Saudi Arabia, and *he* was not a maniac. He even got along well with Jack's shy little sister, Katie, who found his neatly trimmed beard fascinating. He was able to download the Koran, and he started reading it. The holy book had forty-two suras, broken down into verses, just like his own

Bible. Of course, he rarely looked at it, much less read it, because as a Catholic he expected the priests to tell him about the important parts, letting him skip all the work of reading about who the hell begat what the hell—maybe it had been interesting, and even fun, at the time, but not today, unless you were into genealogy, which wasn't a subject of dinner-table conversation in the Ryan family. Besides, everyone knew that every Irishman was descended from a horse thief who'd skipped the country to avoid being hanged by the nasty English invaders. A whole collection of wars had come out of that, one of which had come within a whisker of preventing his own birth in Annapolis.

It was ten minutes later that he realized that the Koran was almost a word-for-word clone of what all the Jewish prophets had scribbled down, divinely inspired to do so, of course, because they said so. And so did this Mohammed guy. Supposedly, God talked to him, and he played executive secretary and wrote it all down. It was a pity there hadn't been a video camera and tape recorder for all these birds, but there hadn't, and, as a priest had explained to him at Georgetown, faith was faith, and either you believed as you were supposed to, or you didn't.

Jack *did* believe in God, of course. His mom and dad had instructed him in the basics, and sent him through Catholic schools, and he'd learned the prayers and the rules, and he'd done First Communion, and Confession—now called "Reconciliation" in the kinder, gentler Church of Rome—and Confirmation. But he hadn't seen the inside of a church for quite a while. It wasn't that he was against the Church, just that he was grown up now, and maybe not going was a (dumb) way of showing Mom and Dad that he was able to make his own decisions about how he'd live his life, and that Mom and Dad couldn't order him around anymore.

He noted that there was no place in the fifty pages he'd skimmed through that said anything about shooting innocent people so that you could screw the womenfolk among them in heaven. The penalty for suicide was right on the level with what Sister Frances Mary had explained in second grade. Suicide was a mortal sin you really wanted to avoid, because you couldn't go to confession afterward to scrub it off your soul. Islam said that faith was good, but you couldn't just think it. You had to live it, too. Bingo, as far as Catholic teaching went.

At the end of ninety minutes, it came to him—rather an obvious conclusion—that terrorism had about as much to do with the Islamic religion as it did with Catholic and Protestant Irishmen. Adolf Hitler, the biographers said, had thought of himself as a Catholic right up until the moment he'd eaten the gun—evidently, he'd never met Sister Frances Mary or he would have known better. But that bozo had obviously been crazy. So, if he was reading this right, Mohammed would probably have clobbered terrorists. He had been a decent, honorable man. Not all of his followers were the same way, though, and those were the ones he and the twins had to deal with.

Any religion could be twisted out of shape by the next crop of madmen, he thought, yawning, and Islam was just the next one on the list.

"Gotta read more of this," he told himself on the way to the bed. "Gotta."

FA'AD WOKE up at eight-thirty. He'd be meeting Mahmoud today, just down the street at the drugstore. From there, they'd take a cab somewhere—probably a museum—for the actual message transfer, and he'd learn what was supposed to happen, and what he'd have to do to make it so. It really was a pity that he didn't have his own residence. Hotels were comfortable, especially the laundry service, but he was approaching his tolerance limit.

Breakfast came. He thanked the waiter and tipped him two Euros, then read the paper that sat on the wheeled table. Nothing of consequence seemed to be happening.

There was a coming election in Austria, and each side was enthusiastically blackguarding the other, as the political game was played in Europe. It was a lot more predictable at home, and easier to understand. By nine in the morning, he had the TV turned on, and he found himself checking his watch with increasing frequency. These meetings always made him a little anxious. What if Mossad had identified him? The answer to that was clear enough. They'd kill him with no more thought than flicking at an insect.

OUTSIDE, DOMINIC and Brian were walking about, almost aimlessly, or so it might have seemed to a casual observer. The problem was, there *were* a few of those around. There was a magazine kiosk just by their hotel, and the Bristol had doormen. Dominic considered leaning against a lamppost and reading a paper, but that was one thing they'd told him in the FBI Academy *never* to do, because even spies had seen the movies where the actors were always doing that. And so, professional or not, realistic or not, the whole world was conditioned to be mindful of anyone who read a newspaper while leaning on a lamppost. Following a guy already outside without being spotted was child's play compared to waiting for him to appear. He sighed, and kept walking.

Brian was thinking along the same lines. He thought about how cigarettes might help at moments like this. It gave you something to do, like in the movies, Bogart and his unfiltered coffin nails, which had eventually killed him. *Bad luck, Bogie,* Brian thought. Cancer must have been a bitch of a disease. He wasn't exactly delivering the breath of spring to his subjects, but at least it didn't last months. Just a few minutes, and the brain winked out. Besides, they had it coming in one way or another. Maybe they would not have agreed with that, but you had to be careful about the enemies you made. Not all of them would be dumb and defenseless sheep. And surprise was a bitch. The best thing to have on the battlefield, surprise. If you surprised the other guy, he didn't have a chance to strike back, and that was just fine because this *was* business, not personal. Like a steer at the stockyards, he walked into a little room, and even if he looked up he'd just see the guy with the air hammer, and after that it was off to cattle heaven, where the grass was always green and the water sweet, and there weren't any wolves around...

Your mind is wandering, Aldo, Brian thought to himself. Both sides of the street served his purpose just fine. So he crossed over and headed for the ATM machine directly across from the Bristol, took out his card, and punched in the code number, to be rewarded with five hundred Euros. Checked his watch: 10:53. Was this bird coming out? Had they missed him somehow?

Traffic had settled down. The red streetcars rumbled back and forth. People here minded their own business. They walked along without looking sideways, unless they were interested in something specific. No eye contact with strangers, no instinct to greet people at all. A stranger was supposed to stay that way, evidently. He appreciated it here even more than in Munich, just how *in Ordnung* these people were. You could probably eat dinner right off the floor in their houses, as long as you cleaned up the floor afterward.

Dominic had taken up position on the other side of the street, covering the direction to the opera house. There were only two ways for this character to go. Left or right. He could cross the street or not. No more options than that, unless he had a car coming to pick him up, in which case the mission was a washout. But tomorrow was always another day. 10:56, his watch said. He had to be careful, not look at the hotel's entrance too much. Doing this made him feel vulnerable...

There—bingo! It was the subject, all right, dressed in a blue pin-striped suit and a maroon tie, like a guy going to an important business meeting. Dominic saw him, too, and turned to approach from the northwest. Brian waited to see what he was going to do.

FA'AD DECIDED to trick his arriving friend. He'd approach from across the street, just to be different, and so he crossed over, in the middle of the block, dodging the traffic. As a boy, he'd enjoyed entering the corral for his father's horses and dodging among them. Horses had brains enough not to run into things unnecessarily, of course, more than could be said for some of the cars heading up Kartner Ring, but he got across safely.

THE ROAD here was curious, with one paved path like a private driveway, a thin grass median, then the road proper with its cars and streetcars, then another grass median, and the final car path before the opposite sidewalk. The subject darted across and started walking west, toward their hotel. Brian took up position ten feet behind and took out his pen, swapping out the point and checking visually to make sure he was ready.

MAX WEBER was a motorman who'd worked for the city transit authority for twenty-three years, driving his streetcar back and forth eighteen times per day, for which he was paid a comfortable salary for a workingman. He was now going north, leaving Schwartzenberg Platz, turning left just as the street changed from Rennweg into Schwartzenberg Strasse to go left on the Kartner Ring. The light was in his favor, and his eye caught the ornate Hotel Imperial, where all the rich foreigners and diplomats liked to stay. Then his eyes came back to the road. You couldn't steer a streetcar, and it was the job of those in automobiles to keep out of his way. Not that he went very fast, hardly ever more than forty kilometers per hour, even out at the end of the line. It was not an intellectually demanding job, but he did it scrupulously, in accordance with the manual. The bell rang. Somebody needed to get off at the corner of Kartner and Wiedner Hauptstrasse.

THERE. THERE was Mahmoud. Looking the other way. Good, Fa'ad thought, maybe he could surprise his colleague, and have a joke for the day. He stopped on the sidewalk and scanned the miniroad for traffic before dashing across the street.

OKAY, RAGHEAD, Brian thought, closing the distance in just three steps and—

OUCH, FA'AD thought. It was quite literally a slight pain in the ass. He ignored it and kept going, cutting through a gap in the traffic on the street. There was a streetcar coming, but it was too far away to be a matter of concern. Traffic was not coming from his right, and so . . .

BRIAN JUST kept walking. He figured he'd go to the magazine stand. It would give him a good chance to turn and watch while he ostensibly made a purchase.

WEBER SAW the idiot making ready to dash across the tracks. Didn't these fools know only to do that at the *Ecke,* where he had to stop for the red lights like everyone else? They taught children to do that at the *Kindergarten.* Some people thought their time was more valuable than gold, as though they were Franz Josef himself, risen from the hundred-year dead. He didn't change his speed. Idiot or not, he'd get well clear of the tracks before—

—FA'AD FELT his right leg collapse under him. What was this? Then his left leg, and he was falling for no reason at all—and then other things started happening faster than he could understand them, and as though from an outside vantage point he saw himself falling down—and there was a streetcar . . . coming!

MAX REACTED a little too slowly. He could hardly believe what his eyes told him. But it could not be denied. He tromped his foot down on the brakes, but the fool was less than two meters away, and—*lieber Gott!*

The streetcar had a pair of bars running horizontally under its nose to prevent exactly this, but they hadn't been checked in several weeks, and Fa'ad was a slender man—slender enough that his feet slid right under the safe bars and his body then pushed them vertically upward and out of the way—

—and Max felt the dreadful *thump-thump* of his passage over the man's body. Somebody would call for an ambulance, but they would be far better off calling a priest. This poor schlemiel would not ever get to where he was going, the fool, saving time at the cost of his life. The fool!

ACROSS THE street, Mahmoud turned just in time to see his friend die. His eyes imagined more than saw the streetcar jump upward, as though to avoid killing Fa'ad, and just that fast his world changed, as Fa'ad's world ended for all time to be.

"JESUS," BRIAN thought, twenty yards away, holding a magazine in his hands. That poor fucker hadn't lived long enough to die of the poison. He saw that Enzo had moved down the opposite side of the street, perhaps figuring to pop him if and when he'd gotten across, but the succinylcholine had worked as advertised. He'd just picked a particularly bad place to collapse. Or a lucky one, depending on your point of view. He took the magazine and crossed the street. There was an Arab-looking guy by the drugstore whose face was even more upset than the citizens around him. There were screams, a lot of hands to mouths, and, damned sure, it was not a pretty sight, though the streetcar had stopped directly over the body.

"Somebody's going to have to hose down the street," Dominic said quietly. "Nice pop, Aldo."

"Well, I guess a five-point-six from the East German judge. Let's get moving."

"Roger that, bro."

And they headed right, past the cigarette store, toward Schwartzenberg Platz.

Behind them there was a little screaming from the women, while the men took it all more soberly, with many turning away. There was not a thing to be done. The door-man at the Imperial darted inside to summon an ambulance and the *Feuerwehr*. They took about ten minutes to arrive. The firemen got there first, and for them the grim sight was immediate and decisive. His whole blood supply, so it seemed, had spilled out, and there was no saving him. The police were there, too, and a police captain, who'd arrived from his station on nearby Friedrichstrasse, told Max Weber to back his streetcar off the body. It revealed much—and little. The body had been chopped into four irregular pieces, as though ripped apart by a predatory creature from prehistory. The ambulance, which had come, was stopped not quite in the middle of the street—the street cops were waving the cars along, but the drivers and passengers took the time to look at the carnage, with half of them staring with grim fascination and the other half turning away in horror and disgust. Even some reporters were there, with their cameras and notepads—and Minicams for the TV scribblers.

They needed three body bags to collect the body. An inspector from the transit authority arrived to question the motorman, whom the police already had in hand, of course. All in all, it took about an hour to remove the body, inspect the streetcar, and clear the road. It was done rather efficiently, in fact, and by 12:30 everything was back *in Ordnung*.

Except for Mahmoud Mohamed Fadhil, who had to go to his hotel and light up his computer to send an e-mail to Mohammed Hassan al-Din, now in Rome, for instructions.

By that time, Dominic was on his own computer, composing an e-mail for The Campus to tell them of the day's work, and ask for instructions on the next assignment.

CHAPTER 22

SPANISH STEPS

"YOU'RE KIDDING," Jack said at once.

"God, grant me a dumb adversary," Brian responded. "That's one prayer they teach at the Basic School. Trouble is, sooner or later they're going to get smart."

"Like crooks," Dominic agreed. "The problem with law enforcement is that we generally catch the dumb ones. The smart ones we rarely even hear about. That's why it took so long to do the Mafia, and they're not really all *that* smart. But, yeah, it's a Darwinian process, and we'll be helping to breed brains into them one way or another."

"News from home?" Brian asked.

"Check the time. They won't even be getting in for another hour," Jack explained. "So, the guy really got run over?"

Brian nodded. He'd gone down and been run over like the official Mississippi state animal—a squashed dog on the road. "By a streetcar. Good news is that it covered up the mess." *Tough luck, Mr. Raghead.*

* * *

IT WASN'T even a mile to the St. Elizabeth's *Krankenhaus* on Invalidenstrasse, where the ambulance crew carried in the body parts. They'd called ahead, and so there was no particular surprise at the three rubberized bags. These were duly laid on a table in pathology—there was no point in their going to casualty receiving, because the cause of death was so obvious as to be blackly comical. The only hard part was to retrieve blood for a toxicology scan. The body had been so mauled as to be largely drained of blood, but internal organs—mainly the spleen and brain—had enough to be drawn out with a syringe and sent off to the lab, which would look for narcotics and/or alcohol. The only other thing to look for in the postmortem exam was a broken leg, but the passage of the streetcar over the body—they had his name and ID from his wallet, and the police were checking the local hotels to see if maybe he'd left a passport behind, so that the appropriate embassy could be notified—meant that even a broken knee would be almost impossible to discover. Both of his legs had been totally crushed in a matter of less than three seconds. The only surprising thing was that his face was placid. One would have expected open eyes and a grimace of pain from the death, but, then, even traumatic death had few hard-and-fast rules, as the pathologist knew. There was little point in doing an in-depth examination. Maybe if he'd been shot they could find a bullet wound, but there was no reason to suspect that. The police had already talked to seventeen eyewitnesses who'd been within thirty meters of the event. All in all, the pathology report could just as easily have been a form letter as a signed official document.

"JESUS," **GRANGER** observed. "How the hell did they arrange that?" Then he lifted his phone. "Gerry? Come on down. Number three is in the bag. You have to see this report." After replacing the phone, he thought aloud, "Okay, now where do we send them next?"

That was settled on a different floor. Tony Wills was copying all of Ryan's downloads, and the one at the top of the download file was impressive in its bloody brevity. So, he lifted his phone for Rick Bell.

IT WAS hardest of all for Max Weber. It took half an hour for the initial denial and shock to wear off. He started vomiting, his eyes replaying the sight of the crumpled body sliding below his field of vision, and the horrible *thump-thump* of his streetcar. It hadn't been his fault, he told himself. That fool, *das Idiot,* had just fallen down right before him, like a drunk might do, except it was far too early for a man to have too many beers. He'd had accidents before, mostly fender work on cars that had turned too abruptly in front of him. But he'd never seen and hardly heard of a fatal accident with a streetcar. He'd *killed* a man. He, Max Weber, had taken a life. It was not his fault, he told himself about once a minute for the next two hours. His supervisor gave him the rest of the day off, and so he clocked out and drove home in his Audi, stopping at a *Gasthaus* a block from his home because he didn't want to drink alone this day.

JACK WAS running through his downloads from The Campus, with Dom and Brian standing by, having a late lunch and beers. It was routine traffic, e-mail to and from people suspected of being players, the majority of them ordinary citizens of various countries who'd once or twice written magic words that had been taken note of by the Echelon intercept system at Fort Meade. Then there was one like all the others, except that the addressee was 56MoHa@eurocom.net.

"Hey, guys, our pal on the street was about to have a meet with another courier, looks like. He's writing our old friend Fifty-six MoHa, and requesting instructions."

"Oh?" Dominic came over to look. "What does that tell us?"

"I just have a Internet handle—it's on AOL: Gadfly097@aol.com. If he gets a reply from MoHa, maybe we'll know something. We think he's an operations officer for the bad guys. NSA tagged him about six months ago. He encrypts his letters, but they know how to crack that one, and we can read most of his e-mails."

"How quick will you see a reply?" Dominic wondered.

"Depends on Mr. MoHa," Jack said. "We just have to sit tight and wait."

"Roger that," Brian said from his seat by the window.

"I SEE young Jack didn't slow them down," Hendley observed.

"Did you think he would? Jeez, Gerry, I told you," Granger said, having already thanked God for His blessings, but quietly. "Anyway, now they want instructions."

"Your plan was to take down four targets. So, who's number four?" the Senator asked.

It was Granger's turn to be humble. "Not sure yet. To be honest, I didn't expect them to work this efficiently. I've been kinda hoping that the hits so far might generate a target of opportunity, but nobody's prairie-dogging yet. I have a few candidates. Let me run through them this afternoon." His phone rang. "Sure, come on over, Rick." He set the phone down. "Rick Bell says he has something interesting."

The door opened in less than two minutes. "Oh, hey, Gerry. Glad you're here. Sam"—Bell turned his head—"we just had this come in." He handed the rough printout of the e-mail across.

Granger scanned it. "We know this guy..."

"Sure as hell. He's a field ops officer for our friends. We figured he was based in Rome. Well, we figured right." Like all bureaucrats—especially the senior ones—Bell enjoyed patting his own back.

Granger handed the page across to Hendley. "Okay, Gerry, here's number four."

"I don't like serendipity."

"I don't like coincidences either, Gerry, but if you win the lottery you don't give the money back," Granger said, thinking that Coach Darrell Royal had been right: Luck didn't go looking for a stumblebum. "Rick, is this guy worth making go away?"

"Yes, he is," Bell confirmed, with an enthusiastic nod. "We don't know all that much about him, but what we know is all bad. He's an operations guy—of that we are a hundred percent sure, Gerry. And it feels right. One of his people sees another go down, reports in, and this guy gets it and replies. You know, if I ever meet the guy who came up with the Echelon program, I might have to buy him a beer."

"Reconnaissance-by-fire," Granger observed, patting himself very firmly on the back. "Damn, I knew it would work. You shake a hornet's nest, and some bugs are bound to come out."

"Just so they don't sting your ass," Hendley warned. "Okay, now what?"

"Turn 'em loose before the fox goes to ground," Granger replied instantly. "If we can bag this guy, maybe we can really shake something valuable loose from the tree."

Hendley turned his head. "Rick?"

"It works for me. Go-mission," he said.

"Okay, then it's a go-mission," Hendley agreed. "Get the word out."

THE NICE thing about electronic communications was that they did not take very long. In fact, Jack already had the important part.

"Okay, guys, Fifty-six MoHa's first name is Mohammed—not great news; it's the most common first name in the world—and he says he's in Rome, at the Hotel Excelsior on the Via Vittorio Veneto, number one twenty-five."

"I've heard of that one," Brian said. "It's expensive, pretty nice. Our friends like to stay in nice places, looks like."

"He's checked in under the name Nigel Hawkins. That's English as hell. You suppose he's a Brit citizen?"

"With a first name of Mohammed?" Dominic wondered aloud.

"Could be a cover name, Enzo," Jack replied, pricking Dominic's balloon. "Without a picture, we can't guess about his background. Okay, he's got a cell phone, but Mahmoud—that's the guy who saw the bird go down this morning—must be supposed to know it." Jack paused. "Why didn't he just call in, I wonder? Hmm. Well, the Italian police have sent us stuff that came from electronic intercepts. Maybe they're watching the airwaves, and our boy is being careful . . . ?"

"Makes sense, but why . . . but why is he sending stuff out over the 'Net?"

"He thinks it's secure. NSA has cracked a lot of the public encryption systems. The vendors don't know that, but the boys at Fort Meade are pretty good at that stuff. Once you crack it, it stays cracked, and the other guy never knows." In fact, he didn't know the real reason. The programmers could be, and often had been, persuaded to insert trapdoors either for patriotism or for cash, and, often enough, for both. 56MoHa was using the most expensive such program, and its literature proclaimed loudly that *nobody* could crack it because of its proprietary algorithm. That wasn't explained, of course, just that it was a 256-bit encryption process, which was supposed to impress people with the size of the number. The literature didn't say that the software engineer who'd generated it had once worked at Fort Meade—which was why he'd been hired—and was a man who remembered swearing his oath, and, besides, a million dollars of tax-free money had been a hell of a tiebreaker. It had helped him buy his house in the hills of Marin County. And so the California real-estate market was even now serving the security interests of the United States of America.

"So, we can read their mail?" Dominic asked.

"Some of it," Jack confirmed. "The Campus downloads

most of what NSA gets at Fort Meade, and when they cross-deck it to CIA for analysis, we intercept *that*. It's less complicated than it sounds."

Dominic figured a lot out in a matter of seconds. *"Fuck..."* he breathed, looking up at the high ceiling in Jack's suite. "No wonder..." A pause. "No more beers, Aldo. We're driving to Rome." Brian nodded.

"Don't have room for a third, right?" Jack asked.

"'Fraid not, Junior, not in a 911."

"Okay, I'll catch a plane to Rome." Jack walked to the phone and called downstairs. Within ten minutes, he was booked on an Alitalia 737 to Leonardo da Vinci International, leaving in an hour and a half. He considered changing his socks. If there was anything in life that incurred his loathing, it was taking his shoes off in an airport. He was packed in a few minutes and out the door, stopping only to thank the concierge on the way out. A Mercedes taxi hustled him out of town.

Dominic and Brian had hardly unpacked at all and were ready to go in ten minutes. Dom called the valet while Brian went back to the outside magazine kiosk and got plastic-coated maps to cover the route south and west. Between that and the Euros he'd picked up earlier in the day, he figured they were set, assuming Enzo didn't drive them off an Alp. The ugly-blue Porsche arrived at the front of the hotel, and he came over as the doorman forced their bags in the tiny forward-sited trunk. In another two minutes, he was head-down in the maps looking for the quickest way to the Sudautobahn.

JACK GOT aboard the Boeing after enduring the humiliation that was now a global cost of flying commercial—it was more than enough to make him think back to Air Force One with nostalgia, though he also remembered that he'd gotten used to the comfort and attention with remarkable speed, and only later learned what normal people had to go through, which was like running into a brick wall. For the moment, he had hotel accommodations to worry about. How to do that from an airplane? There was a pay phone attached to his first-class seat, and so he swiped his black card down the plastic receiver and made his first ever attempt to conquer European telephones. What hotel? Well, why not the Excelsior? On his second attempt, he got through to the front desk and learned that, indeed, they had several rooms available. He bagged a small suite, and feeling very good about himself, he took a glass of Tuscan white from the friendly stewardess. Even a hectic life, he'd learned, could be a good life, if you knew what your next step was, and for the moment his horizon was one step away at a time.

GERMAN HIGHWAY engineers must have taught the Austrians everything they knew, Dominic thought. Or maybe the smart ones had all read the same book. In any case, the road was not unlike the concrete ribbons that crisscrossed America, except that the signage was so different as to be incomprehensible, mainly because it had no language except for city names—and they were foreign, too. He figured out that a black number on a white background inside a red circle was the speed limit, but that was in kilometers, three of which fitted into two miles with parking room left over. And the Austrian speed limits were not quite as generous as the German ones. Maybe they didn't have enough doctors to fix all the screwups, but, even in the growing hills, the curves were properly banked and the shoulders gave you enough bailout room in case somebody got seriously confused with left and right. The Porsche had a cruise control, and he pegged his to five klicks over the posted limit, just to have the satisfaction of going a little too fast. He couldn't be sure that his FBI ID would get him out of a ticket here, as it did all across the U.S. of A.

"How far, Aldo?" he asked the navigator in the Death Seat.

"Looks like a little over a thousand kilometers from where we are now. Call it ten hours, maybe."

"Hell, that's just warming-up time. May need gas in another two hours or so. How you fixed for cash?"

"Seven hundred Monopoly bucks. You can spend these in Italy, too, thank God—with the old lira you went nuts doing the math. Traffic ain't bad," Brian observed.

"No, and it's well behaved," Dominic agreed. "Good maps?"

"Yeah, all the way down. In Italy, we'll need another one for Rome."

"Okay, ought not to be too hard." And Dominic thanked a merciful God that he had a brother who could read maps. "When we stop for gas, we can get something to eat."

"Roger that, bro." Brian looked up to see mountains in the distance—no way to tell how far off they were, but it must have been a forbidding sight back when people walked or rode horses to get around. They must have had a lot more patience than modern man, or maybe a lot less sense. For the moment, the seat was comfortable, and his brother was not quite being maniacal in his driving.

THE ITALIANS turned out good airplane drivers in addition to good people for race cars. The pilot positively kissed the runway, and the rollout was as welcome as always. He'd flown too much to be as antsy about it as his father had once been, but, like most people, he felt safer walking or traveling on something he could see. Here also he found Mercedes taxicabs, and a driver who spoke passable English and knew the way to the hotel.

Highways look much the same all over the world, and for a moment Jack wondered where the hell he was. The land outside the airport looked agricultural, but the pitch of the roofs was different than at home. Evidently, it didn't snow much here, they were so shallow. It was late spring, and it was warm enough that he could wear a short-sleeve shirt, but it wasn't oppressive in any way. He'd come to Italy with his father once on official business—an economic meeting of some sort, he thought—but he'd been ridden around by an embassy car all the time. It was fun to pretend to be a prince of the realm, but you didn't learn to navigate that way, and all that stood out in his memory were the places he'd seen. He didn't know a single thing about how the hell he'd gotten there. This was the city of Caesar and a lot of other names that identified people whom history remembered for having done things good and bad. Mostly bad, because that was how history worked. And that, he reminded himself, was why he was in town. A good reminder, really, that he was not the arbiter of good and bad in the world, just a guy working backhandedly for his country, and so the authority to make such a decision did not rest entirely on his shoulders. Being president, as his father had been for just over four years, could not have been a fun job, despite all the power and importance that came with it. With power came responsibility in direct proportion, and if you had a conscience, that had to wear pretty hard on you. There was comfort in just doing things other people thought necessary. And, Jack reminded himself, he could always say no, and while there might be consequences, they would not be all that severe. Not as severe as the things he and his cousins were doing, anyway.

Via Vittorio Veneto looked more business than touristy. The trees on the sides were rather lame looking. The hotel was, surprisingly, not a tall building at all. Nor did it have an ornate entrance. Jack paid off the cabdriver and went inside, with the doorman bringing his bags. The inside was a celebration of woodwork, and the staff were welcoming as they could be. Perhaps this was an Olympic sport at which all Europeans excelled, but someone led him to his room. There was air-conditioning, and the cool air in the suite was welcoming indeed.

"Excuse me, what's your name?" he asked the bellman.

"Stefano," the man replied.

"Do you know if there is a man named Hawkins here—Nigel Hawkins?"

"The Englishman? Yes, he is three doors away, right down the corridor. A friend?"

"He's a friend of my brother's. Please don't say anything to him. Perhaps I can surprise him," Jack suggested, handing him a twenty-Euro note.

"Of course, signore."

"Very good. Thank you."

"Prego," Stefano responded, and walked back to the lobby.

This had to be dumb operational art, Jack told himself, but if they didn't have a photo of the bird, they had to get some idea of what he looked like. With that done, he lifted the phone and tried to make a call.

"YOU HAVE an incoming call," Brian's phone started saying in low tones, repeating itself three times before he fished it out of his coat pocket.

"Yeah." Who the hell was calling him? he wondered.

"Aldo, it's Jack. Hey, I'm in the hotel—the Hotel Excelsior. Want me to see if I can get you guys some rooms here? It's pretty nice. I think you guys would like it here."

"Hold on." He set the phone down in his lap. "You'll never believe where Junior's checked in to." He didn't have to identify it.

"You're kidding," Dominic responded.

"Nope. He wants to know if he should get us a reservation. What do I tell him?"

"Damn . . ." Some quick thought. "Well, he's our intel backup, isn't he?"

"Sounds a little too obvious to me, but if you say so"—he picked the phone back up—"Jack, that's affirmative, buddy."

"Great. Okay, I'll set it up. Unless I call back and say no, you come on in here."

"Roger that one, Jack. See ya."

"Bye," Brian heard, and hit the kill button. "You know, Enzo, this doesn't sound real smart to me."

"He's there. He's on the scene, and he's got eyes. We can always back out if we have to."

"Fair enough, I guess. Map says we're coming up on a tunnel in about five miles." The clock on the dash said 4:05. They were making good time, but heading straight at a mountain just past the town or city of Badgastein. Either they needed a tunnel or a big team of goats to clear that hill.

JACK LIT up his computer. It took him ten minutes to figure out how to use the phone system for that purpose, but he finally got logged on, to find his mailbox brimming with bits and bytes targeted at him. There was an attaboy from Granger for the completed mission in Vienna, though he hadn't had a thing to do with it. But below that was an assessment from Bell and Wills on 56MoHa. For the most part, it was disappointing. Fifty-six was an operations officer for the bad guys. He either did things or planned things, and one of the things he'd probably done or planned had gotten a lot of people killed in four shopping malls back at home, and so this bastard needed to meet God. There were no specifics about what he'd done, how he'd been trained, how capable he was, or whether or not he was known to carry a gun, all of which was information he'd like to see, but after reading the decrypted e-mails he reencrypted them and saved them in his ACTION folder to go over with Brian and Dom.

THE TUNNEL was like something in a video game. It went on and on to infinity, though at least the traffic inside wasn't piled up in a fiery mass as had happened a few years before in the Mont Blanc tunnel between France and Switzerland. After a period of time that seemed to last half of forever, they came out the other side. It looked to be downhill from here.

"Gas plaza ahead," Brian reported. Sure enough, there was an ELF sign half a mile away, and the Porsche's tank needed filling.

"Gotcha. I could use a stretch and a piss." The service plaza was pretty clean by American standards, and the eatery was different, without the Burger King or Roy Rogers you expected in Virginia—the men's room plumbing was all *in Ordnung,* however—and the gas was sold by the liter, which well disguised the price until Dominic did the mental arithmetic: "Jesus, they really charge for this stuff!"

"Company card, man," Brian said soothingly, and tossed over a pack of cookies. "Let's boogie, Enzo. Italy awaits."

"Fair enough." The six-cylinder engine purred back to life, and they went back on the road.

"Good to stretch your legs," Dominic observed as he went to his top gear.

"Yeah, it helps," Brian agreed. "Four hundred fifty miles to go, if my addition's right."

"Walk in the park. Call it six hours, if the traffic's okay." He adjusted his sunglasses and shook his shoulders some. "Staying in the same hotel with our subject—damn."

"I've been thinking. He doesn't know dick about us, maybe doesn't even know he's being hunted. Think about it: two heart attacks, one in front of a witness; and a traffic accident, also with a witness he knows. That's pretty bad luck, but no overt suggestion of hostile action, is there?"

"In his place, I'd be a little nervous," Dominic thought aloud.

"In his place, he probably already is. If he sees us in the hotel, we're just two more infidel faces, man. Unless he sees us more than once, we're down in the grass, not up on the scope. Ain't no rule says it *has* to be hard, Enzo."

"I hope you're right, Aldo. That mall was scary enough to last me a while."

"Concur, bro."

This wasn't the towering part of the Alps. That lay to the north and west, though it would have been bad on the legs had they been walking it, as the Roman legions had done, thinking their paved roads were a blessing. Probably better than mud, but not that much, especially humping a backpack that weighed about as much as his Marines had carried into Afghanistan. The legions had been tough in their day, and probably not all that different from the guys who did the job today in camouflaged utilities. But back then they'd had a more direct way of dealing with bad guys. They'd killed their families, their friends, their neighbors, and even their dogs, and, more to the point, they were *known* for doing all that. Not exactly practical in the age of CNN, and, truth be told, there were damned few Marines who would have tolerated participating in wholesale slaughter. But taking them out one at a time was okay, so long as you were sure you weren't killing off innocent civilians. Doing that shit was the other side's job. It was really a pity they could not all come out on a battlefield and have it out like men, but, in addition to being vicious, terrorists were also practical. There was no sense committing to a combat action in which you'd not merely lose, but be slaughtered like sheep in a pen. But real men would have built their forces up, trained and equipped them, and then turned them loose, instead of sneaking around like rats to bite babies in their cribs. Even war had rules, promulgated because there were *worse* things than war, things that were strictly forbidden to men in uniform. You did not hurt noncombatants deliberately, and you tried hard to avoid doing it by accident. The Marines were now investing considerable time, money, and effort in learning city fighting, and the hardest part of it was avoiding civilians, women with kids in strollers—even knowing that some of those women had weapons stashed next to little Johnny, and that they'd love to see the back of a United States Marine, say two or three meters away, just to be sure of bullet place-

ment. Playing by the rules had its limitations. But for Brian that was a thing of the past. No, he and his brother were playing the game by the enemy's rules, and as long as the enemy didn't know it would be a profitable game. How many lives might they have saved already by taking down a banker, a recruiter, and a courier? The problem was that you could never know. That was complexity theory as applied to real life, and it was *a priori* impossible. Nor would they ever know what good they'd be doing and what lives they might be saving when they got this 56MoHa bastard. But not being able to quantify it didn't mean it wasn't real, like that child killer his brother had dispatched in Alabama. They were doing the Lord's work, even if the Lord was not an accountant.

At work in the field of the Lord, Brian thought. Certainly these alpine meadows were green and lovely enough, he thought, looking for the lonely goatherd. *Odalayeee-oh...*

"HE'S WHERE?" Hendley asked.

"The Excelsior," Rick Bell answered. "Says he's right up the hall from our friend."

"I think our boy needs a little advice on fieldcraft," Granger observed darkly.

"Think it through," Bell suggested. "The opposition doesn't know a thing. They're as likely to be worried about the guy who picks up the wash as about Jack or the twins. They have no names, no facts, no hostile organization— hell, they don't even know for sure that anybody's out to get them."

"It's not very good fieldcraft," Granger persisted. "If Jack gets eyeballed—"

"Then what?" Bell asked. "Okay, fine, I know I'm just an intel weenie, not a field spook, but logic still applies. They do not and *cannot* know anything about The Campus. Even if Fifty-six MoHa is getting nervous, it will be undirected anxiety, and, hell, he's probably got a lot of that in his system anyway. But you can't be a spook and be afraid of anybody, can you? As long as our people are in the background noise, they have nothing to worry about—unless they do something real dumb, and these kids are not that kind of dumb, if I read them right."

Through all of this, Hendley just sat in his chair, letting his eyes flicker back and forth from one to the other. So, this was what it must have been like to be "M" in the James Bond movies. Being the boss had its moments, but it had its stresses, too. Sure, he had that undated presidential pardon in a safety-deposit box, but that didn't mean he ever wanted to make use of it. That would make him even more of a pariah than he already was, and the newsies would never leave him alone, to his dying day, not exactly his idea of fun.

"Just so they don't pretend to be room service and whack him in the hotel room," Gerry thought aloud.

"Hey, if they were that dumb, they'd already be in some German prison," Granger pointed out.

THE CROSSOVER into Italy was no more formal than crossing over from Tennessee into Virginia, which was one benefit of the European Union. The first Italian city was Villaco, where the people looked a lot more German than Sicilian to their fellow Italians, and from there southwest on the A23. They still needed to learn a little about interchanges, Dominic thought, but these roads were definitely better than they'd run for the famous Mille Miglia, the thousand-mile sports car race of the 1950s, canceled because too many people got killed watching it from the side of the country roads. The land here was not distinguishable from Austria, and the farm buildings were much the same as well. All in all, it was pretty country, not unlike eastern Tennessee or western Virginia, with rolling hills and cows that probably got milked twice a day to feed children on both sides of the border. Next came Udine, then Mestre, and they changed highways again for the A4 to Padova, switched over to A13, and an hour more to

Bologna. The Apennine mountains were to their left, and
the Marine part of Brian looked at the hills and shuddered
at the battlefield they represented. But then his stomach
started growling again.

"You know, Enzo, every town we pass has at least one
great restaurant—great pasta, homemade cheese, Vitello
Francese, the wine cellar from hell..."

"I'm hungry, too, Brian. And, yeah, we're surrounded
by Italian soul food. Unfortunately, we have a mission."

"I just hope the son of a bitch is worth what we're missing, man."

"Ours is not to reason why, bro," Dominic offered.

"Yeah, but you can stick the other half of that sentence
up your ass."

Dominic started laughing. He didn't like it, either. The
food in Munich and Vienna had been excellent, but all
around them was the place where good food had been invented. Napoleon himself had traveled with an Italian chef
on his campaigns, and most of modern French cuisine had
evolved directly from that one man, as racehorses were all
linear descendants of an Arabian stallion named Eclipse.
And he didn't even know the man's name. Pity, he thought,
passing a tractor-trailer whose driver probably knew the
best local places. Shit.

They drove with their lights on—a rule in Italy, enforced by the Polizia Stradale, who were not renowned for
their leniency—at a steady 150 kilometers per hour, just
over ninety miles to the hour, and the Porsche seemed to
love it. Gas mileage was over twenty five—or so Dominic
guessed. The arithmetic of kilometers and liters against
miles and gallons was too much for him while concentrat-
ing on the road. At Bologna, they joined up with the A1
and continued south toward Firenze, the city of origin for
the Caruso family. The road cut through the mountains, going southwest, and was beautifully engineered.

Bypassing Florence was very hard. Brian knew of a fine

restaurant near the Ponte Vecchio that belonged to distant cousins, where the wine was *bellissima,* and the food worthy of a king, but Rome was only two more hours away. He remembered going there by train that one time in his undress greens with the Sam Browne belt to proclaim his professional identity, and, sure enough, the Italians had liked the United States Marines, like all civilized people. He'd hated taking the train back to Rome and thence to Naples and his ship, but his time had not been his own.

As it wasn't now. There were more mountains as they headed south, but now some of the signs proclaimed ROMA, and that was good.

JACK ATE in the Excelsior's dining room, and the food was everything he'd expected, and the staff treated him like a prodigal member of the family come home after a protracted absence. His only complaint was that nearly everyone here was smoking. Well, perhaps Italy didn't know about secondhand smoke dangers. He'd grown up hearing all about it from his mother—who'd often aimed the remarks at Dad, who was always struggling to quit the habit once and for all, and never quite made it. He took his time with dinner. Only the salad was ordinary. Even the Italians couldn't change lettuce, though the dressings were brilliant. He'd taken a corner table to be able to survey the room. The other diners looked as ordinary as he did. All were well dressed. The guest services book in his room didn't say a tie was required, but he'd just assumed it, and, besides, Italy was the world headquarters of style. He hoped to get a suit while here, if time permitted. There were thirty or forty people here. Jack discounted the ones with wives handy. So, he was looking for someone about thirty years old, eating dinner alone, registered as Nigel Hawkins. He ended up with three possibilities. He decided to look for people who didn't look Arabic in their ethnicity, and that weeded one out. So, what to do now? Was he supposed to do anything at all? How could it hurt, unless he identified himself as an intelligence officer?

But...why take chances? he asked himself. *Why not just be cool?*

And with that thought, he backed off, mentally at least. Better to ID the guy another way.

ROME WAS indeed a fine city, Mohammed Hassan al-Din told himself. He periodically thought about renting an apartment, or even a house. You could even rent one in the Jewish Quarter; there were some fine kosher restaurants in that part of the city, where one could order anything on the menu with confidence. He'd looked once at an apartment on the Piazza Campo di Fiori, but while the price—even the tourist price—had not been unreasonable, the idea of being tied down to a single location had frightened him off. Better to be mobile in his business. The enemies couldn't strike at that which they could not find. He'd taken chance enough killing the Jew Greengold—he'd been tongue-lashed by the Emir himself for that bit of personal amusement, and told never to do anything like it ever again. What if the Mossad had gotten a picture of him? How valuable would he be to the Organization then? the Emir had demanded angrily. And that man was known by his colleagues for his volcanic temper. So, no more of that. He didn't even carry the knife with him, but kept it in a place of honor in his shaving kit, where he could take it out and inspect the Jew blood on the folding blade.

So, for now, in Rome, he lived here. Next time—after he went back home—he'd return and stay at another, maybe that nice one by the Trevi Fountain, he thought, though this location suited his activities better. And the food. Well, Italian food was richly excellent, better in his estimation than the simple fare of his home country. Lamb was good, but not every day. And here people didn't look at you like an infidel if you had a small sip of wine. He wondered if Mohammed, his own eponym, had knowingly allowed the Faithful to drink spirits made from honey, or simply hadn't known that mead existed. He'd tried it while at Cambridge University, and concluded that only someone who desperately needed to be drunk would ever sample it, much less spend a night with it. So, Mohammed was not quite perfect. And neither was he, the terrorist reminded himself. He did hard things for the Faith, and so he was allowed to take a few diversions from the true path. If one had to live with rats, better to have a few whiskers, after all. The waiter came to take away his dishes, and he decided to pass on dessert. He had to maintain his trim figure if he was to maintain his cover as an English businessman, and fit into his Brioni suits. So, he left the table and walked out to the elevator lobby.

RYAN THOUGHT about a nightcap at the bar, but on reflection decided against it and walked out. There was somebody there already, and he got in the elevator first. There was a casual meeting of the eyes, as Ryan moved to punch the 3 button but saw it already lighted. So, this well-dressed Brit—he looked like a Brit—was on his floor...

... wasn't *that* interesting...?

It took only a few seconds for the car to stop and the door to open.

The Excelsior is not a tall hotel, but it is an expansive one, and it was a lengthy walk, and the elevator man was heading in the right direction, Ryan slowed his pace to follow from a greater distance, and sure enough, he passed Jack's room and kept going, one... two... and at the third door he stopped and turned. Then he looked back at Ryan, wondering, perhaps, if he was being tailed. But Jack stopped and fished out his own key, then, looking down at the other man, in the casual, stranger-to-stranger voice that all men know, said, "G'nite."

"And to you, sir," was the reply in well-educated *English* English.

Jack walked into the room, thinking he'd heard that accent before…like the Brit diplomats whom he'd met in the White House, or on trips to London with his dad. It was either the speech of someone to the manor born, or who planned to buy his own when the time came and who'd banked enough pounds sterling to pretend to be a Peer of the Realm. He had the peaches-and-cream skin of a Brit, and the upper-class accent—

—and he was checked in under the name of Nigel Hawkins.

"And I got one of your e-mails, pal," Jack whispered to the rug. "Son of a bitch."

IT TOOK almost an hour to navigate through the streets of Rome, whose city fathers may not have been married to the city mothers, and none of whom had known shit about city planning, Brian thought, working to find a way to Via Vittorio Veneto. Eventually, he knew they were close when he passed through what may once have been a gate in the city walls designed to keep Hannibal Barca out, but then a left and a right, and they learned that in Rome streets with the same name do not always go straight, which necessitated a circle on the Palazzo Margherita to return back to the Hotel Excelsior, where Dominic decided he'd had quite enough driving for the next few days. Within three minutes, their bags were out of the trunk and they were at the reception desk.

"You have a message to call Signor Ryan when you get in. Your rooms are just next to his," the clerk told them, then he waved at the bellman, who guided them to the elevator.

"Long drive, man," Brian said, leaning back against the paneled walls.

"Tell me about it," Dominic agreed.

"I mean, I know you like fast cars and fast women, but next time how about a damned airliner? Maybe you can score with a stew, y'know?"

"You friggin' jarhead." Followed by a yawn.

"This way, signori," the bellman suggested, with a wave of his arm.

"The message at the desk, where is he?"

"Signor Ryan? He is right here." The bellman pointed.

"That's convenient," Dominic thought aloud, until he remembered something else. He let himself get moved in, and the connecting door to Brian's room opened, and he gave the bellman a generous tip. Then he took the message slip out of his pocket and called.

"HELLO?"

"We're right next door, ace. What's shaking?" Brian asked.

"Two rooms?"

"Roger that."

"Guess who's just down from you?"

"Tell me."

"A British guy, a Mr. Nigel Hawkins," Jack told his cousin, and waited for the shock to subside. "Let's talk."

"Come right on over, Junior."

That took no more time than Jack needed to slip into his loafers.

"Enjoy the drive?" Jack asked.

Dominic had poured his minibar wine into a glass. There wasn't much left. "It was long."

"You did all the driving?"

"Hey, I wanted to get here alive, man."

"You turkey," Brian snarled. "He thinks driving a Porsche is like sex, except better."

"It is if you have the right technique, but even sex can wear a man out. Okay." Dominic set his glass down. "Did you say ... ?"

"Yeah, right there." Jack pointed at the wall. And moved his hand to his eyes. *I've seen the mutt.* The reply was just nods. "Well, you guys get some sleep. I'll call you tomorrow, and we can think about our appointment. Cool?"

"Very cool," Brian agreed. "Ring us up about nine, okay?"

"You bet. Later." And Jack headed for the door. Soon thereafter, he was back on his computer. And then it hit him. He wasn't the only guy here with one of those, was he? That might be valuable...

EIGHT O'CLOCK came earlier than it should have. Mohammed was up, bright-eyed and bushy-tailed, and on his machine checking his e-mail. Mahmoud was in Rome as well, having arrived the previous night, and near the top of 56MoHa's mailbox was a letter from Gadfly097, requesting a meeting site. Mohammed thought about that and then decided to exercise his sense of humor.

RISTORANTE GIOVANNI, PIAZZA DI SPAGNA, he replied: 13:30. BE CAREFUL IN YOUR ROUTINE. By which he meant to employ countersurveillance measures. There was no definite reason to suspect foul play in the loss of three field personnel, but he hadn't lived to the age of thirty-one in the business of intelligence by being foolish. He had the ability to tell the harmless from the dangerous, he thought. He'd gotten David Greengold six weeks earlier, because the Jew hadn't seen the False Flag play even when it bit him on the ass—well, the back of the neck, Mohammed thought with a lowercase smile, remembering the moment. Maybe he should start carrying the knife again, just for good luck. Many men in his line of work believed in luck, as a sportsman or athlete might. Perhaps the Emir had been right. Killing the Mossad officer had been a gratuitously unnecessary risk, since it courted enemies. The Organization had enough of those, even if the enemies did not know who and what the organization was. Better that they should be a mere shadow to the infidels... a shadow in a darkened room, unseen and unknown. Mossad was hated by his colleagues, but it was hated because it was feared. The Jews were formidable. They were vicious, and they were endlessly clever. And who could say what knowledge they had, what Arab traitors bought with American money for Jewish ends. There was not a hint of treachery in the Organization, but he remembered the words of the Russian KGB officer Yuriy: Treason is only possible from those whom you trust. It had probably been a mistake to kill the Russian so quickly. He'd been an experienced field officer who'd operated most of his career in Europe and America, and there'd probably been no end to the stories he could have told, each of them with a lesson to be learned. Mohammed remembered talking to him and remembered being impressed with the breadth of his experience and judgment. Instinct was nice to have, but instinct often merely mimicked mental illness in its rampant paranoia. Yuriy had explained in considerable detail how to judge people, and how to tell a professional from a harmless civilian. He could have told many more stories, except for the 9mm bullet he'd gotten in the back of the head. It had also violated the Prophet's strict and admirable rules of hospitality. *If a man eat your salt, even though he be an infidel, he will have the safety of your house.* Well, the Emir was the one who'd violated that rule, saying lamely that he'd been an atheist and therefore beyond the law.

But he'd learned a few lessons, anyway. All his e-mails were encrypted on the best such program there was, individually keyed to his own computer, and therefore beyond anyone's capacity to read except himself. So, his communications were secure. He hardly looked Arab. He didn't sound Arabic. He didn't dress Arabic. Every hotel he stayed at knew that he drank alcohol, and such places knew that Muslims did not drink. So, he ought be completely safe. Well, yes, the Mossad knew that someone like him had killed that Greengold pig, but he didn't think they'd ever gotten a photo of him, and unless he'd been betrayed by the man whom he'd hired to fool the Jew, they had no idea of who and what he was. Yuriy had warned him that you could never know everything, but also that being overly paranoid could alert a casual tail as to what he was, because professional intelligence officers knew tricks that no one else would ever use—and they could be seen to use them from careful observation. It was all like a big wheel, always turning, always coming back to the same place and moving on in the same way, never still, but never moving off its primary path. A great wheel...and he was just a cog, and whether his function was to help it move or make it slow down, he didn't really know.

"Ah." He shook that off. He was more than a cog. He was one of the motors. Not a great motor, perhaps, but an important one, because while the great wheel might move on without him, it would never move so quickly and surely as it did now. And, God willing, he would keep it moving until it crushed his enemies, the Emir's enemies, and Allah's Own Enemies.

So, he dispatched his message to Gadfly097, and called for coffee to be delivered.

RICK BELL had arranged for a crew to be on the computers around the clock. Strange that The Campus hadn't been doing that from the beginning, but now it did. The Campus was learning as it went, just as everyone else did, on both sides of the scrimmage line. At the moment it was Tony Wills, driven by his personal appreciation that there was a six-hour time difference between Central Europe and the American East Coast. A good computer jockey, he downloaded the message from 56 to 097 within five minutes of its dispatch and immediately forwarded it to Jack.

That required fewer seconds than it took to think it. Okay, they knew their subject and they knew where he was going to be, and that was just fine. Jack lifted his phone.

"You up?" Brian heard.

"I am now," he growled back. "What is it?"

"Come on over for coffee. Bring Dom with you."

"Aye, aye, sir." Followed by *click.*

* * *

"I HOPE this is good," Dominic said. His eyes looked like piss holes in the snow.

"If you want to soar with the eagles in the morning, buddy, you can't wallow with the pigs at night. Be cool. I ordered coffee."

"Thanks. So, what's up?"

Jack walked over to his computer and pointed to the screen. They both leaned down to read.

"Who is this guy?" Dominic asked, thinking *Gadfly097 . . . ?*

"He came in from Vienna yesterday, too."

Across the street somewhere, maybe? Brian wondered, followed by, *Did he see my face?*

"Okay, I guess we're up for the appointment," Brian said, looking at Dom and getting a thumbs-up.

The coffee arrived in a few more minutes. Jack served, but the brew, they all found, was gritty, Turkish in character, though far worse even than the Turks served. Still, better than no coffee at all. They did not speak on point. Their tradecraft was good enough that they didn't talk business in a room that hadn't been swept for bugs—which they didn't know how to do, and for which they did not have the proper equipment.

Jack gunned down his coffee and headed into the shower. In it was a red chain, evidently to be pulled in case of a heart attack, but he felt reasonably decent and didn't use it. He wasn't so sure about Dominic, who really did look like cat puke on the rug. In his case, the shower worked wonders, and he came back out shaved and scrubbed pink, ready to rumble.

"The food here is pretty good, but I'm not sure about the coffee," he announced.

"Not sure. Jesus, I bet they serve better coffee in Cuba," Brian said. "MRE coffee is better than this."

"Nobody's perfect, Aldo," Dominic observed. But he didn't like it either.

"So, figure half an hour?" Jack asked. He needed about three more minutes to be ready.

"If not, send an ambulance," Enzo said, heading for the door, and hoping the shower gods were merciful this morning. It was hardly fair, he thought. Drinking gave you a hangover, not driving.

But thirty minutes later, all three were in the lobby, neatly dressed and wearing sunglasses against the bright Italian sun that sparkled outside. Dominic asked the doorman for directions and got pointed to the Via Sistina, which led directly to the Trinità dei Monti church, and the steps were just across the street, and looked to be eighty or so feet down—there was an elevator serving the subway stop, which was farther down still, but going downhill was not too outrageous a task. It hit all three that Rome had churches the way New York City had candy stores. The walk down was pleasant. The scene, indeed, would be wonderfully romantic if you had the right girl on your arm. The steps had been designed to follow the slope of the hill by the architect Francesco De Sanctis, and was the home of the annual Donna sotto le Stelle fashion extravaganza. At the bottom was a fountain in which lay a marble boat commemorating a major flood, something in which a stone boat would be of little use. The piazza was the intersection of only two streets, and was named for the presence of the Spanish Embassy to the Holy See. The playing field, as it were, was not very large—smaller than Times Square, for example—but it bustled with activity and vehicle traffic, and enough pedestrians to make passage there a dicey proposition for all involved.

Ristorante Giovanni sat on the western side, an undistinguished building of yellow/cream-painted brick, with a large canopied eating area outside. Inside was a bar at which everyone had a lighted cigarette. This included a police officer having a cup of coffee. Dominic and Brian walked in and looked around, scoping the area out before coming back outside.

"We have three hours, people," Brian observed. "Now what?"

"We want to be back here—when?" Jack asked.

Dominic checked his watch. "Our friend is supposed to show up at about one-thirty. Figure we sit down for lunch about twelve forty-five and await developments. Jack, can you ID the guy by sight?"

"No problem," Junior assured them.

"Then I guess we have about two hours to wander around. I was here a couple years ago. There's good shopping."

"Is that a Brioni store over there?" Jack asked, pointing.

"Looks like it," Brian answered. "Won't hurt our cover to do some shopping."

"Then let's do it." He'd never gotten an Italian suit. He had several English ones, from No. 10 Savile Row in London. Why not try here? This spook business was crazy, he reflected. They were here to kill a terrorist, but beforehand they'd do some clothes shopping. Even women wouldn't do that except maybe for shoes.

In fact, there were all manner of stores to be seen on the Via del Babuino—"Baboon Street," of all things—and Jack took the time to look in many of them. Italy was indeed the world capital of style, and he tried on a light gray silk jacket that seemed to have been custom-made for him by a master tailor, and he purchased it on the spot, for eight hundred Euros. Then he had to carry the plastic bag over his shoulder, but was this not beautiful cover? What secret agent man would hobble himself with such an unlikely burden?

MOHAMMED HASSAN left the hotel at 12:15, taking the same walking route that the twins had done two hours earlier. He knew it well. He'd walked the same path on his way for Greengold's killing, and the thought comforted him. It was a fine, sunny day, the temperature reaching to about 30 degrees Celsius, a warm day, but not really a hot one. A good day for American tourists. Christian ones. American Jews went to Israel so that they could spit on Arabs. Here they were just Christian infidels looking to take photographs and buy clothes. Well, he'd bought his suits here as well. There was that Brioni shop just off the Piazza di Spagna. The salesman there, Antonio, always treated him well, the better to take his money. But Mohammed came from a trading culture as well, and you couldn't despise a man for that.

It was time for the midday meal, and the Ristorante Giovanni was as good as any Roman restaurant, and better than most. His favorite waiter recognized him and waved him to his regular table on the right side, under the canopy.

"THAT'S OUR boy," Jack told them, waving with his glass. The three Americans watched his waiter bring a bottle of Pellegrino water to the table, along with a glass of ice. You didn't see much ice in Europe, where people thought it something to ski or skate on, but evidently 56 liked his water cold. Jack was better placed to look in his direction. "I wonder what he likes to eat."

"The condemned is supposed to have a decent last meal," Dominic noted. Not that mutt in Alabama, of course. He'd probably had bad taste anyway. Then he wondered what they served for lunch in hell. "His guest is supposed to show at one-thirty, right?"

"Correct. Fifty-six told him to be careful in his routine. That might mean to check for a tail."

"Suppose he's nervous about us?" Brian wondered.

"Well," Jack observed, "they have had some bad luck lately."

"You have to wonder what he's thinking," Dominic said. He leaned back in his chair and stretched, catching a glance at their subject. It was a little warm to be wearing a jacket and tie, but they were supposed to look like businessmen, not tourists. Now he wondered if that was a good cover or not. You had to take temperature into account.

Was he sweating because of the mission or the ambient temperature? He hadn't been overly tense in London, Munich, or Vienna, had he? No, not then. But this was a more crowded—no, the landscape in London had been more crowded, hadn't it?

There are good serendipities and bad ones. This time, a bad one happened. A waiter with a tray of glasses of Chianti tripped on the big feet of a woman from Chicago, in Rome to check out her roots. The tray missed the table, but the glasses got both twins in the lap. Both were wearing light-colored suits to deal with the heat, and—

"Oh, shit!" Dominic exclaimed, his biscuit-colored Brooks Brothers trousers looking as though he had been hit in the groin with a shotgun. Brian was in even worse shape.

The waiter was aghast. *"Scusi, scusi, signori!"* he gasped. But there was nothing to be done about it. He started jabbering about sending their clothes to the cleaners. Dom and Brian just looked at each other. They might as easily have borne the mark of Cain.

"It's okay," Dominic said in English. He'd forgotten all of his Italian oaths. "Nobody died." The napkins would not do much about this. Maybe a good dry cleaner, and the Excelsior probably had one on staff, or at least close by. A few people looked over, either in horror or amusement, and so his face was as well marked as his clothing. When the waiter retreated in shame, the FBI agent asked, "Okay, now what?"

"Beats the hell out of me," Brian responded. "Random chance has not acted in our favor, Captain Kirk."

"Thanks a bunch, Spock," Dom snarled back.

"Hey, I'm still here, remember?" Jack told them both.

"Junior, you can't—" But Jack cut Brian off.

"Why the hell not?" He asked quietly. "How hard is it?"

"You're not trained," Dominic told him.

"It's not playing golf at the Masters, is it?"

"Well—" It was Brian again.

"Is it?" Jack demanded.

Dominic pulled his pen out of his coat pocket and handed it across.

"Twist the nib and stick it in his ass, right?"

"It's all ready to go," Enzo confirmed. "But be careful, for Christ's sake."

It was 1:21 now. Mohammed Hassan had finished his glass of water and poured another. Mahmoud would soon be here. Why take the chance of interrupting an important meeting? He shrugged to himself and stood, walking inside for the men's room, which had pleasant memories.

"You sure you want to do this?" Brian asked.

"He's a bad guy, isn't he? How long does this stuff take to work?"

"About thirty seconds, Jack. Use your head. If it doesn't feel right, back away and let him go," Dominic told him. "This isn't a fucking game, man."

"Right." *What the hell, Dad did this once or twice,* he told himself. Just to make sure, he bumped into a waiter and asked where the men's room was. The waiter pointed, and Jack went that way.

It was an ordinary wooden door with a symbolic label rather than words because of Giovanni's international clientele. *What if there's more than one guy in there?* he asked himself.

Then you blow it off, dumbass.

Okay . . .

He walked in, and there *was* somebody else, drying his hands. But then he walked out, and Ryan was alone with 56MoHa, who was just zipping up and starting to turn. Jack pulled the pen from his inside jacket pocket and turned the tip to expose the iridium syringe tip. He resisted the instinctive urge to check the tip with his finger as not a very smart move, and slid past the well-suited stranger, and then, as told, dropped his hand and got him right in the left cheek. He expected to hear the discharge of the gas but didn't.

Mohammed Hassan al-Din jumped at the sudden sharp

pain, and turned to see what looked like an ordinary young man— Wait, he'd seen this face at the hotel . . .

"Oh, sorry to bump into you, pal."

The way he said it lit off warning lights in his consciousness. He was an American, and he'd bumped into him, and he'd felt a stick in his buttocks, and—

And he'd killed the Jew here, and—

"Who are you?"

Jack had counted off fifteen seconds or so, and he was feeling his oats—

"I'm the man who just killed you, Fifty-six MoHa," he replied evenly.

The man's face changed into something feral and dangerous. His right hand went into his pocket and came out with a knife, and suddenly it wasn't at all funny anymore.

Jack instinctively backed away with a jump. The terrorist's face was the very image of death. He opened his folding knife and locked onto Jack's throat as his target. He brought the knife up and took half a step forward and—

The knife dropped from his hand—he looked down at his hand in amazement, then looked back up—

—or tried to. His head didn't move. His legs lost their strength. He fell straight down. His knees bounced painfully on the tile floor. And he fell forward, turning left as he did so. His eyes stayed open, and then he was faceup, looking at the metal plate glued to the bottom of the urinal, where Greengold had wanted to retrieve the package from before, and . . .

"Greetings from America, Fifty-six MoHa. You fucked with the wrong people. I hope you like it in hell, pal." His peripheral vision saw the shape move to the door, and the increase and decrease of light as the door opened and closed.

Ryan stopped there and decided to go back. There was a knife by the guy's hand. He took the handkerchief from his pocket and grasped the knife, then just slid it under the body. Better not to dick with it anymore, he thought. Better to—no, one more thing entered his mind. He reached into 56's pants pocket and found what he sought. Then he took his leave. The crazy part was that he felt a great need to urinate at the moment, and walked fast to make that urge subside. In a matter of seconds, he was back at the table.

"That went okay," he told the twins. "I guess we need to get you guys back to the hotel, eh? There's something I need to do. Come on," he commanded.

Dominic left enough Euros to cover the meal, with a tip. The clumsy waiter chased after them, offering to pay for laundering their clothes, but Brian waved him off with a smile, and they walked across the Piazza di Spagna. Here they took the elevator up to the church, and then walked down the street toward the hotel. They were back to the Excelsior in about eight minutes, with both twins feeling rather stupid to have red stains on their clothes.

The reception clerk saw this and asked if they needed a cleaning service.

"Yes, could you send somebody up?" Brian asked in reply.

"Of course, signore. In five minutes."

The elevator, they felt, was not bugged. "Well?" Dominic asked.

"Got him, and I got this," Jack said, holding up a room key just like theirs.

"What's that for?"

"He's got a computer, remember?"

"Oh, yeah."

When they got to MoHa's room, they found it had already been cleaned. Jack stopped off in his room and brought his laptop and the FireWire external drive that he used. It had ten gigabytes of empty space that he figured he could fill up. Inside his victim's room, he attached the connector cable to the port and lit up the Dell laptop Mohammed Hassan had used.

There was no time for finesse; both his 'puter and the

Arab's used the same operating system, and he effected a global transfer of everything off the Arab's computer into the FireWire drive. It took six minutes, and then he wiped everything with his handkerchief and walked out of the room, wiping the doorknob as well. He came out in time to see the valet taking Dominic's wine-stained suit.

"Well?" Dominic asked.

"Done. The guys at home might like to get this." He held up the FireWire to emphasize his point.

"Good thinking, man. Now what?"

"Now I gotta fly home, fella. Get an e-mail off to the home office, okay?"

"Roger that, Junior."

Jack got himself repacked and called the concierge, who told him there was a British Airways flight at Da Vinci Airport for London, with connecting service to D.C. Dulles, but he'd have to hurry. That he did, and ninety minutes later was pulling away from the Jetway, sitting in seat 2A.

MAHMOUD WAS there when the police arrived. He recognized the face of his colleague as the gurney was wheeled out of the men's room, and was thunderstruck. What he didn't know was that the police had taken the knife and made note of the bloodstains on it. This would be sent to their laboratory, which had a DNA lab whose personnel had been trained by the London Metropolitan Police, the world leaders in DNA evidence. Without anyone to report to, Mahmoud went back to his hotel and booked passage on a flight to Dubai on Emirate Airways for the following day. He had to report today's misfortune to someone, perhaps the Emir himself, whom he'd never met and knew only by his forbidding reputation. He'd seen one colleague die, and watched the body of another. What horrendous misfortune was this? He'd consider this with some wine. Allah the Merciful would surely forgive him for the transgression. He'd seen too much in too little time.

* * *

JACK JR. got a mild case of the shakes on the flight to Heathrow. He needed somebody to talk to, but that would take a long time to make happen, and so he gunned down two miniatures of Scotch before landing in England. Two more followed in the front cabin of the 777 inbound to Dulles, but sleep would not come. He'd not only killed somebody but had taunted him as well. Not a good thing, but neither was it something to pray to God about, was it? The FireWire drive had three gigabytes off 56's Dell laptop. Exactly what was on it? That he could not know for now. He could have attached it to his own laptop and gone exploring, but, no, that was a job for a real computer geek. They'd killed four people who had struck out at America, and now America had struck back on their turf and by their rules. The good part was that the enemy could not possibly know what kind of cat was in the jungle. They'd hardly met the teeth.

Next, they'd meet the brain.